Praise for Denzil Meyrick and the DCI Daley thriller series:

'Absorbing . . . no run-of-the-mill tartan noir'
The Times

'You'll have a blast with these'
Ian Rankin

'A top talent, and one to be cherished'
Quintin Jardine

'Spellbinding . . . one of the UK's most loved crime writers'
The Sunday Post

'Universal truths . . . an unbuttoned sense of humour . . .
engaging and eventful'
The Wall Street Journal

'A compelling lead . . . satisfyingly twisted plot'
Publishers Weekly

'Touches of dark humour, multi-layered and compelling'
Daily Record

'Striking characters and shifting plots vibrate with energy'
The Library Journal

'Daley is a character complete with depths, currents and
sudden changes of the Atlantic ocean that crashes against
K̶̶ harbour walls. The remote peninsula and the
̶̶̶̶̶̶ ̶̶ ̶̶̶ life are perfectly painted.'

A note on the author

Denzil Meyrick was born in Glasgow and brought up in Campbeltown. After studying politics, he pursued a varied career including time spent as a police officer, freelance journalist and director of several companies in the leisure, engineering and marketing sectors. Denzil's debut novel, *Whisky from Small Glasses*, was Waterstones Scottish Book of the Year in 2015, and in 2018 *The Relentless Tide* was one of the *Scotsman*'s Books of the Year. Denzil lives on Loch Lomond side with his wife Fiona.

Also available in the D.C.I. Daley thriller series

eBook only

A BREATH ON DYING EMBERS

A D.C.I. DALEY THRILLER

Denzil Meyrick

Polygon

First published in Great Britain in 2019 by Polygon, an imprint of Birlinn Ltd.

Birlinn Ltd
West Newington House
10 Newington Road
Edinburgh
EH9 1QS

www.polygonbooks.co.uk

1

ISBN 978 1 84697 475 5
eBook ISBN 978 1 78885 205 0

British Library Cataloguing-in-Publication Data
A catalogue record for this book is available on request from the British Library.

Typeset by 3btype.com
Printed and bound by Clays Ltd, Elcograf S.p.A.

To Raymond and Margaret Dow –
here's to all the good times, happy memories and friendship

'On wrongs swift vengeance waits.'

—Alexander Pope

PROLOGUE

1972

The boy watched the soldier corner his older brother against what was left of the ruined building's wall; there was simply no chance of escape. Soon, another camouflage-uniformed man joined his companion, panting after the chase, heavy rifle slung across his shoulder on a webbing belt.

They began shouting, hurling abuse at the teenager, who was now cowering on his haunches, hands held in front of his face to fend off the blows he knew were to come.

'Stop!' the little boy shouted, running towards his brother.

One soldier turned his head. He was laughing, talking to his comrade quickly in a way the boy's young ears couldn't comprehend. These men weren't from where he lived.

He tried to grab the leg of one of the soldiers, which made the man laugh even harder. Hard as the boy tried, he couldn't move the older man, pull him back from his brother, who screamed as the other soldier kicked him hard in the thigh.

'Run, quick – go get Father!' his brother shouted, just before another blow, this time from a rifle butt, sent him sprawling, blood trickling down his face and onto the dusty ground.

The little boy stared at the unmoving figure for a moment. The buckles on the soldiers' belts and the grey metal of their weapons glinted in the hot sun; their breath was heavy as one patted the other's shoulder companionably. But his brother didn't move.

The big soldier grinned at the little boy, displaying one gold tooth at the front of a row of yellow teeth. He picked up the struggling child and laughed in his face. His breath stank. Effortlessly, he threw the boy across the rubble of the old yard, where he landed with a thud that set stars spinning in his eyes, took his breath, and sent a sharp pain along his leg.

The soldier shouted again as he struggled to his feet, and took a step towards him.

The little boy took one more look at his motionless brother, then ran, ran as fast as he could, to find his father.

1

Detective Chief Inspector Jim Daley sat at his desk in his glass box, blinds down. With two fingers of his left hand, he was taking the pulse on his opposite wrist. His heart was thudding in his chest, and the wheeze of his breath troubled him.

He was already regretting his decision to walk to and from work every day. It had been a week now, and he felt no fitter; truth be told, he felt worse.

Pulse taken – it was far too fast – he moved his chair closer to the big desk, inadvertently knocking a pen to the floor. When he bent to pick it up, a flurry of white dots sparkled across his vision and he felt momentarily dizzy.

Shit, he thought. High blood pressure, the curse of his family – well, his father's side at least. He sat back in the chair and the dizziness passed. Daley took deep breaths, anxious now. His father had died young, and he wasn't keen to follow in the family tradition.

The big detective booted up his desktop computer and searched 'high blood pressure'. Each result he read was more apocalyptic than the last. Quickly, he returned to his home page, desperately trying to force thoughts of his own mortality from his mind. He checked his pulse again – faster still. He began to breathe more heavily – short, sharp gulps of air now.

He could feel that his face was red hot; there was a slather of clammy sweat across his brow.

A sharp knock on the door and it swung open: Detective Sergeant Brian Scott, framed in the bright light of the main CID office.

'Do you know how much a pint of milk is noo? I'm sure it's no' that price back in Glasgow. Bloody daylight robbery doon here.' He sat on the other side of Daley's desk, loosening his tie. 'Here, I'll away and get us some coffee in a minute.'

'No coffee,' said Daley, more sharply than he intended.

'Eh? Don't ask me tae get you a dram at this time of the morning. I'm telling you, next thing you know it'll be that wee Mexican band at the bottom of the bed.'

'Mariachi.'

'Mari who?'

'That's the name of the bands – the Mexican ones with the big guitars.' Suddenly Daley felt slightly better.

'Aye, well, if you don't want coffee, it's tea or that white shite they call mushroom soup from thon machine: that's all that's left. What's it to be?'

'Just a glass of water, please, Brian.'

Scott hesitated for a minute. 'Oh, I get it. Big night last night, eh? Bit thirsty, are we?'

'I just want some water. How hard can it be?'

'Hang on, big chap. Cool your jets – you'll gie yourself a heart attack. Your coupon's as red as a beetroot, by the way.'

Daley sighed. 'It's this bloody cruise ship. It's been preying on my mind all night.'

'Och, that's nothing compared to what we've had tae face in the last few years. A bunch of overfed business types off on

4

a jolly round Britain, playing golf and getting pished at the country's expense. What's there to worry about?'

'It's a trade delegation, Bri. Government ministers, top civil servants, business folk from across the world – there's even a minor royal. It's part of the big push for world trade. And they're here for three days.'

'Och, there'll be special protection officers from the Met – spooks and all sorts. Anyway, herself is on the way doon, is she no'? This is her pigeon.'

'Symington? She'll be all braid and polished buttons. Trust me, all the hard work will land on us.'

'What hard work, Jimmy? They sail in the loch, have a party . . .'

'A reception.'

'Right, a *reception*, then – still just a big party tae me. It's like *The Love Boat* wae Glenmorangie and putters.'

'They'll be to and fro to the golf clubs, wandering around the town – you know what this place is like. It'll be on me when a Japanese billionaire gets a black eye in the Douglas Arms.'

'Is that one o' they euphoniums?'

'Euphemisms. And no, it's not. The whole thing makes me uneasy.'

'Everything makes you uneasy.'

'With good cause, wouldn't you say?'

'Well, it's true we've no' had the easiest of billets here so far.'

'So far!'

'Och, it's not been too bad. If you discount the resurrected gangsters, murdering druids, rapists, assassins, Nazis and serial killers, it's been a breeze.'

'Funny.'

'Oh, and they archaeologists.'

Before Brian Scott could detail any more of the unexpected horrors they'd faced in Kinloch, the phone on Daley's desk burst into life.

'Yes, sir,' said Daley, automatically sitting up straighter in his seat to take a call from the Acting Chief Constable. He mouthed the rank to Scott, who grimaced, got up and went in search of coffee and water.

'Now, Jim,' said Haskell, in temporary charge of Police Scotland while his superior faced allegations of inappropriate behaviour with a lap dancer in a club owned by the Paisley mob. 'I know you're the very chap to have your finger on the pulse of all this VIP stuff.'

Daley raised his eyes at the unfortunate metaphor, but merely muttered in the affirmative.

'Just heard that the Foreign Secretary will be making a flying visit while the *Great Britain* is in port at Kinloch.'

The medium-sized but luxurious cruise liner *Calypso Star* had been requisitioned by HM Government and rebranded to accommodate a selection of mega-wealthy business people from across the globe. Palm trees and Caribbean sunsets had been hastily replaced by Union flags and bucolic scenes of the British Isles as every stop was pulled out in an effort to attract business to a country on the lookout for new cash and trading opportunities. As the ship was now a temporary ward of the Royal Navy, many of their number were on hand to make sure things went well. The *Calypso Star*'s captain and some of the crew were still in place, but an RN lieutenant commander stood on the bridge, scrutinising every move, while the White Ensign flew proudly at its stern.

'How's the Foreign Secretary arriving, sir?' asked Daley.

'On the police helicopter with your divisional commander. They'll be there in an hour or so.'

'Shall I meet them, sir?'

'Yes, of course – your little kingdom, Jim.' Haskell hesitated. 'And, as you have a dual role – head of CID and sub-divisional commander – better get a uniform on, eh? Number ones, DCI Daley. Symington will brief you further when she arrives. Good luck!'

As Daley heard the call click off, he felt his heart rate rise. Would his uniform fit? It had been touch and go the last time, and that was a while ago. 'Shit,' he said under his breath.

2

They say it's hard to hate for a lifetime; that old age turns angry, turbulent youths into servile, contented old men, the fire in their eyes long extinguished.

I don't agree.

I'm writing this by way of an explanation rather than an excuse. Why excuse yourself for something that has always been your intention? The very notion is perverse. Mistakes, accidents – a lack of forethought: those are the things that can be excused. I seek no such forgiveness.

An old man from the village where I was born taught me a lesson at a young age: 'Everything happens for a reason.' Though belief and conviction can be painful, demanding and at times sickening masters, one can never deny the hold they have over you.

My beliefs, my seeking of true, elemental justice, have taken me to a place I never thought I would travel and forced me to do something unimaginable to the young man I once was. My mind, my thoughts – my very soul – were all forged in the white heat of hatred and man's inhumanity to man.

Justice must be done before my days are over. Otherwise, my life – and many other lives – will have been lived in vain.

As you read what I write, you will, hopefully, gain

understanding. I desperately want you to know, maybe agree with why I do what must be done. I don't know who you are – I will never know. But you must try to see through my eyes, to feel my pain, my hatred; to endure the voices, the faces, the screams and the horrors that have plagued me all these years.

To you, my reader, I tell all. Please be kind enough to be my confessor.

I will tell you more when the thoughts come.

As he wrote the last words, he could feel a gentle calm descend. The first step in any journey is always the most arduous, he reasoned. Whether mountains are to be climbed, rivers crossed, or obstacles overcome, the will to set the wheels in motion creates the momentum that will run, rumble and lead you on until the end.

He laid the old pen down, sat back in his seat and took a deep breath, inhaled until his ribs ached. He held this breath for a few moments then let it out slowly, expelling the tension from his body. He was fit for his age – had worked hard at it for years – and was happy when he contrasted his wellbeing to that of other men of his vintage, despite the poverty that had haunted his youth, and the gnawing hunger he could still easily recall.

He picked up the picture on his tiny desk. The familiar, open, pretty face stared back at him with a monochrome, enigmatic smile frozen in time – frozen like his heart. He traced the lines of her face with the tip of his finger through the glass of the frame. Though he'd done this countless times, when he closed his eyes the movement reminded him of touching her face: smooth, soft, warm. A gentle, kind face; the face he'd loved then and would love until the end of his days.

He put the frame to his lips and kissed the image. But where once there had been soft sweetness now there was only cold, unyielding glass.

He opened a small drawer and placed the frame face down inside. He closed the drawer and sighed. He did not wish her to witness what was to come.

Then the thought came to him in a flash. The letter he'd begun wasn't for some faceless interlocutor – no, it was to her. His mother. He would explain and justify his reasons to his dead mother. She would be certain to understand; and through that comprehension, his soul would be at peace at last.

Via the prism of a son's letter to his mother, the world would understand why he did what had to be done.

'Ouch! Touch and go there, big man,' said Scott as he observed his superior squeezing into his best uniform. 'I cannae understand why anyone thinks they T-shirts look smart, eh?'

'No, I'm with you there,' replied Daley, desperately trying to fasten his uniform trousers under the bulge of his stomach.

'Bad news, Jimmy.'

'Eh?'

'You going for the under-the-belly strategy. That's the last step on the road. It'll be they elasticated troosers next. The battle's lost, old buddy.'

Daley's face was crimson by the time he managed to secure the trouser button. With a firm grip, he hauled at the zip until it was almost in position – almost. 'There,' he panted. 'Uniform on.'

'Mair like a second skin. Hope you've no' tae take a bow or that in front o' this fifty-second cousin o' the Queen.'

'Why? I don't have a problem with it. It's just part of protocol.'

'Aye, and is your arse hanging out the back o' your breeks protocol tae? I take it you've got a clean pair o' scants on, or it'll no' be pleasant for the poor bugger behind you.' Scott laughed heartily at his own observation.

'When's the last time you wore a uniform?'

'When they had silver buttons and a whistle. Those were the days, right enough – none o' this T-shirt and zip nonsense. Proper kit, wae a proper tie – looked the part.'

'Shame half the cops that were slopping about in them were pished on vodka.'

'You couldnae beat the old voddie. Few glasses o' that and a couple o' Mint Imperials and no bastard knew you'd had a drink.' Scott adopted a distant, wistful look.

'Until you fell over.'

'Och, that only happened twice – and one o' they times it was down tae a bad curry I ate at a doss.'

The door of Daley's office was rattled by a sharp knock and Sergeant Shaw appeared. 'That's Chief Superintendent Symington and the Foreign Secretary arriving now, sir.'

'Thanks, Sergeant. Please tell her I'm on my way.'

'Aye, as soon as he can get some WD40 on they troosers tae help them bend at the knees.'

'Fuck off, Brian.'

'Here, I hope you don't go spouting that kind o' language tae the Duke o' Dingwallshire, or whoever it is. It'll be the Tower for you, Jimmy boy.'

Daley glared at his old colleague malevolently as he walked stiffly from the office in his skin-tight uniform.

Scott sat behind his desk, chuckling to himself. Bugger

that promotion lark, he thought. I would hate to be doing the kind of shit he has to do.

He was just about to get down to the business of the day when the phone on Daley's desk rang.

'DCI Daley's office.'

'Sergeant, I've got a woman on the line – she sounds quite upset,' said DC Potts, answering calls as Desk Sergeant Shaw attended to the Foreign Secretary's visit.

'What's her name, son?'

'I couldn't quite make it out. She's crying, you know.'

'Och, put her through. But if this is a cat up a tree, or a wean with his heid stuck in a railing, you'll hear all about it, Potts.'

Scott listened to the clicks as the call was transferred. Sure enough, he could hear faint sobs on the other end of the line.

'Yes, madam, DS Scott speaking, how can I help you?'

'Brian, where's Jim?'

For a second, Scott was lost for words. Then: 'Liz, is that you, dear?'

'Brian, I'm in a terrible fix. Please help me. I need to speak to Jim.' And DCI Daley's wife convulsed into sobs once more.

3

Govanhill, Glasgow

The man finished his piece to camera in heavily accented English, finger wagging as he spoke.

Rant over, his companion behind the camera pressed a button on the side of the device and the red light blinked off. They began to talk quickly in a Somali dialect.

'You did well, Faduma. Your passion will strike fear into our enemies when our job is done.'

'More than that, I hope, Cabdi. It will send ripples around the world. It will make every one of the Infidel fear us more than ever. What we do will change everything.'

Faduma stood easily from a cross-legged position. He was stocky but spare, his dark hair slicked back above a sallow, clean-shaven face. Though he was a Somali, he could have passed for someone from southern Italy.

In contrast, Cabdi was African. He'd shaved off his tight curls, but boasted a long, untamed black beard. He was taller than his companion, with a straight-backed bearing and graceful, long-limbed gait that afforded him an air of elegance, enhanced by his calm, thoughtful mien. He strode across the spartan room and unpinned the black flag that had formed the backdrop of the video. He folded it reverently then kissed it, before placing it in an old chest of drawers.

'This is what they will find,' snorted Faduma. 'Then, they will know.'

Both men looked startled when the old letterbox sounded in the hall.

'It is the post. Quickly. This could be what we were waiting for,' said Faduma.

For the initial phase of their mission, the pair had eschewed all forms of modern communication. No mobile phones, computers, or internet connection. In case of emergencies they had an old fax machine, one of the few methods of contact that couldn't be monitored by the authorities. Their digital footprint was non-existent, with all their instructions coming via the Royal Mail. Ostensibly these missives looked for all the world like letters from family, asking after their wellbeing, or about life in the UK – even pleas for money. In reality, though, they were carefully coded messages, managing their every move.

The British were too busy tracing mobile phones or browsing history. Ironically, it would be the efficiency of their own postal service that would lead to destruction and death.

Both men worked quietly, competently and well: Faduma in a garage, Cabdi as a junior doctor in a Glasgow hospital, where his caring manner, sound medical knowledge and friendliness were respected by patients and colleagues alike. Their flat was almost empty, save for two beds, a fridge, a table, a small chest of drawers, a radio and a few chairs. They walked lightly in the world, with basic bank accounts, legitimate documentation and passports. They were careful to lead ordinary, unassuming lives. They paid their rent and other bills on time, were on good terms with their neighbours, and even volunteered at a local food bank.

The old Transit van parked outside in the crowded Glasgow street was their only means of transport. Though battered and rusting, it was mechanically sound, thanks to the attentions of Faduma, who had learned his trade as a mechanic in Somalia.

Faduma opened the letter, his eyes widening as he read the words. 'I was right. This is it, Cabdi!' He passed the letter to his friend, hands shaking with excitement.

The old van was about to take them on a long and winding journey, a journey that would lead to martyrdom, eternal paradise, and for some – many – deserved sorrow.

'Pleased to meet you,' said Daniel Brand, the short, stout Foreign Secretary, shaking Daley's hand with a firm grip. 'I see you have the same problem as me.' He patted the stomach that hung over the waistband of his dark suit trousers.

'Yes,' said Daley. 'The perils of middle age.'

'Oh, I've tried all the diets out there, trust me; from that bloody no-bread nonsense to the one where you eat bugger all for a couple of days a week, and anything else you want for the rest of the time. All bloody nonsense.' Brand had a broad Mancunian accent, and – to Daley at least – was not what he'd expected. At least the big detective was relieved that he wasn't alone in having a paunch.

'When would you like to visit the vessel, sir?' asked Symington, dressed as Daley had expected in a neat, perfectly presented uniform, the braid on her hat shining brightly.

'I could do with a decent cup of tea and a sandwich before we go. I'm not keen on being on water, Chief Superintendent, and I'm not sure how my stomach will cope with eating and drinking when we're aboard. If you could provide something for my protection officers too, I'd be much obliged.' Brand's two Met protection officers had been consigned to Kinloch Police Office's family room while he chatted with Symington and Daley.

'We'll round up something from the local bakery,' said Daley. 'Any preferences?'

'Pies – every local bakery does a good pie. I dare say it's all bloody hummus and tiny bits of lamb in a bloody *jus* on the *Great Britain*. Honestly, you sit down for a four-course meal in these places and come back hungrier than when you arrived. Fine dining, my arse!'

Symington smiled with everything but her eyes. It was clear to Daley that Brand wasn't quite the political sophisticate she'd been expecting, though he himself had instantly warmed to the man. It was strange meeting well-known people who were seen regularly in the media. Quite often, in his experience, they were the polar opposite to any preconception he'd had prior to seeing them in the flesh. Brand certainly came into that category; Daley had always reckoned him to be a rather dour, hard-nosed individual. But it was always hard to define the man or woman behind the politician. He did know that for a fact.

Symington answered a call and turned to Daley. 'It's DS Scott, DCI Daley. Something important. Can you see him before we head down to the pier? I'll organise something to eat with Sergeant Shaw.'

'Certainly, ma'am. I'll be as quick as possible,' said Daley, wondering just what was of such importance that he had to be dragged away from the Foreign Secretary. 'Excuse me, sir.'

Brand nodded and smiled as Daley left the room in search of Brian Scott.

'What's up, Brian? I'm under pressure here.' The big man sounded rather irritable, Scott thought.

'It's Liz, Jimmy. Just had her on the phone. In some state, so she was.'

'Huh. Looking for a babysitter at short notice. It's not as though we haven't spent enough time and money on lawyers working out who gets James and when. She's out of luck this time. If she wants to bugger off on holiday with her posh boyfriend she'll have to find someone else.'

'It's not that, Jimmy. She sounded . . .'

'She sounded the way she always sounds. Surely you get it by now, Brian. She's a manipulator – ask your Ella. I know she's never liked her; I wish I'd been as smart. It would have saved me a lot of heartache.'

'I'm telling you – I've known her for a long time tae. There was something different about her this time. Fair sobbing, she was, big man.'

'Histrionics, Brian.'

'Who?'

'It's all an act. I'll phone her when I get a minute.'

'I think you should.'

'Okay, got it. Right, I need to get back and head on to this bloody cruise ship. What happened to normal policing, eh?'

'It stopped in 1987.'

Daley rushed out of his glass box, leaving Brian Scott with an uneasy feeling – a feeling that, over the years, he'd learned to hate, and with good reason.

4

With what they needed packed tightly into the van, Faduma and Cabdi left the sprawl of the central belt as they headed on to Loch Lomondside.

The traffic was slow. Cabdi wound down the window, and the pair luxuriated in the clean smell away from the city. Both of them had grown up in Somalia's countryside, and felt much more at home away from the urban crush.

Faduma checked his new satnav. 'Still more than two hours of driving, I think. We can swap in an hour or so, if you want?'

'No, I enjoy this,' said Cabdi. 'Driving frees my mind. It's like a trance.'

'We are nearer to paradise in the open places.'

'That is true.'

'You look so different without your beard, my friend.'

'It marks me out too easily. Though, I admit, to part with it struck at my heart.'

The pair continued on their journey for a few more miles, before Cabdi slowed the vehicle down.

'What is wrong?' asked Faduma anxiously.

'Up ahead – can you see? A flashing blue light.'

'The police?'

'Yes, I think so.'

Faduma squinted into the distance. His eyesight was poor, and he hated wearing glasses. That spoke of weakness, and he was not a weak man.

As the slow line of traffic snaked on, eventually the reason for the flashing blue light became clear. One car, a white family saloon, was on its side, a large dent on the bonnet. On the opposite side of the road, a large lorry was parked at a precarious slant on the grass verge, large front bumper buckled and battered.

Ahead, a police officer indicated that they stop. He made his way to the driver's side of the van, indicating that Cabdi should wind down the window.

'Can I help you?' asked the Somali in as casual a manner as he could muster.

'As you can see, gentlemen, there's been an accident. We're operating a convoy system, so if you wait, a police van will lead you past the scene. Okay?' The policeman was eyeing the old van with curiosity.

'Yes, of course. I hope no one's hurt. I'm a doctor, and would be happy to help, if required.'

'Thank you, but medical assistance has arrived. No serious injuries. People are still a bit shocked, and the car driver has a broken wrist, but they've been lucky.'

'Thank God,' replied Cabdi. 'We shall wait for the escort vehicle.'

'Good. Thank you, sir – doctor,' the policeman said, correcting himself. He smiled and walked past them towards the car behind.

'Why did you tell him you were a doctor?' asked Faduma. 'We must try to remain as invisible as we can.'

'Did you not see him looking at the van? As soon as

I mentioned I was a doctor, he stopped. Everyone trusts a man who saves lives.'

The pair waited to be escorted past the accident under the shadow of Ben Lomond. On the loch, a passenger steamer made slow progress to its destination as a dark shadow passed across the sky; the eyes of its passengers focused on their unfortunate land-bound fellow travellers.

Soon, the pair were back on the move behind a police van.

'Were you scared, Faduma? Did you think they were looking for us?'

'For a moment, yes.' The reply was flat.

'We are being watched over by a higher power. Have faith, brother.'

As always in Kinloch, word had spread that the Foreign Secretary was in town, and crowds were gathering on the pier from where the party was to embark onto the *Great Britain*.

'Man, but she's a fine sight, indeed,' said Hamish, puffing on his pipe.

'I hope you don't mean Elsie Macmillan, Hamish. You're too old tae have a glint in your eye,' observed Annie.

'No, nor glint in my eye. I mean that cruise ship. Lovely lines. A fine vessel.'

'I canna see it for a' that smoke from your damned pipe. You should try that vaping.'

'Vaping? Is that they young fellas wae the beards who blow oot great clouds o' steam that smell like strawberries? If you ask me, it's mair like the *Flying Scotsman* than enjoying a good smoke.'

'Aye, they do make them in different flavours. Oor Cissie swears by the apple and cinnamon yins.'

'Well, if they start doing them in a whisky flavour, I'll consider it. In the meantime, I'd much rather have a good black shag.'

Annie observed her oldest customer with a raised brow for a few moments. 'It's the only shag you'll be getting this side o' the pearly gates,' she muttered.

'I might be a grand old age, Annie, but there's bugger a' wrong wae my lugs.'

'Naw, jeest the rest o' you that's falling tae bits.'

'Talking of falling tae bits, there's oor chief inspector. Man, he looks fair done in – pale as a ghost.'

'Aye, and that uniform could do wae a bit o' letting oot.'

'Och, what he's needing is a good woman. Too many drams and junk food. The only time a decent meal crossed his lips was when I was up there on the hill feeding him.'

'It was always going to be a temporary arrangement, Hamish.'

'True, true. But it's a fine view he has from the decking. The toon looks right bonnie in any weather fae up there.'

'You're lucky no' tae be in an old folks' home – you should count your blessings.'

'If it was up tae that niece o' mine I'd be tied tae the toilet in one o' those places, fair filled wae drugs tae keep me right pliant.'

'Instead you're filled wae whisky every night you leave the County. Oh, there's the Foreign Secretary – there, beside thon Symington lassie.'

'Another one who could benefit fae a diet o' fish.'

Annie stood on her tiptoes. 'You're right. He's no' very big, is he? Well, up the way, at least.'

'Away, ya fat bastard!' shouted a member of the crowd.

'Och, that's no way tae greet a dignitary at all. When I was young they'd have had you up in front o' the sheriff for less.'

'See Mr Daley fair pulled his stomach in when he heard it.'

'It's a' this caper aboot body image. I read it in a magazine at the dentist. Folk have a different idea o' themselves than the reality. Some better, some worse. Poor Mr Daley is in the latter category, I'm thinking.'

As the Foreign Secretary waved to the crowds before stepping aboard the launch that would take him to the *Great Britain*, there was a feeble round of applause.

'Don't worry, you'll no' droon,' shouted another wag. 'Float like a seal, so you will!'

Hamish shook his head again. 'An' this used tae be a fair genteel wee toon.' He turned to Annie, looking for a reply, but she was scanning the dignitaries as they boarded the small boat. 'Missing Sergeant Scott, are you?'

'Eh?'

'You know fine whoot I mean. Since that nice wife o' his moved tae the toon you've been like a sore wae a bare heid.'

'You've got that the wrong way round, Hamish.'

'You think?'

'And anyway, I'm quite fond of Ella. She's a right nice woman.'

'Shame she didna marry someone else though, eh?'

'You're havering – it'll be the lack o' booze. I need tae get back to work anyway. Are you coming?'

'Och, pension day's no' until Tuesday. It'll be a dry sail for me until then.' Hamish looked wistfully out to sea as he took one last draw on his pipe.

'A dry sail, indeed. Come on, you'll need a dram tae get over a' this excitement – government ministers an' that.'

'Jeest a fat wee barrel, if you ask me.'

'Whoot happened tae a' the dignity?'

'The poor bugger can't hear me now, so it won't rip his knitting in any way. Right, let's get up the road and I can take advantage o' that dram you just promised me.'

As Annie and Hamish headed back to the County Hotel, the launch made its way through the choppy grey water, heading against the tide towards the cruise ship anchored near the head of the loch. No one noticed that one of the passengers was desperately trying to avoid presenting his back to the company. DCI Daley's uniform trousers had finally split as he clambered aboard.

5

She winced as she secured the toddler in the car seat in the large SUV. The child fussed and moaned about wanting to be in the front, but she brushed this off with a sharp 'No!'

Gingerly, she took her seat behind the wheel, automatically checking her face in the mirror then grimacing at the woman who gazed back. One of her eyes was swollen, a bruised red, turning purple and yellow at the edges; not closed, but not far from it. Her brow was marked by small cuts and scrapes and one of her cheeks was swollen, giving her face a lopsided look.

She felt her throat tighten as tears blurred her vision. Taking a deep breath, she wiped them away, cleared her throat, and tried to compose herself. She knew she had to leave soon; her mother would make her daily visit at any time, and she didn't want to be seen in this state.

She gripped the wheel, her right hand still sore from where he'd stamped on it. The painkillers had taken more than an hour to help her headache, and she reckoned that she'd have to buy something stronger from a chemist en route to ease the rest of her aches and pains.

She looked at her son in the mirror. He seemed to be growing by the day – probably he'd be big like his father.

Her thoughts drifted for a moment: memories of old times – different days. She knew she'd been a fool; recent experiences had taught her that. She'd thrown everything away just to play the field, find the next quick shag or pointless affair.

This lifestyle had come at a price. The image of a lonely old woman filled her head. No lovers knocking at the door, or sending her messages on the phone. No fancy cars, or big holidays. A few old friends left who would always treat her kindly, but with suspicion; she'd tried it on with most of their husbands.

But she wasn't alone, was she? Her estranged husband had had an affair – perhaps more than one, who knew? She'd been rocked to the core when she found out that the man she'd married was seeing another woman. How could he, she'd thought. But she soon realised that his one dalliance was dwarfed by her sexual indiscretions.

The pretty face of the young woman with the auburn hair popped into her mind. It was obvious that he'd opted for a younger version of her – even she could see the resemblance. But that tragic girl had been a kinder, better person than she'd ever be.

Could she change – was it possible? She looked again at her reflection in the mirror, forcing herself to take in not only the injuries she'd sustained at the hands of her brutal, controlling lover, but what lay underneath. Her face was beginning to betray the inevitable signs of age: lines getting deeper on her brow; creases beside her eyes and at the corners of her mouth; a grey, almost drawn look; the absence of youth's bloom. The answer was simple: she would have to change her ways.

Where there had once been confidence, a certainty that all

eyes would be on her when she entered any room, there was now doubt. Thoughts of the pity or scorn with which she would soon be greeted haunted her. She'd seen it a hundred times herself: *Oh, look at her. Fuck, she's lost it. Who'd have thought?* This would be her fate.

As she felt the tears again, she opened her expensive designer handbag and pulled out a pair of large sunglasses. They covered her swollen eye and almost obscured the swelling on her cheek. But that would bruise soon, and unless she wore a mask it would be impossible to hide. She brushed her hair down over her forehead to cover the scratches and cuts, checked her son once more in the rear-view mirror, then started the car.

Just as she pulled out of her driveway she saw her mother's car heading up the street. She waved enthusiastically, sure that a combination of the sunglasses, tinted windows and her mother's failing eyesight wouldn't reveal her plight. That had been a close call – too close!

'Right, James, next stop Kinloch,' said Liz Daley to the child already nodding off in the seat he'd almost outgrown.

They thought the road would never end. Their route snaked between high peaks, past lochs and glens, through small villages and towns, all the time twisting and turning as they wound their way to their destination.

'Another lorry,' said Faduma, exasperated by their slow progress. 'How many is that now?'

'Many,' replied Cabdi. 'Even the magic you have worked on this old van will not be enough to allow us to pass them. Be calm, my brother; our journey is only as long as it will be.'

'I do not have your self-possession, my friend. But my satnav tells me we are close to our destination – perhaps only ten miles or so.'

'Good. But remember, the road we seek is not signposted, so we have to be alert.'

'Look for a cottage with a red door on the right, then turn left into a small lane. We will be away from cameras well before we reach Kinloch.'

Though their progress behind the big timber lorry was exasperatingly slow, the miles counted down. At last, they saw a sign that said Kinloch was only five miles away.

'There is the cottage,' said Cabdi.

'Yes, we must turn here.' Faduma pointed to a gap in the fence that ran along the left side of the road, and Cabdi steered onto the rough track, which was clearly little used, grass sprouting from the ridge between the deep wheel ruts. The old Transit van began to bump and lurch alarmingly, sending items in the back tumbling.

'The equipment is secure, my friend?' asked Faduma.

'Yes, yes – no need to worry. It will only be some of our camping equipment.'

Still, despite this assurance, as the vehicle bumped and rattled along the single track, Faduma grabbed the door handle tightly, mouthing silent prayers.

6

On board the *Great Britain* in Kinloch harbour, the reception was in full swing in the wood-panelled ballroom, which was festooned with paintings and photographic images from all corners of the British Isles. A gallery of chairs and tables ran round the room, bordering the dance floor, and a magnificent chandelier sparkled amidst the brightly coloured lights that hung from the ceiling. Smartly dressed waiters moved amongst the gathered elite, handing out tiny canapés or glasses of champagne and orange juice.

Daley looked on as the Foreign Secretary worked the room. He appeared completely at ease, despite his large girth and short stature. On the other hand, the big policeman was keeping to the fringes of the event, standing as close to the portholes on the seating gallery as he could in an effort to hide the gaping hole in his uniform trousers.

'You okay, Jim?' asked Symington, braided hat in the crook of one arm, glass of wine in her other hand.

'Yes, ma'am; just not my kind of thing, really.'

'Well, they're here for a few days, and from what I hear a lot of the passengers are keen to sample the delights of our distilleries and golf courses. So it pays for us to get to know who's who, if you get my drift.'

As Daley nodded in agreement, a tall, patrician figure made his way towards them. His white uniform shirt was pristine, bearing the epaulettes of a Royal Navy commander.

'Now, you must be from the local constabulary,' he observed in haughty tones. 'I'm Commander Brachen – call me Tim – and I'm sure our paths will cross over the next three days, or so. Nothing to worry about, I wouldn't think. Plenty of Royal Marines and some undercover intelligence and protection officers on hand.' His smile was broad but lacked sincerity.

Symington introduced Daley, then herself. 'You can understand that we're rather nervous – you know, with all these VIPs aboard. Especially knowing most of them will want to come ashore at some point.'

'Oh, yes. They're a lively bunch – especially the Japanese, would you believe? We had a hard time with them in Glasgow. Had to put in longer than we'd planned because of the storm. They're fine on spirits, whisky and the like, but give them proper beer and they're bloody miraculous.'

'I've read about that,' said Daley. 'It's a genetic thing. Beer wasn't a tradition in Japan, so they find it hard to hold.'

'You're on the ball, DCI Bailey.'

'Daley, sir.'

'Ah, yes, of course.' Brachen waved his hand airily, eyes focused on what was happening in the rest of the room. 'You'll understand that while I'm not in nominal command of this vessel, it's all things through me, do you see?'

'Yes,' said Symington. 'I believe the shipping line wanted to retain their own captain, am I right?'

'Yes, unfortunately. That's him over there.' Commander Brachen nodded across the room to where a man in an ornate Merchant Navy uniform with a gaudily braided cap was chatting easily with Charlie Murray, Kinloch's own political tour de force. 'Captain Banks – nice chap. Bloody good seaman, I'll give him that.'

'I sense a *but* coming,' said Symington.

'Oh, you know how it is. I dare say you have a similar view of private security firms: fine in their own way, but hardly professional. He and his *crew* – mostly Asians – are doing the legwork when it comes to cooking, cleaning, service, and the like. My men observe, of course, but I'd have been much happier with a fully professional seafaring crew.'

'By that you mean a Royal Navy one?' said Daley.

'Bang on, Bailey. Still, one can't always get what one wants in this life. Rest assured that if anything were to go wrong, I'd take command and consign the merchant squad to their quarters. But, as I say, nothing's likely to happen. We're shadowed by a frigate, as well as the onboard security I've mentioned. I make sure that Banks sticks to his guns, so to speak, and off we go. Quite the jolly for me, in fact.'

'Well, when your guests are ashore, I'd appreciate a briefing from whoever is in charge of security. If that's possible, Commander Brachen?' said Symington.

'Oh, certainly.' He craned his head to look round the large room. 'Her name is Annabelle Tansie; I think one would best refer to her as a spook – MI5, you know. I don't see her, but I'll dig her up before you go and arrange a meeting. Now, must circulate, you know how it is.' He paused for a moment. 'You don't appear to have moved from that spot, Bailey. No sea legs, eh?'

'Something like that.'

The police officers watched Commander Brachen as he made his way through the crowd.

'Arrogant prick,' said Symington quietly.

'At least he got your name right.'

'True. Are you sure you're okay, Jim? You do look a bit pale.'

'I've had a bit of a uniform malfunction, ma'am.'

'A what?'

'I've ripped my trousers.'

'Oh.' Symington struggled to stifle a laugh. 'Yes, I did notice your uniform was on the *neat* side.'

As she looked away in an attempt to hide her amusement, Captain Banks made his way towards them.

'DCI Daley. Jim.' The policeman held out his hand and received a firm handshake in return. 'This is my superior, Chief Superintendent Symington.'

'Carrie,' she said, also shaking the captain's hand.

'Banks – Magnus Banks. I used to be in charge of this vessel.'

'You still are, surely?' said Symington.

'In name only. I saw you chatting to Brachen. He's the real OIC.' Banks shook his head.

'A clash of personalities?' asked Daley, instantly warming much more to the captain than he had to the Royal Navy commander.

'You could say that. I've got a good twenty years on him – he's just a boy, really.'

Daley noted that he had a Scottish accent – watered down, with some anglicised vowels, but Scottish nonetheless. 'What part of Scotland are you from, Captain?'

'Oh, please call me Magnus. I'm an East coaster – Peterhead. Brought up to be on the water, one way or another. I've sailed this coast many times, but this is the first time I've put in at Kinloch. It's a beautiful loch. I can't wait to get ashore.'

'You and the passengers, I gather,' said Symington warily.

'Ha, I can see why that would make you nervous. It's like the Tower of Babel on board. Mind you, it usually is, but unusual to have such an exalted passenger list.'

'How many nationalities?' asked Daley.

'Twenty-four, at the last count. All with their own likes and dislikes. I must say, for business people, it's bloody hard to get them to mix. Love to stay in their own little groups.'

There was a murmur in the crowd.

'Look out,' said Banks. 'Here's the duke and duchess. We'll all be invisible from now on. The allure of these people never fails to amaze me. Pleasant enough, mark you. But they seem utterly detached from the real world. Maybe it's just me. The sovereign does her job – no doubt about it. But these distant cousins . . . Anyway, I'd better go and do my duty.'

'I'll come with you,' said Symington, smoothing down her uniform skirt, and making Daley's heart sink at the memory of another woman he'd known who did just that habitually.

For some reason, memories of Mary Dunn had been crossing his mind more often recently. He supposed that now the initial period of shock and grief was over, he was able to think about her without his heart breaking. Sometimes it still did, and sometimes it was as though she'd never been.

'I take it you're staying put, Jim,' said Symington with a grin.

'Yes, ma'am. For the best, I think. I'll just observe from the sidelines.'

'Very wise, DCI Daley.' She smiled broadly at him before turning to follow Captain Banks, heading for the growing throng around the duke and duchess.

7

Cabdi and Faduma had unloaded most of the contents of the old Transit van, and were now erecting a large tent. They did this quickly and efficiently, as they'd practised many times. They were working to a tight schedule. Everything had to be in place if their mission was to be a success.

The tent secure, Faduma opened an aluminium case. Within was a large drone, together with a control handset. Having made sure the device was intact, he set the case down on the camping table his partner had just unfolded.

Cabdi smiled. 'Ready for the test flight? Good. That is a job best left to you, brother. You are the expert. My mission is to put everything in place. Now I want to have a walk and take a look at our surroundings.'

'Agreed. I will wait here for you. I expect we'll receive instructions soon.'

'Yes, brother, I'm sure we will.' Cabdi took a cheap mobile phone from his pocket and inserted the SIM card and battery, which he had removed earlier.

'It looks so old-fashioned.'

'It is, Faduma. But it works, cannot be traced to us. From here we will get our instructions.'

'So they will come through you?'

'One device is enough. The more phones there are, the more likely it is that we will be caught.'

'Yes, I understand. But here in the West, where so many people have their heads stuck in mobile phones, I wonder how one device could be traced.'

'Very easily, trust me. They are controlled, these people, Faduma. They are told what to think and what to feel. They have lost contact with what is important in life.' Cabdi muttered a prayer.

'While you are away I shall pray, too.'

'Do so, brother. Pray for us all and that our mission goes well.'

'Of course!'

'And remember, always Somali. Even if someone is listening to us, what chance is there that they will have our tongue?'

'You are wise, brother.'

'But you, Faduma, are a genius with electronics and mechanics.' Cabdi nodded over to the old van.

'Please. I am a modest man. I do what I can, that is all.'

'And no one can do it better. Of that I am certain.'

'Thank you for your kindness. Good luck, brother.'

Cabdi left the tent, the small phone in his long-fingered hand. He sniffed the air; in a way, it reminded him of home. He could smell animals – sheep, he thought. They smelled like the goats his father had kept.

His father. Without the hard, ceaseless work of that man, he would never have had the chance to become a doctor. He'd have been a goatherd, just like his forefathers. While they had known little of the world, he knew much. And what he knew had taken him down the path he was now treading – the path that would take him where it would.

He studied the landscape: the small lake; the gently rolling fields where animals grazed peacefully; the hill behind their campsite – rounded at the top.

Cabdi began to climb steadily uphill, his long limbs eating away at the metres. Every so often, he would stop and look round, making sure he wasn't being observed. When he was sure, he continued on the narrow path, no doubt beaten down by many, many feet over hundreds of years. He'd seen such paths at home, trails pushed into the landscape by numberless feet over the ages. In a way, he felt more at home in this place than he'd been for years. But he had to focus, concentrate on what had to be done – what he had to do. Again, he offered thanks.

He was surprised when he reached what he thought was the summit of the hill and found it was a false one. He loped down the other side. Ahead a similar hill, though taller this time, stood waiting to be climbed. But he liked exercise, liked being out in the fresh air – out in the world, as was intended. Breathing heavily, though not out of breath, he finally reached the summit proper.

Everything before him now opened out. Below was a large bay, around which huddled a town. He could see tiny cars moving far below, as if in a child's dream. A trail of smoke wound its way into the grey sky from a small farmhouse further down the rise, and he moved out of view behind a large rock.

He took a tiny pair of binoculars from his pocket and turned to his left.

At the head of this sea loch a loaf-shaped island stood sentinel. There was only one clear channel into the bay, on the right side of the island. Across the other a stone causeway snaked through the waves like a giant serpent, effectively a barrier to any vessel.

Turning the binoculars this way and that, he could see the town's twin piers, while further out in the bay a large vessel sat at anchor near the island. Its sleek lines, red, white and blue paint, raked funnels and distinctive flags marked it out as the ship he was seeking. Their target.

He crouched behind the rock, leaning on it to steady his hands as he held the binoculars to his eyes. It was exactly as the images had portrayed. All, that was, apart from the colour of the vessel. The green and yellow livery they'd been shown in the photographs had been replaced by the colours of the United Kingdom. He stared at the sight of the Union Jack flapping in the breeze.

Cabdi dialled the only number in the phone's memory and put it to his mouth. He only had to wait a few seconds for the call to be answered, as the calm voice he had last heard over a year ago replied.

'You are there?'

'Yes. It is just as we were told. Perfect for our enterprise.'

'You will be able to do what you came to do?'

'Yes. I await your instructions.'

'It is important that you do nothing until I order it. Anything else will ruin all we have planned.'

'Do not worry, my brother, I will wait to hear from you. I know the time is not yet right.'

'Good.'

'Will you pray for us?'

'I will.'

Cabdi placed the phone and the binoculars back in his pocket. Again, he looked around, anxious that no one should see him as he made his way back to the camp. He backed away from the rock, crouching, just in case. Behind him, the ground fell away, and soon he was he was out of sight of the farmhouse, and could no longer see the loch, the ship, the island, or the town. Cabdi turned on his heel and with his long, graceful stride made his way down towards the dip between the two hills.

The old man had been watching the bird, fascinated, almost mesmerised by its flight, its shape. The prehensile wings and markings spoke of a gull far from its normal habitat across the broad Atlantic.

He paused to think. The storms had been unseasonable, and had lasted over a week. The bird that he found so alluring had obviously been brought across a wind-tossed sea. But, as they said, every cloud had a silver lining. Most storms brought new and unexpected species to delight him, but this little gull was one of the most exciting finds he'd ever made.

To the layman, it would have looked like any other seabird. But to him, the American grey gull was a thrill. A bright spark from a far shore on a dull day.

He fixed the location of the bird in his mind, looking for a landmark he could use to find it again quickly, in the short time it would take him to put down his Swarovski binoculars and get the camera to his eye.

There was a rock only twenty metres or so from where the little gull sat on a tiny boulder. But before he could put down his binoculars he saw something move behind the large rock.

Shit, he thought, as he made out the head of a man. Another birder? He didn't think so. This man had his eyes fixed on the loch. Following his line of sight, the ornithologist could see that he was gazing at the cruise liner in the loch. It looked as though he was hiding himself, a theory instantly confirmed when the dark figure crouched its way backwards.

He followed the man's progress, and sure enough, once hidden by the dome of the hill, the man turned, stood upright and made his way quickly down from the peak.

Still wondering what was going on, the birdwatcher turned his binoculars back to the spot where the little seabird had settled. But it had gone. Bastard! he said to himself, desperately searching for another sighting, but to no avail.

Disappointed, Cameron Pearson's thoughts returned to the furtive dark figure he'd seen. There had been something about the man's behaviour that troubled him. He'd spent time in the army long ago, and he recognised the stance an individual took when trying to remain unseen.

He scanned the area for the unusual seabird once more, cursed his luck for losing it, and decided to follow his nose and investigate the actions of the man he'd seen behind the rock. At the very least, it could make a good story in the pub for later, in the absence of any photographic evidence of his feathered quarry.

Cautiously, as if homing in on a bird he didn't want to frighten away, Pearson moved from the shelter of the fallen tree and followed the man he'd seen on the hill overlooking Kinloch.

8

Though she was used to the long drive, the ache in her injured hand had turned the journey into a tortuous one.

As she drove through the familiar outskirts of Kinloch, her thoughts were all about what to do next. He hated being disturbed at work, she knew that, but though she still had a key to his house on the hill, surely he must have changed the locks by now?

She parked on a side street. Their son was still fast asleep in the back, hanging by the straps of his car seat, mouth open, eyes flickering, lost in dreams.

She bit her lip, thinking hard, then turned her head away from the person who was walking along the pavement beside her expensive car, taking it in with great interest, as she knew the locals here were bound to do. She made sure her big sunglasses were tightly in place on the bridge of her nose. The last thing she wanted was for him to discover she was back in town from some gossip – and gossip travelled here at the speed of light.

She pushed the button to restart the engine. She'd decided to take the chance that her key would still fit the lock of the house in which she'd once lived. Checking the wing mirror briefly, she pulled away and headed for the steep road that would take her to her old home.

'I'm glad that's over,' said Daley, as he slumped in the big leather chair in his glass box. He'd undone the button at the waist of his trousers, and now his belly bulged in his black uniform T-shirt.

'Aye, I bet, Jimmy,' said Scott thoughtfully.

'What, no witty banter about me ripping the arse out of another pair of breeks? You're slipping up, Brian.'

The Detective Sergeant merely sighed.

'Right, spit it out, Bri. You're in some kind of trouble, aren't you? I know that face.'

'No, no' me, big man – something else.'

'Is it Ella – the kids?' Suddenly Daley looked concerned. He wasn't used to Scott being troubled, even though over the years he'd had plenty of cause to be.

'Right. I'm just going tae come out with it, Jimmy.'

'Fuck, you're not going to tell me you're gay, are you? Don't worry, we're not in the Dark Ages now, Brian. Though I don't know what your Ella will have to say.' When this elicited not even a smile from Scott, Daley realised there was something wrong. 'Come on, Brian, put me out of my misery!'

'Your Liz is up in the hoose.'

'What hoose – house?'

'Whose dae you think?'

'What, mine? Och, I'm so fed up with this. She's a selfish . . .'

'Wait, Jim. This isn't the normal stuff – and, aye, your wee boy's fine,' said Scott hurriedly, recognising the look that

40

crossed his friend's face. 'But if I was you, I'd get up there quick smart. I'll deal wae Symington.'

Suddenly, Daley felt his heart race, pounding in his chest. He began to feel dizzy. 'Could you get me a glass of water, Brian, please?'

'Aye, sure, big man. You okay?'

'Just a bit squeamish after being on the boat, you know.'

'Aye, go tell that tae somebody who doesn't know you so well. You need tae get tae the doctor, Jimmy. I'll fetch the water.' Scott hurried out of the glass box, a worried expression etched across his face.

As Daley took deep breaths, in then out, he began to feel normal. His heart rate slowed, and the spots that had appeared across his vision cleared.

Scott rushed in with a mug of water. 'There you go. Get that doon you.'

'Thanks, Brian.'

'Right, I'll drive you up the road – no arguments.'

'Don't make a big deal of it. It was hot on the ship, and choppy on that wee boat on the way back. Plus, I'd to wear this bloody costume,' said Daley, pointing to his overstretched uniform.

'And the band played believe it if you like. Right, let's get going. You need a break, that's for sure.'

As he watched Daley getting his things together, Scott fretted. His big mate was at a bad age to be taking turns. Heart attacks and strokes were the main occupation of middle-aged men in the West of Scotland, and Daley did all the right things to be of their number. Scott reckoned it would be best that he went up to the house with his old friend. It wasn't going to be a happy reunion, he knew.

9

I find that writing these missives makes me calmer, although it's still only a temporary release from the doubts that pursue me.

Doubts: oh, I'm riddled with those, my dear mother. You saw to that. How well I remember the feeling of inadequacy you lodged in my young mind.

'You don't walk properly . . . your head's too big . . . I think you're beginning to look deformed . . . how your nose has grown – no one in the family has a nose like that . . . you're the ugliest child I've ever seen.'

You said all of those hurtful – devastating – things to me, but I loved you. I still do, though I often wonder why you felt it necessary to persecute me in that way. What made you want to torture the little boy you loved so much – a form of control, perhaps?

It worked, certainly it worked; these scars that no one can see haunt me to this day. I've had to work at becoming someone else all these years in order to escape them. Do you know how hard that has been? Do you know how you turned a bright little boy into a wasteland of despair? A place so desolate that the man I became is a mere façade, a carapace placed between the world and my self-loathing.

But back to doubts, those gnawing, prodding thoughts that

I cannot escape. I know well that I'm perfectly capable of doing what I must do, but the little boy in me still hears your words. 'You'll never be able to do that, not you. What on earth made you think you could? People will just laugh. Go on, get back to your books and that old wireless – dream your days away. Forget these ridiculous ambitions and stay with me.'

The mask I wear is a hard and immovable thing now. It will remain welded to me for the rest of my life, hiding the timid, nervous child who overcame your slurs just to be able to live a normal life.

No doubts can stop me now. Your power has finally ebbed away; only its deadly flotsam remains.

He took the old photograph from the drawer. This time, though, instead of caressing the image, looking for and remembering every line of the face it displayed, he spat. For a moment, his spittle obscured her; she became a blur, the faded memory of a face. Then, as his saliva slid down the glass, there she was, back looking as she always had.

He sobbed quietly as he polished the glass with his sleeve.

Daley looked at the cruise liner as they drove round the head of the loch, Scott at the wheel. Distantly, he could see people on the deck, no doubt having taken the reception he'd attended outside in the clean, clear, sea-tanged air. Scott had his window down, and the occasional voice or laugh carried across the water.

'Looks like they're having a ball out there,' said Scott.

'Bugger them, Brian. Why are you being so mysterious about Liz – and come to that, why did she call you and not me?'

'You never answer the phone.'

'That's why we're paying our respective lawyers a fortune: to communicate. She shouldn't be calling me directly at all, legally speaking.'

'Aye, well, we all know the law's an arse.'

'Ass.'

'Eh?'

'The law's an ass, Bri. That's the saying.'

'I think my version is mair like the truth.'

'Great, coming from a policeman.'

'I'm no' just any policeman, as you well know.'

'That, my friend, is for certain sure.'

They took the hill, the tone of the car's engine turning to a whine. A woman waved at them as they passed and Scott returned the gesture enthusiastically.

'Right wee local now, eh?'

'I'm just doing my bit for community relations. You know how much we're programmed to dae that these days, Jimmy.'

'But you and Ella have taken to this place like ducks to water.'

'It's better than being holed up in the County, especially when you're on the wagon. No' much fun sitting in thon bar wae a ginger beer and lime.'

'But you always had Annie to talk to.' Daley looked for Scott's reaction from the corner of his eye, but there was no change in his sergeant's expression, and he chose not to respond to the comment.

'So, if my son's fine, what is it that's so urgent that she has to drive all the way down here?'

'That's between you and her, Jimmy. It's no' my place to say anything.'

'Oh, I give up!' Daley slammed his fist against the dashboard.

'See, if you do that in cars noo thon airbags will burst oot and suffocate you.'

'Might be preferable to an encounter with my dear wife.'

They turned into the steep lane that led to Daley's house, where, parked under his decking, sat a large SUV, gleaming red in the early autumn sunshine.

'Huh. There's another thing I'm paying for,' remarked Daley ruefully.

Scott pulled up beside Liz's car, unclipped his seatbelt, and turned to his passenger. 'Noo, listen tae me. You keep your cool in there, got it?'

'Now I'm worried.'

'Just don't blow a gasket, Jimmy. I don't want tae spend my whole day rushing tae get glasses of water for you.'

The pair left the car and took the steps to Daley's front door. Though he was still in uniform, Daley held his braided cap in his meaty left hand.

The door was open. With Daley in the lead, they walked down the hall.

'Liz, where are you?' shouted the big policeman.

'In here.' Her reply came from the lounge

'Take it easy, big man,' whispered Scott.

Daley swung the heavy oak door open. His wife was sitting on the large leather couch, their son asleep beside her.

'Hi there, Jim,' she said weakly.

'Take off the sunglasses, Liz.' Daley's tone was commanding.

She did as she was told and removed them gingerly, revealing a bruised, swollen left eye that matched the swelling on her right cheek, with various cuts and bruises the accompaniment.

'Who did this?'

'Listen, Jim.' Liz stood and reached out to him.

He threw his uniform cap to the floor, ignoring the clutch for his hand. 'Who did this?' This time the question was bellowed, making James Daley junior stir on the couch then burst into tears.

'Here, I'll take the wean through tae the kitchen.' Scott hefted the child in his arms. 'You're getting a big boy, eh? Come on, an' Uncle Brian will get you some juice, eh? I'm sure Daddy's got biscuits.' He carried James from the lounge, closing the door behind him, and took his son into the kitchen. There was a radio on the counter, and he turned it on to mask the noise coming from the lounge.

'Why are Mummy and Daddy shouting, Muncle Brian?'

'Och, that's no' shouting, son, that's them singing. Just a funny kind o' song, that's all. Here, there's some o' they Jammie Dodgers, Jamie. You like them, don't you?'

'I want milk with them. And my name is James.'

With his charge in one arm, Scott opened the big fridge. There was a rack of bottled Budweiser, a lump of cheese, a packet of bacon, and a pot of jam. On the shelf in the door sat a solitary carton of milk. Scott sniffed it, and raised his brows. 'I don't think Daddy needs as big a fridge as this, eh, James?'

'They're still singing, Muncle Brian.'

'Aye, Mummy and Daddy like a good song, son. You sit here and I'll gie you milk tae go wae your biscuits.' He popped the child on the counter, took a mug from the dish rack beside the sink and poured a drink for the boy, who was swinging his legs in time to the song on the radio.

Just as he'd handed James a biscuit and placed the mug

beside him, the shouting from the lounge suddenly stopped. There was a short pause, then a scream. Liz rushed into the kitchen, automatically grabbing her son and lifting her into her arms.

'Quick, Brian, get an ambulance!' Tears were flooding down her face.

Scott rushed into the lounge, searching for the mobile phone in his trouser pocket. He knelt over the recumbent figure lying face down on the floor and placed two fingers against the side of his neck. He found a pulse, but it was weak.

'He just collapsed. Stopped speaking, and then his eyes went into the back of his head and he dropped like a stone.'

'He's okay.' Scott pressed the screen of his phone and fumbled it to his ear. 'Ambulance now, at Fairfield Villa.' He'd called the hospital direct, and recognised the voice on the other end. 'Yes, it's for DCI Daley – he's collapsed. Fucking hurry up!'

'Brian, what's happened?' said Liz, her voice barely audible through the wails of her son.

'I should have known better. He's been having these turns, Liz.' He leaned into Daley's ear. 'Okay, big man, take it easy. Help's on its way.' Despite himself, Brian Scott felt his eyes brim with tears.

10

When Cabdi reached their little camp, he found no sign of life. He poked his head through the tent and then the back of the van – nothing. He looked around and called out in Somali, but answer came there none.

Just as he was beginning to panic, he heard a noise behind him. Turning round swiftly, he felt his heart sink. Faduma was walking down the hill from a different direction. A man was held tightly in the crook of one arm, and his hand was pressing a large knife to his unfortunate captive's throat.

'What is this, Faduma?' Cabdi snapped.

'This man, he was following you. I saw him.'

Faduma's captive looked to be elderly – perhaps in his seventies. He had a fat, florid face, wispy grey hair, and a pair of expensive binoculars and a camera swung over an ample gut that bulged through a Barbour jacket.

Cabdi felt sick inside. He knew how hot-headed Faduma was, and cursed himself for leaving him alone.

The man was trying to speak, but Faduma was holding him so tightly that only a desperately strained whisper crossed his lips.

'Let him go.'

'I cannot, brother. He is a danger. He must have seen what you were doing on the hill. He will expose us.'

Cabdi shook his head. 'No. We can handle this, I'm sure.'

'You must ask for instructions.'

Cabdi turned to Faduma's captive and spoke in English. 'Why were you following me?'

Faduma loosened his grip, allowing Cameron Pearson to gulp in air and breathe properly for the first time since he was taken by surprise and felt a knife against his throat.

'I'm an ornithologist – a birdwatcher,' he replied, his voice weak and trembling. 'I wasn't following you. I was watching a rare bird – an American gull. It must have been blown off course in the storms last week.'

'He's lying,' said Faduma in Somali.

Cabdi walked up to the captive. 'We thought you wanted to steal from us. We have very little, and where we come from bandits roam freely.' He searched the man's eyes for the truth, but saw only panic.

'You must call,' said Faduma, tightening his grasp on his captive's neck once more. Cameron Pearson screamed.

Cabdi turned on his heel and removed the mobile phone from his pocket. He pressed a button on the top of the device and held it. Soon, the tiny screen and small keypad lit up. He dialled. After a moment, the call was answered, and Cabdi moved away, speaking quickly but softly to the person on the other end of the phone.

As Faduma watched, he could see that Cabdi didn't like what he was hearing. His voice rose, and he began gesticulating with his long thin arms.

Suddenly, the call had ended. Cabdi was breathing heavily as he held down the button on top of the phone until the light went out, then slipped the device into his pocket. He walked away from Faduma and Pearson, shaking his head, alternately cursing and praying.

'Tell me, Cabdi, what must we do?' Faduma called.

Cabdi stopped in his tracks. He turned to his partner, grim-faced. 'We must do what has to be done.'

In the distance a cow lowed plaintively. Faduma glared at the old man, the knife held still under his double chin. Cameron Pearson felt the warm stream of urine run down his leg and onto his climbing boots as Cabdi walked towards him.

'There is no other choice.'

Daley came slowly back to consciousness, as though emerging from a nightmare. Instinctively, he tried to sit up.

'No, Jim, stay still.' It was Liz, but he couldn't work out why she was there. He looked down at his chest. It appeared to be covered in sticky pads, from which wires led to a screen that bleeped at his side.

'What happened, Liz?'

'You collapsed, Jim. The doctors are trying to work out why now.' She smiled at him.

'What's happened to your face?' Daley reached out to touch her, but she drew away.

'Nothing for you to worry about. Just try and get some rest. The doctor said he'd be back as soon as he could.'

Daley laid his head back on the pillow, desperately trying to remember how he'd ended up in hospital. He recalled entering his house, but then things were a blur, although he thought he remembered Scott whispering in his ear to take things easy.

The door of the side room swung open, and a young doctor, stethoscope round his neck, strode into the room.

'Up the road for you, Mr Daley, I'm afraid.'

'What's wrong?' Liz asked desperately.

'There's no need to worry, Mrs Daley. It's far too early to diagnose what's happened to your husband.'

'So why are you taking him away?'

'Merely as a precaution. We wouldn't have the right equipment or expertise here if . . .'

'If what?' she said in a rush.

'If your husband required any kind of procedure.'

'Have I had a heart attack?' Daley was looking the clinician straight in the eyes.

'You have raised troponin levels, but not by much. It's too early to say.'

'Troponin?'

'It's a measure of the level of protein in the blood. When cardiac arrest takes place, it's above normal – a classic sign. But the levels are usually higher than yours. We have to make sure we can deal with any eventuality, so it's best we helicopter you to the RAH in Paisley.'

'I want to go with him.'

'Yes, of course. If there's room in the aircraft you can accompany your husband. But try not to worry. Even if it's a heart attack, it's a mild one, and that's worst case scenario. We have to make sure he gets the best possible care until we diagnose what the issue has been.'

'Can I speak to Brian Scott?' Daley asked.

'Yes. He's outside; I'll tell him. The nurses and porters will be in shortly to get you ready to leave. Try and stay calm, both of you.' He took a reading from the machine Daley was wired up to, wrote it quickly on the chart at the end of the bed, then moved quickly to the door, reassuring them again that all was well.

No sooner had he left than Scott burst into the room.

'You're okay, big man. Just a shock, eh?' He looked pale and concerned.

'Listen, Brian. I want you to get hold of Symington. Tell her I fainted – probably after the heat on the boat. But don't mention it might be my heart.'

'Your heart! I knew it, Jimmy. You should have calmed down the booze – lost some weight.'

'Maybe, Brian. We don't know yet.'

'Oh, do leave it, Brian. He's just come round.'

'Aye, but what aboot Symington? She can ask questions herself, Jimmy. The lassie's no' stupid – well, no' that stupid.'

'Patient confidentiality, Brian. Just tell her I'm off to have some tests.'

Before Scott could reply, three nurses and a porter entered the room.

'You'll have to leave while we get Mr Daley ready for his trip, please,' said the charge nurse. 'The helicopter is on its way.'

Liz and Brian were ushered out into the corridor, where they found seats against the wall.

'He's going to die,' said Liz, head in her hands.

'Go Team Daley, eh? Have some faith, Liz. My uncle George had four heart attacks before he died. You've got tae keep positive.'

'What age was he?'

'Thirty-eight – but, man, he'd done all the wrong things. Drank too much, overweight, no' enough exercise, poor diet. You know the score.'

'Sounds just like Jim – and he's older.'

'Och, this was years ago. They can dae wonders these days.'

A nurse appeared from Daley's room. 'Nearly there, Mrs Daley. We'll be off soon.'

Liz nodded, doing her best to swallow her tears.

'Look after him, Liz,' said Scott.

'I've never done anything else.'

Scott shook his head. 'Is that right? So a' they affairs were your way o' making sure he was okay, eh?'

'He had an affair too, you know!'

'No' until you'd driven him tae distraction. Don't come the Little Miss Innocent wae me.' He paused. 'You know, all this time I've kept my mooth shut – said nothing. It's your business, no' mine – or so I thought. But you led him a merry dance, hen. You bloody well know it, too. He'd have done anything for you, but you threw it in his face, time after time.'

'As you say, none of your business, Brian,' she replied haughtily.

'Huh, don't come the old soldier wae me. If you want him back – really want tae make a go of it, no' just a place tae run to when you're in bother – well, you'll have tae change your ways, Lizzie.'

Before she could form a reply to this unexpected outburst, the door to Daley's room opened and the trolley bearing his large frame was pushed out into the corridor. He'd been wired to a mobile heart monitor being carried by a nurse. The rate of its bleep appeared to hasten the nearer they pushed him towards Liz and Scott.

'Can you follow us, please, Mrs Daley?'

'Yes, of course.' She turned to Scott, being careful not to

catch his eye. 'Is it still okay for Ella to look after James – until things are more clear, that is?'

'Aye, of course.' Scott looked past her. 'Hey, big man, just you ca' canny, right? Nothing for you tae worry aboot here. I've got your back.'

'Don't make me worse, Bri.' Daley attempted a laugh, but a pain in his chest cut it short.

As Scott watched them push his friend away, he felt his throat tighten with emotion once more. 'God bless you, old buddy,' he said under his breath.

11

Captain Banks bowed deeply as the duke and duchess ascended the ornate staircase. He'd made sure that their equerry was advised to remove them to their quarters before things became raucous and some of the ship's guests forgot their manners. This party would last into the wee small hours, and he was determined to ensure that everything went smoothly.

As he admired one of the American delegation, a statuesque blonde, his head steward Hutchinson made his way towards him through the throng.

'Sir, we have a small problem.'

'Don't tell me the bubbly's run out. Mind you, I wouldn't be surprised, the rate this crowd knock it back.'

'No, sir. One of my staff has gone missing.'

'Who?'

'Majid, sir. Joined us at Newcastle.'

'Are you sure?'

'Yes. His possessions are not in his cabin, sir.'

'How the hell did he get off the ship? I'm assuming he didn't swim with his goods and chattels in tow.'

'At this stage, we've no idea. Shall I pass it on to security, sir?'

'No, leave it with me for the moment.' Banks hesitated. 'Where was he from, this Majid?'

'Lives in the UK, sir, but his family are still in Pakistan.'

'Right, thank you, Hutchinson. Please carry on.'

Banks whispered into the ear of one of his officers, then discreetly took a side door out of the ballroom. As he ascended the gangway, the noise of the revellers disappeared, vanishing when he took the last few steps onto the bridge.

'Thank you, bosun, I have the bridge. You're relieved.'

'Yes, sir, thank you, sir.' The grizzled older man removed a pair of binoculars from round his neck and handed them to Banks.

The captain nodded to the spotty-faced midshipman, the Royal Navy's representative on the bridge, then set the binoculars to his eyes. Carefully, he scanned his surroundings. The ship was at anchor, prow facing the town of Kinloch that sprawled around the head of the loch. He could see smoke rising from chimneys and streetlights bursting into life as the last light of the early autumn day began to fail.

He cursed quietly to himself. He'd handpicked the merchant crew for this assignment. Though he didn't know them all personally, he had studied their records with the company and taken them on this prestigious trip based on that and recommendations from fellow officers who served the line. He brought Majid's face to mind.

Banks ordered one last search of the ship – quietly, by his men. Soon he would have to inform Brachen. In this rarefied company a missing crewman would be bound to rock the boat – literally.

He bit his lip, considering the best course of action.

'Your name, young man?' he asked the midshipman.

'Truly, sir, Andrew Truly.'

'Been in charge on the bridge before?'

'No, sir.' Truly looked hesitant.

'Well, this is your big moment. I know we're lying at anchor, but you are now in charge of the vessel, understand?'

'I should inform Commander Brachen, sir.'

'For what reason? I'm the captain of this ship, and I've just given you an order. Jump to it, lad!'

Banks left the pale-faced youth and took the short route to his own cabin.

'Now, Commander Brachen, let's see what you're made of, eh?' he muttered to himself. He picked up the phone and dialled one for the ship's communications operator. 'Get me Kinloch Police Office. Urgently!'

The man sat beside the bonfire, staring at the flames.

In their midst, the skin of the severed head was bubbling and bursting, melting in the heat. The unfortunate ornithologist's eyes appeared to slip down the blistered skin of his cheeks. Soon, only the blackened skull stared back at the watcher through the red, yellow and blue flicker as it began to crack in the petrol-fuelled cauldron of the flames.

He looked on, unimpressed. He felt no pity or sorrow for the victim. Some things had to be.

'What do we do now?' said Faduma. He was staring almost unblinkingly at the starlit sky. The Milky Way arched over the hill towards the glimpse of sodium light spilling from the town. 'Our work will soon begin, Cabdi. But maybe sooner after this, I think.'

'What happens when is none of our concern. Our master will decide.'

Faduma looked round. There was no sign of life under the stars. 'But we can't stay here, surely?'

'You are right. If we are unlucky people will come searching. All that should be left here are the marks of our campsite. We must leave nothing behind to identify us.'

'I have changed the wheels. But you haven't answered my question.'

Cabdi stood. 'There wouldn't have been a question if you'd not been so impetuous. We could have easily explained away our presence here. I'm a doctor; people believe in doctors in this country. I told you that before. Your actions were rash!'

'They shouldn't believe doctors.' Faduma's face was a shadow in the starlight.

Cabdi lunged for him, grabbing the smaller, younger man by the throat. 'Listen to me, Faduma. You never – ever – do anything like this again, do you understand. You take orders from me.'

'I do not!' Faduma struggled from Cabdi's clutches. He was stocky and strong, and his tall, lean companion lost his grip. 'I did as I was told – as I was ordered to do. Why do you treat me this way?'

'Because of the action you took. Do you think our master is happy you did what you did? I can assure you, he is not.'

Faduma sulked, looking back at the stars. The sky was dull now; a cloud had edged across the sky, blocking out the starlight. 'I ask again, what do we do now?'

'We move camp tonight. We will find another place near the bay. There are hills on the other side of the loch. Even if anything goes wrong, we have a plan to escape.'

'You are wise, my brother.'

'You are not, Faduma. Do something stupid again and our master may not be so tolerant.'

Faduma looked unhappy. He stood and took one last look round their campsite. 'What is that, brother?'

'What do you mean?'

'That glow over the hill – lights?'

'Quickly. We have to leave this place!'

'Can I speak to DCI Daley?' said Captain Banks. He'd liked the big detective when they'd met earlier in the day. After many years in the Merchant Navy, he could spot someone focused on their job, not on the slippery process of climbing the ladder to promotion and success. His boss – Symington – had worked the room like a politician, not a police officer. Banks was sure Daley would be the right man to quietly assist him.

'I'm sorry, sir.' The voice on the other end of the line was hesitant.

'Sorry for what?'

'DCI Daley is unavailable, sir. Can I direct you to anyone else?'

'He must have an assistant, surely?'

'Yes, sir. I'll put you through to Detective Sergeant Brian Scott.'

The line clicked and popped, then a rough, accented voice said, 'DS Scott, can I help you?'

'Ah yes, Sergeant Scott. Captain Magnus Banks of the *Great Britain*. I have a small problem.'

'Don't we all.'

'Sorry?'

'I beg your pardon, sir. Just thinking aloud – you know what it's like, eh? What's your problem?'

Banks described the missing crewman.

'Am I no' right in saying that you have your own security on board? Half o' MI5 an' the SBS, so I heard.'

'Not quite, Sergeant. But I'd rather keep this between ourselves for the moment, if you don't mind. I'm sure you know what a fuss these people can make. My guess is that the man has simply done a bunk, holed up in some hostelry in Kinloch, or in the arms of a young lady he met on a previous voyage. If I flag this up now it'll be like the D-Day Landings. The place will go on red alert, and your job and mine will become infinitely more difficult.'

Scott thought for a moment. 'Aye, right enough. I'm no' a man for fuss myself, I must admit. You email me a picture o' this Majid, and I'll get oor uniform boys on the job. But if we can't turn anything up, I'm thinking you'll have tae press the panic button.'

'Fair enough, Sergeant Scott. I'll do that now.'

'Good man. I'll dae what I can. If this bugger's in Kinloch, I'll find oot aboot it, nothing surer, trust me.'

'I'm pleased to hear it. Why don't we get back in touch in the morning?'

'Aye – no' too early, mind. I've a lot on my plate.'

'Maybe I can have a word with DCI Daley tomorrow? I met him earlier at the reception. Seemed like a sound chap.'

'That'll no' be possible, Captain.'

'Oh? Why not?'

'I'm afraid DCI Daley took unwell no' long after he came off your boat.'

'Ship.'

'Aye, that's what I said.'

'No, it's a *ship*, Sergeant – not a boat. Nothing serious, I hope?'

'Tae be honest with you, I'm not sure. He just collapsed.' Scott took the phone from his face and swallowed hard. 'In any case, the show must go on. I'll dae my best tae find this Ranjeet guy.'

'Majid, Sergeant.'

'Aye, that's your man. Send me that photo as soon as you can, please.'

Captain Banks replaced the phone then called his comms officer again to arrange for an image of Majid to be sent to Kinloch Police.

As he made his way back to the reception – now even more rowdy, judging by the noise as he approached – Banks wondered what had happened to the big police officer.

12

Margaret Pearson tried her husband's mobile phone yet again. He'd been due home over four hours ago, and now it was dark she was beginning to worry.

She took the stairs to their bedroom. Counting his pills, she saw he'd taken the morning ones she'd set out for him. But his next dose was due, and the last thing she wanted was for her spouse of almost fifty years to have an asthma attack out on the hill.

Fretting, she hurried back down the stairs and called his voicemail once more.

The number you are calling is currently unavailable. Please try later.

She'd already sent half a dozen texts, with no reply. She sat by the phone and bit her lip, trying desperately to remember where he'd said he was going that day. Machrie, she was sure. Then she remembered that another birder had told him that a rare gull had been spotted on Ben Saarnie.

Her hand hovered above the receiver for a few moments. Sighing with worry, she lifted it, and dialled the number imprinted on her mind.

The phone rang three times before it was answered.

'Peter, is that you?'

'Aye, Maggie. What can I do for you?'

'It's Cameron. He went out this morning looking for that bloody gull you told him about. It's been dark a while now, and he's still no' back. It's jeest no' like him.'

'Did you phone? He's always footering aboot wae that phone when he's wae me.'

'What do you think? Aye, of course I've phoned – damn near a hunner times. I've left messages, tae – nothing, no' a squeak. He's due his pills and inhaler soon. I'm worried, Peter.'

'He was looking for shots o' that American gull I spotted up at Ben Saarnie. He's got better equipment than me. Every chance he'd have got a great image.'

'Never mind the bloody gull! What dae you think I should dae? Why are you so out o' breath, by the way?'

The line went silent for a while as Peter Scally considered the problem. 'Och, I was upstairs in the bath when you called. I tell you what, Maggie. Me an' young Kevin will take a wander up. He knows the hill as well as me, and we can take that SUV o' his up tae the end o' the track.'

'I hope he's okay – I mean, what do you think could have happened?'

'Och, maybe jeest a wee fall.'

'What?' she squealed. 'An' if he's had a fall, why no' jeest phone?'

'Any number o' reasons, Maggie. The signal comes an' goes up there – he might have run oot o' battery.'

'Aye, I suppose.'

'Or when he fell, he might have broken the bloody thing.'

'Will you shut up aboot him falling!'

'You're right worried, Maggie. I'm surprised – hurt, even.'

Margaret Pearson whispered a reply. 'Jeest you shut up.

Phones is no' safe. There could be anyone listening in at thon exchange. Mind Iza Donnelly – she knew aboot every phone call in the toon when she was the operator. She used tae sit in the Copper Kettle an' hold court wae a' the stories o'er a cup o' tea and an iced bun. None o' it at her expense, mark you.'

'You're livin' in the past, woman. The exchange closed years ago. It's all automatic noo.' He thought for a moment. 'Here, you don't think Cameron's got wind o' – wind o' us, eh?' Suddenly Peter Scally's voice was all concern.

'Jeest haud your wheesht, man! Get off this phone an' go and find him.'

'Aye, right, Maggie. Calm doon. I'm no' wantin' you tae have a stroke.'

'Find him, Peter – please!'

Daley was sitting up in bed watching the small television on the wall of the side room they'd put him in at the Royal Alexandra Hospital in Paisley. He was still wired to various machines that bleeped, chimed and buzzed with alarming frequency, while his heart rate was displayed in neon blue on a screen at his side. Even he could see that his pulse was fast, and somewhat irregular.

In truth, the programme he'd been staring at had washed over him completely, as he worried about what had happened to him back home in Kinloch.

This could change everything. This could be the end.

As he tried desperately to banish these thoughts, the door swung open and a young man in a shirt and tie with his sleeves rolled up and a file in his hand swept into the room.

'Now, Mr Daley, I'm Guy Cummings, duty cardiologist.'

The man smiled at Daley, who was shocked by how young the doctor looked – no more than late twenties, he reckoned.

'Please, call me Jim.'

'Yes, of course. I answer to Guy – or virtually anything.' He sat at the end of Daley's bed. 'You'll no doubt be worried about what happened to you earlier, yes?'

'Yes, of course. I'm terrified, to tell you the truth. What did happen to me?'

'Well, I have both good and bad news, Jim.'

'Good news, please,' said Daley, desperate for some.

'The good news is you haven't had a heart attack –well, not as such.'

'That's the good news?'

'Yes, pretty positive, I'd say.'

'So what's the bad news?'

'You've had something – in that I mean something led to your collapse.'

'What?'

'Well, we've X-rayed your chest, and run a few cardiographs, and everything looks reasonably normal.'

'Reasonably?'

'Well, you do have a slightly enlarged heart – we think.'

'Surely it's enlarged or it's not?'

'Not always as easy as that. Everything's open to inter-pretation in my line of work.'

'Mine, too.'

'You're a police officer, right?'

'Yes, I am.'

'Stressful, I imagine.'

'It has its moments.'

'It's hard to tell from X-rays, so this is where we come to

65

the bad news. We'll have to keep you in overnight – run some tests. Echo cardiogram, kidney and liver tests. We have to get to the bottom of this.'

'I can see my heart rate is fast, and a bit jumpy too.'

'You're tachy, yes –I mean your heart rate is quite quick, as you've observed. However, given your age – general fitness and so on – that's not all that unusual.'

'Well, that's good, isn't it?'

'No, not really good, Jim. I'm guessing a lot of stressful work, bad diet and too much booze. Would that be close to the mark?'

Daley shrugged. 'What do want me to say?'

'It's important you tell me the truth, okay?'

'Okay, then you're right on all points.'

'Thank you. It's nothing to be ashamed of, Jim. We all have our stresses and strains – little guilty pleasures. But at your time of life those have to change.'

'Any guesses?'

'Don't hold me to this, but I'd say you have an arrhythmia issue.'

'What?'

'An irregular heart beat. Again, as you've noticed yourself. In itself, it's quite normal in some people . . .'

'But?'

'*But*, in some cases, it's the manifestation of something else.'

'Like what?'

'Well, I don't want to speculate any further. We can have a word tomorrow after the other tests. I want you to try and get some rest, agreed?'

'If you say so. Easier said than done, mind you.'

'I understand. But don't worry – you're being monitored constantly. I'll see you bright and early tomorrow.' Cummings got up. 'I better get on with my rounds, Jim.'

'Sure. Thanks for coming in, Guy.'

As the young clinician closed the door quietly behind him, Daley closed his eyes and sighed. One thing was certain. He'd get no sleep.

He reached out to the cabinet by his bed, being careful not to dislodge the wires taped to his chest. Seconds later, he heard the familiar voice of Desk Sergeant Shaw in Kinloch Police Office over his mobile phone.

Peter Scally and his grandson reached the end of the rough track that led up Ben Saarnie. Kevin pulled on the parking brake, and reached into the side pocket of the driver's door. He removed a black case, which he opened to reveal what looked like a pair of binoculars.

'You'll no' see bugger a' wae them in this light, Kevin. I thought you'd know that, you being a gamekeeper an' all.'

'They're night vision binoculars, Papa. Have a look.' Kevin clicked a switch and handed them to his grandfather, who put them to his eyes.

'Bugger me, these things is brilliant. Must cost a bob or two, eh?'

'Aye, but the estate gives us them tae look for poachers an' that.' He turned in his seat and lifted a long leather case from the back seat.

'Here, we're going tae find Cameron, no' shoot him, son.'

'You never know, Papa. I don't go up the hills at night without my rifle.'

'Fuck me, it's no' Afghanistan, Kevin.'

'Aye, even so. There's teams o' they bastards coming doon fae Glasgow, taking sheep an' a' sorts. Don't worry, I'm fully licensed to carry it.'

'Well, if you say so. Right, I telt Cameron that I'd seen the gull jeest up at the peak, thonder.'

'Did you really see this gull?'

'Aye, of course. Why do you say that?'

'Thought you might jeest be wantin' Cameron oot o' the way, if you know whoot I mean?' Kevin winked.

'Eh?'

'Come on, Papa. The whole toon knows you're having it off wae his wife. Ew!' he exclaimed, a look of disgust on his face as he shuddered.

'Well, the whole toon's wrong. I've been friends with Cameron Pearson since we was at school, so jeest keep your hand on yer ha'penny. See, the rumours in this toon.' Peter Scally shook his head.

'If you say so, Papa.'

'Aye, I say so! Anyhow, it's no' three years since your granny passed away. What kind o' man do you think I am?'

Kevin stifled a laugh. 'Dae I need tae answer that?'

'Enough o' this shite! Cameron's up here somewhere wae nae pills. Forget gossiping like an auld fishwife and let's find the poor bugger.'

As he watched his grandson slide off the seat of the SUV, Peter Scally bit his lip. 'See, this place,' he muttered under his breath, shaking his head.

13

Scott had recalled four constables to duty, and with another pair already on shift he'd set them on the hunt for the missing *Great Britain* crew member, Majid.

Their first ports of call would be Kinloch's many licensed premises, armed with a photograph of the errant sailor. If that failed, he'd have to become more inventive. But he was confident that local vigilance would be sufficient unto the day. Not many strangers went unnoticed in Kinloch.

He was sitting in Daley's glass box, behind the desk, when the door swung open. He was absorbed in reading some background on Majid provided by Captain Banks, and without lifting his head he said, 'What the fuck now? And don't think you needn't knock just because the gaffer's no' here.'

'What on earth's been going on, DS Scott? And why wasn't I informed?' Symington was framed in the doorway in a jogging suit and a pair of very white training shoes. 'I had to learn that my sub-divisional commander had been rushed to hospital, presumed dead, from one particularly gloomy member of the public!'

'Who telt you that?' said Scott, blanching at the information.

'The man running beside me on the treadmill at what

passes for your gym down here. Now, I assume that had DCI Daley expired somebody would have been good enough to inform me. So, tell me what actually happened.' Her tone was sharp and commanding.

'Aye' well, we was up at the hoose when Liz – Mrs Daley – and the wean arrived. They started arguing, so I took the wee fella intae the kitchen, gied him some biscuits an' that . . .'

'Spare me the preamble, DS Scott. What's wrong with him?'

'Right, aye. I was going to tell you, but the last I heard you was still on the boat, like. So I didn't want to disturb you.'

'I've been off the boat – *like* – for hours. I went back to my hotel to freshen up and have something to eat, then decided to go for a quick session at the gym – then this!'

'Aye, well, it's no' all bad news, ma'am. Jimmy – DCI Daley – collapsed, and the docs here reckoned he was better off up the road in Glasgow. Just in case, you know. He phoned a while ago, but I was oot organising the boys to search for this missing crewmen fae the boat – ship, ma'am.'

'Missing crewman? I have to say, DS Scott, we're in a small town with half the government and some of the royal family, not to mention some of the richest people in the world, on board a cruise ship, when, my officer in command is taken ill and flown to hospital in Glasgow, a member of the crew of this *boat* goes missing, and you don't see fit to inform me. I look like a fool, Brian!'

Scott chewed the end of his pencil for a few moments, reminding himself of the many times at school he'd been asked awkward questions as to his behaviour, or occasionally his work – or more likely the absence of it. 'Aye, I just assumed you was still afloat, so tae speak. Actually, he's in Paisley, by the way.'

'Glasgow, Paisley – what's the odds?'

'I wouldnae say that in Paisley, ma'am.'

'Even if I had still been *afloat* you should have made sure that I was informed about the collapse of my DCI. How is he?'

'They doctors are still running tests, ma'am. He telt Sergeant Shaw he was feeling fine an' dandy. Och, likely just a wee turn. You know what men oor age are like – off wae the blue light flashing at the drop o' a hat. Happened tae my faither. Mind you, he'd drunk ten pints o' lager and a bottle o' whisky . . .'

'Get me the hospital, and tell them I want an urgent update. I'll be in my office.' She turned on her heel and slammed the door to Daley's glass box, making the blinds rattle and attracting concerned looks from a pair of detectives in the CID suite.

'Right, Potts,' shouted Scott, poking his head through the door. 'Get the RAH in Paisley – somebody senior, no' just some nurse – and tell them tae contact her majesty pronto aboot DCI Daley's condition.'

'Yes, Sergeant. But first I think we've found our man Majid.'

'Oh aye, I didnae think it would take long here. Where is the bastard?'

'He's been spotted entering a flat on Long Road, Sergeant.'

'Okay, gie me the details, an' I'll get doon there. Meanwhile, you do the necessary for the queen o' Sheba doon the corridor.'

Scott ducked back into Daley's office, flung his jacket over his shoulders, and hurried out, DC Potts pressing the scribbled note of the Long Road address into his hand as he went.

*

Peter Scally and his grandson made their way slowly up the hill, torches pointing to the ground to make sure of their footing. The clouds had parted and it had turned back into a clear starlit night, but still, rabbit holes, boulders and lumps and bumps in the ground were unforgiving. Scally had seen too many twisted ankles and broken legs in his time as a poacher to ensure he kept himself safe while prowling the hills at night. Not that he was about to tell his gamekeeper grandson any of that.

Without warning, an owl swooped low overhead hooting as it went, no doubt disturbed by the pair and their torches.

'No' long tae go now,' he gasped. 'That's us nearly at the false peak.'

Kevin smiled in the dark. 'You're fair knackered tonight, Papa. Been at the gym?'

'Gym, my arse!' Scally was about to say more, but his grandson held up his hand.

'Hold on,' he whispered.

'What?'

'Over there. I can hear an engine.'

'How so? We came as far as we could on the track. How could anyone get a vehicle this far?'

'There's another track that comes off the west road – you must know it, Papa. It takes you further up the hill, but no' as near tae where you telt me you saw this bird.'

'Aye, right enough. It's been a long time since I've been up it. Your memory gets fair buggered when you get tae my age. So who can it be?'

'Pound tae a penny it's poachers.'

'Naw, no' up here. What's there tae poach?'

'Some fine sheep up here on the pastures still tae be

brought doon. Anyhow, what dae you know aboot poaching, eh?'

'Och, jeest nothing at all. I'm a birder, and fine you know it. Jeest ignore it, Kevin. Cameron won't be o'er there.'

'We'll try and get closer. Look, there to the left, that wee mound. If we can get there unseen, I can use the night vision glasses. But we'll need tae be right quiet.'

'Don't worry. I can creep aboot wae the best o' them, son.'

Kevin gave his grandfather a knowing look before leading the way up the hill, crouching against its contours in the shadow of the gibbous moon. He soon waved Scally to a stop, pointing upwards, and the pair crawled up the small mound, staying as low as they could.

'They've had a fire, anyway. I can still see the dying embers,' whispered Peter. 'And the tail lights. What can you see?'

Kevin had the night vision binoculars to his eyes. 'Two men wae hooded tops standing near the back of a van. They're checking the fire oot.'

'Whoot for?'

'I don't know. It's hard to see, because the rear lights are flashing out my view. They jeest seem tae be poking aboot in the fire.'

'They've likely had a barbecue.'

'Oh, aye. You could barbecue half the toon in a fire that size.'

'You're getting too big for your boots!'

'Quiet. They're getting ready to leave.'

Sure enough, the tone of the van's engine rose a notch and soon the full beam illuminated the path in front of it. Slowly, the vehicle pulled away, the rattle of a venerable engine plain on the night air.

'What will we do now?'

'Hang on for a few moments, Papa. We don't want to go down there in case they come back. Be patient.'

They stayed crouched to the ground for a few moments, Kevin using the time to remove his rifle from its leather sleeve.

'What are you doing?'

'Better safe than sorry, Papa. These poacher guys don't mess aboot. And if they see this it might gie them second thoughts if they fancy a go, you know whoot I mean?'

Slowly, with only one shaded torch to guide them this time, they made their way down into the dip where the van had been. Kevin stopped a few times, but could hear no movement ahead. When they reached the spot where they'd seen the van, he pointed his torch at the ground. 'They're clever, that's for sure.'

'Why?'

'No tyre tracks.'

'How did they manage that?'

'They get onto a gravel track like this, then change into an old set of tyres with no tread. The gravel gives them purchase, and they don't leave any trace.' Kevin was now crouching beside the remains of the fire the men had left behind. 'Kinda strange, is it no'?'

'Whoot?'

'Well, poachers don't often light fires. They've used petrol, I can smell it.'

'Aye, you might be right, son.' Scally made his way to the fire, and began poking about in the warm ashes.

'Whoot's the white stuff, Papa?'

Scally knelt down and picked a piece of charred material from the heart of what must have been a hot blaze judging by the way the ground had been burned and charred. He examined the rounded remnant in his gloved hand. 'I'd say that was bone o' some description. See, they have had a barbecue. Deer – maybe a sheep?'

'You don't roast meat on a petrol fire. Everything just tastes of fuel.'

'Aye, good thinking, Kevin. But you must know how stupid some folk are. City boys up on the rattle, if you ask me, off wae a taste o' petrol in their mooths.'

Peter Scally hefted the charred object in his palm, then took his glasses from his pocket and examined it under the light of the torch.

'What dae you think, Papa? Is it hot?'

'Aye, jeest that, son. That was part o' a deer skull, I'd bet my life on it.' Peter Scally was breathing heavily.

'How do you know?'

'Twenty-two years in Kinloch's retained fire brigade, that's how. You were jeest a wean when I retired. Och, you see all sorts.'

'We better get the polis, Papa.'

As Peter Scally rubbed his chin, still breathing heavily, Kevin cocked his head. 'Quick, Papa. They're coming back. I can hear the engine!'

The pair dived back up the slick slope in the direction they had come. Scally lost his footing, but with strong arms his grandson pulled him up, until they were safely over the rise.

As they looked down, the same van pulled up beside the fire.

14

The flat where missing crewman Majid had been spotted was on the first floor of a run-down block of flats on Long Road. Scott and three uniformed constables made their way up the dilapidated stone staircase as quietly as they could. As they were only one floor up, Scott had stationed another cop on the pavement below the flat, just in case this Majid decided to make a break for freedom by jumping out the window. As far as he could ascertain, there was no other route out of the apartment, bar the door.

'This place stinks of piss,' said a young constable, screwing up his face.

'You'll have my boot up your arse if you don't shut it, piss, or no',' said Scott in a loud whisper. 'The last thing we want is this bugger getting on his toes 'cos he hears us coming.' He turned to a tall, thin PC with a spotty face. 'Right, Davison, when I nod my heid you chap the door. We'll hide roon the corner here in the shadows.'

'How will I see you nod your head if you're in the shadows?'

'I'll poke it oot intae the light, dumbo. Just get on wae it!'

Constable Davison took his allotted position at the front door of the flat, which was on an open landing, the only light coming from the moon and the dim sodium glow of street lights to the front of the building. He looked anxiously into the shadows until Scott's head appeared, nodding vigorously.

With a gloved fist, he rapped on the door. 'Is there anybody in? It's the police. Open up right now!'

Scott shook his head and made a slashing motion across his throat as he hurried across to the doorway. 'What did I say? Don't let on we're the polis!'

'Sorry, Sergeant. Just we get told to identify ourselves at police college.'

'Aye, well you're not at police college now. Wait.' Scott put his ear to the door. 'Right, there's somebody moving about.' He pushed Constable Davison out of the way, and thumped on the door with his fist. 'We know you're in there, Mr Majid. Open the door, and let's get you back aboard that bloody boat – *ship*,' he roared, not forgetting to correct himself.

He listened again. Someone was definitely moving about in the hall. 'One last chance. Come out, or I'll have no choice but to force entry!' Banks had alluded to the fact that Majid was in possession of some equipment belonging to the *Great Britain*. And for security reasons alone, they had to find their man.

Beside him the radio Davison was carrying burst into life. 'Three-six-one to DS Scott. A light's just come on in one of the rooms. I can see it from the street, over.' It was the officer on the pavement in front of the building.

'Right, boys, get the door in. Use the rammer!' commanded Scott. He stood back and the two stouter constables – not Davison – got to work on the flat's door with a metal ram. After a few lunges, wood splintered and the door broke open. Soon police torches threw bright beams of light across the hallway, where a small dark-haired man cowered against a table.

'Please, do not kill me!' he shouted in an Asian accent.

'Grab him!' shouted Scott. Quickly, they burst into the hall. One of the cops located a light switch and the scene was fully illuminated by a bare bulb at the end of a cord flex. Davison dashed forward and grabbed their quarry by his stained vest. The unfortunate captive wailed, appearing more intent on keeping his boxer shorts from falling to his feet than evading justice. 'I surrender. Please, don't harm me!'

'Wait!' shouted Davison. 'That's Mr Sanjeev from the Indian Star.'

'Eh?' said Scott.

'He's the guy that owns the Indian restaurant on the seafront. He does a brilliant lamb pathia.'

Scott stared at the small man. 'So it is, Davison. Right, you, where's your friend Ranjeet?'

'Who?' Mr Sanjeev was wide-eyed with fear.

'Majid, Sergeant,' said Davison.

'Aye, where's this Majid?'

'Ranjeet, Majid? I don't know anyone with those names. Not in Kinloch, anyway,' said Mr Sanjeev desperately.

'Right, come clean, noo,' said Scott. 'I'll have none o' this nonsense. You should know better, you a local businessman an' all.'

Just as he was about to order a thorough search of Mr Sanjeev's house, another voice sounded from behind.

'Aye, good, you got him.' An elderly man in a red tartan dressing gown was standing at the doorway of the property, a broad smile spread across his craggy, unshaven face.

'What dae you mean, *got him*?' said Scott.

'Yer man there. One of your constables showed me a picture of him in the Douglas Arms earlier. I was looking out o' my flat window across the road when I saw him here heading up the close. I jeest got right on the phone tae the station. Is he one o' they extremists?'

'You know who I am, Mr Duncan. I served you with a chicken curry and extra chips on Saturday. You're a regular customer!'

Scott looked at the man in the dressing gown. 'Is this right? Dae you know Mr Sanjeev?'

'Aye, I dae so. Does the best curry this side o' Glasgow, so he does.'

'So how then did you tell us this was the man in the photograph?'

'Och, it was his spitting image.'

'This was the man I showed you, Mr Duncan.' One of the constables produced an image of a gaunt-faced male, no older than thirty-five, with a full long beard.

'How could you think this was the man we were after?' said Scott.

'You know fine how slippery these buggers are. I reckoned that he had a false beard on in that photograph.'

'And lost twenty years in age. You've led us on one o' they wild goose hunts!'

'Have you checked his shoes? They put the bombs in them, you know.'

'That's just racism, Mr Duncan,' said Davison.

'Aye, it is that. You apologise to Mr Sanjeev here – come on!' said Scott with a scowl.

'I'm no' going near him. Likely have explosives in his knickers. They're wily as fuck. I'm surprised at you lot.'

'You will have no more extra chips in my establishment,

Mr Duncan,' shouted Sanjeev. 'In fact, you're banned from my restaurant for ever.'

'Oh no, you canna dae that. Am I no' right, Sergeant?'

'No, you're no',' said Scott irritably. 'Just get back doon they stairs and home before I charge you wae being in possession of an offensive dressing gown.'

Duncan looked around at the police officers and shook his head. 'No wonder innocent folk get killed wae you polis no' caring aboot these exterminists.'

'Extremists!' said Scott.

'See, you even know it yourself. Free curries, is it? Well, don't blame me when the whole town is lying in ruins.'

'If you ever come to my shop again, I will shit in your curry,' yelled Sanjeev.

'And what dae you have to say about that, Sergeant? A plain threat to my health – not tae mention they hygiene regulations. What dae you intend to do, eh?'

'I'll shit in it tae.'

Duncan's mouth flapped open and closed, its owner momentarily lost for words.

'Right, Constable Davison, show Mr Duncan home.'

'I'm staying put. It's my right as a concerned citizen.' Duncan jutted out his chin, pulling tight the cord on his dressing gown as if to emphasise his determination.

'Fine, have it your own way, Mr Duncan. Constable Davison, throw Mr Duncan doon they stairs,' said Scott.

Duncan hesitated for a moment, then turned quickly and rushed down the winding staircase as fast as his carpet slippers would allow.

'They definitely didn't teach that at the police college,' said Davison.

Peter Scally and his grandson looked on as two men exited the old Transit van and inspected the remains of the fire, poking their toes into the ashes. The bright moon now illuminated the scene; Kevin had no need of his night vision glasses.

'What do you think they're doing?' whispered Scally.

'I think we're about tae find oot.'

One of the men, tall and thin, picked up something from the charred grass then walked across to the van and opened the passenger door to get back into his seat. Scally and Kevin looked on as the smaller man stared at the ashes of the fire before he too returned to the vehicle.

'They'd forgotten something, I reckon,' murmured Kevin.

'Och, maybes they're jeest being environmentally friendly, son. You know what it says on all they posters you see noo – you know, tidy up after yourself when camping. Likely that's what they're doing.'

'Huh, you've fair changed your tune. Thugs fae Glasgow oot on the drink having a fly barbecue – now they're members o' the Green Party.'

'Och, I'm no' right sure now, Kevin. I think maybe a' the excitement o' the night jeest made me a wee bit dramatic. And anyhow, you know fine what my eyesight is like these days. You've got right suspicious since you started this gamekeeping lark.'

'I can't tell you whoot they were at. But I'm here tae gamble they're up tae no good, that's for sure.'

'Wait noo, Kevin. Your mind can fair work up tae mischief up here in the hills in the dark. Best left tae their ain devices, if you ask me.'

'Well, if you say so,' said Kevin doubtfully.

'Anyhow, the last thing we need is tae get involved wae a gang o' poachers. You'll know better than me, but I hear they can be ruthless bastards.'

'So, it's poachers, noo. You change your mind fae one minute tae the next, Papa.'

As they looked on from the height of the knoll, the lights of the van flashed into life and the old engine rattled back into operation. They turned the vehicle round on the grass near the fire then made their way back down the rough gravel track.

'I'm no' happy, Papa. There's something no' right aboot what they were up tae.'

'Och, I widna be fretting o'er much, Kevin. Some strange things happen in the hills. Auld Bertie Mason used tae go up Ben Saarnie every month and howl at the full moon – regular as clockwork.'

'He did?'

'Aye, absolutely, he did. Sure that's how he got the nickname the Howler.'

'Is he still at it?'

'No, he's been deid a few years now. He got drunk one night when he was at that caper and fell in thon wee loch. They found him the next day, the empty bottle of whisky fair floating by his body. That was the end o' the howling.'

'And what aboot Cameron? We've still no' seen hide nor hair o' him, Papa.'

'We'll have another poke about, but I'm thinking he'll be tucked up in bed beside Maggie right this very minute.'

'You'll no' be happy at that, eh?'

'I'm perfectly happy. You should do yourself a favour and

stop listening tae the gossips in this toon. Anyhow, I'm no' keen tae spend much mair time up here, no' wae these two strange buggers floating aboot in that van. We'll take a look o'er at where I saw the gull and follow the path a whiles. I reckon that's us done oor bit.'

'Well, if you say so. Mind, if Cameron's no' hame, we'll have tae call the polis by the morning.'

'Jeest you leave that tae me, son. I'll sort things oot. Come on, let's get going. I'm too auld for a' this night-time adventuring.'

There was nothing to be seen at the top of the hill, on the path Cameron Pearson would likely have taken. As they trudged back towards Kevin's SUV, Peter Scally looked up at the night sky. Life was strange, he thought. 'They say there's billions o' suns up there – countless numbers, Kevin.'

'Is this you at the philosophy, Papa?'

'Ach no, I suppose I was jeest wondering where I fit intae it all. You're a young man wae the world stretching oot in front o' you. Me, my adventures are mostly by.'

'Apart fae a quick roll in the byre wae Mrs Pearson, eh?'

'See, if you were normal height instead o' being one o' they giants that kids grow intae, noo, I'd get up and skelp your lug good and proper.' But when he thought of Cameron Pearson, the smile on Peter Scally's face was soon gone.

15

Liz Daley sat beside her husband's hospital bed, holding his hand as he slept. She'd spent a restless night at home in Howwood, ignoring continuous phone calls from her mother.

James Daley junior was safe with Ella Scott back in Kinloch, and she was determined to make up for the argument that had led to Jim's collapse. She'd done it again – made everyone's lives worse.

'Liz,' said Daley, coming to, moistening his dry lips as the machine at his side bleeped and occasionally chimed.

'Hi, Jim. How do you feel?'

'Fine – normal. I just want to get out of here.'

'I spoke to one of the nurses when I arrived. You'll go for a few tests today, and depending on what they find you might be discharged later on.'

Daley sighed. 'But what *will* they find?'

'You have to be positive, Jim. People collapse for all kinds of reasons that aren't serious. I've fainted loads of times.'

'But you never got helicoptered to hospital and wired to this . . . this bloody thing.'

'It's better to be safe than sorry,' she replied, a tear winding its way from behind her sunglasses.

'And you still haven't told me who did that to you, Liz.

I'm a detective, remember; I have friends in the police across the country. I'll be able to find out. You'd be better just telling me and getting it over with.'

She shook her head. 'Listen, I want you to forget about this. I should never have come to Kinloch. It was just . . .'

'Just what?'

'Oh, nothing – just ignore me.'

'It was just because you didn't want anyone to see you, Liz. Remember how long I've known you. I want you to tell me who did this.'

Daley tried to sit up in bed, and the monitor at his side began to chime repeatedly.

A nurse dashed into his room, a worried look on her face.

'I'm fine,' he said.

'Your heart rate has just shot up, Mr Daley.' The nurse checked the machine. 'If you don't mind, Mrs Daley, I have to get your husband ready to go for his echo scan and X-rays.'

'Yeah, sure. I'm sorry.' She kissed Daley on the forehead. 'I'll wait until you come back. Hopefully I can take you home.'

'To Howwood?'

'Yes, of course.'

'Howwood's not my home, Liz. I don't think it ever was, to be honest.'

As the monitor chimed again, the nurse looked at Liz. 'Please, Mrs Daley, if you don't mind.'

She swept out of the room, head lowered so no one could see the tears now flowing down her face.

Brian Scott sat at the breakfast table facing James Daley junior. Despite the resemblance to Liz across the eyes, he could see much of his old friend in the wee boy's face.

He sighed, thinking about Daley lying in his hospital bed. He remembered placing two fingers against Daley's neck in his house on the hill. It was something he'd done many times in his career as a police officer, but never had he been so relieved to feel the pulse of a still beating heart.

He thought of all the things he'd witnessed in his long career. The dead and dying: eviscerated corpses, people burned black or mangled beyond recognition in car accidents, decapitated murder victims – the list just went on and on.

He understood why Daley could become morose; it was a miracle that he'd not gone the same way. Despite it all, Scott held what meant most to him close to his heart – his family, his friends and the good times in his life. Things Daley seemed incapable of doing. Of course, his big pal had never been blessed with the stable marriage he enjoyed. He watched Ella busy at the sink. She'd never wanted to be anything other than a mother to her children, a homemaker. He knew that type of attitude was frowned upon nowadays, but he could never quite understand why. What could be more important than bringing up children, making them feel safe and loved and cared for – teaching them what was important in life?

Of course, he'd done his bit. However, the police service was a cruel master, with its long, unpredictable hours, the pressure of cases carried back home – something he'd always tried not to do, but had, in the main, failed to avoid.

Then there was his drinking; of that he was ashamed. Night after night spent carousing with his mates, rather than being at home watching his children grow up. How he wished he could scroll back and change all that. But as his mother had always said, wishes were like dreams, they rarely came true. Aye, she was a cheery bugger, his mother, he thought. But with a husband who spent his time either at work or in the pub before handing her a pittance on which to bring up the family, she'd had every reason to be less than happy, he supposed.

'You daydreaming again?' said Ella, drying her hands on a tea towel.

'Just thinking aboot the big fella,' he replied, nodding to James to make sure that the child wouldn't hear anything that would make him worry.

'I telt you when I first came here that he looked dreadful. Of course, add *madam* to the mix and hey presto, your man's in the hospital.'

'She's been through the mill hersel', Ella. Took a right battering, by the look o' her.'

'Well, no woman deserves that – no' even her. But why did she head straight doon here? She's a family at hame wae a big hoose and nae shortage o' money. Why no' just go to them for help?'

'How keen were you tae go to your mother when there were problems?'

Ella Scott thought for a moment. 'Aye, true. But I'd no' been tae bed wae half o' Strathclyde Police – aye, an' bugger knows who else, tae.'

'Who's bugger?' said James, looking up from his breakfast cereal, face slathered in chocolate milk.

'Och, just a person Auntie Ella doesnae like too much, son.'

'Hameby says there's a lot o' buggers down on the pier, Muncle Brian.'

'Aye, well, don't you worry what Hameby has tae say.'

'Yes, just you listen tae your Uncle Brian, son. You'll no' go wrong there,' said Ella, her eyes raised to the heavens.

'Muncle Brian's funny, Auntie Ella.' The wee boy laughed.

'Oh aye, just hilarious, son – a laugh a minute,' she replied unsmilingly.

Scott was about to reply when his phone vibrated on the breakfast table. Wondering if it was news about Jim Daley, he fumbled it into his hand, then mouthed 'Symington' to Ella before walking out to take the call.

'Yes, ma'am?'

'Another success last night I hear, DS Scott.'

'Sorry, ma'am?'

'Mr Sanjeev. He's made a complaint against us and a local resident this morning. After you broke down his door in the middle of the night and terrified the wits out of the poor man.'

'I was just acting on information aboot the missing crewman, ma'am.'

'Flawed information, DS Scott – seriously flawed!'

'Yes, ma'am.'

'Anyway, we can speak about that when you come in. When are you coming in, incidentally?'

'Just on my way, ma'am.'

'Good. Well, get here as quickly as possible. I have something urgent we need to discuss. Some good news about your friend, but I suppose you'll have heard.'

'No, ma'am.'

'Well, he's stable. Just had a heart scan. They reckon he might have a slight arrhythmia problem, but easily fixed with drugs, they hope. Might be out of hospital later today. But he'll have to go back in a while to have more checks, so he won't be coming back to work any time soon.'

'Great news, Carrie!' said Scott, forgetting protocol in the relief of hearing Daley was out of danger.

'Yes, well, he'll have to be replaced – temporarily, at least. That's what I want to talk to you about. So get in as soon as, Brian.'

Before he could say goodbye the phone went dead. He smiled, delighted by the news about Daley, but the joy was soon replaced by the familiar feeling of being in trouble again. Och well, you can't have everything, he thought as he took his jacket from the stand in the hall and flung it over his shoulders.

'That's me away, Ella. Oor man might be getting oot o' hospital later today,' he said, poking his head round the kitchen door.

'What's been the problem?'

'Eh, I'm no' sure what she said – sounded like diarrhoea.'

'What? First time I've heard o' anyone passing oot wae that.'

'I don't know. I've felt like passing oot a few times I've had the runs.'

'Charming. That's just because you were mostly to the nose the night before.'

'Listen, I have tae rush. Her majesty wants me in PDQ.'

He hurried down the hall and out into the drizzle of a grey September morning, a bounce in his step, despite the roasting he was more than likely about to receive at the hands of his boss.

But Brian Scott was well used to being hauled over the coals.

16

Captain Banks was on the bridge of the *Great Britain*. He'd spent a restless night thinking about Majid. He knew that when the police in Kinloch failed to turn anything up, he'd have no choice other than to inform Commander Brachen, and that was likely to ignite the kind of furore only Her Majesty's Royal Navy could initiate. He stroked his chin in contemplation. Why were people so stupid, he wondered?

Kinloch had almost disappeared in the heavy smir of rain, but the ship was quiet. Most of his passengers were sleeping off the party that had carried on until just after four in the morning, when Banks had ordered his head steward to put an end to proceedings.

He envisaged a morning filled by meetings with Brachen and Tansie. Looking at his Omega wristwatch, he decided to hang on for half an hour or so before setting things in motion.

The door of the bridge swung open to reveal Brachen in full uniform.

'A word please, Captain, if you don't mind.'

'Certainly. You have the bridge, Steele,' he said to the first mate. 'In my cabin, Commander?'

'Yes, I think that would be appropriate,' Brachen replied sharply.

The pair made their way down from the bridge and into Banks's large cabin, located directly underneath.

'Can I get you some coffee, tea, Commander Brachen?'

'No, you can bloody well tell me what you think you've been doing since you found out that one of your crew has gone missing!' Brachen's tone was sharp.

'May I remind you that I'm the captain of this vessel? It's not your job to upbraid me. I hope that's clear.'

'I'll do what the bloody hell I like. For fuck's sake, man, even basic seamanship tells you that you raise the alarm if one of the crew goes missing. He could have fallen overboard!'

'He didn't fall overboard.'

'How do you know?'

'He was on one of the launches that were ferrying dignitaries to and fro yesterday. He jumped off at the pier. Told the bosun he had to get something done in the town – family stuff. He had a bag with him. Though the rest of the crew waited, he didn't return, so they had no choice except to carry on with what they were doing without him.'

'Brilliant!'

'I've informed the local police, who have a full description of him, plus a photograph. I thought it prudent, given what was happening aboard yesterday, to make as little as possible of the incident. You people do overreact. Just think what it would have done for the reception.'

'You should have informed me immediately. The actions I'd have taken would have been wholly appropriate, I can assure you – unlike yours!'

'May I remind you once more, *Commander* Brachen, that I remain the captain of this vessel. One of *my* crew is missing, not yours. I did as I saw – and see – fit, and that for me is the end of the matter. Should the police in Kinloch be unable to trace him, then I had every intention of informing you. However, I await information from them, so if you please, I have work to do.' Banks stood, holding his arm towards the cabin door. 'Good morning, Commander.'

'I hope for your sake they've found him, or I will take charge of the situation.' With a furious look, Brachen left the cabin, slamming the door behind him.

Ned Paterson and his nephew were hauling lobster creels out in the Sound. The Isle of Arran looked grey and unwelcoming in the drizzle, and the sea dark, matching Paterson's mood. Only one lobster all morning, and it was undersized and had to be thrown back.

He swore under his breath as he let the coil of rope suspending another empty creel back into the brooding Sound, to lie in wait for an unsuspecting crustacean under a small pink float, or so he hoped.

'No' good the day, Uncle Ned, eh?'

'No, Billy, it sure is not. Only another four creels tae check, and nothing. I blame that bloody great cruise ship. Noise an' lights a' day and night. Puts the lobsters off. We might have tae think about moving the creels.'

He stared the few hundred yards to where the next float bobbed, praying that the creel beneath held something worthwhile.

'What's that?' said Billy.

Following his nephew's line of sight, Ned squinted through the smir at a grey-looking object a few yards from the boat. 'It's too big for a dead fish, unless it's a shark. Might be an unfortunate seal or dolphin, I suppose. C'mon, we'll take a look.'

He fired up the small inboard diesel engine, and the lobster boat chugged in the direction of the motionless floating shape. 'Gie it a tug wae the boathook, Billy!' he shouted above the rattle of the engine, as the now soaking rain hissed off his wet weather gear. Some days at sea were a joy; this certainly wasn't one of them.

'Whootever it is, it's bloody heavy,' said Billy, as Paterson shut off the engine and let the vessel float nearer to the object. 'I've got a grip on it, mind you.'

Paterson made his way to the front of the boat as his nephew strained with the boathook. He leaned over the side of the vessel in order to get a better look at the thing that had caught their attention. 'Wae a bit o' luck it'll be a beluga whale, Billy, eh?'

Quickly, though, the expression on his face changed; on closer inspection, the object in the water was no seal, whale or dolphin. As Billy pulled, the grey mound upended itself. Both fishermen recoiled at the sight of an ugly stump of a neck, bloodied, where a human head had once been.

'Oh, for fuck's sake!' Billy shouted.

'Steady, son. We'll need tae call the harbourmaster. Keep a haud o' it as best you can.'

As Paterson rushed to the tiny wheelhouse for the radio, his nephew leaned over the rail, face averted from the headless torso bobbing in the water. He was still spewing up as his uncle, voice quaking, spoke to Kinloch's harbour master.

Still in his cabin, Banks answered the phone on his desk. 'Yes, Captain Banks speaking.'

He listened carefully to the caller, shaking his head as he did so. 'And what's next – in terms of finding him, I mean?'

He nodded silently at the reply, thanked the caller, and replaced the handset in its cradle.

He drummed his fingers on the desk for a few moments and lifted the phone once more. 'Ask Commander Brachen to come to my cabin, please, Reggie.'

He leaned back in his chair, stared at the ceiling of the cabin. Now the Royal Navy and MI5 would swing into action, and his life would become infinitely more difficult.

17

Scott pressed the entry code into the panel next to the back door of Kinloch Police Office and rushed inside, glad to be out of the rain.

'Hey, where's the fire?' he said as DC Potts dashed towards him, hefting a raincoat around his shoulders.

'They've found a body just off Kilconnan Head, gaffer.'

'This'll be oor man Majid, likely, eh?'

'I'm just going out with the harbourmaster in the lifeboat to bring the remains to shore. I suppose we'll soon find out.' He was about to head for his car when he stopped. 'Oh, the boss is looking for you. Right agitated, she is – especially after this.'

Scott nodded. 'Aye, I know. I've seen plenty agitated bosses in my time, don't worry. Just you get oot on that lifeboat. Last time I was on it I lost my breakfast – aye, an' my dinner the night before, intae the bargain. Keep me up tae speed.'

Without bothering to go to the CID suite, he turned left along the corridor and stopped at Symington's office. He straightened his tie then knocked on the door, hearing the sharp invitation to enter before he turned the brass handle.

Symington was behind her desk, typing quickly on a

laptop. She looked up and nodded to the chair at her desk. 'Sit down, DS Scott.'

Scott did as he was asked, and watched her type with no little admiration for the speed at which she could do so. He waited silently for the onslaught.

Symington closed the lid of the laptop and stared at her Detective Sergeant. 'You'll have heard they've found a body.'

'Yes, ma'am. Out at Kilconnan. DC Potts just informed me.'

'Pound to a penny it's our man Majid, Brian.'

'Possibly,' said Scott, secretly pleased that she'd used his Christian name, always a good sign from a senior officer, in his experience.

'Well, I suspect we're about to become very busy, so I won't bang on.'

'No, ma'am.' Here we go, thought Scott.

'My information is that DCI Daley will indeed be discharged from hospital later today.'

'Oh, great!'

'Yes, good news. But he won't be returning to duty – not until they've investigated fully what caused his collapse, and it's being properly treated.'

'No, ma'am. I guess you'll have tae fill in for him? Him being the sub-divisional commander, an' all.'

'I have a division to run, but someone will have to fill in for DCI Daley, that's true.'

'Some young high-flyer, no doubt. Och, I've seen them come and go.'

'I sincerely hope the person I have in mind will want to stay in Kinloch.'

Scott thought for a moment. 'But what about DCI Daley,

ma'am? I thought you said he'd be returning tae duty once he gets sorted an' that.'

'I hope that will be the case, but he's not out of the woods yet – healthwise, that is.'

'I see.' Scott could now feel his heart in his boots. He'd felt encouraged by Symington's earlier manner, but now things didn't seem as rosy.

'Now, I'm not going to mention the unfortunate incident last night, despite the fact that I believe you threatened to,' she consulted her notes, 'shit in Mr Duncan's dinner, then ordered him to be thrown bodily down a stone staircase.'

'Noo that was just a figure o' speech, ma'am. You see, this auld guy was . . . och, it's a long story. You had tae be there.'

'You can tell me this *long story* in your report. Meanwhile, as you know, we have other pressing matters at hand.'

'Aye, right enough, ma'am. I'll get that report tae you later this afternoon.'

'Good. I'll be interested to hear why one of my officers finds that the threat of defecation in a member of the public's meal is the right way to go about his business. But I know you'll find a creative excuse.'

Scott nodded but said nothing, figuring he was in a better position than he'd expected to be. Saying something – anything – in his defence was likely to make matters worse.

'Now, as to DCI Daley's replacement, I've been speaking with the ACC. He and I are on the same page as far as this is concerned.'

'Oh, aye.'

'First, we intend to give DC Potts a temporary promotion to Acting Detective Sergeant.'

'Eh? He's a fine lad, aye, and he likely deserves a promotion. But what aboot me? There's no' room for two detective sergeants here, I widnae have thought.'

'Indeed, absolutely correct. Kinloch doesn't justify it in terms of size and so on.'

'Right, so I'm back off up the road. Just when Ella was getting settled in, tae.' Scott shook his head and looked at the floor. 'I suppose young Potts has a degree. The only degrees I've got are from the . . .' He paused. 'Well, never mind, ma'am. Just a wee club I belong tae.'

She raised an eyebrow. 'What you do in your own time is your business – as long as it's lawful, that is.'

'Oh, aye. Nothing unlawful about the Lodge – er, the club, ma'am.'

'Right, to the point. I want you to move your things this morning . . .'

'Aw, come on,' said Scott, breaking into her sentence.

'Move them into DCI Daley's office, Acting Detective Inspector Scott.'

Scott opened his mouth then closed it again. 'Aye, an' I just came here in Apollo 24. You're no' so good at the jokes, ma'am.' He laughed.

'I can assure you, there's no joke involved. You'll replace DCI Daley in his capacity as head of CID and nominally as sub-divisional commander when, or indeed if, he returns. I'll be close at hand to take care of divisional matters. We're in for a bloody hard time with all this, as you know. Every eye will be on us. But, as far as it goes, I'm sure you're more than equal to the task.' She stood and held out her hand. 'Congratulations, Acting DI Scott.'

Bewildered, Scott took her hand, and shook it enthusiastically. 'Thank you, ma'am. I've got to say, that was a title I never thought I'd hear.'

'Remember, you're *Acting* DI, but it's still a feather in your cap – long overdue, in my opinion. Let's try not to make an arse of it, Brian.' She smiled. 'Right, no time like the present. You get on with things, and we wait to find out what this body is all about.'

'Aye, right, Carrie – ma'am. Oor Ella won't believe this!'

'Somehow, I'm sure that's true.'

Scott got to his feet and headed for the door.

'Oh, and Brian . . .'

'Yes, ma'am?'

'Send your measurements to HQ. You'll need a uniform – even if it's only for ceremonial purposes.'

'Aye, right, ma'am.'

Scott left the room wondering when he'd last worn a police uniform. No' this century, anyhow, he reckoned.

The new campsite was concealed deep within a thick pine forest on the opposite side of the loch. At first, they'd struggled to find the track outlined in their new orders, but with maps, satnav and many false starts, Cabdi and Faduma eventually reached the small clearing where they had parked and erected their tents.

Faduma was now sullen. He realised that he'd been rash in taking the elderly man captive, and that Cabdi wasn't at all happy with him. Still, though, he resented being subordinate to his companion. No one had his zeal, his will to fight for the cause. He yearned to avenge those killed by the Infidel with a passion that made him feel as though he was already heading for paradise.

Also, he was worried about Cabdi. Did he have the same hatred for those who were trying to destroy their people and everything they believed in? Faduma wasn't sure. The man was too squeamish when it came to punishing those who must surely die. Secretly, Faduma was becoming more and more concerned about Cabdi's will to end the task they had begun, a task that would almost certainly end in their glorious martyrdom and the paradise that followed.

He watched his companion as he prepared food over a camping stove. The thin man's long legs were folded in on themselves as he squatted to stir a huge pot.

'It smells delicious, my brother. You have skill with food, there is no doubt.'

'Taught me by my mother,' replied Cabdi. 'Take your time, love what you do, use spices and herbs, and make the food sing. That is what she always told me.'

'She was a good teacher.'

'I think we must practise with our equipment. I want to make sure that everything goes as planned. We have already made one big mistake – there must be no more. Our mission cannot fail.'

'You worry too much. Once we have eaten, I will test the equipment. Our leader has been clever; this is an even better place from which to work. These tall trees give us cover, and the track leads to a high point from where we can do what must be done.'

Cabdi didn't take his eyes from the pot he was stirring, merely nodding at Faduma's enthusiastic comments.

'Have you nothing to say?'

'No, I am concentrating on our meal. We pray, eat and

then test the equipment. You remember the words of our leader – you obey me in everything, now.'

'We were partners, now you are my master. How is this fair?'

'It's fair because of what you did. You are lucky still to be alive. Be thankful, my brother, for you know our leader would not hesitate to have you killed if he chose. It is only because of your expertise with the machine that you are still alive, I think.'

Without speaking, Faduma stared at the man cooking his meal. Resentment was rapidly now turning into hatred. Faduma knew that he was the instrument of destruction. Cabdi was a tool, a mere cog in the machine that he would set in motion. Ultimately, he would decide when things would be done. He would bide his time.

18

The prospect of the drive from the hospital in Paisley to Kinloch had worried Liz, but Daley had been determined to return to where he now called home, and to his son. Though not keen on the idea, the doctors at the Royal Alexandra Hospital relented, trusting that the clinicians in Kinloch could cope with the solution of drugs needed to stabilise Daley's heart just as well as those in Paisley.

Despite the assurances that he was fit for the journey, she kept checking the wellbeing of the man to whom she was still married. Just in case, though, she drove the hired car much more carefully than usual towards remote Kinloch.

At one point he dozed off, head lolling against the passenger window. Anxiously she took his arm and pulled on one of his fingers, and was relieved when he opened his eyes.

They drove on, the tall hills on either side obscured by low cloud on this grey day, as the rain splattered off the windscreen and kept the wipers busy with an irritating yet hypnotic squeal.

They were roughly halfway to Kinloch before Daley spoke.

'We'll pick up James and go back to the house. I'll get Ella on the mobile.'

'Oh,' said Liz.

'Oh what?'

'Just . . . just that I wasn't sure if you'd want me in the house.'

'Where else would you go?'

'I could book into the County, if you feel it would be better.' She hated the conversations she had with her estranged husband now; the long pauses, silences, unfinished sentences – unspoken hatred on his part, she thought. 'Though I suppose that my being in the house would be better for you. You know, just in case . . .'

'In case what – I die, you mean?'

'No! Oh, for heaven's sake, Jim. It's like treading on eggshells every time we speak. Can't we at least be civil, even if it's just until you recover?'

'I'll be fine.'

She turned to look at him, eyes flashing. 'No, you won't just *be fine*. You heard the cardiologist. This is a real wake-up call. You have to start looking after yourself – right now!'

'Yes, dear, thank you so much for your concern. Until some bastard beat you up, you weren't bothered whether I lived or died. What's changed?'

'Do you want your son to grow up without a father, is that it? Are you pining so much for that girl that you've forgotten you have responsibilities to your own flesh and blood?'

Daley shook his head. 'That's so typical of you, Liz. You've shagged your way right through our marriage – and not with me, either. Now all you can think about is that I was capable of finding happiness elsewhere. Pathetic.'

'She was half your age!'

'She was a beautiful person – nicer, kinder, better than you'll ever be – ever be capable of being!' He banged his fist against the glove box, then grimaced, putting one hand to his chest.

'What is it? Are you okay?' Her face had drained of colour, the red anger of only moments before gone.

'It's fine, just a twinge. They told me that would happen until the drugs kick in properly.'

He pulled his mobile phone from his pocket and dialled Ella Scott.

The body, minus feet, hands and head, lay on a gurney in the mortuary at Kinloch Hospital. The pathologist, who had been flown in from Glasgow, was examining the remains with the detached efficiency that epitomised her profession.

In gowns and masks, Scott, Potts and a local doctor who was assisting looked on.

'Certainly in late middle age, possibly older,' said pathologist Yanka Omelia, her voice heavily accented.

'Thought that myself,' said Dr Terence Brady, Kinloch's newest GP, clearly not immune to the allure of the blue-eyed Latvian woman working on the remains.

'You don't have to agree with everything I say, Doctor Brady. Just do your job, please.'

Nice put-down, thought Scott, grinning behind his mask. 'So, you can find oot his identity wae DNA and that, eh?' he asked.

'I can certainly extract DNA from the remains, but unless you have a match for him, it doesn't mean we'll find out who he is.'

'Aye, but he's Asian, right?'

She stopped what she was doing and stared at Scott. 'Whatever makes you think that?'

'The guy we're looking for is Asian.'

'This man's skin is pale – does he look Asian to you?'

'Aye, but being in the water an' that, you know . . .'

'You think it's washed his skin white, is that it, Inspector?'

For a split second Scott hesitated, wondering who the inspector was, then quickly realising it was himself, shook his head. 'Naw, that's no' what I meant at all. I've seen loads o' bodies come oot o' the sea. Nearly all o' them are bloated, white and puffy – do you get what I mean?'

She stared at him for a couple of seconds, then went back about her business. 'Yes, this person – or these remains, at least – have been in the sea, but not for long. I'd say no more than a few hours. And as far as the identity of the individual is concerned, I can almost definitely say he's not Asian.'

Scott reckoned that he didn't want to pick a fight with Yanka Omelia. 'So can you guess a wee bit, though?'

'Guess? My job is not about guessing, Inspector. If you want a considered opinion, that is easier to give, but guess, no.' She looked at Dr Brady. 'And you can please stop nodding. I find it distracting.'

Even under his mask, the blush on the young clinician's face was plain.

'Aye, a *considered opinion*, then, please,' said Scott.

'A white male, between mid-sixties and mid-seventies in age. Adding on feet and a head, I'd say probably five feet six to five feet seven inches tall. Though the hair on his chest is mostly grey, I'd say that this man would have had blond or red hair when he was young. No particular scars or tattoos that may help identify him, though he has a large mole just below his left shoulder blade. In my opinion, most certainly not of Asian extraction.'

'And what about his feet, head and hands?'

'Removed roughly, most probably with a knife. Most likely

one with a serrated edge – and not particularly sharp, by the look of things. The cut marks on the bones indicate this. Clearly done to hide his identity.'

'I'm no' Sherlock Holmes, but I kinda reckoned that mysel',' said Scott.

'Very well done, I'd say,' said Brady.

'Thanks, son,' said Scott.

'N-no, I was meaning Ms Omelia, actually, Inspector.'

'You have experience in pathology, Doctor Brady?' she asked.

'Well, no, not directly, but . . .'

'In that case, how would you know if the job I'm doing is good or bad? I just wish you would all let me get on with what I have to do. You will have a full report within twenty-four hours, Inspector.'

Scott thanked the irritable pathologist, and left her and the unfortunate Dr Brady to their task. He and Potts removed their masks and gowns and washed their hands in the anteroom adjoining the mortuary.

'Let that be a lesson tae you, Potts. Just because you spy a pretty woman, doesnae mean tae say she'll no' be able tae bite your throat oot.'

'I noticed that, though it didn't seem to put the good doctor off at all.'

'He's got no chance there.' Scott flung on his jacket, checked his pockets, and hooked out his mobile phone. 'Right, we've got a missing Asian man, and a deid geriatric ginger. Just the kind o' thing you don't want to happen when you've just been promoted, temporarily or no'. Are there any local missing persons?'

'No, gaffer, not to my knowledge.'

'Well, if she's right and the body has only been in the sea for a few hours, it didnae come fae far away, so we'd better get asking questions.'

'And still nothing on this Majid.'

'No. Captain Banks phoned me earlier. We've flung oot the net, but he could be anywhere by now.'

'I hope he's still got his head.'

'You know how tae cheer a man up.' Scott looked at his watch. 'You picked a fine time tae leave me, big Jimmy.'

'Is that not a song?'

'No, but "Move your arse before you get my boot up it" is one of my favourites.'

The pair left the hospital, now with two mysteries to solve.

Having picked up James from Ella Scott, the small, dysfunctional Daley family made its way back up the hill to Daley's home. The little boy sang to himself in the back seat as they took the steep lane, the engine of the hired car whining at the gradient.

'Mummy, what's a right shithouse?'

'James! Don't say that. Where did you hear it?'

'Muncle Brian said it last night.'

'Don't listen to what *Muncle* Brian has to say. And certainly don't repeat it.' She looked across at her husband. 'Time you'd a word with your pal, is it not? What kind of man speaks like that in front of a child?'

'The kind that doesn't beat women black and blue,' replied Daley flatly.

'I'm going to take James back home.'

'Okay.'

'So, you don't want to see your son?'

'No, that's not the case at all. What I don't want – what I'll never let happen again – is for you to manipulate me all the time. If you want to go back to Howwood, that's fine. I can keep James. I don't have anything else to do, that's for sure. You can get on with your exciting new life.'

'Thanks. Thanks a lot, Jim.'

'What do you want me to say?'

'Oh, forget it! Anyway, I'm not leaving you alone after all this.'

'Do what you want, Liz. That's what you've always done, and that's what you always will do.'

In silence, they pulled up under the decking balcony of Daley's bungalow, unloaded the car and entered what had once, albeit briefly, been a proper family home.

19

Peter Scally fretted as he walked down Long Road heading for the centre of Kinloch. While he was tired, he was even more worried. Maggie Pearson was going to report her husband as missing.

He'd tried to persuade her that Cameron would turn up, but she would have none of it. Most likely scenario was that he'd fallen in the dark and was lying at the bottom of a cliff, either dead or badly injured, she reckoned.

He knew he'd been selfish; that he should have alerted the authorities about his missing friend after what he and his grandson had witnessed the night before. But he didn't want to face yet more gossip, and probably questions from the police when Pearson failed to appear.

He thought of the two mysterious men in the van he and Kevin had seen. There was something about them that made him uneasy – very uneasy.

He had his hands in his pockets, and his thumb brushed the rough edges of the fragment of bone he'd found amongst the ashes the previous night. He'd been looking at it all morning. He hated lying – one lie just led to another, and before you knew where you were the truth became a stranger.

But who'd want to kill Cameron Pearson? He'd always been a popular, well-doing man, respected throughout the community. He knew that's what they'd say.

No, there was only one man upon whom suspicion would fall – him, Peter Scally.

'Hey, Papa!' The voice came from the other side of the street.

Scally watched his grandson wait for a lorry to pass then run across the road in his direction.

'Right, Kevin, lad, whoot's happening?'

'Have you no' heard?'

'Heard whoot?'

'Ned Paterson found a body in the Sound this morning. They're saying a headless corpse.' The young man looked at his grandfather desperately.

'They've found bodies in the water roon here before now. Look at that poor lassie at Machrie a few years ago. We're right beside the Atlantic, Kevin. Bodies can wash in fae America.'

'It's time tae come clean, Papa. We saw they two guys last night. I don't know whoot they were up tae, but Cameron was your pal. If they fellas we saw last night did something to him and we stay quiet, we're as guilty as them.'

Scally shook his head. 'Now, wait a minute, son. Jeest forget we saw anything last night. You know whoot they say about volunteers – always the first tae get their heids blown off, right? Maggie's going to report Cameron missing tae the polis today. We'll jeest leave this well alone.'

'No. If you don't tell them what we saw, I will. I want you tae come up tae the polis station wae me right now. Now, Papa!'

Peter Scally looked at his feet, and sighed. 'Right, we do it your way. But listen tae me. We can tell them aboot those blokes an' the fire, but we're no' going tae make a big production of it. That's the kind o' stuff the polis love. The next minute they'll be setting us up wae killing Cameron.'

'So, you do think it is him!'

'No, I don't think that for one minute. But they blokes was up tae something, and you're right, we should tell the polis. But nothing more than we need tae say. We was up the hill looking for him and we saw they men. Anything else they can find oot for themselves, right?'

'Okay, Papa. Come on, my car's parked just doon the road. I'll take you up tae the station.'

'Fine, Kevin, son.'

As they walked to the car, Peter Scally wished he'd left the skull fragment at home instead of in his left trouser pocket, heading for Kinloch Police Office.

The meal had been delicious, Faduma had to admit. Even though he now resented his partner, the man's cooking was as good as any he'd tasted. But even as he'd enjoyed the food it had reminded him of home, and the sadness that he'd never see his family again had overcome him.

He thanked Cabdi for the meal and then made his way to the back of the van.

The steel box was around the size of two beer crates, with stout handles on two sides and rubber stoppers at each corner. It was robust, as it had to be in order to protect what lay inside.

Carefully, Faduma hefted the box from the van and laid it on the rough ground under the canopy of fir trees. He clicked

111

open both catches and lifted the heavy lid. Inside, secure in a tightly fitting foam mould, sat a white drone. It had four limbs, configured in an X shape. Its centre was bulky, broader than a normal drone. This casement was sealed, but Faduma knew what lay inside, and it was deadly.

He removed the drone and the remote control beside it, then, again very carefully, replaced the lid on the box and lifted it back into the van.

He carried the device to an open patch of ground away from the vehicle, knelt before it pressing buttons, and then stepped back, the remote control held in front of him with both hands.

'The machine is ready?' said Cabdi, bounding across the ground towards him, an excited look on his face.

'Yes. I am ready to test it.'

Cabdi looked at the device intently. 'You have not armed it, I hope.'

'Of course not. Look.' He walked across to the drone. 'I arm it by using this button. You don't trust me, Cabdi, and that thought makes my heart sore.'

'You have been foolish. My heart aches, too – aches for what might have happened.' He looked into the sky. 'It is clear. Let's try to fly it – get it off the ground, at least.

Faduma stepped away from the drone again, pressed a button on the hand-held console and watched as small rotors at the end of each of the four arms buzzed into life. With his tongue sticking out between his teeth, he worked the little joystick, and soon, slowly and steadily, the drone rose into the air.

'Look, Cabdi – come and see the screen!'

Cabdi did as he was bid, and looking over Faduma's

shoulder he watched the trees disappear to reveal the broad vista of the loch and the hills behind it.

'How steady it is,' said Cabdi.

'Yes, brother. If we wanted, we could just stay here and launch the drone – to its full purpose, I mean. No one would see us – or it – until it was too late.'

'No. You know what our instructions are. We find a vantage point. Remember, we have to film the drone – the end result. I must use our camera to catch the moment we strike. In minutes the destruction of the *Great Britain* will be all over the world. Many of the world's richest men and women will die with it, and the deaths of our brothers and sisters will be avenged. Now, bring it down. We know it works, and we don't want to attract any more attention.' Cabdi lowered his gaze from the drone to Faduma for a few seconds, then walked away.

Faduma felt his temper rise. Who was this man who could now tell him what to do? They had been partners; now Cabdi was master. Faduma knew what he wanted. *You will see what I can do*, he said to himself. *Oh, yes, brother, you will know my power.*

Peter Scally and his grandson Kevin sat in the waiting room at Kinloch Police Office. They'd told a uniformed sergeant what they'd seen, and now they were to be interviewed by the CID.

Despite himself, Scally fiddled with the piece of bone in his pocket.

'They're taking their time, Papa.'

'Aye, son. It's done on purpose; they want you to feel guilty.'

'For what?'

'Anything, it doesna matter tae these bastards. They'd have you on the way tae the big hoose in a minute, let me tell you, though you'd done nothing wrong. As long as they solve a crime, they're no' bothered.'

'You're no' a big fan o' the polis, eh, Papa?'

'No.'

'Why? What did you get up tae when you were younger?'

'Och, just a wee misunderstanding outside the Douglas Arms. This is way before your faither was born. I was jeest a boy.'

'Tell me.'

'As I say, me an' this other lad had a wee argument – turned intae a bit o' fisticuffs. Auld Tam Douglas – Willie that has the pub now is his grandson – he called the polis.'

'Were you charged?'

'Nah, we jeest got a good kicking. The sergeant in they days was this big bastard fae Skye. Him and his buddy took us intae the cells and gied us a right good leathering. My eye was black for weeks.'

'That's terrible!' Kevin looked genuinely shocked.

'Och, they never wasted court time on lads at the fighting back then. You got half beaten tae a pulp then flung in the cells wae nae blanket for the night. Then they kicked you – aye, *kicked* you – oot the door at six the next morning. That's whoot passed for justice in they days.'

Kevin shook his head in disbelief. 'By the way, Papa . . .'

'Whoot?'

'Who was you fighting wae?'

'Ach, it's too long ago to worry aboot that – ancient history, Kevin.'

'So what's the harm in telling me?'

'You're a right persistent bugger – jeest like your mother. If you must know, it was Cameron.'

'Who, Cameron Pearson?'

'Aye.'

'And whoot were you fighting o'er?'

'A lassie, if you must know.' Scally folded his arms indignantly.

'Wait, were you fighting o'er Maggie – Maggie Pearson?'

'She was Maggie Watson in they days – and yes, that's whoot we were fighting about, you nosy bastard!'

'So, after all these years you're having it off wae her, while her man's lost on the hill. Papa!'

The door swung open, revealing Acting Sergeant Potts. 'Right, gentlemen. If we could see Mr Scally first, please.'

'How no' jeest see both of us?' said Scally.

'That's the way we'd like to do it – please, sir.'

'See whoot I telt you aboot helping the polis, Kevin?'

Together with the detective, Peter Scally walked to the interview room.

20

Patrick O'Rourke woke with a start and looked at his expensive wristwatch. He took a few moments to take in the beauty of his slumbering young wife, yawned, and made his way across their luxury cabin on the *Great Britain* to the well-appointed bathroom.

When he looked at his face in the mirror he sighed. He was fifty-three years old now, and despite the expensive haircut, the brow lift surgery, and the Botox he'd had injected into his cheeks, he was beginning to look every year of that age.

He remembered his father, who'd never reached his forties. In Patrick's mind he was still a pencil-slim man with long dark hair, a drooping moustache and a twinkle in his green eyes. But that was just about the only advantage for those who died young; they would never grow old in the minds of their loved ones. They were frozen in time in the prime of life.

However, on balance, while Patrick hated the lines, the shadows and aches and pains of middle age, he was still glad to be alive. In any case, his life was very different from his father's.

He remembered the wind in Chicago when they arrived from Belfast. The size of the buildings astonished him; the roar of the traffic; the clunk of the trains; the speed at which people lived their lives. In Chicago there was no skulking round corners hiding from the RUC, the British Army or the UVF.

When they first got to the city – Patrick and his mother – they were an incomplete family, but at least they were alive. They stayed in the top two rooms of his uncle's house in one of the better areas. Though he realised, even then, that his mother resented being beholden to her elder brother, neither of them could deny that life was much better than it had been on the trouble-ridden streets of Belfast.

They did their best to forget those who lay still in the soil back in Ireland – including his father, his brother, two uncles and his grandmother. She had been the only one to die of what was described as 'natural causes', but even now, he still thought a bullet to the head a better way to go than the withering agony of her death from cancer.

Automatically, he brushed his teeth with the electric toothbrush, flossed, and was just about to get into the shower when he heard his cell phone ring.

Tying a towel round his waist, he hurried to the bedside table, sighing when he saw the name of one of his senior managers.

'Hell, Steve, didn't I tell you that I wasn't to be bothered by the business while I was out here? Surely you can handle anything that comes up?' He listened impatiently as Steve told him that one of his many car showrooms had been set alight during a street fight in Richmond. 'What the fuck were the cops doing?'

'They were fighting, boss.'

'Get a hold of Thomas at our insurers. Just how hard is that to work out, Steve?'

He ended the call, not interested in Steve's reply. The guy

was paid well to do his job; there were no excuses for him not to do so.

'Honey, what's wrong?' Cortina, his raven-haired Mexican wife, had been roused from her sleep by the call.

'Just a bunch of guys back home I pay too much to do jobs they're incapable of, that's all. I'm going for a shower. Hey, that was some night last night, yeah?'

'It was fine, honey, but I'm still tired.'

'You get some more sleep. I'm going for a round of golf, you remember? You can lie in bed all day if you want.'

She laid her head back on the pillow and waved him away lazily.

He stood naked in front of the full-length mirror, taking in his sagging frame. Too much good living and not enough exercise had turned him to fat, and it was time for some more liposuction on his girth.

He thought about the showroom destroyed by fire. His uncle would have cried at the thought, but for Patrick O'Rourke it was nothing.

He'd worked hard as a child, eventually graduating from Harvard with an MBA and quickly taking over the running of his uncle Tom's car showroom. Soon it was the biggest auto sales chain in the USA, with offshoots in Canada. Now, despite his dislike for the British, he wanted to build the business in the rest of the world. He wanted lots of things, and he was used to getting his own way.

As he let the warm water wash away the last vestiges of his hangover, his thoughts turned to something else that was important to him – more important than business, even. Something he was determined to achieve.

*

'So both you and your grandson saw these men, Mr Scally?' said Potts.

'Aye, we did that. Sleekit-looking pair, tae.'

'They looked at this fire and then drove off, returning – what, you say in about twenty minutes or so?'

'Aye, that would be aboot right, son. Maybe a while longer.'

'And you were on the hill looking for Mr Pearson, a friend of yours?'

'Aye, that's right – an auld friend at that.'

'These men, can you describe them?'

'Hard for me tae say. You'd be better asking Kevin, he had the night glasses. But one o' them was tall – very thin. The other bloke was shorter, stockier. Both were wearing they bloody hoods that they youngsters like so much.'

'Hooded tops, then. You mention they both looked foreign. Why would you say that if you couldn't see them properly?'

'I'm nae expert in creeds an' colours, son. I'd a quick look through Kevin's night sight, mind you. Tae me it was the way they carried themselves – especially the big man. Tall, rangy – you know whoot I mean. Anyhow, it's hard tae make things oot properly using thon things. They distort everything – I mean colours and that.'

'And they had a van – what kind?'

'I'd say definitely a Transit – no' a new yin neither. Looked white tae me, but Kevin reckons it was mair likely light blue or green – looked different in the night glasses, he said.'

'How long have you been friends with Cameron Pearson?'

Scally rubbed his eyes. 'Och, near sixty years. We was at school together, though he was in a different year fae me, right enough.'

'And Margaret Pearson – his wife – you know her well, too?'

'Aye, of course. Do you no' have friends that are man and wife? It's quite normal, I think. Anyway, this is Kinloch: everyone knows everyone. I'd have thought the polis would have picked up on that by now.'

'And you couldn't make out the registration of the vehicle?'

'No. It was as though the plates was splattered wae mud, or the like. Neither me nor Kevin could make them oot. Well, if he canna see them at his age I've nae chance, eh?' Scally's laugh was forced and nervous. 'Anyhow, I've told you what we saw. I've things to be getting on with.'

'Just a couple more questions, please, Mr Scally.'

'Aye, if you must.' He sighed and folded his arms across his chest.

'You're a former firefighter, am I right?'

'Aye, retained fireman. I've been retired for a long time now, but I did it for twenty-five years. A volunteer, mark you.'

'And you examined the fire?'

'For a while – jeest a fire, whoot else can I say, son? Anyway, they came back, and we had tae get on oor toes quick smart, like.'

'In your opinion, nothing unusual about the fire, then?'

'No, no' really. It was dark, mind.'

'The fire officer tells us that a propellant was used – probably petrol. I'd have thought you'd have recognised something like that with your experience, Mr Scally.'

Scally shrugged his shoulders. 'Noo that you mention it, there was a smell of fuel.'

'Right, Mr Scally, thank you very much for your help.' Potts collected his notes and nodded to the DC beside him. 'Interview ends at eleven-thirty hours.'

'Right,' said Scally, picking his cap from the desk in front of him. 'I hope you find Cameron – aye, and soon, tae.'

'Indeed, Mr Scally, indeed.' Potts stood up. 'Oh, just one more thing, sir.'

'Aye, whoot?'

'Why didn't you – or Mrs Pearson, come to that – report Cameron Pearson missing last night?'

Scally shuffled from foot to foot. 'Is it no' true that the polis is no' interested until someone's been missing for over twenty-four hours?'

'Not necessarily, sir. It depends on the circumstances. I'd have thought, what with night falling and him not home, the obvious thing would have been to contact us, no?'

'Maybe you're right, son,' said Scally with a defiant look. 'But we're no' all as clever as the polis.'

On a screen in the CID suite, Acting DI Scott had watched the whole thing, scribbling down some notes as the interview progressed.

He rubbed his chin, realising he needed a shave. 'You're no' telling the truth, Mr Scally,' he murmured under his breath. 'No, no' at all, my man.'

21

Captain Magnus Banks stood on the deck in his best uniform saluting his guests as they passed by, ready to be ferried ashore to the delights of Kinloch and beyond. He had parties heading off to golf courses, distilleries, or just general sightseeing. Banks had just been in another shouting match with Commander Brachen, and though he was smiling, inside he was seething. Each one of his crew – including himself – was to be questioned by the Security Service regarding their knowledge of or acquaintance with missing crewman Majid.

Banks hated not being master of his own vessel. He'd worked hard to get where he was, and the idea that he was subject to the whims of the upstart naval officer infuriated him. Crew members, often from poor parts of the world, desperate to get back home, regularly jumped ship. They missed wives and children, had found a new love on shore, or simply a better way of making money – the possibilities were endless. Now he and his shipmates were being treated as though they were part of some plot against the nation. Perish the thought.

'Mr O'Rourke, good morning to you!' he shouted to the flabby American businessman with the hair weave and the bulging stomach. Despite the man's failing efforts to stay youthful, Banks liked him, finding the car sales billionaire much less pretentious and aloof than many of his fellow passengers.

'And a good day to you, Captain. Fine morning for the magnificent game of golf, eh, buddy?'

'I doubt you'll make the course before afternoon,' said Banks, looking at his watch.

'Yeah, we would have been ashore a whole lot earlier if you stopped throwing such great parties, Captain. Hey, and serving so many fine Scotch malts.'

'We're here to please, Mr O'Rourke. You know you'll be able to see your homeland from the golf course?'

'Hell, if I can see the Windy City from here in Scotland, I'll give you a million bucks when we get back.' He laughed heartily, his face turning red.

'No, not Chicago – Ireland. I remember you telling me you were originally from Belfast.'

For a split second, O'Rourke's face lost all trace of merriment. It was as though a shadow had passed over the large vessel, turning the bright day dull.

'Hey, you're right!' he said, smile restored. 'I should have realised that. From the other side of the peninsula we can see County Antrim, yeah?'

'Yes, absolutely,' replied Banks, suddenly feeling awkward for reasons he couldn't explain.

He was about to change the subject and ask after the health of Mrs O'Rourke when a small, neatly dressed Asian woman, perfectly turned out for the game and sporting a bag full of the most expensive clubs, slapped the large American on the shoulder.

'Are you ready to be soundly defeated, Mr O'Rourke?'

'Mrs Khan. Now you're the perfect example to us all when it comes to abstaining from alcohol. I wish I could take on board that simple advice, as we'd be halfway round the course by now, and I'd be closer to winning our bet.'

'A small wager?' asked Banks.

'Fifty thousand US dollars – if you call that small, Captain?' said Mrs Khan.

'I'm in the wrong business,' said Banks.

'You are very good at your job, Captain. You have made us all feel very welcome and very safe on this beautiful vessel. I can't say I'm a keen sailor, but you have allayed any fears I may have harboured, and now I feel completely at home at sea. It is not a person's worth that makes him or her, but their integrity, and how they go about life and the treatment of others. We learn this from the Prophet, may peace be upon him.'

'I still wouldn't mind having a spare fifty K to risk on a wager.'

'With the money this woman makes selling steel all over the world, fifty *million* dollars is chicken piss, buddy.'

'You overestimate my wealth, Mr O'Rourke.'

'Oh, I make it my business never to underestimate anyone.'

Though he saw the huge grin spread across O'Rourke's face, Banks detected a steeliness; probably the will to win at everything, regardless of the odds. 'Ah, here come your friends from the government,' he said, spotting a tall civil servant dressed appropriately in golf gear.

'Good morning.' Iain McMaster nodded a greeting to all three. 'It's my job today to show you the delights of the golf course at Machrie.' Though his name was Scottish, his accent was crystal-cut upper-class English.

'Show us the delights of the course, as well as promise huge profits for our companies in the United Kingdom, yes?'

'You nailed it there, Mrs Khan,' said O'Rourke.

'Take my advice and don't enter into the wager, Mr McMaster,' said Banks.

'Oh no, that would be impossible in just about every way. I'd like to say it was protocol, but with the stake being more than half my salary I feel it would be a reckless venture – especially given the standard of my game.' He looked at his wealthy charges. 'Right, shall we?'

Though Khan smiled broadly, Banks was sure he could see the merest trace of a sneer on O'Rourke's face – or perhaps it was just a rictus grin, the result of his only too obvious plastic surgery.

Brian Scott sat in Daley's glass box feeling less than comfortable. He'd already had to notch up the height of the swivel chair, and everything on the huge desk seemed too far away. He had to stretch to reach pens, papers – even the computer keyboard. Soon, the belongings of his old friend and boss were gathered in an easy-to-reach clutter around him.

Even the coffee cup he was drinking from, white with a 'J' emblazoned on the side, seemed too big. He supposed this was all redolent of the huge gap the absence of Jim Daley left in his life and work.

While waiting for a visit from Symington, he was taking the time to re-read the notes from Peter Scally and his grandson's interview. Though their statements coincided almost exactly, he knew a man who wasn't telling the truth when he saw one, and Scally had been lying – but about what, and why? Scott was sure he'd do anything to find a missing friend, but there was something amiss.

He shouted through the open door of the glass box. 'Hey, Potts, come in a minute, will you?'

'Yes, Acting Inspector,' said Potts as he entered the room.

'First off,' said Scott, 'stop calling me Acting Inspector. You call me gaffer, an' I'll call you what I like – just the usual.'

'Yes, Ac . . . gaffer.'

'We'll be here a' day if I call you Acting Detective Sergeant Potts, and you return the favour.' Potts stifled a grin. 'Listen, I want you to do something for me.'

'Yes, what?'

'We spoke aboot Scally. Well, I want you tae find oot a' you can aboot him. Past, present, what he likes tae eat, his mother's maiden name – any gossip. Fuck knows, it'll no' be hard doon here. I'd dae it myself, but I'm tied tae this desk waiting for her majesty tae arrive. It's nae wonder oor Jimmy gets so depressed.'

'I always think he's quite cheery.'

'Aye, well, you don't know him like I do, son. What's happening on the good ship bollocks today?'

'Er, just a few excursions to the golf, or distilleries, I believe, sir. All covered by the Security Service. We're to be on alert if there are any problems, but according to one of the Marines I spoke to they've got half the army on standby and a frigate full of commandos out in the Sound. So I don't think our services will be required.'

'Still no sign o' this Majid, then?'

'Guy spotted in Oban fitting his description, but apart from that, nothing. The boys up here are doing the rounds to find out more.'

'And these guys in the van, anything?'

'Nope. I've checked locally, and the uniforms are out asking questions, but nothing.'

'Well, if they exist, they had tae get here somehow. Circulate it to the rest o' the force and start checking every bloody CCTV camera we can get a hold of up and doon that bloody road.'

A small figure appeared behind Potts in the doorway. 'Excuse me, Acting Detective Sergeant Potts,' said Symington, pushing past the detective. Scott raised his brows at the title.

She was out of uniform, wearing a black trouser suit. She looked around the room with a critical eye, and for a moment Scott could picture her predecessor John Donald.

'Oh, something's arrived from HQ for you, gaffer,' said Potts, retreating.

'Aye, well, away and get it, son.'

As Potts closed the door behind him, Symington took a seat. 'You really must use the correct ranks now you're Sub-Divisional Commander, Acting DI Scott.'

'Och, it's an awfy mouthful, ma'am.'

'It's procedure. Please stick to it.' She paused. 'We should have DNA results on our corpse later today. I want to ID this man as soon as we can. Cameron Pearson's son works in Glasgow and has given a DNA sample. He's coming down to be with his mother. I hope it's not him.' She shrugged her shoulders in regret. 'I'll leave you in charge of that, anyway. I've a meeting with the Security Service this afternoon. I know they've spotted someone in Oban fitting Majid's description, but I'm not holding my breath – certainly not after what happened to the owner of our local Indian restaurant, poor man.'

'That was just some racist trying tae rock the boat. I put him in his place, ma'am.'

'Not by shitting in his dinner, I hope.'

'Noo, as I said that was just a turn o' phrase. Och, you had tae be there – I telt you that already.'

'I'm sure. Anyway, before we do anything, I want to take a quick trip up the hill to see how things are with DCI Daley. I'm sure you'll be happy to accompany me.'

'Aye, great. I meant tae go up myself, but you know how things have been, ma'am.'

'Oh yes. It's the old story, Brian. *With power comes responsibility.* I'm sure you've heard it.'

'It was one of John Donald's favourite sayings, ma'am.'

'Yes, well, perhaps he wasn't the best example . . .'

Before she could finish her sentence, there was a sharp knock at the door, and Potts appeared, carrying a large box.

'For you, gaffer.'

'Aye, thank you, Acting Detective Sergeant Potts. Just put it down here.'

Potts did as he was told, with a half-smile at the sudden return of his temporary rank.

'Your uniform, Brian. Better go and try it on. With our distinguished guests out in the loch, chances are you'll need to wear it before long.'

'Right, ma'am. I'll just go to the changing room beside the canteen.'

'Never had you down for a prude, Brian. I'll pull the blinds and turn my back. Hurry up!'

As she closed the blinds around Daley's glass box, Scott opened the box with his ever-present penknife. Sure enough, a hat with silver braid was on top of the rest of the uniform.

Soon, chided by Symington for taking so long, he was changed. Wearing any kind of uniform after all these years felt very odd, especially one with pips on the shoulders – he was more used to chips occupying that particular position.

'Fits like a glove – who would have thought you could look so smart, Brian!'

Scott pulled up one blind and looked at his reflection in the glass. 'I'm like thon bugger Mr Ben.'

'Who?'

'Och, before your time, ma'am. Anyway, I'll get my suit back on and we can head up tae see Jimmy – DCI Daley.'

'Oh, no, definitely keep it on, Brian.'

'Eh?'

'You know what they say: laughter is the best medicine. I'm sure your old friend will love the . . . the sight.'

'Aye, I'm sure.' Scott looked at the face staring back at him from underneath the braided uniform cap and suddenly realised why he'd been happy as a detective sergeant for so many years.

22

Faduma slammed down the bonnet of the van irritably. 'I need proper parts for this, I can keep it running for now, but I don't know for how much longer.'

Cabdi was staring at the sky through the gap in the trees. He acknowledged Faduma with a slight sideways nod of his head, eyes still fixed on the heavens.

'Why do you never answer me, brother?'

'I only answer when there is something to say. The vehicle has done its job, it doesn't have much further to travel.'

'I don't know what you mean.'

'When we launch the weapon, we will do our best to escape. But by now – certainly now a local man is missing – someone will be looking. I heard it on the radio earlier. Maybe not looking for us, but for anyone who can answer questions about his disappearance.'

'So you have new instructions, yes?'

'We flee once our job is done. We take the van to a place near the road, then set it alight.'

'So you are trying to save us? I thought we were to be martyrs!'

As though Faduma had said nothing, Cabdi continued: 'Our job then is to make it difficult for the Infidel to find us

– to use up their resources. Yes, we will be caught, but our masters have something else in mind after our job is done, and to do it we need to become the hunted.'

Faduma scraped the toe of his boot in the dirt. He was tiring of the wait, his soul called out to him every night as he dreamed of the large ship ablaze, with those on board dying in agony amidst their filthy luxury. 'The ship leaves in two days. We must act soon.'

'We will act when our master tells us the time is right, Faduma.'

The smaller man turned on his heel and walked back to the van. He was happier with his tools than he was with his companion now.

He was just about to lift the bonnet when he heard Cabdi's cheap cellphone ring. Faduma watched as the tall man answered the call, nodded, said something he couldn't hear, then returned the device to his pocket.

'So, do we have orders to go ahead?' Faduma's eyes were bright with bloody zeal.

'No. Not today.'

Faduma took in this information for a few moments then roared at the top of his voice, sending birds flying from the surrounding pine trees.

'You want the whole world to know we're here?' said Cabdi, striding towards him, a look of sheer fury on his face. They began to tussle, and this time the wiry, taller man soon had Faduma pinned to the ground by his shoulders.

'Listen to me, Faduma. You have a job to do, and so do I. But both of us are only packhorses, the lowest of the low. We do what we are told to do – we do it. You seem to have a problem with this. Why, brother?'

Faduma struggled, but with surprising strength Cabdi held him tight on the rough ground, staring into his eyes unblinkingly. Soon he lost the urge to struggle any longer and surrendered to Cabdi's will. 'For a doctor, you can handle yourself, brother.'

'I wasn't always a doctor.' The tall man stood, his towering figure now silhouetted against a shaft of sunlight. 'I swear to you once more, do as you are told, Faduma. Only I have kept you alive, you know that?'

'So, I want to kill the Infidel. Is that not why we are here?'

'You were foolish and impulsive. You acted without thought. And, by doing this, you risked all.'

'Why have we not struck back at our enemies? Surely the sooner this is done, the easier it will be?'

'Because this is not what our master wants.'

Faduma pulled himself back to his feet. 'Tell me, Cabdi, who is our master?'

'You ask too much.'

'If you know, why shouldn't I?'

Cabdi stared at his companion, almost looking through him, as though lost in thought.

'Brother?'

'All I know of him is his voice. That's how all of this works, don't you understand, Faduma? We work in groups – cells – of one or two. If we are taken and tortured by the Infidel, all we can tell them is what we were ordered to do, nothing more. No matter what they do to us, the men who are our leaders are safe simply because we don't know who they are.'

'I would never give them away – betray my masters – no matter what the cost. Never!'

Cabdi looked up to the sky once more. 'You would, my brother. At the hands of their torturers you would, trust me.'

Faduma watched Cabdi as he walked away, stopped, then knelt in prayer. Despite the strength of the man, despite his conviction, Faduma was restless. Something was wrong; he could feel it in his soul.

He had to act.

Liz Daley opened the front door of the house on the hill, James Daley junior peering from behind her legs.

'Chief Superintendent, how nice to see you again. Please come in.' She stood aside and let Symington and the uniformed officer with her in. She glanced at the man in the braided cap then took another look. 'Brian?' An astonished expression crossed her face.

'Aye, don't faint, or that. It is me. Just act normal as you can – nothing to see here,' said Scott, removing his cap as he crossed the threshold.

'Muncle Brian!' shouted the toddler, rushing to greet him.

'How are you, son?' Scott picked James up and held him above his head. 'You're getting big, my boy. Too heavy for me, eh?' James chuckled.

'Would it be okay to have a word with Jim, Mrs Daley?' said Symington. 'I know he's on sick leave, but I thought we should pay him a visit, even if it's just to show him this marvel.' She turned to Scott.

'Aye, it would be great to see him, Lizzie.'

Still open-mouthed, Liz turned and led them up the hallway towards the lounge.

Lying across the full length of a leather sofa, DCI Jim Daley had a large hardback book propped on the bulge of his stomach and a pair of round reading glasses perched on his nose, absorbed in the book he was reading. He looked up quickly when his visitors came in.

'Jim,' said Symington. 'You're looking well, I'm pleased to say.'

'Thanks, ma'am.' He laid the book on the floor and made to get to his feet, but Symington stopped him.

'No, stay where you are, Jim. We've just come to say hello.'

Daley took up a seated position, removed his glasses and smiled. 'Thanks for coming, Carrie. You've met my wife, of course.'

'Yes, yes indeed.' The senior police officer smiled at Liz again.

'What, nothing to say tae your old pal, Jimmy?'

Daley squinted in the sunshine pouring through the picture windows that looked across the loch to the hills beyond. First, a broad grin crossed his face, then a chuckle, followed by a full-blown laugh. Though he tried to speak, he doubled over.

'Jim, are you okay?' Liz rushed to his side. But it was soon clear that the tears streaming down the big policeman's face were those of mirth, not pain.

'Is it Hallowe'en?' he managed to say through the guffaws of laughter.

'See, I just knew this was how it would a' play oot,' said Scott flatly. 'One sight o' me wae some pips on my shoulder an' it's like Hallowe'en.'

'Ha,' said Daley. 'Sorry, Brian, but it's the last thing I expected to see.' Helplessly, he burst into another paroxysm of laughter.

'Come here, ya big bugger.' Scott handed James Daley

junior to his mother and rushed over to his old friend, enveloping him in a bear hug. 'Man, I thought we'd lost you the last time I was in this room.' A tear made its way down his cheek, but for different reasons from those of his best friend.

A mobile phone sounded, and Symington thrust a hand into her handbag. She listened for a few moments, thanked the caller, then replaced the phone in her bag.

Sensing her change in mood, both Daley and Scott looked up.

'What's up, ma'am?' said Scott.

'The results of the DNA test on our corpse are through. It's the body of Cameron Pearson. So, we now have a local murder to solve, as well as a missing sailor.'

23

As was the way of things in Kinloch, word had already seeped out that Cameron Pearson was dead and the headless corpse which had been dredged up in the Sound belonged to him.

Still sceptical, in her position behind the bar Annie looked unimpressed.

'And jeest how did you hear this, Neil?' she said to the thin man at the counter.

'I telt you already, Annie. I was just going intae Kerr the bakers for a roll and sausage when this bloke stops me an' asks if I knew Cameron. Aye, says me. The next thing he's asking me a' kinds o' questions. When I asked him why, he said he worked for the papers, and that heidless body was poor Cameron.' He shook his head. 'Och, man, it's enough tae make you want tae get fair pished, so it is.'

'Taking a breath's enough tae make you want tae get *fair pished*. I didna know Cameron very well, but he was always a quiet, decent man – no' much of a drinker, neither.' Annie gave Neil a knowing look.

'You know fine that it's always the quiet ones that are the worst. Sure, honest men like mysel' are too busy working and having a small libation of an evening tae get intae any mischief.

A man like that can have deep, dark thoughts. I widna be surprised if he was involved in some cult, or organised crime, or that.' He drained his glass. 'Another please, Annie – better make it a large one. Jeest tae handle the grief, you understand.'

'You're very quiet, Hamish. You knew Cameron better than any o' us, eh?'

The old man sucked quietly at his unlit pipe, his leathery face wrinkled, slanting eyes closed.

'Bugger me, no' another corpse!' Annie wailed.

Hamish stirred and opened his eyes. 'No, I was jeest engaging my brain. Something you might consider doing yourself, Neil, afore opening that great gaping gob o' yours, that is.'

'Well said,' piped up Annie.

'Cameron was one o' the gentlest souls I ever met. A kind, well-doing man; loved his birds much mair than a glass o' whisky – aye, or even two or three glasses. Man, it's tae be admired when a body can resist the pull o' the bottle wae all its pleasures in favour o' an all-consuming hobby.'

'You've never had much room for the birds, eh, Hamish?' said Neil, winking to his fellow customers.

The old man's eyes flashed. 'I've only loved one woman in my life, and my heart will be true tae her until the day I die!'

A large fisherman rose to his feet and walked across to the bar. 'Apologise noo, you cheeky bastard. There no' one o' us here that will hear a word against the auld fella. Another crack like that, and you'll get a crack – on the heid!'

'Now, now, boys,' Annie put in. 'That'll be enough. A man's deid – one of oor own, tae. We should behave in a fitting manner. Neil?'

'Sorry, Hamish. I was jeest breaking your balls.'

There was a stunned silence in the room, only ended when Annie gave voice to the question on the tip of everyone's tongue. 'You were what?'

'Och, it's an expression fae one o' they gangster movies. It's a Mafia saying.'

'Well, the only Mafia here is me, so if you want tae break any balls, jeest you go and dae it in another establishment. Sounds like the kind o' caper they'd be at o'er at the Douglas Arms, certainly no' in a respectable establishment like this.'

Hamish shuffled to the bar, and automatically Annie moved to pour him a dram.

'Haud your hand, Annie. I've had enough the noo. This news aboot poor Cameron has had the opposite effect on me than it has on Neilly here, obviously. Only the good Lord knows whoot torments poor Cameron had tae suffer. A man that didna deserve them, that's for sure.'

'Stay a whiles,' said Annie, worrying about the old man being alone with his grief. 'Mind we've got that party for they folk off thon big boat tomorrow night. They'll be wanting to hear your tall tales, I'm quite sure. One for the road, eh? Look, I've poured it and everything.'

'No, my dear, but thank you, I'll be off. Aye, and I'll see you tomorrow for sure. Sometimes a man needs a while tae reflect on life, if you know whoot I mean.'

As she watched Hamish leave, she turned to Neil. 'I hope you're proud o' yourself. When you've done wae that dram that's your last for the night. If there's balls tae be broken aboot it, I'll be the one tae do it.'

There followed a ragged cheer as Neil sipped at his last whisky of the day – in the County Hotel, at least.

*

Hamish leaned against the outside wall of the hotel for a while, taking in the bustling town. Alistair the butcher waved to him from his van, while across the road a huddle of young girls was staring at something on a phone, laughing and giggling as they did so. Jean Duncan, pulling a shopping trolley, said hello as she passed by and commented on the dreadful fate of Cameron Pearson.

He watched Archie Dixon haul a sack of potatoes on his back, then bundle it into the back of his car, as his wife Mhairi chided him about something or other. He noted how interesting their conversation was to Amy McKay, purposefully slowing her stride as she neared the car, better to hear just what was being said.

He recalled a night much like this, standing with his old skipper Sandy Hoynes as they chewed the fat after a few drams and shared a convivial smoke before they took their separate paths home. It seemed like yesterday, but it was a long time ago.

As Hamish puffed blue tobacco smoke into the air, he remembered the day when news such as today's would have seen everyone in Kinloch scuttle for hearth and home, keeping their families close, while at the same time thanking God that they weren't the ones lying dead.

That things had changed there was no doubt. But for Hamish nothing seemed to have altered for the better. He feared the day when the wee town where he'd grown up and lived all his life turned into just any other place, where community was of little value, and friends and neighbours were to be found on the screens of new-fangled devices and not across the garden fence, on the street, or over a dram or two at the County.

Maybe he was just getting old, and the way he felt now was the way old men down the centuries had felt about the changes they'd seen in their lifetimes. Och, he wasn't sure – perhaps it was just a touch of melancholy. The glums could hit any man with a taste for the water of life, especially on days like this.

As he reflected on the changes the passage of years had brought, something niggled at his conscience – had done since he'd heard the news.

He'd never been a man to tell tales. He remembered his father giving him a swift clout round the lug when he'd run to tell him that Jamie Morrans had kicked the football in his face deliberately.

Don't tell tales, son, jeest you go back and do something aboot it. His father's voice was as clear in his head now as it had been all those years ago.

Now, though, he felt he must heed only part of the wisdom imparted to him on that day. Instead of turning left down Main Street to begin the long walk home, he turned right, heading up the hill for Kinloch Police Office.

When Patrick O'Rourke arrived at Machrie he took the time to stand and look across the water to the place of his birth. Though he'd never returned to Belfast – or the island of Ireland, come to that – since leaving as a child, the place still burned in his heart. Sometimes it was a warm, comforting feeling; on other occasions – most, in fact – the hatred he felt for what had been done to his family made him feel almost sick.

And there it was; he could almost touch the place.

'Are you ready to lose fifty thousand dollars, Mr O'Rourke?' said Khan, taking short quick steps towards the first tee along with the tall McMaster, their UK civil service minder, the man who wanted to persuade them to invest in UK plc.

'Ready? Sure I'm ready, but not to lose our bet. I just hope for your sake that those steel mills of yours are working as fast as they can,' he replied, smiling broadly.

'All over the world, Mr O'Rourke.'

Before they teed off he turned back to take another look at County Antrim over his shoulder, the smile already gone from his lips.

24

Brian Scott was waiting for a cup of coffee to drop from the machine in the office canteen when Sergeant Shaw appeared.

'A visitor for you, sir.'

'Will you cut oot this *sir* stuff. They pips on my shoulder earlier are like snowdrops on the river, a moment white, then gone for ever.'

'Burns.'

'What, the coffee?'

'No, what you've just said – it's from a Rabbie Burns poem.'

'I thought Jimmy made it up. He's forever saying it. Mind you, just the kind o' cheery stuff you get from him, eh?'

'Now you're at the same patter. Must be something to do with rising in the ranks.'

'I can think o' one o' my own sayings tae answer that.' Scott pulled the cardboard cup from the machine and took a sip of warm coffee. 'So, who's this visitor?'

'Your old pal Hamish.'

'Shit! I'd love to chat wae the old boy, but I've got my hands full here. Can you fend him off?'

'No, I don't think he's in for a yarn. Says he has some important information to pass on.'

'The price o' fish, likely.'

'What's that got to do with anything?'

'Exactly.' Scott winked. 'Tell you what, gie me a couple o' minutes and send him through tae my office.'

'Woo, your office.' Shaw made a gesture with his hands under his chin.

'And you can . . .'

'How far are you into setting everything up for the investigation into Mr Pearson's murder, DI Scott?' Symington had appeared from nowhere.

'Things are in place, ma'am. I'm just about to interview a witness now, in fact.'

'Good stuff. I'm having a quick coffee and a sandwich, and then I'll have to go and tell our Security Service friends on the boat that we have a problem. I want the search for these guys in the Transit van widened. We're looking at NPR around West Dunbartonshire, all approaches to the road down, to see if we can pick up this van.'

'Could have come via Arran, ma'am.'

'Yes, there are a number of places from which they could have sprung. It's our job to find out where they came from and where they are now. I'll let you know how I get on when I'm afloat. Good luck with your witness, DI Scott.'

Cabdi was stretched out on the grass beside his tent in their campsite amongst the trees, fast asleep under a rough blanket. Faduma watched him with simmering hatred.

As far as he'd been led to believe, they'd started out on this enterprise as equals, but now it was obvious just who was in charge. The thought fed his anger, and combined with the inertia made him agitated beyond tolerance.

As he gazed, the echo of the great ship's horn sounded

through the trees. He was frustrated – how was this advancing the cause? They were sitting around doing nothing in an old tent in a damp pine forest, while those he hated so much enjoyed themselves in the lap of luxury.

Cabdi's mouth was gaping open now, his breath heavy; he was clearly in a deep sleep.

Quietly, Faduma got to his feet and made his way to the back of the old Transit. He opened one of the rear doors slowly, knowing that it needed to be oiled and not wishing to wake the other man.

Carefully, silently, he removed the big steel box from the back of the van. He laid it carefully on the ground, closed the door, and hefted the heavy metal box by one of its stout handles. He made his way into the trees, doing his best to do so as quietly as possible.

Now was the time to act; now was the time to avenge his brothers and sisters who had died across the world in the battle against the Infidel. Sitting waiting only increased the risk of being caught. Once his mission was accomplished, he didn't care. Cabdi could kill him – it would be for the best. Faduma knew he was heading for paradise, when he had sent the souls of many unbelievers to hell.

It was time.

Back in his crumpled suit, Brian Scott felt much more at ease. He'd enjoyed seeing his old friend, but was still worried about his health.

Daley had offered to do some work on the murder case from home, but Symington had firmly refused.

He'd noticed that Liz was now making no effort to hide the cuts, lumps and bruises on her face, and he admired the way Symington had ignored them, though he knew she must have wondered what had happened. Whatever her thoughts, she hadn't mentioned anything as they drove back to Kinloch Police Office.

A knock on the door, and Hamish's familiar olive-skinned, wrinkled face appeared around it.

'Am I fine tae come in, Brian – Inspector?' he said.

'No' you as well! Brian will dae just fine, Hamish. Now, come in and take a seat. I'm afraid I cannae offer you a dram, just the bilge that passes for coffee fae oor machine – or tea, if you prefer.'

'Och no, you're fine, Brian. I know you're a busy man, whoot wae poor – well, wae whoot's happened. So I'll no' take up much o' your time.'

Scott studied the serious look on the old man's face, seeing none of his usual bonhomie, or natural charm. That something was troubling Hamish was very clear.

'Right then, fire away, Hamish. I'm all ears.'

'I know you'll no' want tae confirm it, but I know – the whole town knows fine – that Cameron Pearson was the unfortunate soul dragged fae the Sound.'

'You're right, Hamish. I cannae say anything else right now, but we'll be asking questions soon enough – asking everybody in the area.'

'Well, I have some information on the matter.'

'You have?'

'Aye, I do that.'

Scott leaned forward. 'Just what is this information? No' just local tittle-tattle, I hope.'

'No, nor nothing of the kind. It's concerning Peter – Peter Scally.'

Hamish had the detective's attention now. Something about Scally's demeanour – his interview – had set off a warning light in Scott's mind. Maybe Hamish knew why. 'What aboot Mr Scally?'

'Let me tell you, I've thought long and hard aboot this. I'm no telltale, Brian. As far as I'm concerned folk's business is their own.'

'But?'

'But I was very fond o' Cameron. We worked on the same boat for a while – och, when he was jeest a boy. Trouble was, he was mair interested in creatures wae feathers than the ones wae scales. He didna last long as a fisherman. But we've been friends ever since; aye, and me and him have chewed the fat doon the pier most weeks aboot bird migration and the like. The man was an expert, no doubt aboot it.'

'I don't see where you're going, Hamish.'

'Well, now, you see, Peter Scally – a snake by any man's measure – he and Maggie Pearson, Cameron's wife, are more than jeest friendly, if you know whoot I mean. When I heard he was up on the hill looking for Cameron and then a body was found – well, I jeest couldna keep it tae myself.'

'So they're having an affair, eh?'

'They are that, and have been for years. The whole toon will back me up on the subject. I'm no' sayin' Cameron didna know, but if he did, he kept it tae himself, for Maggie was always the apple of his eye.'

'Long way from having an affair tae killing someone, Hamish.'

'Aye, I dare say. But for me, I widna put anything past that bugger Peter Scally, and that's a fact. I'm jeest telling you so as you know. There might be nothing in it, but I can guarantee he said nothing about that when he was speaking to you.'

'I cannae officially say you're right – but you are.' Scott winked. 'This is serious, and if you don't mind, keep it to yourself that you've told me, Hamish, right?'

'Of course. Believe it or not, I know when tae open my gob and when tae keep it shut. Might be hard tae believe, but there you are. I'll say nothing, I swear.' He hesitated. 'Can I ask how Mr Daley is? I've – we all have – been worried aboot the big fella.'

'He's no' bad at all, Hamish. Had me worried, mind you, but hopefully on the mend. I'll tell him you're asking for him.'

The old man stood and nodded at Scott. 'Please do, Brian. I'll be getting back hame. It's getting late, and I'm right melancholy today.'

'Well, thank you, Hamish. I appreciate what you've done. I know it doesnae come easy – giving information to the polis. Where I come fae it was considered tae be worse than stabbing your granny. Can I get you a lift home?'

'Och, no, I'll be fine. Maybe a wee walk will do wonders for the glums. I'll see you aboot. Mind, I'm not saying Scally did the dirty deed, but he'll know more than he's saying, that's for sure. And I hope you catch whoever did this tae Cameron.' Head bowed, he left the glass box, closing the door quietly behind him.

Scott rubbed his chin, thought for a few moments, then reached for the phone on his desk. 'Potts, I want you tae round up Peter Scally and his grandson again, but go canny. Just say we need a wee bit more information, casual like.'

147

25

The expensive, specially adapted drone lay at Faduma's feet. He was standing just beyond the line of trees, with a clear view down from the hill to the loch below and the cruise ship in its midst.

He watched silently, the drone's remote control poised in his hands, as the ship's launches ferried passengers back and forth from Kinloch's pontoons. He'd armed the device, and saw the sun glinting off the deadly weapon with a certain pleasure.

The drone was packed with explosives, and that firepower would be aimed at the *Great Britain*. Such objects were commonplace now. Photographers, hobbyists, all kinds of folk had them, and they went almost unnoticed in the West these days.

Faduma had rehearsed his role a hundred times. He'd worked out the new trajectory to the target earlier that day, and calculated the best moment during the drone's flight to veer for the vessel, aiming for the portion of the ship where most damage was likely to be caused. After hours of practice, the console felt comfortable – familiar – in his hand, almost part of him. He could fly the drone without reference to the hand-held unit, muscle memory and senses doing the job, like a virtuoso musician playing perfectly with eyes closed. It was as though he and the device were now as one. Together they would shake the world, even from this remote place in a country he'd grown to despise.

At first, they'd found him a job in a back-street garage as cover. No expensive modern vehicles there, just old wrecks poor people were desperate to keep going. He'd found the work interesting, but one of the other mechanics was a racist, and he began to hate going there only to suffer the man's jibes.

He had a natural aptitude for fixing things. From childhood his father had encouraged him to become familiar with the workings of the ancient Toyota pickup that they used to take livestock and the few things they were able to grow to market in the nearest town in Somalia. How he'd enjoyed the first day he'd been able to get the old pickup going when his father had fallen ill and it refused to start for his mother. He was only eleven years old, and his father, from his sickbed, had been proud.

But though he'd rallied, Faduma's father was never the same after his illness. He became thin and listless, leaving the work on the farm to his wife and children. Faduma could picture him, with his light skin, just like his own, lounging on the steps of their home and chewing on a long piece of grass while Faduma, his mother and his two younger brothers did what they could to keep the family fed and a roof over their heads.

His father came from Morocco, Faduma knew that – in fact it was about all he did know about his father. It was why both he and his eldest son had lighter skin than his mother and the rest of the village. They were different, and because of it Faduma had suffered a difficult passage in the tiny hut that served as a school, teased and shunned in equal measure because of the lightness of his skin.

But as he grew, he found that the young women of the village found his looks attractive, and he learned the secrets of life from a girl of seventeen years when he himself was only thirteen.

He could still see her as she lay dying a mere two months later.

In the night men had come to their village – white men. They had weapons, and forced the villagers to gather in a little square in front of the schoolhouse. The young women were raped in front of their families. Later, one by one, everyone was killed.

As the horror erupted, he'd backed away from it, unseen by the men with machine guns, who were more eager to take their turn with the next woman than to watch for a skinny teenager making his way silently into the undergrowth behind the school where all the children used to play.

Then, like now, he'd stood motionless, taking in the horrific scene, his eyes brimming with tears. He saw a white man hold a pistol to the head of the girl who had made him a man. Her flesh had already been torn and bruised by her tormentors when they'd raped her. He recoiled in horror as her head disappeared in a flash of crimson blood, grey brain and white, shattered bone.

He had looked across the square to where his father stood, mute, head bowed, and he was ashamed of him. Why did he not fight back? There were weapons in the village – the men outnumbered the small group of killers who were now wreaking havoc amongst all the people he'd ever known. Why did they not fight back?

As the bile rose in his throat at the shame he felt for his father's mute acceptance of the death and destruction that swirled around him, he saw his father raise his hand. No shower of blood and brain this time, just a neat black hole in his temple. He had to stifle a scream as his father's legs gave way and he crumpled to the ground like a rag doll.

Forcing his limbs to move, Faduma crept away, keeping as low as he could. Soon, the screams, the sound of gunfire and the laughter of the white killers who had fallen on his village like a sudden sandstorm retreated. All was quiet, but his life was changed for ever.

Afterwards, he'd heard the term 'mercenaries' for the first time. The men who had raped and murdered his family, the people of his village – everyone he knew or cared about – were mercenaries from the West. The burning hatred of them and their kind had never left him.

It was as though that night had never ended, the sun had never risen. For this moment, here on a high hill above a small town in this strange country, where the sea shimmered in the haze, was, for him, the end of days.

He pressed the ignition button on the handset. Each of the four rotor blades set at the corners of the drone burst into life as he stood on the small promontory just beyond the treeline, a jutting platform of rock, perfect for his mission.

Daley gazed out over the loch, his son in his arms, binoculars trained on the ship on the calm water below.

'Here, do want to look at the big ship, James?' He held the binoculars in front of the toddler's eyes.

The little boy giggled at the new experience. 'It's bigger,

Daddy!' he announced through the laughter. 'How did you make it bigger?'

'Magic, son – sheer magic. Here, let Daddy have another look.'

Daley could see a launch disgorging its passengers at the sea door of the vessel – the same one he and Symington had been ushered through when they had visited. He remembered how the sides had towered over them like a tall building as they stepped off the small service vessel and into the vast ship.

He tried to make out who was who, and was convinced that Symington, dressed this time in her dark trouser suit, was again boarding. He knew that she planned to brief the security people aboard about the murder of Cameron Pearson, and was sure that it was she who now disappeared out of view as though swallowed by some great sea creature.

The binoculars were expensive, a gift from Liz when they'd first moved to the house on the hill. Since arriving back from hospital he'd used them more than ever before, fascinated by the *Great Britain* out on the loch.

He also felt useless.

Seeing Brian Scott had been – as it always was – a tonic. But the sight of the pips on his friend's shoulder reminded him that no one is irreplaceable. He was sure that, left to his own devices and unique style, Scott would make an excellent replacement, but part of him hated the thought that his own career might now be over. Everything he had – his future, such as it was – to be decided on the whim of the medical profession.

Yes, he'd have a generous pension and lump sum. Yes, he'd be able to potter about reading books – maybe even travelling to the places he'd always wanted to see. But he was too young to retire.

His thoughts drifted back to a stooped old man in a shed at the bottom of the garden. Ian Burns, no longer a senior detective, had spent his days there, with only the daily newspaper and the wireless for solace; poor replacements for the world in which he'd been so expert, adept and self-assured.

At least Burns had had a happy marriage.

Though Daley was again sharing a house with his wife, the situation was far from permanent. He and Liz had barely spoken a word to each other since Scott and Symington had left. While he revelled in Scott's temporary promotion – one likely to become full-time, Daley reckoned – he could see only sullen resentment on his wife's face. Even in her reduced state, nothing had changed. She was only here now because she couldn't face her parents, her friends from the badminton club in Bridge of Weir, or the rest of the ladies who lunched, while her face was still battered and bruised.

When he'd first seen her, his blood had boiled. For a fleeting moment he had seen her vulnerability, and the old feelings of protectiveness and a hint of affection had touched his heart.

However, in hospital he'd had time to think. She hadn't come to him for protection, or even some kind of frayed love; no, she'd had nowhere else to go. He was sure that once the physical wounds healed, she'd head back up the road and behave as though nothing had happened. He'd been glad when she'd put on her big sunglasses an hour ago and announced she was going to the shops. He hoped she wouldn't rush back.

Though she refused to tell him who'd attacked her, he now knew – or at least could make a well-informed guess. He had used his contacts – both police officers and informers – to find out who was likely to have been responsible. It had taken a few hours and a dozen phone calls from his hospital bed to discover that her erstwhile boyfriend was a dentist called Alexander Manston. He owned a number of thriving practices throughout the Greater Glasgow area, and lived in some splendour on the Clyde coast – just Liz's type.

And he had form. He'd been cautioned twice over domestic abuse claims, and a case brought against him by a young colleague been found not proven, that notorious quirk of Scottish law that saw far too many guilty men and women escape justice, in Daley's opinion.

So Daley knew the likely assailant's name, his history of similar offences, and where he lived and worked. Though he hadn't confronted Liz on the subject yet, he was going to.

'Daddy, Daddy, what's that flashing?' his son shouted, pointing excitedly across the loch to the hill beyond.

Daley trained the binoculars on the area where the sun appeared to be twinkling on something metallic. He could just about make out the figure of someone standing stock-still on what looked like level ground, and he eased the little lad back to the floor in order to better focus on the spot. He was sure it was a man with dark hair, and on the ground beside him something metallic was indeed catching the late afternoon sun.

He remembered Scott talking about two men in a van seen in the hills the night before; he thought about the murdered man whose body had been found in the Sound. Something wasn't right, he could sense it.

He walked across the lounge, lifted the phone, and dialled the familiar number of Kinloch Police Office.

26

The man made his way through the engine room of the *Great Britain* attracting no attention. His job – on this ship, at least – was to deal with the rubbish. It was a much harder task than many might imagine. With hundreds of passengers, plus crew and security personnel, the waste generated was monumental.

His job was to make sure that the appropriate rubbish ended up in the incinerator, and that what could be recycled was separated out and stored until it could be dealt with at the next large port they docked in on their tour round the British Isles. He would trundle off the ship with a full waste truck and head back with an empty one.

The sight of the man in the green boiler suit was in no way out of the ordinary, so he moved about unseen. He spot-checked every area of the great ship from time to time, just to ensure no waste was building up that could be a potential fire or hygiene hazard. Now, on the latest such trip, he slipped a canvas bag into a small gap between a power console and a bulkhead.

He ducked through an unsealed bulkhead door and into the part of the ship where most of the electrics were contained. It was from this cavernous space that vital functions such as heat, light and kitchen power, as well as navigation, engine ignition and computer systems were to be found. If the large engines were the beating heart of the vessel, this was where its brain drew strength.

He looked about. Not far off, he could see an engineer working on something with a welding torch. Blue sparks flashed through the air as the masked man did his job. He turned to a large fuse box, opened it with an Allen key, then eased open the hinged fascia. In a few moments, his job there was done, and he started walking purposefully along the mezzanine decking. Checking again that no one could see him, he ducked under a huge panel of switches. In less than two minutes that task too was complete.

As he ascended the stairs out of the bowels of the ship, one alarm sounded, then another, which made him smile. Now it was back to rubbish collection – for now, at least.

Faduma looked up as the drone rose high in the air, his heart thudding in his chest.

With his glasses on, he squinted between drone and ship, and was about to move the device forward from its hovering position when he heard a noise coming from the trees behind. Cabdi was running at him, shouting, eyes bulging, a ferocious look on his face.

Faduma laid the handset on the ground, leaving the drone hovering. 'It's time, brother. We just do what we were sent to do!' From his pocket he removed a knife, bringing Cabdi to a halt a few feet from him on the rocky ledge.

'Don't be stupid, Faduma. This will ruin everything! Bring the drone back down. If you do, I promise that no one will know – I will not tell our master, I promise.'

'We came here for one thing and one thing alone. We are to kill these people; we will defend our beliefs and avenge all those we have lost. We must do it now!'

'But what about our master? How do you know he is safe?' Cabdi kept his eyes trained on the blade of the knife as he spoke.

For a split second, a look of puzzlement crossed Faduma's face. It hadn't occurred to him that the man whose orders they obeyed might be aboard the vessel. 'You are just trying to trick me. Why would our master be there?'

'He is. Before we attack, he must make his escape. If he does not, our mission around the world will be in tatters.'

'Liar!' Faduma lunged at Cabdi with the knife.

Daley had his binoculars trained on the scene on the hillside beyond the loch, one hand holding the phone to his ear.

'Jimmy, what's up?' Scott's familiar voice was loud on the other end of the line.

'Brian, something's going on up the hill – Gullion – near the peak. There's a ledge in the clearing beyond the treeline. I can see a drone or something hovering, but . . .'

'But what, big man?'

'There might be two of them, Brian. It's hard to tell against the tress from this distance. I'm remembering what you were told about the guys in the van. Paparazzi – worse?'

'Right, Jimmy. Keep your eyes peeled. I'll get off the line and alert the *Great Britain*. I'll get back to you, big man!'

Scott searched the big desk for his notebook, finding it under a blue file. He dialled the number quickly. 'Captain Banks, son – and it's an emergency!' he said to the comms operator on board.

'Yes, sir.' The line went quiet.

As he listened to some innocuous hold music, Scott reached for the radio on the other side of the desk. 'DI Scott to all stations. We have sightings of one, perhaps two individuals with a drone on Gullion Hill, at the treeline. There's some kind of outcrop just near the summit. I want a team up there PDQ.'

'Banks here, can I help you?' The voice came from the phone held to Scott's ear.

'Sir, we have a problem. A drone's been sighted on the hill to your starboard – I think – the side wae the graveyard on the hill. We suspect it might be photographers, but who knows? Can you inform onboard security – quickly?'

'Yes, certainly. I'll do it now. I'll get back to you!'

Scott could hear the urgency in Banks's voice.

Sergeant Shaw rushed into the glass box. 'Right, Brian. I'll take a team up with DS Potts. I can't say how quick we'll get up there, mind; there's a track so far, but the rest is on foot.'

'Dae your best, son. Here, and you take charge. Potts is too wet behind the ears for this caper. I'll have tae coordinate here – unless you want tae do it, eh?'

'Your call, Inspector.' Shaw shrugged his shoulders.

Scott paused for a heartbeat. 'Right, you get behind this desk. Jimmy's got eyes on from his hoose – you've got his home number, aye?'

'Yes – leave it with me, Brian. Good luck!'

Scott rushed from the CID suite in search of the rest of the team.

Cabdi and Faduma were wrestling on the ground, the buzz of the drone sounding on the air.

Faduma tried to lash out at Cabdi's face, but the tall man was surprisingly quick, and lurched to one side in the nick of time.

'You will have to kill me, Faduma. I will never let you do this now.'

'You are a traitor – you serve more than one master. I've known it all along!'

'You are a fool!' bellowed Cabdi, catching Faduma on the side of the face with a glancing blow and sending him flying to the rocky ground, the knife spinning from his grasp. He thought he was about to be killed, but Cabdi loped away, searching the ground for the drone's handset.

Dizzy, suffering the after-effects of Cabdi's blow, Faduma was desperate now. Frantically, he groped around, looking for the knife. Instead his hand brushed across a rock, and he wrenched it free. Unsteadily, stumbling a couple of times, he managed to get to his feet.

He squinted, trying to locate Cabdi, and spotted him leaning over the place where he'd laid down the handset. His world still in a spin, he limped towards him, the rock he'd dislodged held in both hands.

As Cabdi began to get up, clutching the handset, Faduma brought down the rock, hard against the man's skull.

Cabdi tottered for a heartbeat, but like a tree felled by a woodsman's axe he collapsed to the ground, the light gone from his eyes.

The handset also landed on the rough ground, and without looking Faduma could hear the modulation of the drone's motors.

He looked into the sky, squinting again in the brightness. The machine was dropping, heading in his direction in a skewed, swaying flight. As his vision cleared, he knew what he must do. Not without effort, he stood, holding the handset, trying to get the drone back under control.

It was swinging wildly, but Faduma managed to steady it and redirect it back across the town far below, towards the loch and the *Great Britain*, gleaming white on the blue water.

It was now that his hours of practice bore fruit. Pausing the drone in mid-air, he paused and took a few deep breaths. Eyes moving again from drone to ship, he steadied the small device. After one more gulp of air, he thrust the joystick on his console forward, sending the device accelerating down towards the *Great Britain*.

But as he squinted, desperately trying to focus on the target in order to witness the death of those on board, he heard a noise from behind. Before he could turn round, he felt a heavy push to the small of his back.

Cabdi looked down at the motionless figure spreadeagled two hundred feet below him. Faduma was dead; there could be no doubt. He crouched back on his heels, his one thought now to do what had to be done. But first, he must evade capture.

He pictured the landscape from the memory of the map in his mind. He would head northwest through the pine forest, then find somewhere to gather his thoughts. Though he knew he'd be pursued, he'd been trained when it came to remaining unseen. With his head still splitting, and blood drying on his head and face, he crawled from the ledge, heading for the treeline and safety.

27

Royal Marine officers and members of the crew had managed to clear the foredeck of passengers. Lieutenant Naliss marshalled passengers, Marines and crew in a calm, efficient manner. Whatever was happening, panic would certainly be unhelpful. All she knew was that a drone had been spotted near the vessel and it was her job to make sure this deck was empty of passengers.

'Eleven o'clock, ma'am,' shouted one of her men, just as the last of the guests had been ushered below. She looked skywards and spotted an object hurtling from the sky towards the ship.

'Get down everyone – now!' Her voice rang out along the deck. The Royal Marines responded immediately, in some cases having to drag their merchant colleagues down with them.

Everything was happening so quickly.

From their van, Scott and his team watched in horror as the drone hurtled across the loch. There was no way they could do anything now to stop the device, but Scott knew they had to press on, catch whoever it was who had launched it. For now though, like the Marines on the *Great Britain*, the team of police officers braced themselves as they saw the small aircraft hit the side of the great ship and smash into pieces.

'Situation, Sergeant Shaw?' Scott shouted into his radio.

'Patching you through to Commander Brachen . . .'

'DI Scott, the drone has come into contact with our vessel but left nothing more than a dent. I'm sending a team to help you, but you're closest to whoever flew this into the *Great Britain*. They must be apprehended as quickly as possible. A helicopter from the frigate will be assisting. Do you copy, over?'

'Aye, roger that,' said Scott. 'But how come nothing happened?'

'We're investigating. We'll get divers to fish what's left of the drone out of the loch. My guess it's some newspaper stunt gone wrong. But find the people who did this, and quickly, DI Scott!'

Daley watched from his window. At first, when he saw the drone streak through the air towards the cruise ship, he stood back instinctively, awaiting a deadly tumult that never came.

As he tried to make sense of the scene, perhaps sensing the tension, his son began to wail. 'I want Mummy!' he roared.

Daley picked the child up in his arms. 'It's okay, James – I think,' he added quietly as he took in the bustle aboard the *Great Britain*, and watched the grey frigate that had been anchored in the Sound make its way into the loch, a huge wave at its prow. Already two RIBs were bouncing across the waves from the warship towards the shore.

He picked up his binoculars again, setting his still wailing son down on the floor at his side. There was no sign of activity on the rocky outcrop.

Nothing makes sense, he thought.

Behind him, a familiar voice. Furious.

'What the hell are you doing?' Liz lifted their sobbing son off the floor.

He lowered the binoculars. 'I don't know – I really don't know.'

When Scott and his team arrived on the outcrop of rock, they saw a body lying motionless on the rocky grass far below. Even from this distance, Scott could see that the man was dead. Dark blood had oozed and congealed on the grass around him.

'He's dead,' said Potts.

'Aye, top marks, son. There's no' anything gets past you,' replied Scott waspishly. He looked around, but of the second man Daley thought he might have seen there was no sign.

Potts was kneeling on the grass. 'Look, sir, leading into the trees.' He was pointing to a rough trail where the grass and scrub had been recently disturbed. 'There's blood.'

'Come on!' said Scott, hurrying along the track into the woods. They followed it carefully, until it suddenly ended. Scott looked around. 'What happened?' Automatically, he looked up.

'Maybe he flew,' said Potts, equally baffled.

'Right, we keep going.' Still in the lead, Scott made his way forward slowly, brushing aside tree branches, footsteps muffled by the scented pine needles that formed a carpet beneath them. After a few minutes of slow, careful trudge, the trees thinned out into a small clearing, where sat an old blue Transit van and a rough-looking tent.

Carefully, batons drawn, the small group of police officers checked the van and the tent, but there was no sign of life.

'Right, pull back,' said Scott. 'Trace your steps back the way you came. We want to disturb this scene as little as possible. We've got evidence all over the place, so there's bound tae be plenty for SOCO tae go on.'

'Sir – on the grass.' A uniformed constable pointed to an area just beside the tent. Lying beside an old blanket was a rudimentary mobile phone.

Scott put the radio to his mouth. 'Sergeant Shaw, patch me back to Brachen, will you?'

28

Brachen stared at Symington. 'Why on earth didn't you inform me about what had been spotted on the hillside?'

'I was in the process of conducting another investigation: we found a murdered man in the Sound. As far as I was concerned, this was a civilian matter, and I still think that. I can see nothing to connect a drone's being flown into the side of your ship with the death of a local birdwatcher.'

'As far as you were concerned? That's a load of bollocks!' Brachen took a seat and visibly tried to calm himself. 'The drone – what was left of it – has been recovered by naval divers, and found to contain nothing more dangerous than the battery used to propel it.'

'I take it that it was equipped with cameras?'

'Yes, of course.'

'And that's why you've termed this *an exercise*, Commander?'

'We have to reassure our passengers; anyway, it was on orders from the Ministry. There's no harm done, but that doesn't mean you're off the hook, Chief Superintendent. You should have informed me of suspicious characters on the hillside, not hushed it up!'

'Now, *hushed up* . . . there's a term I heard recently.'

'What do you mean?'

'I mean that my orders to keep the murder of the local man and the sighting of the men in the van quiet came from the Foreign Secretary. So if you want to end any careers, he's your man.'

Brachen thumped the desk in front of him. 'This is intolerable. How are we to protect these people when police and politicians are going behind our backs? I'm going to take this up with my superiors, of that you can be sure.'

'Please do, Commander. As a police officer, I take instructions from my superiors, too. In any case, we are following another line of inquiry as regards the murder, and we are unsure if these men in a van have anything to do with it.'

'Bit of a coincidence, isn't it?'

The door opened and Captain Banks walked into the large cabin.

'This ship is pretty well soundproofed, but the way you pair are conducting yourselves every passenger aboard will know that we were under attack a short while ago. I'm sure that's not what you want.'

'If you don't mind, Captain. I'm meeting with the Chief Superintendent – in private. It's a security matter. And there's no suggestion this was any *attack*. Probably over-enthusiastic press photographers.'

'Oh, that sounds plausible.' Banks shook his head. 'Well, please conduct your meeting in your own quarters. This is my cabin, and despite recent events I'm still captain of this vessel. And we have a problem that I have to attend to urgently.'

'Something you haven't informed me of, *Captain*. What on earth can be so important that requires your urgent attention?'

'You may have noticed the lights flickering, Commander. It seems a large part of the ship is without power for some reason. That means – though your team wish it were otherwise – we can't sail.'

'We can't what?'

'We can't sail. I would have thought that was reasonably self-explanatory the first time round.'

'Superintendent, will you excuse us?' said Brachen, still glaring at Banks.

On Kinloch's second quay, the usual crowd of observers had gathered. Word had spread that something was awry aboard the *Great Britain*, and half the town had gathered to see what the problem was, and speculate in a way only they knew how.

The road that wound down to the causeway had been closed, and residents – including Hamish – had been evacuated in what was termed as Commander Brachen's 'exercise'.

'This'll no' dae any good for oor chances as a tourist destination,' said Donald Major, locally known as the crazy captain, a play on his name, and the regimental way in which he walked. 'Who'll want tae come tae Kinloch and get blown tae kingdom come?'

'Ach, yer arse,' said Annie. 'I didna hear any explosions, did you? Aye, and you know whoot they say: there's no such thing as bad publicity.'

Donald shook his head and took a swig from the hip flask in his pocket. 'Well, in my opinion, since that Daley character arrived here, there's been nothing but bother, one way or other. That's a' I'm saying.'

'Good, we're a' glad that's a' you have tae say,' said Annie, a sentiment echoed by many of her fellow townsfolk.

'It's they Alkies,' said the Trencher. How he had acquired this nickname had disappeared into the mists of time, but no one called him anything else, most people having forgotten his original name in the first place.

'Alkies?' The question was on many lips.

'Och, you know fine whoot I mean: they Alkie Eeda buggers.'

Hamish sucked on his pipe, sending clouds of tobacco smoke across the gathered crowd. 'Well, now, you see, my understanding is that one o' they drones hit the ship, and there could be any number o' reasons for that. Anyway, if it's Alkies they're looking for there's no shortage of culprits here, and that's a fact.' His eyes settled on Donald Major, who was taking another long draw on his hip flask.

Once the hilarity had died down, a young woman with a baby said, 'But what aboot poor Cameron Pearson? Is it they Alkies that killed him?'

Again a murmur swept through the assembly.

'Ach, I'm thinking it's best no' tae speculate on that,' said Hamish, a look of grim resignation on his face.

'Here, look!' said a spotty youth bearing a large smartphone. 'Someone's put this up on YouTube.'

'And jeest what's View Tube?' asked Hamish.

'It's YouTube.'

'And whoot's that a' aboot?'

'You can see stuff on it: videos, TV shows, your mates at the banter – that kind o' thing.'

'So you *view* these things,' said Hamish with a half-smile.

'Aye, well, of course that's whoot you dae, Hamish.'

The old man nodded his head sagely. 'Aye, well, there you are; they should have called it View Tube, then a body might have known jeest whoot the hell it was all aboot. Here, gie me a look.'

The lad pushed his way through the crowd and handed the phone to Hamish. 'See, there you are.'

The footage featured the *Great Britain*. On deck, there appeared to be a commotion as camouflaged figures rushed to and fro. For a split second, there was a flash from the bow of the vessel.

'Och, that'll be they special effects. Somebody oot tae profit fae jeest nothing at all. One o' they false faces, likely. They've got a wild job wae that o'er in America right noo,' said the old man, as he took another puff of his pipe and handed the phone back.

'It's false news,' said Annie.

'Aye, but look,' said the youth. 'It's been put up by the *Kinloch Herald*, so it canna be wrong.'

Hamish canted his head to one side and looked at the young man steadily. 'If you believe a' you read in the papers you'll no' drink a drop o' whisky, eat meat, smoke or have relations wae the opposite sex in case you're taken tae an early grave. Aye, an' forbye that, if it's like oor local newspaper, a' the names will be wrong, and they'll have Christ crucified at Calgary, like they did in the Easter edition last year.'

At this there was a general murmur of agreement.

'Whoot I'm saying is, if a' they well-to-do folks is on that boat, it makes sense that they carry oot such measures tae ensure their safety. Man, folk in this toon would make Ben Hur oot o' Tom and Jerry. Jeest nothing but drama in the extreme, that's it in a nutshell.'

The crazy captain, who had seen enough, and in any case had drained his hip flask, marched off in high dudgeon.

'And there goes that bugger,' said Hamish. 'All he needs is a military band tae accompany him tae the Douglas Arms.'

Brachen was in his cabin preparing for the security meeting to be held in the officers' dining room. A naval rating knocked at his door and entered on the commander's request.

'Sir, have you seen this?' He handed the officer his smartphone.

Brachen looked at the footage, then handed the phone back to the seaman with a word of dismissal. When the door had closed behind the young man, he placed his elbows on the desk in front of him and rubbed his eyes. What had been intended as a jolly round the British Isles was rapidly turning into a bloody nightmare – one that could have been so much worse had the drone that hit the *Great Britain* been more than just a drone.

He picked up the phone on his desk. 'Get me Vice-Admiral Hutchins. Tell them it's priority,' he said wearily.

29

It's truly wonderful what happens when you set something in motion. The theory of chaos applies to everything, no matter how detailed the preparation.

Sometimes – often – this works against the best laid plans. However, in some circumstances, chaos augments intention, and the end result is better than could have been wished for.

He put down his pen and smiled. Though things had indeed not gone to plan, the fiasco that had ensued had had more impact then he had expected, and now that he'd seen the mobile phone footage he could have stood and clapped his hands in glee.

He put pen to paper again.

But this is just a beginning, a small starter to a meal of many courses. And when this particular meal ends, everything will be changed.

He could feel a pain in the small of his back when he leaned forward. It was pain that he relished, a constant reminder of why he sought to do what must be done. This pain had accompanied him for most of his life, and though sometimes its severity would keep him awake at nights, its mere presence galvanised him again and again.

The time had never been right – until now.

Gathered round the large table were Captain Banks, Commander Brachen, Annabelle Tansie, representative of the Security Service, Commander Naysmith from the frigate now moored beside the *Great Britain* on the loch, Chief Superintendent Symington and Sir Edward Chapelhouse, a senior civil servant from the Home Office.

'We need to move as soon as possible,' said Brachen agitatedly. 'What is the situation with the *Great Britain*, Captain Banks?'

'I'm waiting for a team of engineers. They will be with us later today, I hope. As to how long it will take to fix the problem, I have no idea.'

'Surely some of your men know how to service their own ship!' Brachen's impatience was clear.

'I'm informed it is a highly specialised electrical matter, involving complex computer diagnostics, only held by the original shipbuilder. If you want, we could get under way, but there would be no hot food, no hot water, no heating and very limited lighting. As it is, if we stay put – as we are scheduled to do – we can provide these things using mechanical backup systems, as long as the ship is at anchor, that is.'

'I say we sail out to sea. What do you think, Tansie?' said Brachen.

'I agree.' The security coordinator was sitting to Brachen's right in pristine blue fatigues, her hair pulled back into a tight bun. 'We are sitting ducks here for a future attack – if that is what it was. Definitely, we should make way, with all urgency.'

Symington frowned. 'I know you had people here prior to your arrival in Kinloch. I thought they were checking out the lie of the land?'

'Yes,' replied Tansie. 'They were. The loch was considered to be a safe haven – as safe as anywhere else, that is. This type of thing could have taken place anywhere around the British coast; we took risk into account then planned the schedule based on our assessment. I'm sure it's a process – as a senior police officer – of which you are well aware.' She glared at Symington.

'As far as HM Government is concerned, all's well that ends well. Apart from the YouTube footage, which is easily explained away as being fake, or the product of an over-enthusiastic photographer. The body found on the hillside is D-listed, so need-to-know basis only, as you are all aware. If questions are raised then this was a planned exercise. It is my duty – on behalf of the government – to ensure that our guests enjoy a trouble-free tour of these islands, in order to encourage them to invest in our country. We have been successful to date, and I see no reason why that cannot continue.' Sir Edward sat back, as though he felt his contribution had brought the discussion to a conclusion.

'We are equipped to combat anything like this,' said Commander Naysmith from the frigate. 'That's why we should have been stationed alongside the *Great Britain* in the loch instead of in the Sound.'

'And that, Commander, would have made our friends on board feel welcome and safe?'

'Yes, of course.'

'No, it would have engendered a siege mentality. As though an attack of some description was expected at any moment. I assure you, that is not the kind of ambience we are anxious to cultivate.'

Symington looked at the patrician civil servant. He was

tall, probably in his sixties, and had been assistant to the British ambassador in the USA for ten years; a career diplomat to his bootstraps, and good at it, too. His well-cut pinstripe suit, pristine silk shirt, ruby signet ring and easy, superior manner marked him out as the epitome of the establishment. Around the table, there were many well-adorned uniforms on display, but there was little doubt that the man in the suit was in charge.

'We have Royal Marines and police officers in the hills around the loch in case this second-man theory is correct. However, I wish to scale that back, as I see no real evidence of the existence of another man and word of such things spreads. The last thing we want is our passengers becoming unsettled. We continue with the itinerary as planned. And if the engineers need more time to fix the problem with the electrics, well, I can't think of a better place on our tour to stay a little longer.' He smiled at those gathered around the table, as if to say *This meeting is over*.

'I'm afraid I don't agree,' said Naysmith, Brachen and Tansie nodding in support. 'The *Great Britain* has been attacked; if she can't get under way immediately, then plans should be made to transfer the passengers to another vessel and sail as soon as possible, under our close escort.'

Sir Edward smiled benignly, but there was steel behind his blue eyes. 'The *attack* you mention was merely the work of an over-enthusiastic photographer – who paid a hefty price for his effort to seek ill-gotten gains. Our friends at Police Scotland have roadblocks checking every vehicle leaving the town. We have – I reiterate – Royal Marines searching the hillsides for this missing accomplice who have found nothing. Whatever risk there was has passed. We proceed as planned.'

'But we stay on station in the loch, yes?' asked Naysmith.

'No, you return to the Sound. Your presence here has been explained as part of a drill.' Sir Edward collected his notes and stood. 'These are the wishes of the government. Of course, if you require orders from your individual superiors, that isn't a problem. But I think that would be rather a waste of time, don't you?' He looked at them one by one, all now mute around the large table. 'Good! Now let's get on with what we're here to do.' He nodded to Captain Banks, turned on his heel, and left the room.

'What about the phone we found, Sir Edward? And the sighting of two men with a van similar to the one found on the hill today?' said Symington.

'The phone will be analysed and whatever it contains taken into account. As for the van – well, vans are ten a penny. There is no evidence as far as I can see connecting one van with the other. Indeed, I think I'm correct in saying that the witness you have said he thought the van was white – this one is blue. Happy?'

As she headed back to shore on the launch, Chief Superintendent Symington was anything but happy. Like the majority of those at the meeting, she was far from convinced that all was well. She had a murder inquiry on her hands, an errant crewman, and now an accomplice in the drone affair she was almost sure was not hypothetical. The fact that it was Daley who thought he'd seen another man was enough to convince her.

The mobile in her handbag rang, and she took it out and put it to her ear.

'Ma'am,' said Sergeant Shaw. 'As you know, we had the

phone found on the hillside cloned before handing it over to the Security Service.'

'Yes, and?'

'Calls were received from and made to only one number – untraceable.'

'No surprise there, then.'

'But they've triangulated the signal, ma'am. Every call on the phone found on the hill was made to or came from the *Great Britain*. They have their own mobile facilities on board and all calls and internet go via the ship's communication systems because the locals masts are blocked for security reasons, so the job was reasonably easy.'

Symington's mind was working overtime now. 'So whoever was operating the drone that hit the *Great Britain* was in contact with someone aboard?'

'That's what forensics think, too.'

'I'm on my way back to the office. I'll call them.' She ended the call and thought about Sir Edward Chapelhouse. If a police forensic team had managed to reach such a conclusion, she was sure that the Security Service had done likewise.

As the boat bounced across the waves towards Kinloch, she stared at the hill from where the drone had been launched, deep in thought.

30

'Why that dress?' he asked, looking her up and down.

'Oh, don't you like it? It cost a small fortune.'

'Your tits are hanging out.'

'It's revealing, but my tits, as you call them, are hardly hanging out. Anyway, this is the dress I'm wearing, end of story.'

'Change – change now. We don't have much time. Come on!'

'I don't have anything else with me.'

He sat on the end of the bed, bow tie undone over a dress shirt, head bowed. 'Just do what you're told.'

'I beg your pardon?'

'This is a big night for me. Everyone who's anyone will be there tonight to see me get this award. I don't want to be sitting next to someone who looks like a cheap tart at the top table.' He glared at her, eyes flashing with temper.

'Fine, go on your own. I'm damned if I'm going anywhere with you in this mood.' She walked towards the door. 'Enjoy your night.'

Liz stared at herself in the mirror. She'd just showered, and was wearing no make-up. If anything, the cuts and bruises on her face looked worse – vivid yellow, purple and black now – and much more noticeable, though mercifully the swelling on her cheek had gone down a bit and was less painful.

She remembered reaching for the door handle, then being grabbed around the neck and pulled back into the room. The rest of what happened was a flurry of blows, pain and shock, which left her, head spinning, on her hands and knees on the carpet, watching the blood from her nose drip onto the deep pile carpet.

'And you can fucking clean that up before I get back,' he'd shouted before leaving the room and slamming the door.

She'd known what he was like. She'd seen him humiliate employees, hotel staff, waitresses, but she'd never thought that his arrogant cruelty would be directed at her, and with such violent fury. But here she was, staring at a face she barely recognised, in a house that belonged to a man she'd shamelessly cheated on and treated like shit for years. She opened her make-up box and began the job of trying to make her face look passable enough to go out of the house.

She saw him standing in the doorway. 'What?' she said, almost aggressively.

'I know who did it, Liz,' said Daley.

'No, you don't.'

'Alexander Manston. I know his address in Inverkip, the name of his yacht, what cars he drives, where his dental surgeries are – even how much he earned last year.'

She turned and stared at him. 'Why did you bother to find all that out?'

'Because I hate scum like him.'

She turned back to the mirror. 'It's none of your business, Jim.'

'No, but here you are, in my house, with my son. How long do you think it would have been before he took his temper out on James, eh?'

'He would never harm a child – and anyway, I'd never have let him.'

'Oh yes, you were obviously in control of the situation.'

'Just leave it!' She banged her fists down on the dressing table.

'No, I won't leave it. I want you to report him.'

'No.'

'So, you're happy for this to happen to someone else? Surely to fuck you don't plan to go back to him?'

'Oh, so now you're going to start. What is it with men that they think everyone has to do what they want? Please enlighten me, because I'm mystified.'

'But this isn't just about you, Liz, it's about our son. Or have you forgotten that?'

'Of course I haven't forgotten that! I just want nothing more to do with Alex, so you've no need to worry, have you?'

'Of course not. You're only down here out of the way until the bruises heal, then it's back to business as usual up the road, with the next psycho you pick up. Well, if you think I'm going to allow my son to be put in harm's way, you'll have to think again, Liz.'

'What does that mean?'

'It means that I don't care what expensive lawyers your family can afford. I'll fight you for custody of James, and I'll win.'

'Huh, so you can leave him in the charge of some decrepit fisherman, or with Brian Scott? That'll be the day.'

'No, so that he's safe from the next man you choose to buy

179

you fancy clothes and take you on expensive holidays, just so he has something pretty hanging off his arm. Anyway, you weren't too bothered who looked after him when you left him with me a while ago at a moment's notice, were you? You knew I was working.'

'And around we go again, Jim.'

Daley shook his head wearily. 'Do everyone a favour and report this bastard. Because if you don't, I will, got it?'

'Well, I won't be giving evidence. I just want to forget it ever happened – that I ever met him.' She stood and walked across to the wardrobe, bundling clothes onto the bed.

'Oh, the grand gesture, as always.'

'It's clear you don't want us here, Jim. It's fine; I'll make other arrangements.'

'You do what you like. My son stays here.'

'And just how are you going to achieve that? I'll take him where I want. He's in my care.'

'In that case, I'm going to report this incident to social services. I'll tell them what condition you were in when you turned up here, and that I'm worried that our son will be endangered if he remains in your custody.'

'My lawyer will shred that nonsense, and you know it.'

'Your father's lawyer – but I'm guessing he doesn't know anything about this, am I right?'

She blinked at him across the room. 'Please don't do this, Jim. Please, I beg you. I've been through enough, don't you think?'

He walked over to his estranged wife and embraced her. 'I'm sorry for what's happened to you – you know how I hate bastards like Manston. Do the decent thing, Liz. Report him and save someone else from this – or worse. There's more than just your pride at stake here.'

She buried her head in the chest of the big man she'd married and sobbed.

Cabdi was cold – very cold. He'd walked for miles, staying low over the summit of the hill then creeping from bush to bush, or along drystone walls. He'd spotted a farmer working distantly on a field on his tractor and had managed to duck into a hollow before being spotted, where he'd stayed until the coast was clear.

Eventually, he'd arrived at the ruins of a cottage. There was no roof, but he was sheltered from the wind and out of sight, and he'd have time to think. He was confused, too. Though Faduma had gone against their instructions, the device should still have exploded, and the fact that it hadn't made him question everything.

He'd realised that in his haste he'd left the mobile phone behind at their campsite and cursed himself for it, but otherwise they'd been careful. The van had been bought for cash and registered using false papers; nothing in their belongings could point to who they were, or where they'd come from.

They had trained to do this on so many occasions. Each time, the drone had exploded, though using a much smaller charge. Why had nothing happened this time?

He thought of the voice on the other end of the phone – a man he had never met face to face. He knew that Faduma had betrayed his trust, but now he began to wonder if he too was a mere pawn, an unwitting player in someone else's game.

Cabdi felt his head. Though it still ached, the flow of blood had stopped; using his medical knowledge he concluded that he was suffering from nothing more than minor concussion and contusions.

He thought about Faduma. Perhaps he shouldn't have taken his life; perhaps leaving him dead on the hill was a wicked thing to do. But in the time he'd known the man, Cabdi had recognised an individual who was out of control. This had become more and more obvious as time had gone on. Now Cabdi thought that Faduma would never have accepted the failure of their mission, and would have tried something insane in order to bring death and destruction to the great ship.

He knew that people would be searching for him, and that time was short. He had to get away from this isolated place, but first he had to think of a way of completing the task he'd been given, regardless of how he now felt about the faceless individual who had set him on the path. It was the most important point in his life; all he had ever wanted to do.

But now he must rest. Leaning his still pounding head against the cold stone of the wall, he let tiredness overcome him, and he drifted into a troubled sleep, Faduma's face haunting his dreams.

31

Brian Scott was sitting beside DS Potts with Peter Scally facing them across the desk in the interview room, his lawyer at his side.

'Come on, Peter,' said Scott. 'You were having an affair with Cameron Pearson's wife – admit it, man!'

Scally's lawyer opened his mouth to intervene, but his client stopped him by speaking first.

'Aye, you're right. Me an' Maggie are close – have been for a long time, as you say. Cameron was mair interested in his birds than paying attention tae his wife. But as far as I know having it off wae a married woman isn't a crime, or have I missed something?'

'Good. Now we're getting somewhere, Mr Scally.'

'But I'm telling you – and my grandson will back me up on this: I did not kill Cameron Pearson, plain and simple. Me and Maggie was going tae tell him – come clean, like. She's always felt sorry for him, but life's too short, and neither o' us are spring chickens.'

'Don't worry, we'll be having a wee word wae Mrs Pearson tae.'

Scally scowled at the acting DI. 'She might no' have wanted tae stay married, but the woman still has feelings for Cameron.

Can you no' jeest leave her oot o' all this? There's nothing to it, nothing at all.'

'And what about this? For the tape I'm showing Mr Scally production number one, which I'm reliably informed is part of a human skull, charred fae a fire.' Scott stared at Scally. 'Now, we're just waiting on the results of tests on this, but I'm willing tae bet my hoose on the fact that this is part of the deceased's skull. It was found in your house, Mr Scally. What is it – some gruesome keepsake, eh?'

'I must protest,' said Wilkinson, Scally's lawyer. 'Nothing has yet been determined in connection with these remains. For all we know they could be animal bones. I will not allow my client to be asked questions based on mere supposition.'

'I can explain how I came about that,' said Scally. 'When me and the boy saw they two guys had left the fire – as I telt you – we went doon and took a nosy aboot. Yes, I saw the piece o' skull, and like you I think it's likely Cameron Pearson's, though I'm heartsore tae say it. They men killed Cameron – I've no doubts aboot that.'

Just as Scott was about to reply the door opened. 'A word, DI Scott,' said Symington.

Scott paused the interview and followed his boss from the room. 'Aye, ma'am? What's up?'

'I don't think Peter Scally was responsible for the death of Cameron Pearson, Brian.'

'Eh? He's admitted having an affair wae the man's wife for years – he's got every reason tae want Pearson deid. He'd half o' his heid in a kitchen drawer!'

'No, I think he and his grandson did come across two men – one of whom you found dead on the hillside. I don't think for a minute those guys were trying to get a picture or two to sell to the papers. The fact that one of them is dead is enough to persuade me of that.

'So, the emphasis is now on what Scally and his grandson saw. I want to know everything they noticed about those men. I know they've given statements, but once you tell Scally that you believe him, perhaps it'll help jog his memory.'

'Right. So no' paparazzi, then?'

'No, not in my opinion.' She paused. 'Something came to light at the meeting on board the *Great Britain* – something significant.'

'Like what?'

This question was left unanswered. 'End the interview with Scally. Tell him he's no longer under suspicion but we still want to talk to him about the men he saw the other night. Let him and his grandson have a chat about it in the family room. Give them coffee – something to eat. I don't want them to feel under any pressure.'

'You seem awfy sure, ma'am.'

'Yes, I think I am.' She looked her new detective inspector straight in the eyes. 'Have you and Ella ever been on a cruise?'

'No, no way. I've always hated boats . . . wait, why are you asking me that?'

She smiled. 'Sort out Scally then come to my office, please, Brian.'

As Scott watched her walk briskly down the corridor he muttered to himself, 'I don't care how fancy the boat is, I'm no' going on it.'

Roughly a hundred and fifty of the *Great Britain*'s passengers sat in the ballroom. Sir Edward Chapelhouse was addressing them using a PowerPoint display on a large screen at his back.

'Now, the good people of Kinloch have, I hear, gone to great lengths to make this visit to their town an enjoyable one. As we've seen there are a number of eateries, bars and shops, and the distilleries have thrown open their doors to all comers. Feel free to enjoy the delights of this unique little town – another example of the diversity and allure of our great country.' He smiled broadly, looking around the room as his words were translated into a dozen or so languages for those who didn't speak English by a team of unseen translators via individual headsets.

Segre Avine, a Belgian hedge fund manager, stood to speak. 'So we can go anywhere and mix freely, yes?'

'Oh, certainly. As usual, measures have been taken to ensure your safety while ashore, but Kinloch is a quiet place, so relax.' Though Sir Edward smiled beatifically, he recalled the police van arriving at the quayside in Glasgow with a van full of very drunk, very rowdy Japanese businessmen. But he'd seen his fair share of pissed presidents, sozzled sovereigns and tipsy tyrants in his time as a diplomat. Despite the hard sell, of which he was in charge, it was essential that these influential men and women on board were afforded ample opportunity to let their collective hair down between the discussions that were designed to bring much needed business to the nation.

'What about these insects?' asked one tall, red-haired woman in a New York drawl, the senior executive of an American fashion conglomerate.

'Insects?' Sir Edward tilted his head like a mystified dog. 'Do they call them midges?'

'Ah yes, the fabled Highland midge. Nothing to worry about on that score – out of season, Mrs Hapstein.'

'I have delicate skin, Sir Edward. The last thing I need is to spend the rest of the trip covered in lumps and bumps.'

'You have nothing to worry about; I assure you the locals don't bite either.' The laughter pleased him. 'Now, if you're all ready, it's time to take the short trip to Kinloch. The launches will ferry you to and fro, and will always be on hand, so you can return here whenever you want. If you please, ladies and gentlemen . . .' He gestured to the door, where members of the crew were ready to escort their guests to Kinloch.

Watching them go, Chapelhouse was pleased that the numbers willing to take the trip were healthy without being large; just about right in terms of management and security. Behind his broad smile, the incident with the drone still troubled him, and though he'd brushed off the concerns of the onboard security team he'd been around too long not to recognise a threat when he saw one. However, in the opinion of Number Ten, whatever risk there had been was now spent. Sir Edward could only trust that the missing man on the hill would soon be found, if indeed he existed at all.

O'Rourke stood in line waiting to board the small vessel that would take them to Kinloch. He was looking forward to socialising with some normal people for a change, instead of his preening, snooty fellow passengers on the *Great Britain*. In any case, he needed a drink – a proper drink and a chance to mull over his thoughts and plans. Seeing his homeland – albeit distantly – had brought so many feelings to the surface that had long lain buried. He wanted to deal with these before he made any more plans.

A voice spoke at his shoulder. 'Ah, there you are, Patrick,' said Khan. 'I hope you don't mind if I join you. No hard feelings about losing all that money?'

'Hell, no! I enjoyed throwing away every dollar,' he lied. 'C'mon, my friend, let's see what this Kinloch has to offer.' He'd hoped to spend time alone in some bar, but Khan was tolerable company, and he'd soon lose her if the need arose.

As for Harid Khan, she looked serene. He'd seen the fire in her eyes as she thumped him at golf, but now she looked as though everything in her world was good. He was sure he detected a look of anticipation on her face, and for the first time he worried if this beautiful woman planned on getting to grips with him at something other than golf.

As they shuffled along towards the sea gate, O'Rourke felt the phone vibrate in his pocket. He read the message and smiled.

'Good news, Patrick?'

'Hell, I only listen to good news, my friend.'

Khan smiled back. In reality, the last thing she wanted to do was to spend time in what she considered a miserable little town. But she had things to do.

Cabdi found a stream and managed to clean himself up, though the gash on his head would be obvious to anyone who gave him more than a passing glance.

He'd taken the decision to hide in plain sight. He wasn't sure if he'd been spotted on the hill, but he had to take the chance that he hadn't. He figured that with so many new faces from so many different parts of the world coming off the cruise ship, it would be possible for him to blend into this small community unnoticed. Though it was a huge risk, he'd calculated that it represented his only chance.

Reaching the top of a ridge he spotted a cluster of houses huddled round a rocky bay. Immediately below him, a man who had clearly been digging ditches was walking away in the direction of this small community. He'd left a shovel thrust into the ground, and a red baseball cap was perched on the handle, presumably because the sun was now well hidden behind high white clouds and he no longer needed it.

Cabdi held back until the man was out of sight, then scrambled down the side of the hill and grabbed the hat from the shovel. He placed it carefully on his head and looked around. A road snaked past the village.

Cabdi climbed over a fence and walked across a field towards the road. He had money in his pocket, and by his reckoning couldn't be far from Kinloch. Though his strategy was risky, he had come too far to leave things unfinished. And in any case, questions – many questions – needed to be answered.

As well as the cash, he could feel the reassuring heft of the pistol in his pocket.

32

Jim Daley watched the district nurse take his blood pressure as he sat on the leather recliner in his lounge. His son looked on with wide eyes as the black band inflated on his father's arm and the nurse squinted attentively at the gauge.

'Still a bit high, Mr Daley, but not as bad as yesterday, which is good. You're taking the medication as directed, yes?'

'Yes. Well, I don't want to collapse again, and the last place I want to be is in hospital.'

'I'm sure.' She smiled. 'Your pulse is steadier, too. I'll need to take some bloods, if you don't mind.' She looked pointedly at the toddler.

'James, go and find Mummy. She's in her bedroom, son,' said Daley. Liz had chosen to stay out of sight when the nurse arrived, not wanting any questions asked about the condition of her face.

'He's gorgeous,' said the nurse, when James junior had gone.

'Yes, and a right little monster – I wish I had his energy.' Daley bit his lip. 'I know it's not your decision, but can I ask you a question?'

'Yes, of course. If I can answer it, I will. If I can't . . .' Her voice tailed off.

'I'm guessing I'm not the first patient you've ever had with this condition, right?'

'Not by any means. Heart problems, sadly, are not unusual in our community. I'm sure you don't need me to tell you that.'

'So, with this . . . I mean what I've been diagnosed with . . .' Daley hesitated.

'Go on, I won't bite your head off.'

'Well, will I recover – I mean recover enough to go back to work?'

She packed away the blood pressure monitor and removed a yellow box from her bag. 'Advances in treatment of heart conditions like yours are improving rapidly, Mr Daley. We're seeing effective new medications arriving all the time. Let's face it, here in Scotland we've had plenty of willing subjects to practise on.'

She took a syringe from the yellow box, checking it carefully as she removed the plastic packaging in which it was housed.

'So do you think I'll be able to go back to work?'

'I think your condition will improve dramatically. The drugs are already taking effect. But I don't know what rules they have in the police. All I will say is that I have many patients with managed heart disease who go about very demanding jobs in an almost entirely normal way. But let's not rush things, eh, Mr Daley?'

Daley nodded, baulking at the title. He was used to having a rank, and DCI Daley sounded so much better than plain 'Mister'. 'Thank you. I'll hold on to that, then.'

'Now, you'll feel a little scratch.' She had applied another tight band around his upper arm, and was poised with the syringe.

'Don't you say a little prick any more?'

'No, for precisely the reason you've asked.' She found a vein and began to draw dark blood from Daley's arm. 'Listen, it's normal to be anxious – everyone is when they hear they have heart problems. But if you keep taking the medication, have regular exercise, watch your diet and let us keep an eye on you, it should be fine. Oh, and try to avoid stress.'

'Fat chance of that.'

'Losing some weight will definitely help, too.' She smiled.

'Yes, I know,' replied Daley wearily. 'I know a warning when I see one. Trust me, you're preaching to the converted.'

'Right, that's us finished. I'll get this sent up the road. I'll be back tomorrow – will the same time be okay?'

'Thank you, yes,' said Daley, feeling utterly miserable. He recalled how many times he'd bemoaned the fact that he was a police officer, but now that his career was at stake he wanted nothing more than to be back at work.

You don't know what you've got until you lose it. The words rang in his head.

'I'll show you out,' he said, lowering the recliner.

'No, don't worry. I can see myself out – I remember the way. You should just sit quietly for a while after I've taken your bloods. Oh, and it's Mary, by the way.'

Daley, who'd been lost in his own thoughts, looked up, momentarily out of kilter, a confused look on his face.

'My name. It's Mary. I'll see you around the same time tomorrow.'

'Yes – yes, sure, Mary.' The name almost stuck in his throat, but he swallowed hard and banished thoughts of another Mary.

He heard the nurse close the front door firmly and head off in her car.

What would he do if he couldn't continue as a police officer? Would he even survive to be anything? Thoughts of his own demise, memories of his dying father, and the last time he'd seen Mary Dunn's face as she smiled at him round the bedroom door of her tiny cottage, all flashed through his mind.

The truth was, no one knew their fate. Some had a better idea than others, but in the main, life was a lottery. Some won, some lost, but no one could go on living for ever. This realisation was the curse of middle age. The young – unless they were ill – never let thoughts of their own mortality cross their mind. He certainly hadn't. But as grandparents, parents, even friends began to die, thoughts of one's own end came almost daily, for him, at least.

He'd started listening to music again in the hospital. Though there were some songs he still couldn't bear, he was pleased that at least he could pass the time doing something he loved again. It had been a pleasure denied him since the death of Mary Dunn.

Daley reached for the tablet on the floor by his chair. He made sure that the Bluetooth was on and connected to his sound system.

He scrolled down a list of his favourite songs.

As the first bars of Journey's 'Don't Stop Believing' boomed from the speakers, he closed his eyes and thoughts of the past soon began to appear again. The pair of them sitting in a café eating burgers with onion rings; her blue eyes flashing, looking straight into his.

The truth was, he'd stopped believing a long time ago; stopped believing he'd ever be happy again.

Just as the song's second chorus was about to begin, the

door swung open. Liz shouted at him to turn down the music; she had a sore head.

As the band sang 'stop', he switched the tablet off. The moment was gone.

'No, I'm no' doing it, and neither is my wife,' said Scott, crossing his arms over his chest determinedly. 'Anyway, you cannae place a civilian like Ella in harm's way.'

Chief Superintendent Carrie Symington stared at him, a hint of disapproval on her face. 'Of course, this isn't the kind of thing I can order you to do, Brian. But I'd hoped that you'd see the sense in it.'

'Oh aye, I see the sense in it, fine. But how is it when it comes tae going on a boat, my name's always the first oot the hat?'

'I've been aboard twice – and Jim was on the *Great Britain* too.'

'Aye, look how he fared after his wee jaunt.'

'He has a medical problem. Nothing to do with being on the *Great Britain*.'

'Well, I've got a medical problem, tae: I don't like boats!'

'That's not a condition, just an irrational fear.'

'Irrational! Do you know how many times I've near copped it on the wet stuff since I came doon here? Anyway, it doesnae make sense. I'm the acting boss here. Why no' stick Potts on the boat?'

'Two reasons: first, he's not married; and second, he doesn't have your experience or eye for something that's not right.'

'Don't you try tae butter me up – ma'am,' said Scott, remembering in the nick of time to whom he was talking.

'And most important, no one on board knows you.'

'Ha! I've spoken tae the captain – thon Banks fella.' He sat back in the chair with a smile on his face.

'Oh, he'll never put a face to the voice. And in any case, all I want you to do is observe. Someone was in touch with the men who operated that drone, and whoever it was was on board. Now, as I told you, the government is trying to play this down as a paparazzi stunt gone wrong. But taking into account the man left dead at the scene, as well as the possible connection to the murder of Cameron Pearson, not to mention the fact that they've slapped a D-Notice on it all, I think they know it was a terrorist attack gone awry.'

'The fool on the hill, eh?'

'Yes, exactly.'

'Well, I'm no' going tae be the daftie on the deck.'

She sighed, looking through some papers while she thought of another strategy to persuade her recalcitrant Acting DI to be her eyes and ears on the *Great Britain*. 'Think about it, Brian. Someone on board that ship was in touch with the man, or men, on the hill. There were no explosives in that drone, yet someone who operated it is lying dead. So we have to ask the question, surely?'

'The answer's easy. Either it was a wind-up that went badly wrong, or it was hopeless from the start. Ma'am, we're not even allowed tae ask questions about the dead man. Don't you think we should leave all that tae the Security Service?'

'No. They're on cover-up manoeuvres, and you know it. That's why I want us to do something.'

'Like what?'

'That's what I want you to find out. And since this has been closed down by the MOD, I think it's our duty to probe further. It's our patch, Brian!'

'No, my answer's the same. I'm no' posing as some businessman on there. For a start, what kind o' businessman would I make? They'd suss me oot in seconds.'

'Oh well. As I say, I can't force you and your wife to do this, but it would have been so helpful.'

'I'm usually the man that stands still while every other bastard takes one step back – if you'll pardon the French, ma'am. No' this time. I'm no' volunteering. Anyway, I've got a sub-division tae run.'

'Very well, Brian. Your choice, and I respect that.'

Symington watched him leave the room. Once he'd closed her office door she picked up her phone. 'Sergeant Shaw, can you put me through to DI Scott's home number?'

'He's in the office somewhere, ma'am. I saw him about twenty minutes ago.'

'Yes, I know that. It's Mrs Scott I'd like to speak to, please.'

Symington replaced the receiver and waited with a smile for the phone to ring.

33

'You have no idea how it feels, Jim. You feel helpless, scared, shocked – horrified that you've let yourself become so vulnerable. I wake up in the middle of the night after seeing his face in my dreams – smelling him, even.' She looked away to hide her tears.

'I understand – well, I'm trying to, Liz.'

'You can't ever understand. The feeling of being at the mercy of someone who could kill you; the outright ordinariness of it all once it's over, as he sits back down and ties his tie as though nothing happened.'

Daley watched her take a gulp of wine. He'd investigated so many cases like this – women attacked by brutal husbands or boyfriends, or a tiny number where the female had been the aggressor.

He remembered being told as a young cop to steer clear of domestic disputes; what happened behind closed doors between man and wife was their business, not that of the police. Fortunately, those days had gone, but what could he do when Liz refused to take the matter further?

'Let's just forget this happened, Jim. Though I suppose Brian will have been asking questions.'

'He hasn't said a word. You know Brian: he only gets involved when it becomes his business.'

'Good, faithful Brian. Maybe I should have married someone like him.'

'You think?'

'Who knows? You and I haven't exactly been couple of the century, have we?'

'I tried.'

'You were – still are – married to the police, Jim. What are you going to do when both me and the job you love so much are gone?'

It was like a stab to the heart. He knew he was only her target by proxy, but it brought the thought that had haunted him since his short time in hospital back to the forefront of his mind.

'I'm sorry, that was unfair. I shouldn't have said it.' She gave him a weak smile and reached across the table for the wine bottle.

'It doesn't matter,' he lied. 'And that won't help. Booze will just make everything seem worse, trust me.'

'Oh, are we back to one of your mother's old maxims? *Never drink when you have a problem, son.* I hate all that homespun philosophy, Jim, and you know it.'

He'd promised himself that he would stay calm, try to talk her into bringing her attacker to justice, but he could see he was getting nowhere.

'Mummy!' James junior was toddling into the lounge after his nap.

'Can you deal with him, Jim? Take him outside for a walk or something. The nurse told you to take regular exercise – don't you think it's time you took some? Or are you just going to sit on that recliner and feel sorry for yourself, playing old songs and watching the TV?'

'While you get drunk, you mean?'

'So what? You going to have go at me too? Why not, eh? Just wallop me here.' She pointed to her right cheek. 'He missed that bit.'

Daley picked up his son. 'Right, Jimmy boy, time you had a walk with Daddy.'

'Don't call him that. His name is James. You sound like Brian bloody Scott.'

'Could be worse – I could sound like you, Liz. And please, don't talk to me like that again. You know I'd never harm you.'

'What does harm mean, Daddy?'

Daley lifted their son high above his head, ignoring the twinge of pain he felt for an instant in his chest. 'Let's get your coat on and go for a walk. We can see the big ship better from the top of the hill.'

'Yay!' The little boy smiled broadly as his father carried him out of the room.

Liz heard the door slam, took another gulp of wine, then searched in her handbag for her mobile phone. She dialled a number and waited for a reply.

'This is *lovely*,' said Ella Scott, taking in the splendid cabin they'd been allotted on the *Great Britain*. 'Look, we've got a balcony, and a separate bedroom and lounge. It's bigger than the flat we had when we got married.'

'Aye, well, don't get too used tae it. I'm here tae work, no' enjoy myself, Ella.'

'Nothing to stop me having a good time, is there? Aye, and

if you want tae look the part would it no' be better if you weren't cloaking aboot wae a face like a wet weekend in Paisley?'

'This is serious! You both knew fine I didnae want this job, yet you and Carrie Symington conspired against me.'

'Made you see sense, you mean.'

'Whatever.'

'So, the story is that you're a local businessman on board for a few days tae make contacts, aye?'

'Wind energy, Ella.'

'Aye, well, you've plenty o' that. Carrie knows you well, right enough.'

'Oh, *Carrie* is it noo?'

'What dae you want me tae call her – ma'am? She's no' my boss.'

'Aye, but she played you like a fish.'

'At least I've no' got a face like one – a deid haddock, at that.'

'I'm no' sayin' anything.'

Ella Scott threw herself back on the huge bed. 'Oh, this is right comfy – and look at the size o' it! You could have a game o' tennis on here.'

'New balls, please,' replied Scott, his mouth downturned. 'Anyway, when's the last time you played a game o' tennis?'

'1978, if you must know. I went tae the council courts quite a lot then wae my friend Teeny.'

'Teeny's no' playing much tennis noo, I bet?'

'Naw, she married an Australian. You want tae see the hoose they've got oot in Adelaide.'

Scott sighed. 'You're getting mair like Liz Daley every day.'

'Aye, and talking of Liz Daley, what's happening there?'

'What do you mean?'

'She appears oot o' nowhere, just as bold as brass. Wae a face like that, I think we all know what happened tae her. Jimmy's got a big heart, that's all I can say.'

'Hardly appropriate, Ella, especially since his heart nearly stopped the other day. Anyway, it's none o' oor business.'

'You're a policeman. And whatever I think of her, she doesnae deserve that. Och, you know fine what I mean aboot Jimmy having a big heart.' She patted the bed beside her. 'Here, it's a while since we . . .'

'We don't know what happened to her. It could have been a car crash – anything.' He paused. 'Since we what?'

'You know – the jolly old thing. Dae I need tae spell it oot?'

'I'm working, Ella!'

'Oh aye. And you were working when you were winching me up a close in the Toonheid – uniform, the lot. I cannae see any potential terrorists in here. Come on, we don't get luxury like this very often in oor lives.'

'You're a wicked woman, Ella Scott.' He began to unbutton his shirt.

'And don't you be shouting oot "Annie!" in the throes o' passion, neither.'

'Eh?'

'Think I'm daft? I see the way she looks at you – they puppy dug eyes. I like the lassie fine, but it's as obvious as the nose on your face that she's got the hots for you.'

'You fair know how tae dampen a man's fire. Just put on thon leopard onesie and that'll be the job done. I'm no' like Jimmy, running aboot wae young things.'

'Och, that was a shame. Poor Jimmy.'

'So he has it away wae some lassie half his age and it's a *shame*, while I get accused o' something I never did. That's just typical.'

'He deserved some happiness. You've had a happy marriage for years.'

Scott looked at the ceiling,

'Aye, and before the next half an hour is by, I'll know why Liz Daley is here, tae.' She smiled. 'Come tae bed, Brian.'

34

Cabdi thanked the old woman. She'd given him a lift to Kinloch in her ancient car. He was pleased by the easy way she'd just assumed that he was a passenger on the *Great Britain*. In return, he'd taken a look at a lump on her wrist and diagnosed a ganglion, something she appeared to be inordinately happy to have.

'Saves me a trip tae the land that time forgot,' she said.

'Sorry?'

'The health centre. Och, they jeest tell me I'm getting auld and tell me tae drink plenty fluids and take an aspirin. They're no' bothered if you live or die once you get past a certain age in this country.'

Cabdi thought about this. Old people were venerated in Somalia; valued for their wisdom and respected by one and all. In the West, as with so many things, life was different. Working in the hospital in Glasgow, he'd seen bored relatives argue around the bedsides of elderly relatives about who would get what when the patient died. It made him feel sick.

'I'll jeest leave you here, son. My hoose is up in the scheme, there. If you jeest follow this road a whiles it'll take you right into the toon centre.'

Cabdi thanked her, and strode off towards Kinloch. He knew his strategy was risky. He couldn't be sure he hadn't been seen. However, he was also reasonably certain that there was little evidence to connect him to Faduma, the man he'd left dead on the hill.

He had to go on. He had a mission to complete, and there would be many strange faces in Kinloch with the cruise ship in the harbour. Though he cursed himself for leaving the phone behind on the hill, he'd had little choice. Faduma, by virtue of his own stupidity, had killed himself, and as a result, Cabdi had almost failed in his task.

He shivered at the memory of pushing Faduma from the ledge. But he had a job to do, and though he'd never met the man on the phone – didn't even know his name – he would recognise his voice. Of that, he was sure.

With this in the forefront of his mind, he pulled the stolen baseball cap down over his eyes and turned the corner into Main Street.

'What is this pony? A small horse, yes, but what does it have to do with whisky?' asked Henning Schroeder, a German freight magnate, a confused look on his face.

'Noo, you see, a pony's something that you have wae your first few drams, especially if you've a drouth fae the night afore,' Hamish replied.

The bar at the County Hotel was thronged with visitors from the *Great Britain*. They had put on a cold buffet in the function suite upstairs, and the distant notes of an accordion could be heard as the bar door swung open and closed.

'So you drink this pony, yes?'

'Aye, here, I'll show you whoot I mean.' Hamish leaned

across the bar. 'Annie, can we have two ponies for me an' my new friend here?'

'You can hold your horses, Hamish. There's only the three of us behind the bar here, and that's six hands. I'll get tae you when I've a second.' She scowled at the old fisherman, then smiled broadly at his German companion.

'How ye getting on?'

'Sorry?' said Henning, stroking his tidy beard as he tried to decipher the local dialect.

'I'll be wae you in a wee minute,' said Annie, like Scott deploying her usual strategy of speaking slowly and loudly to any foreign guests who happened upon her domain at the County.

'Och, she's jeest useless,' said Hamish. Just as he was about to comment further a tall Japanese businessman lurched into them, spilling some of his dark beer on Hamish's dungarees. The visitor bowed and muttered something the old man couldn't understand. However, he returned the bow and soaked up the spillage with a large handkerchief.

'Too much to drink, yes?' said Henning.

'No, I've only jeest started.'

'No, I meant the man who spilled the beer on you, Hamesie.'

'Och, if I'd a pound for every time I've had a drink spilt on me in this establishment, I'd be on that boat wae all of you – fair minted, I'd be. Once we get oor ponies, we'll head tae the shindig upstairs, aye?'

'All these new words.'

'Zie accordion,' replied Hamish in his best German accent.

'Here's your ponies,' chimed in Annie. 'Two lights.'

'This is beer in a wine glass,' said Henning with a look of surprise.

'Aye, it is that,' replied Hamish.

'And the lady behind the bar called it light, yes?'

'Aye, that's light beer.'

'But it is dark, no?'

Hamish thought for a moment. 'It is, but it's light at the same time – if you know whoot I mean.'

'With these ponies and light beer that is dark, I don't think I will pick up Scottish so easily.'

'You're doing jeest fine. And anyhow, your Scottish is a lot better than my German, and that's a fact.'

'Ah, this is good to hear!' A broad smile spread across Henning's face.

'All I know aboot German is fae the war movies. Did you ever see *Where Eagles Dare*?'

'No, I have missed that one.'

'Die, Englischer!' Hamish shouted, mimicking a bayonet thrust.

'Oh.' Henning looked uncomfortable.

Before Hamish had the chance to run through his repertoire of German phrases, he had to fend off another Japanese businessman. This one was smaller and he was doing his best to sing an Elvis Presley song.

'Come on, me an' you will go upstairs, Henning. The chances o' staying dry in here are worse than being caught in an Atlantic squall.' The old man eased himself down from his bar stool, and, followed by a bemused German carrying a whisky in one hand and a wine glass full of dark beer that they called light in the other, wound his way out of the main bar of the County Hotel and up a short flight of stairs to the function suite, where the music was now bellowing.

*

Chief Superintendent Symington knocked at Jim Daley's front door. When no reply was forthcoming, she was about to turn on her heel and leave when the door opened a crack.

'Oh, hello,' said Liz, staring through the chink. 'Jim's out with our son. Will I get him to give you a call when he gets back in?'

'No, it's okay. I'll see him soon. Just thought he could help me with something to keep him occupied. I know how hard it is to be laid up with nothing to do.' She hesitated. 'Are you okay, Mrs Daley?'

Behind the door, Liz lowered her head for a moment, then let it swing fully open. She was slightly unsteady on her feet because of the wine, and still hadn't applied any make-up to her battered face.

'What happened to you?'

'Don't worry,' said Liz. 'It wasn't Jim, if that's what you're thinking.'

'I wasn't thinking anything.'

'Yes, you were. Listen, please come in. I'm afraid I've had a few glasses of wine, but I'm not drunk – yet. It would be nice to have some female company. This isn't something I normally do – the drinking, I mean.'

Symington nodded and crossed the threshold into the hall.

'In here,' said Liz, leading her into the lounge.

Symington sat on the large couch and watched Liz Daley open another bottle of wine. 'It won't help, you know.'

'Ha, you sound like Jim. I suppose he's discussed this with you.'

'No, not at all. But it's not hard to tell, is it? I'm a police officer, Mrs Daley. I know an abused woman when I see one.'

'Call me Liz.' She offered Symington a large glass of wine,

which was refused with a shake of the head. 'I know that you – Jim – have all dealt with women in my position. But you don't know what it's like, I assure you, Chief Superintendent.'

'You might be surprised what I know. And please, it's Carrie.'

'You knew about Mary Dunn, I take it?'

'Yes, I did.'

Liz snorted a mirthless laugh. 'Never thought he had it in him.'

'In my experience – and clearly yours – you never know what's really *in* anyone.'

'Jim wouldn't harm a fly – oh, he has a temper, but this kind of thing is the last thing he'd do.' A tear meandered down Liz's bruised cheek.

'What are you going to do about it?'

'You really are as bad as my husband! All you police officers can think about is charges and courts. Do you have any idea what that would entail for me? I would never be able to go home again.'

'And just how is this your fault? I'm assuming a man did this to you?'

'Good work, detective.' Liz put her glass on the large coffee table. 'I'm sorry. I didn't mean to be rude.'

'No, but it is my job. Whoever did it needs to be brought to justice, Liz.'

'I told you, I can't! I just want to forget it ever happened. Why don't you and Jim understand?'

'I do understand.'

'How could you?'

'A man – a colleague, in fact – raped me.' This was delivered with an emotionless steady gaze.

The sentence hung in the air.

'Oh – I'm sorry. I had no idea . . .'

'Very few people have. Like you, I couldn't face doing anything about it. And anyway, it was complicated.' Symington raised her head defiantly.

'So what did you do?'

'I let it eat away at me for years. It ruined every relationship I've had since. Oh, I know there are good, kind men out there – like your husband. But I can never take that chance.'

'Did it happen a long time ago?'

'Yes – long enough.'

'And you still think about it?'

'Every day. I think about it every day.'

'And it doesn't get easier – with time, I mean?'

'Good and bad days; but on the whole, no, it doesn't get better with time. It festers in your soul, and unless you have the strength to do something about it, it will destroy you.'

Liz swallowed hard. 'I'm so sorry – really, I am.'

'Don't be sorry for me, be sorry for yourself. I got myself into a place I should never have been in, at the hands of a monster. But you have the chance to do something. It's too late for me now, but you can help put things right, for your own piece of mind, and for those who will suffer at this man's hands, again and again.' Symington stopped, hearing the front door open.

'We're back, Liz!' called Daley.

'You can come and talk to me any time,' said Symington quietly, as James junior appeared in the doorway.

'Ma'am,' said Daley with surprise, coming in behind him. 'I didn't see your car.'

'No, I got a lift up. The driver will come back for me when I'm ready.'

Daley stared between Liz and Symington. He could sense tension in the air, and wondered what had passed between them.

'Can I have a word, Jim?'

'Of course.'

'I'll take James through.' Liz picked up her son and made to leave the room.

'Okay. I hope I'll see you again soon, Liz.'

'Thanks, Carrie. Much appreciated – I mean that.' She closed the door, leaving the two police officers alone.

'She's had a hard time, Carrie,' said Daley.

'You don't need to say anything, Jim. I understand.' She opened her handbag. 'Listen, if you want, there's something you can do for me – if you feel up to it, that is.'

'Great. It's driving me mad just sitting here.'

'That's what I thought.' Symington handed Daley a memory stick.

'What's on here?'

'Answers, I hope. As you know, the phone we found near where the dead man had only communicated with one number. Untraceable, of course, but we know it came from the ship.'

'And?'

'On the memory stick is a detailed list of the passengers and crew on the *Great Britain* – their jobs, short biographies and so on. Don't ask how I got it.'

'So you still think this wasn't some paparazzi job gone horribly wrong?'

'With two dead men – yes, I do. The Security Service realise this too, but they think the danger is over.'

'But you don't.'

'No, I don't. You saw the other man on the hill.'

'Yes, I think, but not clearly enough to describe him. I was making calls when I saw movement. I'm sure there were two men fighting.'

'Well, they'll probably find him. They've certainly got enough manpower on the job. But what about the contact on the ship?'

'Majid? Perhaps got cold feet and buggered off before the attack?'

'No, there are calls after he disappeared. There's somebody on that ship who knows something. Somebody who may be dangerous; I can feel it, Jim.'

'Pity we can't get someone aboard – clandestinely, I mean. I know that the spooks won't be keen.'

'I've managed to place somebody on board. Captain Banks is a very friendly man – as worried as me, as it turns out.'

'Good going, ma'am.'

'If you go through the passenger list – have a dig, flag up anyone who even sounds remotely suspicious – you'd be doing me a huge favour, Jim.'

'Sure – absolutely.'

'Good. Thanks, Jim. And remember, if it's too much, just stop.'

'No, I welcome any diversion right now.' His face was dark.

'Give her time, Jim, yes?'

Momentarily, Daley was confused. 'Liz, you mean?'

'Yes.'

'I'm trying. I take it you two have spoken – about what happened, I mean.'

'Briefly, enough for me to know bits and pieces.'

'If I could get my hands on him . . .'

'That's not the way, DCI Daley, and you know it.'

'No, ma'am.'

Symington pulled out her mobile and called for a car back to Kinloch Police Office. 'I'll leave you to it.'

'Okay, I'll boot up the computer now.' He hesitated. 'By the way, who have you placed aboard the *Great Britain*?'

'Come on, there was only one man for the job.' She smiled.

'You're kidding?'

'Nope, Brian Scott – or should I say, Mr William Sinclair, specialist in wind energy.'

'But Brian knows nothing about that kind of thing.'

'He does now – sort of. Enough, I'm hoping.'

As Daley watched his superior head for the door, he wondered just how much information about renewable energy Brian Scott could have assimilated in such a short time. He bit his lip.

35

Cabdi walked around the town, testing the water. If he wasn't in the clear, he calculated he'd soon find out.

He passed two uniformed police officers who nodded a friendly greeting. He was right; they couldn't have identified him. He saw a bakery and suddenly felt very hungry. In fact, he couldn't remember the last time he'd eaten. Walking in, he bought a large mug of coffee and a cheese roll.

'They no' feeding you on that boat?' asked the woman behind the counter.

'Ah, they feed us very well, but I have a big appetite.' He smiled, patting his belly.

'Well, you don't look like it. You're like a clothes pole.'

'What?'

'Och, nothing. Just you enjoy yourself. Most of the hotels and pubs have music on. You're all very welcome. Have you been rolling in the mud, by the way?'

'No, I went hiking to see more of your beautiful area,' said Cabdi. 'I'll get changed when I go back on board.'

He walked out of the bakery and leaned against a litterbin, taking in the sights and sounds of the bustling town as he drank his coffee and ate his roll. Dotted along the streets were groups of men and women who were clearly tourists, and probably from the *Great Britain*. They were looking in shop windows, no doubt hunting for little reminders of their visit to Kinloch, or presents for friends and family to hand out when they returned from their trip.

How foolish they are, he thought. They have no idea what danger lies in wait. This was the easy way of the Westerner: no cares, no worries. When a father, a mother, a daughter, a son – anyone – left their homes in the countries these people came from, their last worry was that they might lose their life. In Somalia, things were very different.

He saw a group of very loud Americans cross the road in his direction, so decided it was time to mingle.

He placed the empty cup and the paper bag in which his roll had been served in the bin, and looked around. A white-spired building stood up the street from where he was standing, to its side a narrow lane. He decided to make his way down this little road, away from the main thoroughfare to somewhere quieter.

The lane opened out to a square, on each side of which shops and bars huddled around a car park. The sign above one of the bars read *The Douglas Arms*. Cabdi heard music and laughter coming from inside, and decided this would be as good a place as any to sit down and rest, to lose himself in a crowd and get warm.

He entered the busy pub.

Acting DS Potts was reading the post-mortem report on Cameron Pearson. Identity confirmed, it was now just a case of trying to find any clue as to the person or persons who had killed the unfortunate ornithologist. But there was little to go on.

Chief Superintendent Symington breezed into the CID suite. She was making for Daley's glass box, but stopped at Potts's desk when he signalled to her.

'Very little from the PM on Mr Pearson, ma'am.'

'I didn't expect there would be. If whoever killed him went to the trouble of removing his head, hands and feet to obscure his identity, it's unlikely that they were going to leave a wealth of evidence as to who they were. The remains were only found by sheer luck.'

'Yes, ma'am. We might be able to isolate the make of knife used to – well, to decapitate him and so on – from the serrations on the wounds. It's a long shot, mind you.'

'Even if we do, you can bet it will be from some chain store which sells thousands of them. But if that's all we have, that's all we have. I just hope our colleagues from the Security Service manage to come across someone up in the hills. It looks like a military exercise on Ben Saarnie – Royal Marines everywhere. Odds on it's this Majid. Just how this has happened given the security surrounding everything, I don't know. Keep digging, DS Potts.'

'Yes, ma'am.' He remembered the yellow Post-it note on his desk. 'Ma'am, there was a call for you – well, for the person in charge; he initially asked for DCI Daley. It's a Mr Manston. He didn't sound very happy.'

'What was it about?'

Potts coughed awkwardly.

'Spit it out, DS Potts.'

'He says he's been receiving threatening calls, ma'am.'

'Surely you don't need me to deal with that! It's not as though we don't have enough on our plate at the moment.'

'It's rather sensitive, ma'am.'

'In what way is it sensitive?'

Potts lowered his voice. 'Apparently the calls are coming from Mrs Daley, ma'am.'

The expression on Symington's face changed, darkening in concert with her mood. 'Give me the number, DS Potts.'

He handed her the Post-it note, and she marched into Daley's box, slamming the door behind her. Soon, she closed the blinds.

The bar was busy as Cabdi stood behind a group of people waiting to be served. He spotted a small room through a door behind the bar. It looked less crowded, so he decided to make for that in the hope of getting a seat. His legs still ached from his hike across the hills.

A short corridor led him into the lounge, where two men in golf gear were arguing over a scorecard in voluble French. He knew the language well, and could hear that the dispute was about their respective scores from an earlier round of the game.

Three young women sat at another table. One of them looked at him and smiled, then said something to her friends that made them giggle conspiratorially. All in all, the place was quieter than the main bar, but most of the seats were filled.

At the end of the narrow room sat an elderly man. He was perched at a table alone, two empty chairs at his side. Cabdi reached the counter at last and ordered a coffee from a harassed-looking barman.

'I'll be with you as soon as I can,' said the young man. 'Take a seat and I'll bring it over to you.' He pointed to one of the chairs at the table where the old man sat staring into space.

'Do you mind?' said Cabdi with a smile.

'Naw, not at all, son. Be my guest. There's no' many will sit beside me just noo.'

'Oh? Why's that?

'Ach, folk in this town – no' as nice as they look, let me tell you. Hey, you off the cruise liner?'

Cabdi was ready for the question, and merely nodded a reply.

'Lucky you, eh? She's some vessel.'

'Yes, a great ship, indeed.'

The old man held out his hand. 'Here, what's your name, son?'

'I'm Nassim,' Cabdi lied.

'Aye, good tae meet you. It's nice tae have someone tae talk to. There's no' too many keen tae pass the time of day with me in Kinloch, as I've said.'

'Oh, small towns, I suppose. Always trouble with some people, yes?'

'Aye, you could say that, son – wae bells on!'

'Sorry, what's your name?'

'Peter, Peter Scally.' The old man and the tall Somali shook hands.

Symington waited for the phone to be answered. 'Yes, may I speak to Mr Manston, please? It's Chief Superintendent Symington from Kinloch Police Office.'

She listened to some inane hold music for a short while until another voice came on the line.

'Must say, I'm glad to see you're taking this seriously. I expected to be palmed off with some constable.' Manston was well spoken and brusque.

'I'm told you've been receiving threatening calls, Mr Manston.'

'Yes, from a deranged woman, and I want them to stop.'

'What is the nature of these calls, sir? I take it the woman is a resident of this area, since you're calling Kinloch?'

'Yes, as a matter of fact she is. However, this isn't just any woman. I believe she is married to one of your senior officers.'

'Really, who?' asked Symington innocently.

'A Detective Chief Inspector Daley. His wife is Liz – Liz Daley.'

'And what kind of things has Mrs Daley been saying to you?'

'Threats – telling me she'd make sure I suffered. All sorts: all irrational, threatening, and she's often drunk. This is happening at all times of day and night. My family – my children – are becoming very distressed.'

'I don't suppose that you have recorded any of these calls?'

'Yes, as it happens, I have. I recorded the calls I received yesterday and today.'

'And you know Mrs Daley?'

'Yes, but I don't want to know her any more.'

'Did you know her through work, or socially?'

'If you must know, we were in a relationship. That relationship is now over, thankfully. The woman is mad, and I want her to stop contacting me. I'm making an official complaint. And before you reply, I know just how you police officers stick together. Well, I'll have you know that I have friends who are very senior figures in Police Scotland, and if my complaint isn't treated properly I'll have no hesitation in pointing it out to them, Chief Superintendent.'

'I see.' Symington paused. 'I assure you, Mr Manston, that I'm taking this matter very seriously indeed.'

'Glad to hear it!' Suddenly he sounded unsure. 'So, you are aware of the issue?'

'Yes, I am. In fact, I was with Mrs Daley – oh, not more than an hour ago.'

For a moment, there was silence, then: 'What has that mad woman been saying? I demand to know!'

'All I'm prepared to say at this stage is that I'm dealing with what is potentially a serious crime. I'm gathering facts at the moment. And as part of that, I'd like to speak to you – quite possibly under caution. Do you understand?'

The tone of Manston's voice changed. Suddenly it was low and menacing. 'Typical. Just as I expected – a cover-up. Well, my lawyer will make mincemeat of you and Liz Daley. In any case, she won't want to take me on. If she's made some kind of complaint, I want to know about it. And you can be sure the information will be passed on to my lawyer.'

'Perhaps you have a lack of understanding of the Scottish legal system, sir. And while some women can submit to being threatened, I'm glad to say that I'm not one of them. In Scotland, it is the police who bring charges, not the complainant. So, if I have reason to believe that a crime has been committed, I have every right to investigate. As I've told you, I'll be looking into this matter closely. And the likelihood is that I'll want to speak with you more formally. Until then, good day, Mr Manston.'

Symington replaced the receiver with great satisfaction, cutting off Manston's protests.

Now it was up to Liz Daley.

36

Brian and Ella Scott were sitting at a table with some of the *Great Britain*'s other passengers. There was an elderly Arab sheik – apparently an oil billionaire – and his beautiful young girlfriend; a striking Frenchwoman and her new wife who together ran an upmarket Cognac house she'd inherited from her mother; an Australian senator who'd had far too much to drink, and a quiet, bookish-looking civil servant from Edinburgh wearing a trouser suit that engulfed her, being several sizes too large. She blinked at the party behind round spectacles, flashing an occasional nervous smile.

'Aye, it's a nice day,' said Scott, remembering Symington's instruction to get to know as many of the passengers as possible, and pick up any gossip and potential intelligence that he could. He'd been a police officer for a long time, and she was placing much faith in his instinct to spot something wrong, out of place.

'Nice day, mate? I nearly froze my bloody bollocks off when I was up on deck earlier. In Australia, this is like the fucking winter – if you'll pardon my language, ladies.'

Chantelle Amion stared at him in disgust. 'But everything is so dry and dusty in your country. I was in Perth – it almost choked me.'

'We make a better drop of wine than you do now, you have to admit that.'

'Monsieur, your wine is cheap and cheerful – not for the connoisseur, I assure you. I'm right, Patti, yes?' She patted her wife's hand affectionately.

'As long as it gets you pished, eh?' said Scott, earning a kick under the table from Ella, who smiled sweetly at the Frenchwoman.

'That's a lovely dress, Chantelle.'

'A Stella McCartney – I feel it is only right to wear what little your country has to offer in haute couture while I'm here.'

'Mine is fae Debenhams,' replied Ella. 'Best dress I've had for a long time. William's no' a big spender, are you, darling?' She had to nudge her husband, who still hadn't got to grips with his cover identity.

'Aye, right – och, I'm no' much for dresses myself. Nane o' that effeminate stuff where I'm from.' Scott smiled, ignoring the French couple's baffled stares.

'You are a very funny man, Mr Sinclair,' said Sheik Ahmad. His accent was that of an English private school rather than his homeland. 'Please, tell me more about your turbine operation. You must understand, your renewable energy holds certain concerns for me, as a man who sells oil for a living. However, I can see which way the wind is blowing, and I am certainly thinking of investing in the future. I hope you'll forgive my little joke.'

Ella Scott braced herself. She'd been coaching her husband in the short time available about the mechanics and nuances behind wind turbine manufacture and usage with the books, pamphlets and websites Symington had provided. To say she wasn't sure that her husband had mastered the subject was putting it mildly.

'Aye, well, it's no' as simple as it looks,' said Scott. 'You see, things go fine when the wind's on the go, but when it stops – well, the wheels fall off the bus, like.'

The civil servant Alison Rutledge coughed. 'But it's so important for the future of energy provision in this country and worldwide, Mr Sinclair. Surely we have systems in place to store energy generated on windy days for just such circumstances?'

Scott thought for a moment, the toe of Ella's shoe pressing hard into his foot. 'You're right – aye, they big accumulators. I mind my mother off tae the wee electrical shop tae get oors filled up. You must mind o' that, tae, Ella.'

'Oh, I thought your name was Nancy?' said Sheik Ahmad.

Ella smiled broadly. 'Och, Ella's his pet name for me.'

'Aye, as in 'ell o' a woman,' said Scott.

'How quaint,' said Chantelle. 'I have a pet name for Patti too, don't I?'

Her wife prodded her. 'But this is between us!' They both grinned.

'Tae get back tae the subject, no matter what you've got – big batteries, anything – you cannae make up for they days when the wind doesnae blow,' said Scott, folding his arms.

Ella focused on a distant chandelier, quietly willing her husband to shut up, while Alison Rutledge shifted uncomfortably in her chair.

'But you blokes are supposed to be at the cutting edge across here,' said Frinton.

'Oh, we are,' said Ella, desperately trying to rescue the situation.

'It sounds as though you know more than your husband, Nancy, *n'est-ce pas*?'

'Och, he likes tae joke around – play the devil's advocate. Don't you, darling?' She kicked him on the leg as hard as she possibly could without drawing attention to the fact. 'What part of France are you from, Chantelle?' she added, in a desperate attempt to stop her husband saying anything more.

'I live in Paris. Do you know it, Nancy?'

'Och, no' as well as I'd like. William's a bit o' a home bird, aren't you, eh?'

'Whistling for the wind, no doubt,' said Sheik Ahmad.

'My faither always said that worked,' said Scott.

Ella glared at him. 'I'm sure we've heard enough about your family, dear.'

'No. The auld dear – my mother – she used tae put the washing oot doon in the green, you know?'

Frinton shook his head.

'Anyhow, if it wasnae a windy day, the auld fella – my faither – well, he would get doon tae the bottom o' the close and start whistling.'

Ella had her head in her hands.

'So this is part of your business strategy, this whistling for the wind?' said the sheik, a smile playing across his lips.

'Naw, it didnae work. My poor mother would have tae haul the whole lot back up the close stairs and try and dry it beside the fire – you know, on one o' they horse things.'

'Oh, for fuck's sake,' said Ella under her breath.

'But you must have a solution to this problem of no wind – if not the whistling, I think?' said Chantelle.

'Well, we was thinking of putting some o' they windmills up in the Arctic – it's fair breezy up thonder.'

'But surely an issue with ownership?' said Frinton.

'Of what?'

'The land, mate. I know UK has some possession up there, but I don't think anyone would sanction wind turbines in such a fragile environment.'

'Och, who's tae see? A few o' they explorers, a polar bear or two and some penguins?'

'I thought you said the Arctic, Monsieur?' said Chantelle. 'Penguins live at the South Pole.'

'He's only having a laugh wae yous all,' said Ella. 'We've got well-developed plans tae make wind energy mair efficient,' she added, trying to remember some of the basic points she'd tried to cram into her husband's head.

A waitress appeared at the table. 'May I take your orders for the starter course? If you would like the alternative tasting menu, please just say.'

'Here, I think we're getting away wae it,' Scott whispered into his wife's ear while the rest of the table dithered over what to eat.

'You've just telt them that penguins come fae the North Pole and that your faither whistled for the wind!'

'Och, these kind o' folk like the banter. Sure, they're stuck in these big office blocks, and that. Must be good tae let your hair doon and have a laugh.'

'You're supposed tae be getting them tae buy oor windmills and blend in normally, no' playing the village idiot. If you go on like this, I'll fling you overboard myself.'

'And what would madam like?' asked the waitress.

'Can I have the Caesar salad, please?' said Ella.

'And you, sir?'

'I'm famished. Lobster for me, lassie, if you don't mind.'

'And would you like bread with that? We have an artisan range.'

'We've just got a normal cooker. My wife wanted one o' they Agas, but I put my foot doon. No, can I have chips wae mine?'

The waitress looked momentarily astonished.

'My husband will have some bread, please.'

The waitress scribbled on her pad and moved on to Frinton.

'Here, I wanted chips.'

'Just try no' tae make a fool o' yourself any mair than you've done already.'

'Huh, says you. Anyway, what dae you want me tae do?'

'Just shut up would be the best strategy.'

'Och, no. I've an idea that'll blow their socks off. I've been looking at the internet. Trust me, dear.'

Ella took a large gulp of her wine, almost draining the glass. 'The first time you said that tae me was aboot nine months before oor eldest was born.'

'See you, you can never let things go – after all these years . . .'

'So, please, tell us more about this whistling, Mr Sinclair,' said the sheik as the waitress trotted away with her orders.

Ella Scott reached for the wine bottle and refilled her glass to the brim.

Cabdi observed what was going on in the Douglas Arms with great interest. Despite the drunken gabbling of the man he'd been forced to sit beside, his ear was tuned to listen for the voice he'd heard so many times over the phone. He'd tried to picture the face, but he knew that was a fruitless exercise.

'What is it you do, son? I've got to say, you don't look like a millionaire,' said Scally.

'I'm in medicine. I work for a company producing the latest treatments for diabetes.' Cabdi had his cover story ready. His medical knowledge would be more than sufficient to fill any gaps, he reasoned.

'Can you fix my knee, eh? I'd a hell o' a job with it the last time I was up the hill.'

'Oh yes, and when was that?' The Somali's interest was piqued.

'Oh, the other night.' Scally downed what was left of his whisky. He leaned into Cabdi. 'I tell you, saw something I didna like, tae.'

'What did you not like?'

'Och, these two strange guys – in an auld van, they were. They had a fire going. Me and my grandson went doon to look at it once they'd gone. I found some bone.' He stopped and took a swig from the glass of beer that had accompanied his whisky. 'The next day, they pulled a body out of the Sound – aye, jeest beyond the island at the loch. Nae heid nor hands – aye, but they've identified him.'

Cabdi felt his heart pound in his chest. Silently he cursed the soul of Faduma. This didn't make sense.

'Friend o' mine, too,' said Scally.

'So, why are people ignoring you?' Cabdi was trying to retain his composure.

'Long story, young man – long story.'

Just as Cabdi was about to reply someone spoke behind him, making him freeze.

'Something the matter, lad? You look like you've just seen a ghost.'

'I'm fine,' he replied, turning to look at a group of people who had just entered the lounge bar.

226

'So, as yous can see, it makes much mair sense tae use tidal energy than it does they windmills. The tide goes in and comes oot right regular. You don't need tae whistle for that, eh?' Brian Scott smiled with self-satisfaction.

'What about the seabed ecology, mate? I mean, we're losing more fish than we can handle already; can't afford to kill off any more,' said Frinton. 'Look at our Great Barrier Reef – bloody tragedy!'

'Och, the fish won't mind aboot oor machines. They're no' daft, you know. Look how long they zoomers stand on the banks o' rivers waiting for the fish tae bite. No, they'll swim round them, dead gallus, like.'

'For a man who makes wind turbines, you don't seem very keen on them, Mr Sinclair.' Sheik Ahmad looked at Scott sceptically.

'It's a bit like yous wae the oil, you know. It's running oot, so you've got tae be ready for the next thing. Every businessman knows that.'

As the sheik nodded thoughtfully, Ella Scott couldn't help being impressed by her husband – and during their marriage, that had been a less than regular occurrence. It seemed that the little coaching he'd been given had rubbed off. She smiled proudly.

'So likely yous will have tae up sticks and pitch your tents somewhere else – near the sea would be my recommendation.'

Chantelle and Patti giggled at the look on Sheik Ahmad's face. Slowly, his mouth had turned down and his expression had darkened.

'I live in some of the most modern, expensive buildings on the planet, Mr Sinclair. I won't be *pitching my tent* anywhere.'

'I thought yous all lived in tents. Thon Colonel Gaddafi was never oot o' his – until he got the rod right up his . . .'

'Och, you're jeest a hell o' a man,' said Ella with a nervous laugh, stopping her husband in mid-flow. 'He's an awful man, right enough.' This time her kick made him yelp.

'Here we are,' said the waitress, looking at Scott warily. 'Your Caesar salad, Mrs Sinclair, and for you the bisque, sir.'

'Wait,' said Scott. 'There's a mistake here – this is soup. I wanted the lobster.'

'It's lobster bisque, sir.'

Scott sighed, looking forlornly at his plate. 'Have you got the bread?'

'Yes, of course.' She handed him a side plate bearing two tiny flatbreads.

Scott blinked at them, then looked back at the waitress. 'I'll need some chips right enough, please.'

37

Daley stared intently at the computer screen. He'd no idea how Symington had come across the detailed information about each passenger on the *Great Britain*, but it was comprehensive and obviously intended only for the eyes of the Security Service.

He had a pad beside him with a short list of names he'd noted down – each possessed what could be considered points of interest, as far as security was concerned, at least. Though he was enjoying the task, just having something productive to do, he wondered why this information hadn't been used by those who compiled it – or perhaps it had? It was clear that there was a small number of passengers on the cruise ship who had – to say the least – shady pasts. However, in most cases they'd been respectable businessmen and women for a number of years.

His mobile rang and he answered.

'Anything, Jim?'

'Yes – too much. Where did you get this, Carrie?'

'Let's say I have a very co-operative source on board.'

'Some of these people have made their money doing some very dubious things.'

'Oh, I knew that. It's the exigencies of business, Jim. Our country has been dealing with mass murderers and dodgy regimes for years, you must know that.'

'I'd hoped that things were improving.'

'The way things are going here, are you kidding?'

'So what you're saying is that our government is perfectly aware of most of this stuff?'

'You saw how they happily ignored the drone – covered it up. I think it's safe to say that we have to look between the lines, Jim. If you come up with any names who jump out at you, let me know and we can have a closer look at them using our own intel.'

'I've found a few already. Give me another couple of hours and I'll get back to you. You never know, we might turn something up, ma'am.' He paused. 'Still nothing on our dead man, or Mr Pearson?'

'No, our corpse on the hill is a mystery. Ordinarily, I'd go to the press, but as you know, with the restrictions placed on us, that's impossible. Though they've been fishing about.'

'And Pearson?'

'Again, nothing. Whoever killed him knew their business well. Not a fleck of forensic evidence. We've taken some DNA from the van and clothing found at the campsite, but no matches. And there's nothing anywhere to identify them – not as much as a note, or a wallet – nothing.'

'What's Brachen saying?'

'He's changed his tune; nothing to worry about now. Obviously pressure from on high – big pressure.'

'And still no sign of the other man I saw on the hill?'

'Not for want of trying. The Marines are all over the place, but they haven't found a thing.'

'Someone knows what they're doing, ma'am. Maybe has help?'

'Yes, I think that too, but what can we do? Our hands are tied – that's why what you and Brian are doing is so important.'

'Yes, because you can be sure that if anything goes wrong the blame will soon land at our door.'

'Undoubtedly.'

'And how's Brian getting on?'

'No idea. He's going to call me later. I'm due back on board tonight for supper with the captain.'

'Very nice. Do you think he'll be able to give you any more intelligence under the counter?'

Symington smiled as she held the phone to her ear. 'Very clever, Jim.'

'It was a process of elimination – it's not as though I haven't done it before.'

She hesitated. 'Jim, can you talk? I mean is Liz there?'

'She and James are having a lie-down – sleeping it off, if you know what I mean.'

'Does the name Alexander Manston mean anything to you?'

As soon as he heard it Daley felt a twinge in his chest. 'Yes, I know who Alexander Manston is, ma'am.'

'I thought you might. Listen, Jim, Liz has been calling him – leaving threatening messages. He called me today to make a complaint.'

'What! Complaint – him! The bastard. If I ever get my hands on him, I swear I'll kill him. I don't give a fuck about the consequences!'

'Calm down, Jim. Think of your health. I hate this guy as much as you – all the men who do this. I saw Liz's face. We spoke; I've a good idea what happened. If we could only get her to open up, we could go on the offensive.'

'She won't do it.'

'Why, is she scared?'

'Scared that people will find out.'

Symington took a deep breath. 'Yes. Yes I can understand that.'

'Ma'am?'

'Oh, I've seen it before with abused women, you know, over the years. You've done this job longer than me, you must have seen your fair share too.' She could feel her throat tighten and hoped Daley hadn't detected it.

'She doesn't want to lose face. Up there, with her family and friends. I'm sure you've seen that before too, Carrie.'

'Oh, yes.' She swallowed hard. 'But if we could only persuade her, Jim. Do you think if I have a word, away from everything? Over a drink, or something – I don't know.'

'You could try, though another drink is the last thing she needs.'

'I'll phone her tomorrow – you know, when she's feeling a bit better.'

'When she's not drunk, you mean.'

'I know it's difficult, trust me. But give her some space, okay? You never know, she might change her mind.'

'Don't hold your breath, Carrie. But I appreciate what you're trying to do. I just hope Manston doesn't try anything. He's got plenty of money, and we all know with money comes influence.'

'Leave him to me. You've enough on your plate. Keep digging, but if for one second it feels too much I want you to stop, and that's an order.'

'Yes, ma'am,' replied Daley with a smile. 'I'll call you soon with any names that come up.'

He ended the call and began to key the computer. The screen flashed into life, and he began to scroll down. The name O'Rourke was next on the random list. He began to read.

'Daddy!' James Daley junior toddled into the room rubbing sleep from his eyes.

'Come on, son. Did you have a good sleep with Mummy?'

'Yes, but she's still tired.'

'What do you mean?' Daley stared at the little boy.

'I tried to wake her up, Daddy, but she just stayed asleep.'

'You stay here. Look, play with Panda for a minute.' Daley handed his son the fluffy toy and left him on the floor humming softly to himself as he rushed off to see Liz.

She was lying with her head to one side, one arm dangling over the bed.

'Liz, Liz!' he shouted, trying to rouse her. When there was no response he took hold of her shoulders and shook her. Though her eyelids flickered, she remained unconscious.

Daley looked on the floor beside the bed. Poking out, just under the spread of the duvet cover, lay two empty blister packs. The paracetamols they had once contained were gone.

'No, Liz. No!' He hefted her into his arms and half carried, half dragged her into the lounge. With one hand he picked up his phone, scrolled down the contact list and pressed call. 'I need an ambulance, now. Please hurry!'

James Daley junior burst into tears.

*

O'Rourke had seen enough of Kinloch. It was just an extension of the forced camaraderie of the cruise liner. He wanted to be alone, and he knew just where he wanted to do it.

He left the crowded Douglas Arms, walked up the narrow lane past the square and ended up back in Main Street. To his right, three taxis sat at a rank. The driver of the first car, a thin man in his early sixties with fading red hair, was leaning in the passenger window of the car behind.

'Hey, buddy, you on hire or what?'

The man hurried back into his cab, taking time to stub out his cigarette on the way.

'How'ye,' came the usual local greeting. 'Where are we for?'

'Machrie. I'd like to take in some fresh sea air.'

'Aye, nae bother. We'll be there in a jiffy. Nice hotel there, noo. Just done up. Me and the wife had a great night for oor anniversary there a few weeks ago.'

'You don't say.' O'Rourke jumped into the back of the cab and the driver pulled off, performing a casual U-turn in the busy street.

'You'll be off the boat, eh?'

'Yeah, that's it. Well spotted.' O'Rourke tried to indicate that he'd rather pass the journey in peace, but the driver persisted.

'Me and the wife are off tae the reception on board tonight.'

'You guys have all the fun of the fair.'

'No' jeest anyone gets an invite, you know. It's because I was on the community council for years. I'm fair looking forward tae it.'

234

'Yeah, me too,' replied O'Rourke sarcastically.

'See how the other half live. Hey, you'll have a few bob aboot you, right?'

'Don't worry, I'll tip you. But do me a favour, buddy, cut the chat. I just want some peace and quiet – appreciate the scenery, you know.'

'Aye, nae bother. Message received and understood, sir.'

Though his driver maintained a bright sense of bonhomie, O'Rourke could see him glowering in the rear-view mirror, his brows furrowed. O'Rourke sat back and took in the scene from the car. The road they were travelling was long and straight, the landscape flat up to the hills that cocooned them. It was like travelling through a massive amphitheatre.

He cracked the window open; the salty smell of the sea filled the car and at the same time jogged his memory. Soon they were in the outskirts of the village of Machrie.

'Where dae you want dropped off?' asked the driver.

'Is there somewhere outside the village, somewhere quiet where I can just sit and think?'

'Aye, sure. Jeest gie me a couple o' minutes.'

They drove past the hotel and golf club, through what was left of Machrie, then onto a single-track road. The driver pulled into a layby and brought the car to a halt.

'Here, you'll no' find much mair quiet than this.'

They had pulled up beside an old wooden bench seat. Time and tide had eaten away at it, but it still looked serviceable.

'This will be fine, thank you, driver.' O'Rourke leaned across the back seat and offered a handful of notes to the man behind the wheel.

'Oh, wait, that's too much.'

'Then don't charge me when you take me back. Give me an hour and pick me up here, okay?'

'Aye, don't you worry. It's time I'd a break anyhow. I'll jeest dodge doon tae the hotel and get a snack. See you in an hour – and thanks for this, very generous.' He held up the money.

O'Rourke stepped out of the taxi and watched it drive away. He stood for a while, breathing in the sea air. It reminded him of being young and visiting a place that looked just like this. He stared across the short stretch of sea to the coast of County Antrim, now looking even closer than it had during his round of golf with the formidable Asian businesswoman. Faces flashed across his mind – happy faces, soaking up the sun, filling buckets with sand, paddling in the cool water, searching for crabs in seaweed-strewn rock pools under shifting skies; blue then grey.

He smiled at the memories.

He made his way down a grassy slope to dark jagged rocks. Only feet away, two seals lounged near the water. One eyed him lazily as he made his way carefully to a tiny outcrop of rock where he found a boulder flat enough to sit on.

The day was bright and sunny, with hardly any wind. He stared into the clear water, watching the strands of kelp and bladderwrack twist and sway gently on the ebb of the tide. One of the seals waddled across the rocks then slipped gracefully into the water with barely a sound.

He remembered the story that his mother used to tell of these creatures, who stole children and took their place. They could only be recognised for what they truly were if they swam in the sea.

You watch out, now. The boy who won't swim is one of the seal children.

He could see her earnest face as she warned them. He also recalled pitching reluctant swimmers into the waves, just to make sure they were ordinary little girls and boys. Though he nearly drowned a few of his classmates, he never found a seal child.

Maybe that's what I am? He pondered this question as he stared at the green coast across the water. Was he a shape-shifter, existing in a foreign skin, far away from the place that he knew was home? True, in a way. He wondered whether, if he jumped into the clear cold water in front of him, he'd return to the skinny Belfast boy he'd once been, rather than the rich fat American he'd now become.

But dreams and stories were just the same: they always ended in the grey wash of harsh reality. Whether it was the first fluttering of the waking eye, or the last chapter of the book, everything came down to the here and now.

He knew who he was, and he knew what he wanted to do.

He took one last look at the coast of County Antrim and made his way carefully back across the jagged rocks and back up the ragged rise.

It was time – time to change things for ever.

38

1972

The little boy ran, his feet aching in his worn-soled shoes as they slapped against the hot, hard road under the bright summer sun. His heart pounded in his chest and his mouth tasted of blood as he shot up the hill as fast as he could and turned left into the cobbled street.

The bar stood amidst a row of shops: a grocer, an ironmonger and a bakery. They all displayed their wares through open, bright windows: a loaf here, a tin of beans there, a yellow plastic bucket in another.

The ironmonger was standing in the doorway of his shop wiping his brow with a handkerchief as the boy caught his breath, hesitating in front of the door to the pub.

'But you're a boy in a hurry, am I right?' said the stout man kindly. 'I saw you bolt up that hill – like an Olympic athlete, so you were.'

He tried to speak, but his mouth was dry, and he was still gasping for breath.

'If it's your daddy you're after, he's in there. But if I were you I'd steer clear, young man. The last I saw of him, he'd a fair head of steam – like the bloody *Titanic*. Aye, and in bad colour, too, young fella.'

The boy stared at the only place in the street with no windows – well, none you could see through. The glass was dark and mottled, and only the ghosts of shapes moving inside were visible from the street. But these were no phantoms of the imagination, for they produced that familiar warm, malty smell and the gaggle of conversation and laughter he'd so often heard coming from this place.

He doubled forward, his hands on his knees. 'It's the soldiers, Mr O'Leary – they've got my brother.'

The ironmonger's expression changed. His ruby-red cheeks sank into his face and his eyes glowered straight into the boy's as he grabbed him by both shoulders. 'Where do they have him?'

'Down by the old gasworks – the place they blew up.'

'Come with me, boy.' O'Leary hauled him by the jumper off the warm, bright street and into the dark mewl of the bar.

At first the boy could see nothing, so dim was the place, but slowly his eyes adjusted.

'Where's Declan?' O'Leary shouted.

'He's through in the pool room,' said one rough-looking man with a green T-shirt, untidy curly hair and long sideburns. 'But if it's conversation you're after, you'd better take a trip elsewhere, Seamus.'

Ignoring this advice, O'Leary dragged the boy through to another room with brewery mirrors and a painting of dogs playing cards on the wall, where two young men he'd seen with his father before were playing pool.

'Young fella,' said one, ruffling his hair. 'If it's your da

239

you're after, that's him there. Sleeping off a fair cargo, so he is. What's your hurry, O'Leary?' he said to the ironmonger.

'The soldiers've got the eldest boy down at the gasworks.' He looked across at the man stretched at full length on a red upholstered bench at the side of the pool table. 'For fuck's sake, come on, Sean. They've got your boy – the bloody Paras. Will you wake the fuck up!' O'Leary punched the recumbent man on the shoulder, but to little effect.

'Away and tell, Mary,' Sean muttered through his beard, turning his back on his son and facing the wall.

'You drunken bum!' O'Leary shouted. 'Come on, lads. The boy's one of our own; you're not going to see him get a kicking, eh?' He looked down at the youngster he still held by the shoulder. 'Now you, just get off and get your mammy. Tell her to get down to the gasworks. Have you got that?'

The little boy watched O'Leary and a few others rush from the bar to the aid of his brother, leaving his father spreadeagled on the bench. One of his platform shoes had fallen to the floor, and there was a hole in his red sock. As the man who'd given him life began to snore, for the second time that day the boy felt a new emotion: the sharp passion of hate.

'I think that went well, Ella,' said Scott, removing a tight shoe while balanced on the corner of the large bed in their cabin. 'Maybe I could get used tae a life at sea after all.'

'I wouldn't bother your arse. Symington will have a fit when she finds oot what you said tae thon sheik.'

'We was just chewing the cud, dear.'

'You telt him he'd need tae pitch his tent somewhere else! Did you no' see his face?'

'Ach, I was just at the banter.'

'You were not. You think they all live in tents, don't you?'

'How come you're an Arabian expert a' of a sudden?'

'Because during a' the time you spent propping up some bar or other I was reading newspapers and books, or watching the TV – finding things oot.'

'Listen tae Paul Gascoigne.'

Ella looked puzzled for a moment, then: 'Bamber. You mean Bamber Gascoigne, Brian.'

'Well, whatever. I'm willing tae bet nane o' these folk at oor table were any threat tae the ship.'

'Good. Your investigation came at a price though, did it no'?

'How?'

'You've single-handedly changed government policy on wind turbines, for a start.'

'Och, a blind dog in the street could see that they tidal machines is far better – mair environmentally friendly, tae.'

'Who are you, Jacques Cousteau or David Attenborough?'

'You're getting right bitter in your auld age, Ella.'

'So what's next? Which British industry will you manage tae put to the wall the night?'

'Symington's coming aboard. She's got Jimmy working on some background o' the passengers – see if he can spot any likely rogues.'

'He's no' well enough tae be back at work.'

'He's just sitting doon at a computer, no' taking on the Taliban.'

'Thank heavens you never mentioned them o'er lunch. We really could have had an international incident.'

'Gie me some credit. I am a senior police officer, you know.' Scott smiled broadly.

'Until they hear you've caused a massive rift within OPEC.'

'Opeck? I'm buggered if I know where you get this stuff fae. Anyway, are we going oot on deck tae mingle?'

'I need a nap. I'm fair knackered after all that food.'

'At least you never got the soup.'

'How many times! Lobster bisque is *soup*. And you're likely the only person in the world that gets chips tae dip in it.'

'You get your nap. I'm off tae dae some undercover work. Which is why we're here – no' for the soup.'

'Right, Mr Bond, I'll see you later.' Ella Scott stretched out on the bed as her husband slipped into something more casual.

39

The paramedics rushed Liz into the Kinloch hospital on a stretcher. They were met at the door by a team of doctors and nurses.

'Is she still conscious?' asked a young doctor.

'Yes, but her pulse is weak and she's drifting in and out,' replied the paramedic.

Daley was still carrying James, whose wailing made the rest of the conversation between the medical professionals inaudible to him. 'Is she going to be all right?' he asked desperately.

'Pupils are responsive. We need bloods taken a.s.a.p. Then prepare her for gastric lavage and IV antidote,' said the doctor calmly, as two nurses transferred Liz to a gurney and wheeled her down the corridor.

'Here, I'll take the wee one,' said another nurse, holding out her arms to take James junior. Daley handed him over and left the crying child with her as he followed the team pushing his wife into the A&E ward.

When they reached the door the doctor turned to him. 'Listen, you stay here and let us do our job. The guys on the ambulance say it's a paracetamol overdose, right?'

'I think so, yes. This is all I could find.' Daley handed him the empty blister packs. 'Could be worse?' he said hopefully, but though he didn't speak the doctor's face said otherwise.

Daley watched as the ward doors swung shut. He stood for a moment, hands on his head, not knowing quite what to do. It was a strange feeling. Having been a police officer for so long, he'd dealt with many poor souls who had resorted to an overdose in desperation, or OD'd accidentally on illegal drugs, but now he was lost. Now it was personal, his training – his reason – had failed to kick in.

Down the corridor, he could hear his wailing son. He hurried in the direction of the sound and persuaded the nurse to hand him back.

'I'll go and get him some sweets and juice. Maybe that will help.' She patted the little boy on the head, but James, although back in his father's arms, continued to sob. For a moment, Daley felt a pain flash across his chest. He stumbled, and spotting a chair in the corridor staggered over to it, sitting down heavily.

As he'd been taught to do during his recent visit to hospital, the big detective took deep slow breaths in and out, and soon the room ceased to spin, the pain in his chest eased, and his breathing steadied.

He sat still for a while, trying to calm his son, who was now shouting loudly for his mother and trying desperately to wriggle free from his father's arms to find her.

The nurse arrived with some crisps, a bottle of orange juice and a packet of colourful sweets. 'I'm afraid this is all they had in the vending machine. I hope he's allowed to have sweets; they might calm him down a bit.' She looked at Daley. 'Are you feeling okay?'

'Yes, yes. Just the shock, that's all.'

'You're sweating, Mr Daley.'

'Oh, it's all been a bit of a rush, you know.'

She looked at him doubtfully. 'If you say so. Here, let me have your son for a moment, and go and get yourself a drink or something. Try and stay calm.'

'Calm? My wife's just taken an overdose. How the hell can I stay calm?'

'Listen, she's still conscious. That's really good.'

'Barely conscious, you mean.'

'But responding. That's the important thing. I think I'd like a doctor to check you over, Mr Daley. I'm aware of what happened to you recently. Do you have your medication with you?'

He shook his head.

'Right, just sit there.'

'I'm fine, honestly.'

'I want to be sure, and in any case you'll need to have your pills.'

Still with his son in her arms, the nurse hurried down the corridor.

Daley had been afraid before in his life, but not like this. He had no control: not of what was happening to Liz, or to himself. As he felt another twinge of pain in his chest, he sat forward on the chair, and again began to breathe slowly, in and out.

Symington was at her desk, nearly ready to leave for the *Great Britain*, when Sergeant Shaw poked his head round the door. 'Ma'am, you have a visitor. Captain Banks.'

'Oh? Please show him in, Sergeant.'

Banks appeared in the doorway a few moments later.

He was in full uniform, smart and tall. He took his cap off as he entered the office.

'Good afternoon, Chief Superintendent.'

'Lovely to see you. To what do I owe this honour?'

'I came ashore to make sure our guests were doing okay in Kinloch. I must say, some of them seem to be having a very good time indeed.' He raised his eyes to the heavens.

'This place can have that effect on people, Captain. As long as things are going along smoothly, I'm happy. I've a full contingent of officers on duty, just in case, and I know that a large security detail from the ship are ashore, too.'

'Well, everyone looks very happy and well behaved. I have some of my stewards on hand too, to make sure that anyone's who's had a glass too many gets back on board in one piece.'

'A very good idea, I'm sure. Please take a seat, Captain.'

'Thank you. I was wondering, can I have a word?'

'Yes, of course.'

'Just interested to know if that information I gave you bore any fruit?'

'I have DCI Daley on it now. In fact he's due to report back to me soon. Trust me, he has a good eye. You can't beat experience.'

'Good, good.' Banks looked around. 'I have to say that the drone incident did trouble me, on top of the disappearance of Majid. I'm a bit shocked that I seem to be the only one now who seems to be bothered.'

'We are taking it very seriously.'

'I'm sure, but I can't help but feel that I don't have the full picture.'

Symington lowered her gaze. 'Oh? Why is that?'

'Just a rumour – you have no idea how rumours spread on

ships, big and small. Especially when they carry the type of passenger we're currently entertaining.'

'So what's this rumour?'

'Probably just gossip, but I heard that a man was found dead on the hill – near where the drone was launched, I mean.'

Symington sighed. 'You know there are some things I can't speak about, Captain.'

'But you're happy enough that I gave you the security report on our passengers, aren't you?' He smiled and smoothed back his hair. 'I could get into all sorts of strife if that were to come out, Chief Superintendent. It was only given to me after many demands. I like to know all of those I have aboard my ship.'

Symington drummed her fingers on the table absently. 'Yes, the rumour is true. The man who flew the drone – we think – was found dead at the scene when my officers arrived.'

Banks's expression was grave. 'And don't tell me, the Security Service shut the information down, right?'

'I'll leave that to you to work out, Captain.' For a moment, Symington was sure she saw a sign of irritation pass across Banks's face, but she could imagine how frustrating it must be being in nominal command of a ship with such an exalted passenger list while being kept in the dark. To a certain extent, she felt the same.

'Thank you very much, Carrie. Though I must admit, that knowledge does make me more uneasy. It stands to reason that if this person was killed, then someone must be at large, yes?'

'I can't say any more, Magnus,' replied Symington, taking her opportunity to dispense with the formalities as he had done. 'And the problems with the ship: how soon until you can sail?'

'The team are now on board. It's electrics and computers, so always a bloody nightmare, but they're confident that we shouldn't be delayed by more than a day or so.'

'Does this type of thing happen all the time on great vessels like yours? The big cruise liners, I mean?'

Magnus Banks raised his chin. 'No. That's just it, Carrie. Of course we have the odd technical problem from time to time, and our engineers are very capable. But this is different.'

'Different how?'

'Different as in I think it was done deliberately.'

Symington took a few moments to absorb this information. 'And you've made your concerns known to Brachen, yes?'

'Yes, of course. But I believe he's under pressure to work quietly behind the scenes. No fuss – absolutely the last thing they want.'

'They?'

Banks smiled enigmatically.

'Sir Edward – the government?'

'That, Carrie, I will have to leave to your instinct and reason.'

'*Touché*, Captain.'

He nodded. 'In any case, let me give you a lift in my personal barge. You're heading across to the ship this evening, yes?'

'Oh, that's very kind. But I've a few things to do before I go.'

'No problem. I'll carry on the grand tour of Kinloch. Here's my card; just give me a call when you're ready to depart.'

Cabdi's mind was working overtime as the local man beside him rambled on, becoming more and more intoxicated.

He had no doubt that the man who'd stood only a few feet away from him not long after he'd arrived in the bar was the same person he'd talked to over the phone. The voice was distinctive and identical. They'd always communicated by fax prior to their mission going live, but he'd carried the pay-as-you-go mobile with him for communications in Kinloch.

But something didn't make sense. The owner of the voice he heard most certainly didn't match the person he'd imagined would be behind it.

As Cabdi's mind raced on, Scally leaned into him again. 'Aye, dae you want me tae tell you why the folk here aren't talking tae me?'

'Yes,' Cabdi replied, feigning an interest he didn't feel.

Scally rambled some more, but suddenly he caught Cabdi's attention again.

'So, as I said, I agreed tae go up there wae my grandson that night tae look for Cameron.'

'Did you find him?'

'Aye. Well, bits o' him, at least.' Scally looked around as though he expected everyone to be listening to him. 'I found a piece o' his skull – burnt to a cinder, it was.'

'Really?'

'Aye, and I saw the men who killed him. They men in the van I telt you aboot – a light blue yin, we think. It was hard tae see in the dark. I reckon I could identify them.'

'But you didn't see them properly?' Cabdi felt he already knew the answer.

'Aye, it was dark. But one of them was tall and thin – a bit like you,' slurred Scally.

'And how do you know they killed him?'

'Who else could have done it?'

Cabdi took in the man as he took another swig at his glass of whisky. He was small, mean-faced, with sharp features and pixie ears. There was something in this face that reminded Cabdi of other people who had lied to him over the years, a venal inscrutability that marked them out as the worst of men. But what was he trying to say? A plan formed in the Somali's mind.

'So they buggered off, and me an' the boy goes doon tae where they'd set the fire. There, in amongst all the ashes were the bones of my friend.' Scally sat back and folded his arms with a contented look of achievement, as though the story had been utterly compelling and accomplished.

'So you knew this man well – the dead man, I mean?'

Scally took a deep breath and again leaned into Cabdi, who did his best not to recoil from the strong smell of alcohol on his breath. 'You see, I've been having it away wae his wife for years.'

'Sorry?'

'Me and her – you know.' Scally made a lewd gesture.

'Oh, I see.' Cabdi forced a smile and began to think. 'Listen, it's very crowded here. I don't like bars so much. I'm interested in your culture; this is my first time in Scotland. I would love to see how you live – your home? I'm sorry if I am being impertinent.'

'No, it's my pleasure, son. I've had enough o' these bastards anyhow,' Scally said, raising his voice and attracting looks from customers and staff alike. 'Me and you will go up the road. Hey, listen. My grandsons are baith tall lads – no' quite as skinny as you – but they're always leaving clothes and stuff at my hoose when they come up for a bevvy. I can lend you some o' their kit, if you like. It looks as though you could do with a change.'

'That is very kind.' Cabdi smiled broadly and thanked him,

even though everything about Scally made him recoil. He knew how the man on the hill Faduma had come across had died.

'Good man! I'll get some food doon ye, tae. You look like you could do wae a good feed.' He paused, then said more quietly, 'You'll be right rich, I'm thinking – especially if you're on that boat, eh?'

Cabdi nodded, his face giving nothing away. 'I have enough, Mr Scally. Now, let me see your home. I should be honoured.' Though he had remained calm, Scally's story had made one thing very clear: he had to get out of sight. He could have approached the man – his contact, his master – done something in the bar, but there had been so many people about. Though they had never met, Cabdi was sure that this man must have recognised him. It made sense. They had lost contact since Cabdi had been forced to abandon the camp when Faduma had failed in his early attempt to attack the ship.

Cabdi still couldn't work out why that had happened. He needed time to think. At least his master now knew he was close. He had to find a way to get near him. The man's face appeared in his mind again. It had been a surprise, but then, all sorts of people shared his hatred of the Infidel.

'Right, follow me, son,' said Scally, taking to his feet rather unsteadily. 'We'll get a taxi, I think. I've done too much walking the last few days.'

40

'So this was the biggest octopush you ever saw,' said Hamish, his voice slurred by whisky. They were at a table in the County Hotel's function suite, where he and Henning had been joined by one of the German businessman's colleagues and an Argentinean businesswoman. 'Och, the damned thing was near as big as the boat – huge!'

'Aye, like your capacity for whisky, Hamish,' said Annie in passing, as she collected empty glasses from the table. 'He's full o' tall tales,' she continued by way of warning to the old fisherman's new companions.

'Oh, but we are enjoying these stories very much,' said Henning. 'They have entertainers on the *Great Britain*, but none as good as Hamesie, I am thinking.'

'Aye, whootever you say,' said Annie, moving to the next table with a growing trayful of empty glasses.

'If I were you I widna listen tae anything she's got to say. Och, she's jeest fair scunnered that she's not holding court behind the bar doonstairs and somebody else is getting a word in. She's a bitter woman, and no mistake.'

'Tell us more about this octopus, please,' said the Argentinean, pushing her dark fringe back from her forehead before taking a sip of red wine.

'Yes, please do,' agreed Henning.

'Whoot octopush?' said Hamish, a puzzled look.

'The one you were telling us about just a moment ago,' said Henning.

Hamish closed one eye and thought for a few moments. 'Aye, right, thon beastie, I've got you noo. As big as two boats.'

'You said one a minute ago.'

'Aye well, you see, Mariana, that's the thing aboot octopushes, they can fair stretch – bugger me, you never quite know jeest whoot size they are, to be absolutely honest wae yous.'

'Did you catch it in your nets?' asked Henning, wide-eyed.

'Well, we thought we'd caught it right enough, but in actual fact it had caught us, if you know whoot I mean.' Hamish paused for a gulp of whisky. 'You see, as I jeest telt you, as we hauled it aboard, oor skipper – Sandy Hoynes, a fine man, God rest him – was fair chuffed, because you don't catch an octopush every day o' the week, by any manner o' meansh. And doon in the likes o' Shpain, a beast like that could fetch a pretty penny.' Hamish nodded sagely.

'How much – relatively speaking, I mean?' asked Henning's colleague Gunther.

'I'm no' right sure aboot the creature's relatives, but this yin – och, enough tae buy a hoose back in they days. A modest one, mind, but a hoose nonetheless,' Hamish added quickly, anxious that no one should think he was embellishing the story.

'I have heard of these animals,' said Mariana. 'Though one has never been caught, they have found huge beaks that can only have come from such a giant creature. So, tell us, what happened next?'

'Beak, did you say? Well, this fella had a beak like one o' thon T-rex's, I'm telling you.'

'They didn't have beaks,' said Gunther. 'They were dinosaurs, with huge teeth.'

'You have the right of it there. But as any right-thinking man knows, a' they dinosaurs turned intae birds, so on the way they grew big beaks.' Hamish gestured with his outstretched arms to indicate the dimensions by way of illustration.

'You are a font of knowledge, Hamesie. Of this there is no doubt.'

'Och, when you've been at the mercy o' the great Atlantic for so many years, if you was tae haul up Queen Victoria in your nets you'd no' be o'er surprised.'

'Back to the octopus, Hamesie. So, you have hauled it on board in your nets. What then did your *Kapitän* do?'

Hamish's face took on a melancholy look. He removed his bunnet, revealing a bald head a good few shades lighter than his face. 'That's jeest the thing.' He sighed.

'So there was some kind of tragedy?'

'Och, tragedy's no' the right word for it, Gunther. It was much worse than that.'

'Oh my goodness!' Mariana put her hand to her mouth. 'You mean, this creature – did it grab him and take him back into the depths?'

'Well, something like that – worse in fact.'

'Come on, Hamesie, don't keep us in this suspense!' said Henning.

'Well, the bugger reached oot o' the net and wae one o' they big tentacles o' his took a grab at Sandy.'

'No!' said Gunther.

'Oh, aye. Jeest fair lashed oot at the poor man, so it did.'

There was silence at the table as Hamish's companions took in the full horror of Sandy Hoynes's predicament.

'And then?' asked Mariana reverently.

'This is the worst part, right enough. Wae one o' its sookers – you know the things they have on the tentacles?'

They all nodded in unison.

'Well, wae one o' they great sookers, it took a hold o' Sandy's bib and braces.'

'It did pull him overboard, then?'

'No' quite, Gunther. But it got a grip o' his wallet – aye, an' his baccy, tae – an' slipped back under the water wae them. A right devilish look on its face, tae.' Hamish nodded his head, a faraway look in his eyes.

His companions looked at each other.

'Mind you, he had his favourite pipe in his other pocket, so it wisna a total disaster.' He shook his head, the same sad look on his face.

Just as Henning was about to make further enquiries, Lamont and his accordion band struck up with another reel.

'One o' my favourites,' shouted Hamish. '"Pipe Major MacPherson Leaving Benbecula" – jeest a fine melody!'

'What is this *baccy*?' asked Gunther, but no one could hear him over the swirl of the accordion.

As Daley sat in the hospital corridor anxiously awaiting news of his wife, a doctor appeared through the ward door.

'Now, Mr Daley, can I have a word?'

'Yes, yes, of course. How is she – my wife?'

'She's responding well. In one way, she's out of danger.' He eyed Daley up and down. 'But I'd like to speak to you more generally.'

James junior had been mollified by the sweets and was chewing away quietly on his father's knee.

'Nurse Stanley, could you take charge of Mr Daley's son, please?'

'Certainly, Dr Lee.' The nurse took the child in her arms, cajoling him quietly as they walked down the corridor.

'My office is this way, Mr Daley.'

The detective followed the doctor down the corridor past a nurses' station and some side rooms until they reached the office.

'Can you please get to the point, doctor? I'm very anxious about my wife.'

'We were lucky. We got her in time, pumped out her stomach and stabilised her. She's out of danger, as I say, but I'm still unhappy.'

'Lasting damage, you mean?' Daley looked worried.

'Well, she certainly has been *damaged* recently. I examined her thoroughly, and she has extensive bruising and contusions to her face, and indeed some bruising to her upper body, too. In other words, she's been beaten – and recently, in my opinion. What do you have to say about that?'

'That it's none of your business,' replied Daley tersely.

'That's where you're wrong, Mr Daley. I've not been in Kinloch for long – only a matter of days – but I know an abused woman when I see one. And I've noted that all too often the husband or partner is the one responsible for such attacks.'

'What are you trying to say?'

'That in this instance, it is my duty to inform the police of my findings.'

'Have you spoken to Liz – my wife?'

'I know how scared women in these circumstances become.

256

But don't think your wife's silence on the matter will save you. I'm sick of these situations . . .'

Daley fished in his pocket and flashed his ID. 'My wife and I have been estranged for some time. She arrived in Kinloch with these injuries – I can tell you the name of the man who did it, if you want, but it's a matter best left between her and the police, don't you think?'

'How do I know this is true?'

Daley stood quietly, then suddenly lurched across the desk and grabbed the doctor by the lapels, his grip tightening. Panic spread across the clinician's reddening face as he tried desperately to speak, but only a throaty squeak could be heard.

The office door swung open.

'Jim, enough!' The voice was Symington's. 'DCI Daley, let him go!'

Daley released his grip, letting the doctor fall into his chair gasping for breath.

'What on earth is going on here?' asked Symington.

'Ask Hercule Poirot here,' said Daley, pushing past his boss.

'Where are you going?'

'To find a doctor who can tell me how my wife is, not accuse me of assaulting her.'

'I want that man arrested,' croaked Lee.

'I want to know what you said to my colleague,' replied Symington, as she watched Daley stalk down the corridor.

After a brief conversation with the doctor, Symington went in search of Daley. She found him sitting with his son, his face still red following his encounter.

'Here to arrest me, are you?'

'Don't be ridiculous, Jim. I heard what had happened to Liz – came as soon as I could.'

Daley nodded his head. 'Thanks.'

'I didn't expect to find my senior officer trying to strangle one of the medical staff,' she said quietly, with a forced smile so as not to upset James Daley junior.

'I'd like to tell you I regret it, but it wouldn't be true, ma'am.'

'Right or wrong, you could have been in serious trouble, Jim.'

'Huh! Do what you like. I'm finished anyway – I won't be able to keep my job with this condition. And as far as Dr Lee is concerned, I have a lawyer, too, and his behaviour was less than professional. So I think it will end up quits, don't you?'

'And Liz, what about her?'

'She's out of danger.'

'She must be really troubled, Jim.'

'We all are.'

'Listen, I've warned Lee about his conduct, and he's agreed not to make a complaint.'

'Oh, that's big of him. You can tell him if he comes near me again he won't be so lucky.'

She shook her head, and held out her arms to hold Daley's son. 'There are men serving with your condition – I've checked. It all depends on the severity, and how you respond to treatment.'

'Really – in my present capacity?'

'If you get the all-clear and your condition is managed, yes.' She was dandling James on her knee, making him giggle.

'If not?'

'Come on, can we at least try to look on the bright side?'

'Yeah, right. I've got a heart condition, my wife's had a good kicking from her boyfriend, and the arsehole down the corridor presumed I did it. Everything's moonlight and roses, ma'am.'

'Everything can be fixed here, Jim. Trust me, I'm on your side.'

He stared at her as she whispered in his son's ear and made him laugh out loud. 'I do believe you. But it's all bloody difficult right now.'

Just as she was about to reply the phone rang in her pocket. She answered, and her expression turned grave. 'I see, Sergeant Shaw. Thanks for letting me know.'

'Don't tell me, Brian's sunk the ship?'

'No, much worse. The press have got hold of the Pearson and drone stories.'

'But they can't publish on a D-Notice.'

'They can if they're in America.'

'Give me James. You have enough on your plate, Carrie.'

'And so do you. I'd better go. Give my best to Liz, yes? . . . Until she does something about that horror of a man, I worry that she might try this again.' She blinked back a tear.

'I appreciate your concern, ma'am, and I admire your empathy.'

'Ah, it's not something I've had to work hard on.'

'Ma'am?' Daley sensed he was missing out on something.

'I'll tell you one day. But I better go now. Sorry I can't stay and chat to Liz, but as I say, please give her my best.'

'Of course I will.' As he watched her walk down the corridor he called her back. 'Ma'am, nearly forgot, something I found that might be of interest.'

'From the list I gave you?' She was back at his side.

'Yes. You might want to take a look at Patrick O'Rourke. Owns car dealerships throughout the States. He's rich –very rich – but he has a past.'

'As in?'

'His father was associated with the Provisional IRA, and some of his close family were wiped out, one way or another.'

Symington bit her lip. 'Good work, Jim. Thank you.'

'I haven't had a chance to finish, sorry.'

'You have your family and your own health to think about. You look exhausted, Jim.'

'I'm fine.'

'Try not to worry. I'm always here for you, remember that.'

As she hurried off, his admiration for the person who had replaced the venal John Donald rose. Yet again, he found that this woman – his boss – possessed all the skills required to do her job well. Not only did she have to navigate the awkward politics that faced senior officers in Police Scotland, she was a more than capable investigator, and knew how to manage her staff.

It's a different world, he thought, as he pondered his early days in the police.

'Mr Daley, your wife would like to speak to you.'

Again relieved of James junior, Daley made his way into the ward.

41

Cabdi looked round Peter Scally's front room. The chair on which he sat was worn in places, and the table in front of him, where Scally had placed a mug of unhealthy-looking pale tea, was dotted with the rings from previous drinking vessels.

In the corner beside a large TV, a rubbish basket was filled with empty beer cans and discarded cigarette packets. There were a few photographs on the walls, one of which showed a young Peter Scally with his bride.

'Aye, she was a bonny woman, my Elaine, eh?' said Scally, who'd just walked into the room bearing an armful of clothes.

'Your wife?'

Scally coughed. 'She was.'

'Oh, I'm sorry.'

'In the past. Long time in the past now.'

'But you are having an affair, yes?'

Scally shrugged. 'Aye, true, but what's a man to dae?'

While Cabdi mulled over the distastefulness of the remark, Scally laid out the clothes on the couch.

'Here, some o' these should do you – until you get back on board and get your own gear, eh?'

Cabdi stood and looked through the rag-tag selection of clothing. Though mostly too large for his thin frame, the trousers and jackets would be a near enough fit in length, certainly better than the clothes in which he was currently standing.

'Thank you, Mr Scally. I may change, yes?'

'Aye, jeest across the lobby, bathroom's on the right. You can get changed in there.'

As Cabdi nodded, an old-fashioned phone sitting on a small table beside an easy chair rang loudly. Scally sidled over to it and answered. 'Hello, son. What can I do you for?'

Cabdi watched him intently, and noticed the change of expression that passed across his face. Suddenly, the rosy glow of alcohol had been replaced by a paler complexion. The older man stole worried glances at his guest.

'Right, aye, right, son. Thanks for letting me know. Funny you should say that, right enough.' There was a pause. 'Och, I'll tell you later.' Scally put the phone down and straightened his jumper before looking back at Cabdi. 'Jeest my grandson,' he said with a smile, but his expression was different. 'You get yourself changed and we'll take a wander down the pier and get you back aboard your cruise ship, eh?'

'I thought we were going to have something to eat?'

Scally shook his head. 'Jeest had a look in the pantry, son. Clean oot o' everything, so we are. You'll be better served having a good feed back on board. Here, I hope I'm getting an invite?' Though he smiled, gone was the drunken bonhomie, and the wary eyes were not in tune with the rest of the face.

'I'll get changed then.' Cabdi grabbed a handful of clothes and made for the bathroom. 'I won't be long.' He pulled the door behind him, but didn't shut it. Instead, he hung back and listened.

In the lounge, he heard Scally cough, then the sound of the telephone being lifted.

Before Scally had a chance to dial 999 Cabdi dashed back in the room and pushed him to the floor, grabbing the receiver from his hand and placing it back in the cradle.

'You bastard! Whoot dae you think you're at?' Though Scally was attempting to be aggressive, Cabdi could hear the tremble in his voice.

'What did your caller have to say, Mr Scally?' He loomed over the older man.

'Jeest my grandson. He was asking me about some family matter, if you must know.'

'I don't believe you.' Cabdi reached into the waistband of his trousers and produced the pistol he'd concealed there. 'Now, what did he really say?' He pointed the weapon straight at Scally's face.

'You've nae chance. You might as well gie yourself up!' wailed Scally, pushing himself back in the chair as though wishing he could disappear through it.

'Tell me what was said, or I will kill you!' Cabdi drew back the trigger.

'Come on – I've helped you!'

'Tell me, or I promise your life is at an end.' Cabdi leaned over Scally and thrust the barrel of the gun into his face.

'You're all over the internet – you and your mate. You killed him after you tried tae blow up the cruise ship. You're nae more a guest than I am – you murderer!' Despite his fear, a mixture of alcohol and desperation had produced a defiance in Scally he hoped would save him.

'Tell me more!' Cabdi pushed the gun further into Scally's face, making him cry out in pain.

'They're looking for you – they described you, aye, and the van. It's you, I know it!' Scally shrank away from the weapon.

'And where was this reported?'

'On that internet. I don't have it, but my grandson does and he's just telt me on the phone. You're a murdering bastard!'

Cabdi pulled back the weapon and in an instant pistol-whipped Scally across the face, smashing his nose in a splatter of blood and sending the older man spiralling into unconsciousness.

'And you know all about death, Mr Scally,' he said under his breath as he hurriedly removed his clothes and replaced them with the ones the stricken man had given him. His mind was whirling. How could this have happened? He thought about it as he pulled on a pair of trousers and drew the baggy waist tight with a black belt that was threaded through the loops of the garment.

There could only be one conclusion: he'd been betrayed, but why?

Symington ran into Kinloch Police Office and made directly for the CID suite. It had taken her only a few minutes to make her way back from the hospital.

'DS Potts, what do we have?'

'Here, ma'am. The initial report was put up on a minor political website, American, but it's been picked up and is now being reported widely on the likes of CNN and MSNBC. Look, I have it here.' He was scrolling down the screen as he spoke.

Symington read:

Reports are coming in that the UK cruise liner Great Britain *has been the victim of a failed attack by a Middle-Eastern terrorist group. The attack is thought to have happened recently when a drone was deliberately crashed into the ship, which is*

*carrying senior businessmen and women from across the globe.
This incident is alleged to have taken in place in Kinloch harbour,
a remote location on the West Coast of Scotland.*

*The UK Government refuses to confirm or deny the story,
though it is believed that both police and military personnel are
searching for a tall, thin Afro-Caribbean male who is responsible
for not only this attack, but also the murder of two people in the
area. More to follow. AP*

'Where did that description come from, Potts?' asked
Symington. 'Majid isn't tall.'

'I have no idea, ma'am. But DCI Daley did report that
there were two people on the hill.'

'Yes, he did. Thank you, Potts. Keep me up to speed on
this. I'll get hold of security on the *Great Britain*.'

She rushed into Daley's office and dialled the direct number
she'd been given for the ship's switchboard. 'Commander
Brachen, please. It's Chief Superintendent Symington from
Police Scotland.' She listened for a few moments. 'I don't care
how busy he is, I want him on the line, now!'

As Symington held on, she heard an indistinct oath,
followed by the familiar patronising tones of Brachen.

'Chief Superintendent, this isn't a good time.'

'Well, make it a good time. Where did this description
that I'm seeing online come from? It doesn't fit Majid, and
although Jim saw another figure on the hill he couldn't really
describe him in detail. The only person who has ever mentioned someone tall and thin is a man we've been questioning.
And what happened to the D-Notice? You assured us the
drone man took his own life, but now he appears to have had
an accomplice, just as DCI Daley said.'

'The information appeared online in the States about an hour ago. Not much we can do about what gets said across there. We have no idea who the source is . . .'

The hesitation in his voice made Symington suspicious. 'What else do you know that you're not telling me?'

'All I know is classified. I'm not at liberty to tell you.'

'Classified? That's a joke. I'll just wait and read it online, shall I?'

Brachen sighed. 'Reports from America have alerted us to the fact that the man we're looking for has been spotted in Kinloch. They haven't made it public yet, but they will do.'

'We're waiting for some political website in Washington to tell us what's happening under our own noses?'

'The picture has changed. It was an anonymous message sent by fax – untraceable.'

'So I have a dangerous terrorist at liberty on the streets of Kinloch, with some of the richest men and women on the planet in the mix, and you weren't going to tell me?'

'We're recalling passengers now.'

'That'll be fun. Half of them are drunk!'

'And we have security and the Royal Marines searching for this man. *If* this is true.'

'People aren't stupid, Brachen. Everyone knew this was no *exercise* to keep the troops fit – that was so obvious. As the senior officer in Kinloch, I should have been given this information immediately. I'm contacting my superiors, but I'm sure that within the next few minutes the whole thing will be declared a civilian matter and I'll take command of what's happening in the town.' She paused for breath. 'I must say, you have dealt with this in a thoroughly unprofessional manner from the beginning. This was no paparazzi stunt gone wrong, but because of the delicate nature of things and the assurances that your people gave, I went along with it. Now I have a terrorist who has probably tried to blow up a ship and has already killed two men loose on the streets of Kinloch. And just where did this detailed description of the man we're looking for come from? DCI Daley only caught a glimpse of him through binoculars!'

'I don't know. It was first reported online by Slugnet.'

'The political website?'

'Yes.'

'Great!'

'So you believe everything that you read on the internet?' He laughed.

'What does that mean?'

'It means, just how much did your DCI Daley see? My understanding is that he's not fit for duty. Is he trying to find a way to supplement his pension? It's amazing what some people will do for money, given the right circumstances.'

'I'm not even going to dignify that pathetic nonsense with a response. First, one of the crew of your ship disappears, now this. There's something not right aboard the *Great Britain*, Commander Brachen, and you know it. I want to speak to my superiors. I'll get back to you shortly!'

Symington was out of breath when she finished the call. As she dialled the ACC in charge of the overall operation regarding the *Great Britain*, she thought about the 'thin, tall man'. Regardless of the Security Service and the Royal Marines, she was now responsible for a potentially major problem.

42

The man in the maintenance uniform was leaning against a rail on the upper deck of the *Great Britain*, casually smoking a cigarette. It was now a sunny day, and he could see the roofs and spires of Kinloch huddled around the head of the loch under a blue sky dotted with cotton wool clouds.

A Royal Marine walked past him and stopped. 'Here, mate, any chance of tapping a fag off you?'

'Sure.' The maintenance man thrust his hand in the pocket of his boiler suit and removed a cigarette packet. 'Here, there's two or three in that one. I've got a fresh packet.'

'You sure? Thanks, mate.' The Marine looked about him before taking one of the cigarettes and lighting it in his cupped hands. 'Nice place, isn't it?'

'It's okay. I've been to better. You can't beat the Caribbean as far as I'm concerned.'

'You blokes are a bit like us: get to see the world, right?'

'Yeah, sure do.'

The Marine took a few deep draws on his cigarette and sent it spinning into the blue waters of the loch. 'Cheers, just what I needed. Thanks again.'

As he walked off, the maintenance man's lip curled.

'Arsehole,' he muttered under his breath. He was about to go back to work when the mobile in his pocket vibrated.

Now, the text read.

Like the Marine before him, he sent the butt of his cigarette spiralling into the waves, then made his way back into the bowels of the *Great Britain*.

'So there *was* another man. Oor Jimmy was right,' said Scott, his mobile phone to his ear. 'What now? Do you want me to come ashore?'

'No,' said Symington. 'I want you to check out a Patrick O'Rourke. He's one of the VIPs on board.'

'Here, I thought it was Arab terrorists we was after?'

'To be honest, Brian, I don't know who we're after. All I know is that we've been lied to from the start by the Security Service. O'Rourke's name was flagged up by DCI Daley. He was going through a passenger list I managed to obtain.'

'Aye, well, tell him tae slow doon. I've only the one pair of hands.'

On the other end of the line Symington hesitated.

'What's up, ma'am?'

'Jim's had to take a break, Brian.'

'Aw, no, no' his heart again?' There was genuine concern in Scott's voice.

'No, not that. It's Liz.'

'What about her?'

Symington sighed. 'I'm only telling you because I know he'd tell you himself. She took some pills.'

'What, Liz – an overdose? I cannae believe it!'

'She's going to be okay, but Jim's with her in the hospital.'

'I should come back, ma'am – phone him, at least.'

'Brian, you have a job to do. And you can't break cover. This line to me is encrypted, but any other calls from the *Great Britain* might be monitored. I need you on there. I can handle what's happening in the town. We have more resources on the way.'

'Tell me one thing, ma'am.'

'What?'

'Is Ella safe? Because, see, if she isn't, I want her off this tub PDQ. I might have orders, but she doesn't – she's no' in the police. Tell me the truth now.'

'To tell you the truth, Brian, I don't know who's safe, or where.'

'You're no' exactly filling me full o' confidence. I mean, what do you think's going tae happen? Catch this guy and you can get it oot o' him.'

'Somehow, I don't think it's going to be that easy, Brian.'

Cabdi tied Scally's hands behind his back with an old rag he'd found and ripped up. His legs were already trussed with some rope Cabdi had found in a cupboard under the kitchen sink. As the older man began to stir, he applied another piece of rag as a gag, ensuring that if he regained consciousness he couldn't cry out.

'He watches us all, Mr Scally. He watches us all.' Cabdi stood over Scally for a few moments. He knew what he was going to do. He'd found a set of car keys on a small hook in the hall; no doubt they would match the old van that was parked in the driveway outside.

The tall Somali stooped through the front door, the red baseball cap pulled low over his face. He ducked into the van, and couldn't help but be relieved when it started first time and he noticed the tank was just under half full.

Indeed, there was a strong smell of fuel in the vehicle. When Cabdi turned to look, he saw two red petrol cans sitting on a filthy blanket in the back.

He shook his head, turned the key in the ignition and made his way slowly, carefully out of Peter Scally's driveway.

The man in the boiler suit nodded to one of his colleagues when he arrived back in the engine room of the great ship. He opened the bag he'd found aboard as arranged and looked inside. It held everything he needed.

He pulled the zip tight on the canvas bag and walked towards his foreman. 'Right, Joe, I'll take a wee look up at the board. Are you ready to switch on and test anything yet?'

'Nearly. Give the panels a good look over, because whoever did this knew what they were doing. There's no one on board could've fixed this – they don't have the right diagnostic tools. Off you go and get sorted. I want out of here as quick as I can, know what I mean?'

'Aye, get your point. Leave these rich bastards to it.'

'Bang on!'

The man strolled along a gangway to the room through which the vessel's electronics were funnelled, turning the lock when he'd closed the heavy steel door behind him. He unzipped the bag, removed its contents, and went to work, quickly and quietly.

'She's still a selfish cow,' said Ella.

'Gie the lassie a break. She near died fae what I hear,' replied her husband.

'Aye, exactly. Him just oot o' the hospital and still ill, and all she can think aboot is herself. I swear sometimes I wish Jimmy had never set eyes on her. Bugger knows how the wee fella will turn out with Liz bringing him up. He'll have a few new daddies before his time's oot, that's for sure.'

'Listen, Ella.' Scott's expression was serious. 'I want you tae stay in the cabin tonight, got it?'

'And miss the reception for the locals? Not likely, Brian.'

'Would you just take my advice for once in your life!'

'You know something I don't, Brian Scott.'

'Aye, that's why I'm telling you tae stay put. On here everything might look normal, but it's no'. That's what they want you tae think – business as usual.'

'What is it?'

'I'm no' saying. And nothing you do will change that, Ella.'

'Ach, I know anyway.'

'Eh? How?'

'I'm no' daft. I listen tae the gossip on the boat. I was out on deck earlier; the place is full o' it.'

'Well, you listen tae me – there might be nothing in it. This O'Rourke guy could be as white as the driven snow.'

She grinned. 'How you ever got tae stay in the polis, I'll never know.'

'Eh?'

'You've never been able to keep a secret – not ever.'

'Bastard! So you didnae know anything?' Scott shook his head ruefully.

'Just you be careful, that's all I'm saying. Nothing's worth your life, and you've come too close too often.'

43

Cabdi knew the layout of Kinloch reasonably well. He'd studied maps of the town just in case their plan went wrong – and it had done so, spectacularly.

He knew he had to get to somewhere he could think, somewhere safe and out of sight. The realisation that he'd been betrayed was slowly dawning, and it was a bitter blow. But why send them on a mission that was bound to fail? It was clear that the drone they'd been told contained explosives had held nothing of the kind. If it had, Faduma would have set it off.

It made sense too that the only man who knew of his existence had leaked his presence in the town. Scally had said it. He knew how the British government – all Western governments – worked; it would all be covered up, unless they thought a significant threat presented itself. The *Great Britain* would surely have sailed away from Kinloch otherwise. But nothing made sense.

Suddenly he felt guilty; but guilt was part of his life, and had been for a long time. He cursed Faduma, cursed his mission, everything. But now the mists were beginning to clear he had to decide what to do. He had a duty to do something to make a difference. He couldn't shift one face from his mind. He knew it was the key to everything.

Cabdi took quiet side streets, avoiding the centre, and eventually found a road that rose out of the town, bordered by grand-looking houses. When he'd reached the top, and was clear of Kinloch's boundary, he could see the island at the head of the loch, and beside it the cruise ship that had occupied his thoughts for so long.

He pulled the van over onto the verge, zipped up the fleece that Scally had given him until it almost covered his face, and made off across a field.

The ground fell away towards a rocky shore. He now had a clear sight of the *Great Britain*. He fished in his pocket and found the tiny transistor radio he'd picked up in Scally's kitchen. He would use the radio to glean what he could about what was going on.

The pistol was still nestled in the small of his back, and as long as he had that, he could do something to make a difference.

When he reached the shoreline, he almost slipped on the rocks, slick with seaweed and wet from the sea. But the tide was out, and he managed to scrabble round towards a structure he'd spotted. It was a squat brick construction, dank inside, with a slit through which he could view the world outside. Cabdi assumed that it had something to do with the war – certainly it was the perfect hiding place. Though the far side of the building was crumbling, the part in which he now nestled would provide shelter from prying eyes, as well as the rain and wind when it came.

Here, Cabdi could plot in relative safety. He was wearing clean clothes and was warm. He'd grabbed some food at Scally's house; predictably the man had lied about there being none. Now he was ready to think, ready to plot, ready to kill.

As he squatted in the corner of his impromptu shelter, only death and destruction were on his mind.

Scott read the email Symington had sent him containing a plan of the ship and the cabin in which O'Rourke was berthed. He decided to take a look around, and when he reached the right floor took a slow walk along its length, pretending to be engrossed by something on his phone.

Symington's email had detailed Daley's findings, and from Scott's perspective the man did have a questionable past.

He stopped at the door marked Cabin 312, knocked on it and called out, 'Mr Sangster, are you in?' He listened quietly for a response, but there was no reply. 'Mr Sangster, it's me?' Still nothing.

Just in case, Scott turned the handle, and was surprised to find the door unlocked. He opened it a crack and leaned his head around it. 'Hello, Mr Sangster. It's me, William. Just wondered if you fancied that chat we talked about last night?' There was no sign of movement in the room, so Scott slipped in and let the door close quietly behind him.

The cabin was untidy, a white bath towel spread along one side of the unmade bed. He walked through into a small lounge, where a couch and an easy chair sat facing an enormous screen. At the other end of the room was a writing desk, facing the exit to a balcony. Through the next door was a small but well-appointed dining room. He looked about, but saw nothing of interest.

On his way back through the suite he pulled open drawers at random, but found nothing save for some information on the car dealerships that O'Rourke ran, some business cards and a top-of-the-range MacBook Pro.

The door to the bathroom was just off the bedroom, and Scott decided to have a quick look inside before he left.

In one corner was a huge bath, in the other a shower, handbasin and WC, and some make-up and toiletries. Something was lying in front of the lavatory, so he bent down to pick it up.

He unfurled an Ordnance Survey map of Northern Ireland showing the coast of County Antrim. Just outside Ballycastle, an area of beach was circled in red pen. Scott studied it, laid it flat on the floor, and with his mobile took a picture of it.

Just as he was folding it away, he heard movement: the handle of a door being turned.

Suddenly, Brian Scott was rooted to the spot.

'We will see you tonight on the ship, yes?' Henning called as they parted ways at the door of the County Hotel.

'Aye, you surely will,' replied the old man, rather unsteady on his feet, but nonetheless disappointed that the guests had been asked to report back to the *Great Britain* early, therefore ending the party he was enjoying. There was nothing better than the chance to tell tall tales on the back of free whisky, as far as Hamish was concerned.

But he'd heard some gossip, and was determined to find out if it was reliable or not before he went home to get ready for the reception to which he'd just been invited.

He wandered up the hill, past Kinloch Police Office and the primary school, and was soon at the entrance to Kinloch Hospital.

'Hamish, what can I do for you? You're not feeling unwell, are you?' asked the receptionist as she noticed the old man stagger.

'Och no, I'm in fine fettle – maybe one dram too many at the County, that's all.'

She smiled. 'Well, I don't think there's much we can do for that.'

'Am I the one that's glad for that. There's no cure for a dram of which I'd care to partake. Anyhow, I've had my three score years and ten, so I'm on borrowed time anyway.'

'You're a fit man for your age – mainly,' she replied, smelling the strong odour of whisky on Hamish's breath. 'So if you're okay, why are you here? This isn't the County Hotel, or have you got lost?'

'No, I'm here to enquire aboot a friend.'

'Who?'

'Mrs Daley. I hear she's no' so well.'

The receptionist looked at her desk. 'Listen, Hamish, there's no visitors allowed to see her at the moment. I'm sure you understand.'

'Och aye, of course. I was just thinking Mr Daley might be aboot?'

'Well, I'm sure he has enough on his plate . . .' She didn't get to finish what she was going to say, as a young voice called out and a toddler charged straight for the old fisherman.

'Hameby!' James Daley junior grabbed Hamish by the legs and might have sent him sprawling had it not been for the prompt actions of his father, who grabbed Hamish by the shoulders, keeping him upright.

'Young James, but you're a wild a boy right enough. My, it's good to see you, son – you too, Mr Daley. I was right worried when I heard you weren't so well.'

'I'm fine, Hamish, thank you.'

'Aye, you look it.' Hamish eyed him up and down. 'A bit

peaky maybe, eh?'

'It's been a hard couple o' days.'

'Aye, I dare say it has. And how is your good lady? I heard she wisna feeling too chipper either.'

'I know this town, Hamish, and I'm sure you know what's wrong.'

'But well intended, I assure you, aye, well intended.'

Daley slapped his friend on the shoulder. 'I know fine. You've been a good friend to me – to all of us – since we arrived. Liz will be okay, I promise.'

'Och, I'm absolutely certain o' it, Mr Daley.' The old man shuffled from foot to foot. 'I've something else to discuss, if that's okay with you.'

'I'm off work, you know, so no fishing for gossip, mind.'

'As if I would dae such a thing. I'll leave that tae Annie behind the bar at the County, if you don't mind.'

'Come on, I was about to take the wee man out for a walk. He's been cooped up in here for hours. There's a bench outside where we can take a seat while he gets a run about and some fresh air.'

'Aye, that would be just fine, fine indeed.'

The three of them made their way out of the hospital and round a corner into a rock garden, a place where patients on the mend could enjoy some sunshine, and in some cases a quiet cigarette.

'You run about here, James. Now, don't touch anything, or run out of sight, got it?' Daley emphasised the point by pointing his finger to his eyes. 'I'm watching you, remember.'

'I won't, Daddy.' The little boy ran off with his hands spread out like the wings of a plane, delighted to be out of the confines of the hospital.

Daley and Hamish took a seat on a wooden bench, and it was the older man who spoke first.

'I'm right sorry tae hear about Liz. But she's got a good heart, and I know she'll be fine.'

'Is this your second sight again, Hamish?'

'You might scoff, but you know well I've got the gift.'

'If you say so,' Daley said with a smile.

'In fact, that why I'm here, Jim.' He fixed the policeman with a serious expression.

'What?'

'I've been having dreams – bad yins at that.'

'What kind of dreams?'

'About you, if you must know.'

'Don't tell me: I'm working on a bin lorry and my police career is over.'

Hamish looked into the middle distance. 'Every one's the same. I see the sea – a boat, tae.'

'Not unusual. You're around them all the time, Hamish.'

'Nah, this isn't a boat fae aroon here. No' a fishing boat. Nor is it oor coast, neither.'

'Anyway, what's so bad about dreaming about that?'

'I saw you plain as day.'

'On this boat?'

'Aye, on the boat. The sky black as thunder – near as dark as your face. In the dream, I mean.'

'And?'

'Well, that's it.'

'I don't really know what's worrying you about it. There's a big ship in the loch, and you know I've not been well. It's just a mixture of these things playing on your mind.'

'It's never what you see, Mr Daley, it's what you feel.'

'And what do you feel?'

'Despair. Aye, I canna put it mair exactly than that: pure despair. Oh aye, an' a great blackness. As dark as auld Horny's waistcoat, it is.' He reached out and caught Daley by the arm. 'Take my advice, Jim. Don't go near the water – no strange tides. Do you get me?'

'I'll try.' Daley tried to suppress a smile.

'Here, I'm serious!' Hamish's grip tightened. 'Oh aye, and there's one mair thing, tae.'

'I'll be running out of places I can go at this rate.'

'Och, this is likely caused by my hatred o' false teeth.'

'What?'

'A big tooth – roots an' all. That's another thing I keep seeing. Jeest like the ones that auld butcher MacCann took out o' me when I was aboot twelve. They called him a dentist, but he wiz mair like a torturer, and that's a fact. I'm sure he took pleasure oot o' inflicting pain on weans.'

Jim Daley took a moment to watch his son caper about. The sun was suddenly hidden behind a cloud, and he shivered.

44

Brian Scott was trying to keep his breathing steady and quiet. He was pressed against the wall near the bathroom door, clearly hearing someone rummaging about in the cabin beyond.

Trying to think what to do, he considered the idea of stepping out from his hiding place, flashing his warrant card and asserting that he was merely taking part in a security check. But, he thought, if O'Rourke was the man they were looking for it would be unlikely to shift him from his course of action, and he might well end up on the wrong side of someone with malign intent. In any case, one way or the other, his cover would be blown.

The sound of movement from outside the bathroom continued. Drawers were opened then closed. Something was dragged across the floor. Scott's mind began to work overtime. Then the distinctive sound of metal on metal, an implement being fitted together.

Gun! thought Scott. He was on a boat – a big one, but a boat nonetheless. He remembered Hamish's tales about people recognising the place where they would die – knowing it all their lives. And Brian Scott had always been scared of boats.

I could make a break for it, he thought. Head down, push my way past. Och, I'd be halfway down the corridor before this O'Rourke knew what was happening. The idea cheered him. He took deeper breaths, getting ready to make a dash for it. He toyed with the idea of pulling his jacket over his head in order to hide his identity, but figured that was going too far. His vision might be obscured and he could fall over. Symington wouldn't be happy, but he'd acted on his own initiative, and what he'd discovered from the map could make a difference if the man who occupied this room was who Daley reckoned him to be.

Then the footsteps outside the bathroom became louder, and, as Scott forced himself against the wall, the handle of the bathroom door began to turn.

Cabdi fiddled with the dial of the small transistor radio. It cracked and whined, but then a station came through loud and clear.

'And the price o' lamb this year is a disgrace. It'll be a cold Christmas for us up at Lossiebeg, Jock.'

'Ach, you've been saying that since 1981, Jock. And look at the belly on you. It'll be the same Christmas at Lossiebeg it a'ways is – you full o' turkey lying sleeping after the best part o' a bottle o' Glen Scotia doon you.'

'Noo the listeners are no' wantin' tae hear that, Jock. My festive domestic arrangements are no' for general consumption.'

'Neither is your whisky! I came up last New Year and got a pixie's thimbleful, while you were sitting wae a great bumper – damn near quarter o' a bottle.'

'I knew you'd the beasts tae set right first thing in the morning. I couldna bear the thought o' they fine coos desperate *tae get milked while you was lying in a drunken stupor after o'er enjoying my seasonal hospitality.'*

Cabdi was utterly baffled by this, but a jaunty jingle soon helped him make sense of what he was hearing.

'You're listening to Kinloch FM's Two Jocks Show.'

Local radio, thought Cabdi. If he was to find out anything about the movements of the *Great Britain*, this would be the place.

'Dae you mind thon party we went to in 1979 – I'm sure it was after the Blaan New Year bowling match in the village hall.'

'Och, I knew fine you'd bring that up.'

'No' as much as whoot you brought up that night, though, eh?'

'I'm no' going tae discuss the distant past wae oor listeners...'

'Right o'er the Reverend's wife, tae. Even I felt sorry for you thon night. I'm no' right sure she did, mind you.'

'Here, I paid for her dry cleaning bill. That green dress o' hers came up good as new.'

'Aye, she wore it for the next ten years, right enough.'

'I've jeest got a message in fae Willie doon at the pier. How'ye, Willie?'

'Whoot's he saying?'

'Noo, apparently there's tae be boats laid on for those lucky enough tae be invited tae the reception aboard the Great Britain *tonight. They're doing it in shuttle runs fae half five, so if you're one o' the lucky few, be there in plenty time.'*

'You'll be going, you being a councillor and a'?'

'No, they only invited Charlie Murray.'

'Likely feart you'd get full o' the amber nectar and deposit the results a' o'er the princess.'

'She's a duchess, Jock – there's a fair difference.'

'Aye, you have the right o' it there. If you was tae barf o'er a princess it would likely be the Tower. For a duchess, och, it would be nothing mair than a slap on the wrist.'

'Anyway, folks. For all o' yous going tae the big night, make sure you're doon the pier in plenty time.'

'Aye, no' a trace o' bitterness in that voice. And I'm reliably informed yous can all ignore that nonsense that was on the internet fae America this afternoon.'

'Fake news, Jock.'

'Aye, like Charlie Murray's election promises, it'll jeest no' happen.

'Here, that's right controversial.'

'Jeest a statement o' fact, Jock. Noo, Kinloch Juniors are playing at hame this Saturday. Whoot dae you think the score will be?'

'If it's thon team fae Paisley, they'll be lucky tae come oot the game alive, never mind score.'

Cabdi clicked the radio off. He'd heard all he needed to. Somehow, he had to get to the pier without attracting attention. And that wasn't going to be easy.

Scott had managed to reach across to the sink and grab a soap dish. He raised it above his head as the bathroom door swung slowly open.

It took the small Asian cleaner a few moments to register the man brandishing the white soap dish above his head behind the door. But when she did, her scream sent the hairs on the back of Scott's neck upright.

'Noo, Miss, there's nothing tae worry aboot.' He fished his warrant card from his pocket. 'See, I'm a policeman – p-o-l-i-c-e,' he said slowly, hoping the woman would understand.

'So what the hell are you doing with the soap dish?'

Scott was momentarily taken aback by her broad Liverpudlian accent. 'Aye, right. Och, I was just looking underneath it – for contraband, like.'

'What kind of contraband could you fit under there?'

'You'd be surprised what criminals can get up tae.'

'But these people are all rich. Why would they need to steal anything?

'You cannae be too careful.'

'Does Captain Banks know about this?'

'Eh, no – strictly undercover, lassie.'

'I bet.'

'Now, if you'll excuse me, I'll need tae be getting on. A lot tae check, I'm sure you understand.'

'Yeah, especially if you're going to look under every soap dish on this ship.'

Scott smiled nervously and made for the door as quickly as he could, being careful to step over the vacuum cleaner as he left the cabin.

He walked out into the passageway and turned left, heading for his own cabin. At the other end, Patrick O'Rourke watched him go.

45

Symington was studying the list that she'd given Daley while a team of detectives checked the town's CCTV records of the day, looking for the man who had been described online – the tall, thin Afro-Caribbean.

O'Rourke's father had been shot by the RUC in the early 1970s, his uncle, too. His elder brother had been arrested, found guilty and consigned to the Maze prison, where at the tender age of sixteen he had died on hunger strike. There could be no doubt that it was these events that had led a young O'Rourke and his mother to seek sanctuary in America. But as Symington knew, deep emotional wounds, however noble or ignoble the cause, were likely to stay with an individual for life.

She recalled the seminar she'd attended when still a serving officer in the Met. The majority of killers had been shaped by events in their past, and resentment, hatred, the need for revenge often lay dormant for decades. Could O'Rourke be such an individual?

From Daley's glass box she noted a flurry of activity in the CID office beyond. DS Potts hurried in carrying a sheaf of papers.

'Ma'am, I think we have him. I've printed out all the images we could find.'

Symington looked at the photographs in order of their timeline. A tall, thin black man, wearing a faded red baseball cap, had walked casually down Main Street and into a bakery, emerged minutes later, and casually consumed a filled roll and a hot beverage.

'Get me the footage please, Potts.'

As he rushed off, she instinctively knew this was the man they were looking for. But something in his demeanour spoke of a person at ease, not afraid to hang about the centre of town, clearly not concerned that he was of interest to the authorities.

Potts appeared back in the office. 'If you don't mind, ma'am.' She nodded her consent as the young detective deftly worked at the keyboard of the desktop computer. 'Here, ma'am. This is what we have from when the subject was first sighted. I think you'll find it very interesting.'

Symington watched as the man walked north on Main Street, and then turned into Monument Lane. His gait was casual and unhurried. The screen flicked to another camera, one of those covering Kinloch's small square. More distantly, but still clearly, the figure was visible entering the Douglas Arms.

'Now we have a time lapse, ma'am,' said Potts. He was fast-forwarding through the footage, making the figures coming in and out of the bar, or merely passing by, look comical, like those in a silent film from the distant past. When the clock on the screen had rushed through almost an hour, he slowed the footage back down.

'Is this it?'

'Yes, ma'am. Two seconds, please.'

The lounge door of the Douglas Arms swung open. First through it was the tall figure of the man they'd seen earlier, followed by a smaller, weasel-faced individual.

'Is that who I think it is, DS Potts?'

'Indeed it is, ma'am. Peter Scally.'

The police officers looked on as the two men made their way companionably back along Monument Lane. Again the scene changed, and now back on Main Street both Scally and his companion with the red baseball cap climbed into a taxi, the first one on the rank.

'Okay, Potts. Get a team together. I want that taxi and its driver identified. As soon as we find out where they were taken, that's where we'll go.'

As Potts hurried out of the office, the phone rang. When Symington answered, she heard the now familiar tones of Commander Brachen.

'We've had more intelligence, Superintendent.'

'Where from this time? The Disney channel?'

'The source is the same as before.'

'And what have they told you?'

'Majid has been spotted. He's in a small boat, last seen in Firdale harbour.'

'How on earth has this information managed to cross the Atlantic and find its way back to you?'

'I think the more pertinent question is why haven't your officers been able to trace him before now? He has clearly been in the area since he disappeared from this vessel. I'm just glad he's been found. You should be, too. He's our second man, no doubt.'

'But that man's tall and thin.'

'So says some dodgy website in America. No, I'm convinced this is our man. The frigate is heading in that direction now. As this Majid is seaborne, we can easily intercept him. Panic over, I'd say. Everything goes ahead as normal.'

Symington was about to tell Brachen about the sighting of the other suspect, but something made her stop. Suddenly everything was beginning to fall into place too easily. And in her experience, if things seemed too good to be true, they probably were.

Liz's face was pale; even the bruises and abrasions looked less vivid. She was attached to a monitor with an IV in her left arm. Daley watched her for a while as James junior played quietly on the floor with a toy truck a nurse had given him. As he looked her eyes fluttered open and she stared straight at him – a wild look, almost as though she was seeing her husband for the first time.

'Liz, how do you feel?' He walked over to her bedside and stroked the hair back from her eyes.

'I'm sorry, Jim.'

'We nearly lost you, you know.'

'It would have been better if you had – both of you.' She looked sadly at her young son.

'How can you say that? I know we've had our differences, but never, not for one second, did I wish you harm. I hope you believe me.'

'But look what I've done to you. I treated you like shit for years, Jim, and you never gave up on me. Then I had the cheek to give you a hard time when you found the happiness you deserved.' She turned her head on the pillow, her auburn hair fanning out across it. 'I'm poison, regular poison – everything I touch withers and dies.'

'You're the mother of my child – our child.'

'And what kind of mother am I? The kind that runs about with one man after another, that's what. Well, I've paid the price for that, haven't I? And deserved it, too.'

'None of this is your fault. Married couples break up every day – find new partners. What happened to you was not your fault, or something you deserved. You were assaulted by a brutal criminal, simple as that.' He closed his eyes to hide the growing anger he could feel building. Liz had known him for a very long time, and in her present state would quite possibly misinterpret his revulsion for the man who'd assaulted his wife as anger directed at her.

She caught his arm and pulled him towards her, until their faces were almost touching. 'I can't do what you want me to do, I just can't.'

'I know it will be hard. But the law is on your side. Trust me, the only way you'll feel any closure over this is if you are part of the process that makes sure he can never do to some other poor woman what he's done to you.'

'I haven't been truthful with you, Jim.' She stared at him.

'What the hell do you mean?'

She held one finger to her lips and looked pointedly at their son.

'Tell me what you mean, Liz,' said Daley more quietly.

'There's more. I couldn't face it – court, I mean.'

'Couldn't face what? You should shout it from the bloody rooftops, the beating this man – this animal – gave you.' Daley's teeth were clenched in anger.

She closed her eyes, took a deep breath, and propped herself up in the bed to whisper into Daley's ear. 'He raped me, Jim. When I wouldn't do what he wanted – after he'd beaten me – he raped me.' She fell back on the pillow, her chest rising and falling as though she was struggling for air.

Daley let go of her arm and took a step back, all colour draining from his face.

'You see? Look at your reaction. How could I face that from everyone I know: my friends – my *parents*, for fuck's sake. The pity, the disgust – I can see it written across your face, Jim. Don't deny it, it's so obvious.' She began to sob. 'And I didn't come to Kinloch just so that the scars would heal and no one would see that I'd been battered. I came because I knew you'd keep me safe. I'm frightened, Jim – I'm terrified of him, can't you see?'

Daley staggered back, finding the edge of a chair and sitting down heavily. 'I'm so sorry – I had no idea,' he said, looking into space.

'How could you have? Anyway, the whole event was brutal; the end was just – just the end. But cuts and bruises heal, even the shock of it all. You can pick yourself up and go on. Well, I think I can, anyway.'

'You don't need to say anything else, Liz. I understand.' Daley could feel his heart pounding in his chest. But this time it wasn't due to his condition, but to the flame of his temper. He had the old sensation of rising out of the chair even though he hadn't moved a muscle.

'So, please understand why I can't do what you and Carrie want me to do.'

Daley looked at her. 'No, I understand. Anyway, you have a lot of recovering to do. The doctors – I – want you to rest.'

'I am so tired,' she said, her voice tailing off.

As she slipped back to sleep, Daley got up and stroked her hair once more. Gone were the feelings of resentment, of being cheated on, cuckolded. All he could see was the beautiful young woman who had bounced into his life and changed it for ever in a dark Paisley nightclub so long ago.

'Come on, James. Mummy needs to rest to make her better. Come with Daddy, there's a good boy.'

As they left the side room and walked down the corridor, anyone who didn't know the man would have seen a doting father with his adorable young son in his arms. What they would never see was the rage, the visceral hatred that he now felt in his heart and could feel burning behind his eyes.

All the tiredness, the listlessness, that had followed his recent collapse had disappeared. Adrenaline had kicked in, and for DCI Jim Daley the fog that had clouded his thoughts for too long had cleared.

46

It's strange how hollow I feel. I suppose you get caught up in plots and plans; the drama of it all carries you along, energises you. When the hard work is done – well, it feels rather flat.

But of course, the thrill of execution may change that.

He looked through the words he'd been writing. He wondered again if the people who would read this could possibly have any notion of the real motivation behind his actions.

I've thought about survival – my own. Feelings of worthlessness that my mother instilled in me initially made this an easy, somehow obvious decision. But now – now, I hesitate, and I can't quite understand why. Am I killing her along with the rest? Will this be the final act of defiance that sets me free from the bonds that have held me tight for so, so long? The knowledge that no matter what I achieve, what station in life I attain, it will never be – can never be – enough. Even from the grave her power has been stronger than my will to be free.

But I'm a coward. Maybe that's what she most despised in me. I knew she always thought me a weak, fretful child. No wonder! I was forced to believe that anything I did was wrong, that my very existence was something of which I should be ashamed.

Well, dear Mother, look on. I'm not going to sacrifice myself at your altar of inadequacy, however much I remember your goading me to end my life. You've gone, and now I end the saga, the first act of my life that has seen me despise myself, no matter what I attain.

Now, it ends.

He took the faded photograph from his pocket and stared at her face. This was all he had left of her now, this sliver of paper bearing the image of the woman whose will had – partly, at least – brought him to this point.

But, he supposed, it wasn't merely the hatred of what she'd made him that drove him. It ran much deeper.

He looked at the face one last time, then let it flutter down to the restless waters of the loch, where it floated for a heart-beat, but was soon consumed by the waves.

Now she was gone, only the final act remained to be played out. Instead of being on stage, though, he would act out the rest of the play under his own direction. The role had changed; this time he was master of his own destiny.

As the waves hissed across the shingle beach and the squealing seabirds soared, Cabdi gathered his thoughts. He cursed his height, his build, his colour. Not that he was ashamed of them in any way; he just wanted to be able to blend in with the crowds he knew were about to gather on the pier.

If he could not do what had to be done, then someone else must.

Suddenly, the answer was clear. We must all answer for our sins, he thought.

He emerged from his hiding place and ran across the rocky foreshore, up the hill and over the fence. Soon he was back in

Peter Scally's van, the reek of petrol somehow even stronger now he had spent time in the clear sea air.

He turned over the engine and headed back to Kinloch.

'Right, DS Potts, are we ready?' said Symington.

'Just about, ma'am. The team are being issued with firearms and vests.'

Her phone rang. 'Symington,' she said. Her expression changed. 'But, sir, we know where the suspect went and who he was with. This is happening on our streets, in our town – in our jurisdiction!' She listened for a few more moments and then ended the call abruptly with a cursory 'yes, sir'.

'Stand everyone down, DS Potts.'

'Sorry, ma'am?'

'This *sensitive* situation is to be handled by the Security Service. We, it seems, are not to be trusted to face such a task.'

'But this is a basic operation, ma'am. Even I'm no stranger to this kind of thing.'

'It's political, Sergeant. The top brass have taken fright. The government is clearly shutting this all down.'

'So the safety of the passengers on the *Great Britain* – of the people of this town – is secondary to how things appear?'

'Well put, Potts, and very true.'

'I know what DS Scott would say.'

'What?'

'Bugger them – if you'll pardon the language, ma'am.'

Symington thought for a moment. 'Fortune favours the brave, Sergeant. Get me a vest. You and I are going to pay Mr Scally and his new friend a call.'

Potts smiled. 'Yes, ma'am!'

*

Back home, Daley stood in his lounge, overlooking the loch. The *Great Britain* still dominated the scene, its sharp modern lines incongruous against the soft backdrop of the hills. It reminded him of the science fiction films he'd seen where an alien craft visits an unprepared Earth. The mega-wealthy passengers on the ship might as well have been from another planet when compared with the local populace.

He looked across at his son, who was lying asleep on the couch. For the first time he realised how much like Liz he looked. Yes, he had some of his father's characteristics, but in the main James junior was the image of his mother.

He couldn't rid himself of the image of her lying frail, bruised and battered in the hospital bed. He swallowed hard in order to try to contain the emotion, but it was no good. Nothing could erase his hatred for the man who had done that.

He sat down at the computer and booted it up. In an attempt to regain some kind of equilibrium, he did the only thing he knew how: sought sanctuary in his work. He'd downloaded the information Symington had given him, and decided that he might as well do something positive. He had covered most of the VIPs aboard, just a few to go. Then, as a cursory check, despite knowing that the crew had been vetted by the Security Service, he thought he might as well provide a second eye. But as he scrolled down the list of names, he could not rid himself of the desperate look in his wife's eyes.

'Bad news, ma'am,' said Potts.

'Is there any other kind in this place? I'm not surprised DCI Daley had heart problems.'

'HQ are asking why we're drawing firearms. Sergeant Shaw was obliged to inform them, ma'am.'

'For God's sake!' Symington banged her fists on the desk in front of her. 'We're not as good at this as DCI Daley and DS Scott, are we?'

'DI Scott, ma'am.'

'Yes, quite right. We're still not as clever as them, whatever their rank.'

'Experience, ma'am – they've plenty of that. And, well . . .'

'What?'

'A sometimes healthy disregard for the rules.'

'Yes, that's true.' She thought for a moment. 'We don't need permission to wear body armour – notify HQ, that is.'

'No, ma'am.'

'How brave do you feel, DS Potts?'

'About the normal level, ma'am.'

'Good enough for me, Sergeant. I'll be Jim and you can be Brian.'

'Great,' replied Potts, not particularly meaning it.

'Just let me make a call.' Symington dialled the mobile number she had for Brachen. He replied almost instantly. 'I have information for you.'

'If it's about this mysterious tall man, I don't want to know,' he barked.

'So you're not interested in the case?'

'We're searching for Majid, Chief Superintendent.'

'But our drone man is a murderer!'

'And we suspect Majid to have been radicalised. If there ever was another drone man it was him. Who do you think poses the greater danger to the *Great Britain*? Yours is a civilian matter, as far as I'm concerned. This man you're after may have murdered your local man, but he presents no danger.'

'Then let me go after him, then.'

'The civilian police leak like a sieve. This suspect is of secondary importance. I'm now in operational charge of all aspects of this case. Stand down, Chief Superintendent – and that's an order!'

Symington slammed down the phone.

'Ma'am?' said Potts.

'We're on our own. I hope you're still feeling brave.'

'Exceptionally so.'

'That's good, because it's you and me. I don't want to risk anyone else with no weapons.'

'Do you think our baseball cap man is armed – with a gun, I mean?'

'We have to treat it as though he is – he could have anything. And I have a feeling we're all being played, but for the life of me I can't work out why, or by whom.'

'I'll get you a vest, ma'am.' Potts hurried off, leaving Symington deep in thought.

47

Cabdi drove as fast as he could into Kinloch, then took a circuitous route to his destination – the house of Peter Scally. Instead of parking near the house, he chose to leave the van further down the street. Again, he pulled the baseball cap low over his eyes, though he suspected this was a futile gesture; if the authorities hadn't identified him by now, they must be utterly incompetent.

He ran the last few yards to Scally's house and slipped round to the back door, the one he had exited from and knew to be open – or at least he hoped it still was. Quietly, he tested the handle, and with no little relief found that the door was still unlocked. He closed it quietly behind him and made for the lounge where he'd left Scally.

At first sight, though, the room was bare. A glass had been knocked over on the filthy coffee table, and there was a dark shadow of blood on the floor where he'd left Scally. But of the man himself, there was no sign.

Cabdi stood, silently contemplating what to do next. Who had rescued Scally – perhaps a neighbour, a relative? He sensed that time – his time – was running out and he would have to think again.

As he was about to leave, he heard a noise that drew his attention to the back of the worn couch. When he looked behind it there was the trussed body of Scally, his eyes wide with fear, face bruised and smeared in his own blood. Cabdi tore the gag from the injured man's mouth, but immediately covered it with his hand.

'Do you know what I do for a living, Mr Scally?'

Has captive shook his head frantically, tears slipping down his bloodied cheeks.

'I am a doctor.' He paused, seeing the reaction. 'That surprises you, yes? Of course it does. Why would a man who has devoted his life to the healing of others act in such a way? I will tell you why, Mr Scally. It is because I hate you – people like you. I know what you've done, but you don't care. For you there is no cause apart from personal gain, no regret, no remorse. Yes, I have come to kill, but I do so for a reason. I do it for my people, and sometimes people like you get in my way. I am righting wrongs; you are merely part of those wrongs.'

Scally tried to reply, but his voice was muffled by Cabdi's hand so he quickly gave up.

'But salvation is possible for all, even those, like you, to whom I don't think God means much.' Cabdi forced Scally's head against the floor, the older man's cry of pain again muffled by the hand forced tight against his mouth. 'For you there is a chance for salvation, an opportunity to atone for the terrible thing you have done. A chance to be free, Mr Scally – do you want this?'

Scally nodded desperately.

'Then you do as I say. You do exactly as I tell you. I know you are no stranger to lies and deceit, so your miserable soul will not be troubled by this act. And once you have done what

I ask, your job then is simple: you blame everything – I mean *everything* – on me. Then you have a chance to live a life of freedom, and I will pray for your soul. You may even be a hero.' Cabdi lifted his hand from Scally's mouth.

'Aye, I'll do anything you want, I promise.'

'Ah, a promise from you, Mr Scally, I fear means very little. But then, you know what lies ahead if you do not do as I say. I know you know what I know.' He smiled.

Scally lowered his gaze. 'Aye, fine.'

'Then, good!' Cabdi smiled, but suddenly grabbed Scally by the throat, almost instantly turning his face red. 'You must realise that as a man of medicine I am intimate with every part of the human body. A doctor knows how to harm, as well as to heal – to cause pain, and make that pain more excruciating than you can imagine.' He let go of Scally's throat.

'I know, I know! I'll do anything you say.'

'If you don't you will suffer, I promise.' Cabdi went to work on the rope binding Scally's feet together. 'Now, though your physical bonds have been removed, my hold on you is tighter than ever, yes?'

'Yes.'

When Cabdi had finished freeing the man he pulled him to his feet. 'Now we clean you up and we go about our business.' The Somali pulled Scally from his lounge into his squalid bathroom.

'This is your chance to say no, Potts. I won't think any less of you. Strictly speaking we are both disobeying orders and putting our lives at risk.'

'I understand, ma'am. I'm channelling my inner Brian Scott, remember.'

'Yes, well, perhaps don't work too hard on that.' She laughed. 'Sergeant Shaw, we're leaving now. You know what to say if anyone wants me.'

'Yes, ma'am.'

'Good stuff. Hopefully we can sort this mess out. Who needs Brachen, eh?'

Shaw looked thoughtful. 'Are you sure you don't want to take some more bodies? I'd be happier if we were mob-handed.'

'It's the only way. If I'm right, the man we're after is the real danger. For some reason, I think this Majid is just a decoy.'

'But for what?'

'I haven't worked that out yet, Sergeant.'

Shaw smiled.

'What's so funny?'

'You're the first female gaffer – superior – I've ever had, ma'am.'

'Really? A rare beast, then.'

'Down here in the sticks, it's always been the way it's been – if you get my drift.'

'I do, Sergeant. Well, I hope I'm not letting you down.'

'Quite the opposite, ma'am.'

'Thank you, Sergeant Shaw. I appreciate that more than you know.'

With that, Symington and Potts hurried through the security door at the rear of Kinloch Police Office and out into the car park. They climbed into a small, unmarked police car and drove through the gates and down the hill to Main Street.

Daley was working away quietly when his young son awoke. He hefted the little boy onto his knees in front of the computer screen.

'I want Mummy,' said James junior, rubbing the sleep from his eyes.

'She's not been well, James. That's why we were up at the hospital earlier on. But she's going to be fine, and she'll be back with us soon, I promise.'

'But will we stay here?' The child looked at him with big eyes.

'What do you mean, son?'

'In this house.' He looked at his father. 'I like the sea out of the window, and Muncle Brian and Auntie Ella – and Hameby.'

Daley felt a lump in his throat. His mother and father had always been together, separated only by death. He hated himself for not taking the feelings of his own son into account when he'd split with Liz. It was clear though that the little boy – his little boy – wanted to be in the place he loved, with the people he loved, all together. It was a nice thought, but contained within that idyllic notion were many flaws.

Daley had been so shocked and consumed by anger at what had happened to Liz he hadn't stopped to think about the future. Everything seemed so uncertain now: his job, his health, his marriage. Even he had become accustomed to waking up to the panorama of the loch and the wee town sprawling around it. But if his career was over he would have to find something else to do – somewhere else to live. He'd never find suitable employment in Kinloch, and the last thing he wanted was to end up in the kind of tedious security job so many of his former colleagues had been forced into in order to support their pensions. Would he even be fit enough to do that?

There seemed now to be too many imponderables in his

life. He supposed that had always been the case: same life, different problems.

'Would you like to watch a movie, son?'

'Yay!' said the little boy, arms raised. 'Can we watch *The Snowman*?'

Daley smiled. 'What, again?'

'Yeah. It's the one me and Mummy like best.'

Daley swallowed hard to stop the tears he felt welling up in his throat. He remembered what Ella had said when his son was born: *Don't miss out, Jimmy. Every moment's precious.*

'Okay, *The Snowman* it is.'

He lifted James from the chair and headed to the couch. The remote controls were lying on the coffee table in front of him. 'Right, just let me find it and we're good to go.'

While the little boy clapped, the cursor on the computer screen behind them hovered over the last name Daley had been looking at.

The man groaned with effort as he reached above his head in order to make sure the device was firmly attached to the underside of the console. He was about to press a button on it when he heard footsteps.

'Hey, Barry, what are you at under there?'

He pulled himself out from underneath the ledge. 'Just thought I smelled burning, boss. Can't see anything, though.'

'You want a hand?'

'Nah, I'm about to give it the once-over. Maybe it's just this ship. I'm probably just smelling some billionaire's expensive aftershave. When will you be ready down your end?'

'Give us half an hour, mate. Banks wants this done and dusted ASAP. It's meet-the-locals night on board tonight.

He can't get going until we're finished. So I'm hoping that everything's going to work when we press the button.'

'It always does, doesn't it?

'This is your first time on my team, mate. It doesn't always go the way we want. It's been a strange one, mind. I swear someone did this on purpose.'

'Nah, don't think so. Just some rookie on the bucket getting it wrong. How many times have you seen that?'

'Yeah, too many. You're probably right. I swear, these buggers come out of school with nothing between their ears, these days. I just want to get back to civilisation. Palace are at home this weekend, me and the boy never miss a game if I can help it.'

'You'll be back in plenty time. I'll be ready in half an hour. Just give me a shout when you want to run the test.'

'Right, my man. I'd better get on, eh?'

'Yeah. See you in a bit, boss.'

Barry watched his manager walk out of the cramped room and let out a sigh of relief. He ducked back under the panel he'd been working on and looked up to the device he'd attached to its underside. Reaching up with his index finger and pressing, he watched three red digits blink into life. 'That's my boy,' he said to himself. The reading stayed steady at 0:00.

One more and he would be finished. He opened the thick steel door and stepped into another, smaller compartment. As he knelt in front of the tall console, he reached behind it. Yes, there was room to work; he'd been worried about that. He could feel the thud of the engine room, only a sheet of bulkhead steel from where he was now. He could picture the massive fuel tanks that abutted this small room.

He reached into his canvas bag and brought out a device identical to the one he'd just fitted. 'And for my final trick,' he said, smiling to himself.

He checked the device and turned it on. Again, the three red digits flickered into life. Device in his hand, he reached behind the console, feeling the satisfying clunk as the magnetic backing attached itself firmly.

His job done, he zipped up the canvas bag and left. He was more than ready to leave the *Great Britain*.

48

'I need somewhere to go, somewhere safe where no one will look for either of us. We need to remain unseen until it is time to act. I need to be able to see the harbour.'

Scally thought hard. 'There's an old net shed on the new pier. My grandson uses it tae practise wae that band of his. Apart fae that, no one's ever in it.'

'And how do we get there?'

'We'll need tae walk some o' the way. But with all that's going on over at the old quay, no one will be looking at us.'

'You'd better be right, Mr Scally. If you give me any trouble I will kill you.'

'Wait!'

'What?'

'Ootside. There's somebody coming up the front steps. I heard the gate. I've been meaning tae oil it for ages.'

Before Cabdi could speak a loud knock sounded on the front door. A man's voice called out, 'It's the police. Are you in there, Mr Scally?'

Scally took a deep breath as though he was about to reply with a shout, but the sight of a gun pointing straight at his face stopped him.

'Quickly, out of the back door – now,' murmured Cabdi.

Staying low, the pair made their way from the bathroom across the hall and into the kitchen. They left the house via the back door, Cabdi tugging Scally by his shabby old jacket. 'We head this way, through the gardens.'

They made their way along a communal path that served the block and soon reached the end house. Cabdi angled his head round the wall and looked. Two figures wearing dark vests with POLICE emblazoned on them were standing at Scally's front door. One was a young man, the other a petite dark-haired woman. Cabdi looked back the way they had come, puzzled – only two police officers? For a split second he considered his options, but soon realised there was only one course of action. 'Over the fence!' he said, stepping over the obstacle blocking access to the path leading past the next block of houses. The older man struggled to get over it, but with some effort and a shove from his strong companion, he succeeded.

As they crept along the path a door opened.

'Hey! Whoot are you pair up tae? Is that you, Peter?' A middle-aged man in grey jogging trousers, with a distended belly protruding from under a filthy T-shirt, called them to a halt.

Cabdi prodded Scally in the back.

'Listen, Davie, big man. The polis is after me. I'd one too many doon in the Douglas Arms and took the motor. We're trying tae get away.'

'Who's your pal?' Davie was looking Cabdi up and down.

'Och, jeest a friend o' one the boys. Listen, we need tae get a move on.'

'On you go, Peter. I'm nae lover o' the polis myself. If they ask me anything I'll say nothing, you can rely on that.'

'Good man, Davie.' The pair hurried on.

'Try round the back, DS Potts,' said Symington, peering through the letterbox. 'Mr Scally, if you're in there you need to come out now. It's just routine. We'd like to ask you some questions.'

She waited, and was just about to call again when she heard the clunk of a lock and DS Potts was framed in the doorway.

'Back door was open, ma'am. No sign, though I've not been up the stairs. There's blood in the bathroom.'

'Shit!' she exclaimed, making Potts raise an eyebrow. 'Let me have a look – you check the back garden.'

She walked quickly along the hall and into the lounge. There was a bloodstain on the carpet, a rope and remnants of torn cloth, some of it bloodied.

She crossed the hall and went into the bathroom: blood in the sink, and discarded clothes. She ran upstairs and checked in every bedroom. One room was pristine, if rather stuffy. The other was a mess: unmade bed, overflowing ashtray and various items of clothes scattered across the floor. The place reeked of sweat and cigarettes. 'Bugger it!' she swore to herself, hurrying back downstairs and out into the back garden. On a path beside a drying green, she could see Potts talking to a fat man over a fence a few yards down, and made her way towards them.

'Nah, I haven't seen anything,' said the fat man. 'Peter keeps his self to his self. I hardly see him. Och, the odd time in the passing an' that. But that's all.'

Symington looked at the path. Dots of red blood ran from Scally's back door to where she was standing. She looked over the fence, and could see they carried on past the man Potts was questioning. 'Forget him, Sergeant. Follow the blood on the path.' Deftly, she straddled the fence and was soon over it, closely followed by DS Potts.

'Hey, haud your horses! This is my property,' Davie shouted.

Ignoring him, the two police officers carried on until they reached the end of the next block. The red dots of blood petered out on a small grassy hill leading down to the road. Symington rushed forward, and looked the length of the street in both directions, but there was nothing to be to be seen, save for a scrawny dog sniffing at the gutter.

The phone in her pocket sounded. 'Yes, Sergeant Shaw?'

'I've had Commander Brachen on the phone, ma'am. They've captured Majid. He would like a word with you. I told him you were out to lunch, ma'am.'

'Thank you, Sergeant Shaw.'

'Did you get anywhere, ma'am?'

'No, but I want you to get as many units as you can muster looking for Peter Scally and the man described online.'

'Tall, thin, black? Our red-hot man?'

'Yes. And tell them to use caution. Scally may be injured – there's blood all over his house.'

'Yes, ma'am. We're already looking for his van.'

'Good work. If Brachen gets back in touch, tell him I'm on my way.' She looked at DS Potts and shrugged. 'We just missed them. I want you to arrest the man we were talking to. He must have seen something, and any piece of information we can get just now is invaluable. I'll send the van to fetch you. I'm heading back to the office.'

As she walked back down the street to where their car was parked, she cursed Brachen for the delay. More than ever, she was now convinced that the second drone man, as she'd come to think of him, was the real danger. Yet things still didn't make sense. To go to the trouble of alerting the authorities by attacking the *Great Britain* with a drone containing no explosives was pointless.

Scott was stretched out on his bed when a knock sounded on the door. A tall man in a dark suit stood before him.

'Sorry to bother you, Mr Sinclair. I'd like a word, if I may.' He flashed an ID card.

'Oh aye? What aboot?'

'If I could come in, please, sir.'

Scott held open the door and let his visitor into the cabin. Ella was off having a swim and a sauna while he tried to make sense of the images he'd taken of the map he'd found in O'Rourke's bathroom.

'My name is Haddon. I'm with security here on board, sir. I'll come straight to the point. We've had a complaint.'

'If it's my wife's snoring, there's bugger all she can do about it. Her ain mother was exactly the same – runs in the family, so tae speak.'

'No, sir, something more serious than that, I'm afraid.'

'Aw fuck, don't tell me we're sinking!' said Scott.

'Just under an hour ago you were spotted in another cabin, sir.'

'Och, see this boat. I get fair confused. I was on the wrong floor, son.'

'And the wrong side of the ship, sir.'

'Aye, I'm hellish when it comes tae directions. My wife will tell you, cannae find my way anywhere. I apologise for my mistake.'

'The cleaner we spoke to was under the impression that there was something suspicious about your behaviour, sir.'

'Like what?'

'You looked *furtive*, she said.'

'See, I've just got that kind o' face, son. I was always being picked up the police, just because of the way I looked when I was a boy,' continued Scott convincingly.

'Well, there appears to be nothing missing from the complainant's cabin, so he's willing to overlook the matter. I must warn you, though, that such is the nature of this trip, if you were to do something like this again we would have no choice but to ask you to leave. I hope that's clear, sir.'

'Aye, crystal clear. Next time I'm on my travels roon the boat, I'll make sure and take my wife wae me. She might be a right bad snorer, but she's got a great sense o' direction – like one o' they dogs.'

'What dogs, sir?'

'They ones that find folk in the snow – big fluffy things wae sad eyes.'

'A St Bernard, sir?'

'Aye, you're right enough, though she's no saint, mind. Easy seen why you're in security, eh? No' much will get past you, I'm thinking.'

'No, sir.' He walked to the door. 'Oh, and it's a ship, sir.'

'Well, I didnae think it was a hoover.'

'No, you called it a boat – it's a ship.'

'Aye, right. I'll stow that away wae the rest o' my nautical knowledge. And let me tell you, there's a lot o' that.'

'If you would just be more careful where you're going, sir, that would be much appreciated.'

Scott watched him go, then leaned out of the door. 'Hey, how did thon cleaner know it was me?'

'You had your name tag on your jacket, sir.'

Scott closed the door and lay back on the bed to examine his phone and forward a copy of what he'd photographed to Symington. Just as he was about to send the email, another knock sounded at the door.

'Fuck me, it's like Sauchiehall Street on a Saturday night!'

When he turned the handle the door was flung open with some force, knocking him to the ground. As he tried to get back to his feet and collect his thoughts, he was bent double by a kick to his stomach, winding him and sending him back to the floor.

Then he felt a strong grip on his throat, stopping his breath.

49

Brachen sat beside Symington in one of the interview rooms at Kinloch Police Office. The Royal Navy commander hadn't been particularly keen on this course of action, preferring to take Majid to the *Great Britain* for questioning, but Symington had insisted. The man had been intercepted in a bay where he'd moored his little craft and erected a tent. He'd set a fire there, bordered by some boulders. And it seemed likely that this was where he'd been since disappearing from the cruise ship.

Majid looked miserable and confused as he sat beside local duty lawyer Arthur MacPhee opposite Symington and Brachen. He was a gaunt-faced man with a wispy dark beard, well below average height, wearing a tatty jumper and dirty jeans, and no more than thirty-five years old.

'Tell us why you left the *Great Britain* without informing your supervisor, Mr Majid?' Symington began.

The man shrugged. 'I was given money. I was told to hide for a time, then go to the village – I can't remember its name – when I received a message. This is what I did.'

'Firdale?'

'Yes, that is it.' Majid's English was hesitant, but good. 'At a certain time I was to go to the local shop on the pier, ask for some items and return in the boat to my campsite.'

Brachen sat back in his chair. He was dressed in civvies and had removed his suit jacket to reveal an immaculately laundered white shirt. He folded his arms across his chest. 'What made you do this? I mean, did you know the person who asked you to leave your job without a word and do what he told you?'

Majid looked at the floor. 'No. I went into my cabin after work one night. In it was a bag.'

'What was in the bag, Mr Majid?' said Symington.

'More money than I can earn in three years, all in US dollars.'

'And what else?' barked Brachen.

'Just a note and a mobile phone. The note told me what to do if I wanted to keep the money.'

'Which was?'

'As I've told you. Go to where I made camp. A car had been left for me in Kinloch – well, just outside the town. I followed the directions and ended up where you found me. I was to wait, then go to the shop and do as they asked.'

'Why do you keep saying *they*?' said Brachen.

He shrugged his shoulders. 'I don't know – he, she, they – I don't know! I was warned that if I took the money and did not do what I was told there would be consequences.'

'Then you have no idea who provided the money and asked you to do this? Surely you must have suspected that something was wrong, Mr Majid – especially when you were threatened in that way? I'm afraid I don't believe you!' Brachen thumped the desk in front of him engendering a concerned look from the lawyer.

'My family in Pakistan are very poor, sir. The only way I have of providing for them is to send money home from my work on the cruise ships. Recently, my daughter was taken ill. She needs an operation. The money is enough to pay for that. What would you do?' He stared at Brachen with a mixture of sadness and defiance.

'And this phone you were given, where is it now?' asked Symington.

'I was told to throw it into the sea on the way back from Firdale.'

'So how on earth were you to learn what to do next?' Brachen snapped.

'I was to stay at the camp for another day, then go back in the car and leave for home.'

'Pakistan?' said Symington.

'I was told to join the crew of a freighter heading to Pakistan. Work my passage. The letter said that everything was arranged and that I would be able to take the money with me, no questions asked.'

'Surely you must have wondered why this was happening? I mean, you don't get handed a big bag of money and asked to go camping for a couple of days and not think that strange?'

Majid lowered his head. 'I wanted to save my daughter. It all seemed very simple, and I couldn't see anything wrong in doing what I did. I have not robbed or harmed anyone, yet here I am being held prisoner.'

'And the note you were given? What happened to that, Mr Majid?'

'I ripped it up and threw it into the sea. That is what I was told to do, and that is what I did.'

Symington leaned forward and pressed a button, ending the interview.

'Am I free to go?' asked Majid hopefully.

'Don't be ridiculous!' said Brachen standing to put on his jacket.

'If I may interject.' This was MacPhee. 'Mr Majid can be held for, oh, another eighteen hours.' He looked at his watch. 'Of course you can ask for an extension, but under the circumstances – certainly as things stand – I see no crime committed here. If the money hasn't been stolen, nor the vessel and vehicle Mr Majid used, then there is no reason for his confinement beyond the accepted terms of detention. In short, if you cannot charge him in the next eighteen hours, in my opinion, he must go free.'

Majid smiled at the lawyer and bowed his head, hands together in a praying motion. 'Thank you, thank you so much.'

'This is now a matter of national security. Do yourself a favour, MacPhee, and shut the fuck up!'

The lawyer stared at him, unmoved. 'As the tape is now off, and the interview officially over, I shall record what you've just said to me in writing, Commander.' He looked at Symington. 'I trust you will witness Commander Brachen's comments, Chief Superintendent?'

Symington nodded, then looked at Brachen, her face like thunder. 'A word with you, please.'

Ella Scott opened the door of the cabin to find her husband lying motionless on the floor.

'Brian!' She rushed to his side, and instinctively tried to lift his head from the floor.

Scott began to stir. 'What the fuck?' he murmured, his voice slurred.

'Come on, I'll help you onto the bed. What the hell happened to you?'

Though he was still unsteady on his feet, with his wife's help Scott managed to stagger onto the bed. As he lay back Ella noticed that his eye was red and swollen and blood was trickling from his nose.

'Who did this to you, Brian?'

'That O'Rourke guy. Listen, Ella, I need tae get hold o' Symington, rapid like.'

'Damn right! This guy needs tae get huckled, big time. Then you need tae see a doctor.'

'Naw, I'm fine. Stop fussing. It's no' the first time I've had a right battering, as you well know.'

'Oh, somebody comes into oor cabin – I take it that it happened here – gies you a good kicking, and everything's fine? No' likely, Inspector Scott!'

'Get me a phone, woman. This is important!'

'A phone! It's a bloody ambulance you need,' she said, looking around nonetheless for his mobile, which she found lying on the floor.

'Thanks, doll.' Scott dialled Symington's number. 'Answer, for fuck's sake!' he said, cursing again when the call went to voicemail.

'Are you no' just going tae leave her a message?'

'Aye, that's it, darling. Here, I'll just write a wee note and send it on a pigeon. This is something she needs to know now!' Scott fumbled again with the phone. 'See these bloody phones! They keep handing me new ones, and none o' the damned things are the same.'

'Here, gie the bloody thing tae me, you stupid bastard.'

'Florence Nightingale here, eh?' Scott touched his bleeding nose gingerly with one hand as he handed the phone to Ella with the other.

'Huh, the polis inspector that cannae work his mobile phone! Are you wanting tae phone the station?'

'No, the cinema.'

'If you don't shut it, you'll have broken teeth tae deal with as well as whatever's happened tae your coupon.' She pressed the screen a few times and handed the mobile back to her husband. 'Here. I take it you'll manage tae speak?'

As he heard the ringing tone Scott looked at her. 'When I'm finished, I'm going tae stick this phone right up your . . . Hello, it's DS Scott here. I need tae speak tae Symington!'

'DI Scott, numb nuts,' said Ella.

'Och, does it really matter?'

Ella Scott shook her head and went to the bathroom to get a flannel and some hot water to attend to her husband's injuries. Whatever had happened to him, she could see he was worried – very worried.

Daley was watching the final scenes of the film when he noticed that his son was fast asleep at his side. He smiled down at the little boy.

'You're tired today, James,' he said quietly. No wonder, he thought. It's been an eventful one.

Gently, he lifted the boy in his arms, ignoring another twinge in his chest. He'd made a conscious decision not to think about what might be wrong with him. What would be would be. He pushed open the door to his son's room and carefully laid James in his bed, tucking him in and switching on his nightlight.

As Daley looked on, James sighed in his sleep, turning his head on the pillow, and muttered, 'Mummy.' Daley felt his throat tighten. Here was his son, and he was determined to stay with him as long as he could. He pictured his own father in his mind's eye, the look on his face as he'd stared at his son in the moments before he died.

'I'm sorry, son,' was all he'd said before his eyes closed for the last time.

Daley walked from the room, closing the door gently as he went. He'd made sure the baby alarm was on. Not that James needed it now, but Daley was over-cautious when it came to something as precious as his little boy.

He decided to call the hospital and see how his wife was.

'She's doing fine, Mr Daley,' said the staff nurse kindly. 'She's asleep again, or I'd let you have a word with her. She's been through a lot, so best that she gets as much rest as possible.'

Daley thanked her and put down the phone. He was relieved that she seemed none the worse for her overdose, and gave silent thanks for it.

Resisting the urge to pour himself a dram, he looked out of the lounge window as the golden light of evening adorned the loch, turning ripples in the water into glittering jewels as boats from the *Great Britain* ferried people to and fro. He remembered that this was the night some locals were to be invited on board, and smiled at the thought of Hamish having a conversation with the duke and duchess.

He'd been warned off alcohol for the time being by his doctor, and now he understood what a gargantuan effort Brian Scott had made to kick his booze addiction. Though Daley hadn't plumbed the depths of alcoholism his friend had sunk to, he still felt the strong desire to sit with a comforting dram to ease his troubled mind.

He picked his iPad off the couch and looked at the music he might play to help him relax. As he scrolled through the tracks in his library, his hand hovered over The Blue Nile's *Hats* album, but he still couldn't listen to that song. Instead he searched for ELO's greatest hits, and played the album through his stereo. The first bars of 'Evil Woman' quietly rang out. For long enough the song had reminded him of Liz.

As the music washed over him, it brought back memories in the way only music could do – memories both happy and sad. Where had the years gone? It seemed these days that no sooner had he raised his glass to bring in another New Year than the next festive season was upon him. Though he tried to stop the thought before it began, he couldn't help but wonder how many more years he'd have to toast the beginning of another one.

Unsettled, melancholy, and missing the soothing effects of alcohol, he decided to do what he always did when everything became too much for him to bear: work.

His computer had gone into sleep mode, but a touch of the keyboard saw the screen flash back into life. He was now at the final stage of his checks, the crew of the *Great Britain*. With a sigh, he pressed a key and began a search he thought to be futile, but nonetheless had to be done.

50

'Just what the hell did you think you were doing in there, Commander?' snapped Symington. 'This is a police office, not some back street torture room. No one gets threatened in my station, got it?'

Barchen yawned theatrically. 'I suggest you spend a little more time on the matter in hand rather than your wearisome morals, Chief Superintendent,' he sneered. 'I'll get the spooks on this, and Mr Majid will be eaten up by the system and spat out whenever it suits. We're not restrained by your ridiculous rules. Please try to remember that.'

'You are one arrogant bastard – also an arrogant bastard who has everything wrong. The second drone man does exist, and he matches the descriptions from America.'

'So what? He's on the run because the pap he was with fucked up, fell down a hill and killed himself after botching a photo opportunity. He's worried in case he gets the blame. We've checked out the man found dead on your hill, and he has no terrorist connections – utterly clean.'

'Who is he?'

'That's classified, I'm afraid.'

'And what's his record as a photo journalist?'

'Surely you're not stupid enough to believe that only the

accredited press search for images they think they can sell on these days? Every bugger and his friend are at it. We had a chap try to get aboard in Glasgow to snap the passengers. This whole thing has been a fiasco. It's unsettled those on the *Great Britain*, and we've been run ragged for no bloody reason.'

Symington smiled. 'So, you've got a crewman who's paid a considerable amount of money to disappear for a couple of days, complete with specific instructions, just for fun. You also have a drone hit the cruise ship you are tasked to protect, leaving one man dead and the other on run, and you think there's nothing to worry about?'

'Yes. It has all been a combination of circumstances that have had no impact on my task. Who knows what this Majid was going to be asked to do when he reached the freighter bound for Pakistan? My guess is he was to end up as some drugs mule. Our men are checking out the vessel on which he was due to take passage.'

'That doesn't make sense. If you're trying to find someone to quietly smuggle drugs – whatever – across continents, you're not going to pick a person the authorities are likely to be looking for because he's just gone AWOL from a ship with the richest passenger list in history. And there's more you don't know, Commander.'

'Oh, do tell,' he said mockingly.

'A local man was caught on the town's CCTV cameras with the second drone man. I visited his home – blood everywhere. We've reason to believe this mystery man you think so innocent has taken him captive. Is that the action of someone who presents no danger?'

'All I know is it's nothing to do with me, or the *Great*

Britain. We just have to get this local yokel reception out of the way and then we can bugger off.'

'So the electrical problems are fixed?'

'Yes, back to normal. If it was up to me we'd sail now, but . . .'

'But it's not up to you.'

'No, but hey-ho. We'll soon be under way.'

'Where's your next port of call, Commander?'

'Belfast, if you must know.'

'I have a theory. I think Majid, the men with the drone and the sudden failure of the *Great Britain*'s electrical systems are no coincidence.'

'Bloody hell! Are police officers like this everywhere, or just in this damnable place? All of you seeing hidden dangers round every corner, like children scared of the dark?'

Ignoring him, Symington continued. 'I think all that has gone on has been done to keep you and your team busy – eyes off the ball, if you like.'

'For what reason?'

'We have information that one of your passengers has connections to Irish Republican paramilitary groups – or did once upon a time.'

'*Once upon a time*. How apt, Chief Superintendent. Your whole theory is a fairy story. Every passenger has been thoroughly vetted, as have the crew. I hope you're not naïve enough to think that some of the wealthiest business people in the world today don't have some skeletons in their closets? I assure you, we're well aware of the risk profile of all our guests, and none of them presents a danger.'

She stared at him. 'So bugger off, Symington – is that it?'

'I couldn't have put it better myself – in the nicest possible sense.' He smiled sickeningly.

324

'Well, I hope for your sake – and for the sake of those you have a duty to protect – that you're not mistaken. As a police officer you get a nose for things that aren't quite right.'

'Like a dog, you mean?'

'Go back to your ship, Commander.' Though Symington's voice was quiet, her face spoke of a much more heated emotion.

'With pleasure. Get Majid ready. I'm taking him with me to be handed to the Security Service.'

'That's not happening. Majid is in my custody, and in it he will remain until I am told otherwise.'

Brachen towered over her as he stood. 'My father was from Dublin, you know.'

'And why are you telling me that?'

'Just to add to your obvious paranoia. Good day, Chief Superintendent.'

As he swaggered out of the room, Symington's phone rang.

'DI Scott for you, ma'am.'

Scally had driven to some broken-down garages at the foot of a hill, where he parked the van.

'We're on foot fae here,' he said to his captor, looking at him nervously.

'Where do we go?'

Scally pointed across the road. 'Thonder is an auld railway cutting; never many folk aboot. It leads tae the seafront. From there it's a few hundred yards tae the new pier and the shed I telt you aboot.'

'And this is the best way to get there – no other route?'

'It was you that said they'd be looking for the van. I came o'er the Doctor's Road and up past the scheme. No cameras on that way. Wae the motor hidden here behind these garages, we can leg it doon tae the shed. It's the only way I can think o'.'

'Okay. That is what we do. But I warn you, Mr Scally, if you do not do exactly as I say, you've been warned of the consequences.'

'Aye, I've got the message.'

'Good. You lead the way.'

As casually as possible, the pair headed across the road and down the old railway cutting, hidden by its steep, tree-lined banks. As they neared the end of it a boy appeared on a bike. He stared at the tall African in the red baseball cap as he approached.

'How'ye, son,' said Scally calmly. 'You watch your tyres, there's some broken glass up there.'

'Aye, cheers, mister,' said the boy, still staring at Cabdi, who smiled broadly back.

'Right, we're jeest aboot tae come oot intae the open. This is the dangerous bit.'

'How fast can you run, Mr Scally?'

'Are you kidding? Anyhow, if we run we'll attract attention. Jeest walk and keep your heid doon. Follow me.'

Suddenly they were out in the open, the loch before them on the other side of a promenade of grass bordered by a pathway. To their right was the island protecting the loch, almost obscured by the sleek lines of the large cruise ship, much nearer across the water. The evening sun was lowering, and Scally shaded his eyes as they crossed the road and walked down a narrow path to the promenade proper.

'See, they're loading folk on and off they boats that ferry everybody oot tae the cruise ship fae the pontoons over on the far side of that pier.'

'And where are we going?'

'This way.'

The unlikely pair turned left on the promenade, passed a small play park, mercifully empty of children, and headed for buildings Cabdi had seen from the hill.

'This is a ferry terminal – there will be people about.'

'Nah, no boats today, only at weekends. We're fine.'

A woman with a small dog was walking towards them, though she was more interested in the *Great Britain*, eyes fixed on it as she passed them by without a glance.

A few yards further on they reached the ferry terminal buildings. Scally was right: though a crowd of people was gathered on the opposite pier, their attention was focused elsewhere, on the pontoons beyond, where guests were queuing, waiting to be transported to the *Great Britain*.

Scally bustled past the ferry terminal, dark within and clearly closed. Beside it were three decrepit buildings. Scally made for a blue door at the gable end and bent down.

'What are you doing?' asked Cabdi.

'Getting this,' Scally said, moving a weight designed to keep lobster creels on the seabed and revealing a rusting mortise key. He thrust the key into a hole in the ramshackle door and with some effort managed to push it open.

The two men entered the musty building, and Scally locked the door behind them. The space was cluttered, full of old fishing nets, floats and other fishing paraphernalia, at odds with the drum kit and two amplifiers placed against the rear wall. At the front of the room were two filthy windows, one with a long crack running diagonally across its length. Through them shone the setting sun, highlighting dust motes as Cabdi did his best to clean the uncracked one using his forearm, sending a large spider scurrying for a darkened corner of the window frame.

'I can't see,' he said, frustration plain in his voice.

'Here, use this.' Scally handed him an old brass mariner's telescope. Though its glass was almost as encrusted with dirt as the window, Cabdi could now make out figures standing on the quayside across the short stretch of water.

'This will do,' he said, focusing on the crowd of people on the pier.

Behind him, Scally eyed an old mallet used by the net makers who had once inhabited the building. He sidled towards it as quietly as he could.

'Take your chance, Mr Scally,' said Cabdi, still looking through the telescope at the scene across the harbour. 'Trust me, I will break your head in two before you can hit me with anything. Get back and sit by the wall. Now!'

Scally sighed in frustration, but knew when he was beaten. He shuffled to the back of the room and perched on an amp. 'Whoot are you looking for? I'm telling you, the place will be crawling wae security and polis. You'll get spotted straight away.'

Cabdi lowered the telescope and turned to face the local man. 'Yes, but I have you, Mr Scally.' His smile was broad, but not encouraging.

51

The excited crowd of locals were waiting their turn to be taken the short distance across the loch to the *Great Britain*. They chatted enthusiastically, their discussions punctuated by the odd flurry of laughter, especially when old MacSporran the newsagent's false teeth fell out and landed in the loch with a plop as he was boarding the launch. He stared back at his fellow townsfolk on the quayside and managed to mash out his feelings on the subject. 'Fuckshake, it'll be the shoup for me the night.'

Councillor Charlie Murray was dressed in an evening suit bursting at the seams. The collar of his shirt, clearly too small for his thick neck, looked likely to decapitate him at any moment. 'Here, I should be at the front o' the queue, whoot wae me being on the council.'

'If you manage to get on that wee boat wae your clothes intact, you should be grateful,' shouted someone from the crowd.

'I'll have you know this suit came fae one o' the finest tailors in London!' Murray retorted.

'Aye, in 1967!' replied his anonymous interlocutor. 'You've near doubled in size since then.'

As laughter rang out, Hamish ran his finger round the collar of his own shirt. It had probably once been white, but was clearly – like Charlie Murray's suit – suffering from the ravages of time and was now a deep ivory colour. He was wearing a blue tweed jacket with leather patches on each elbow, above a faded kilt that had also seen better days. What set off his outfit though was the wide orange tie, knotted awkwardly at his neck. He fumbled around in a sporran hanging far too low, and fetched out his pipe and a small skein of tobacco.

'Could you no' jeest take off that tie, Hamish,' said Annie at his side.

'Indeed not! Whoot kind o' man goes tae meet some o' the wealthiest folk on the planet wae no tie on? You've got some strange ideas, Annie.'

'Better nae tie than that tie,' she told him.

'This is a pure silk tie. It cost me near three shillings when I bought it.'

'In whoot century?'

'Nane o' your cheek – that blue dress you've got on has seen a fair few outings, unless I'm much mistaken.'

'I'll have you know, Hamish, that this dress is haute couture. I got it in a charity shop in Glasgow. It's all the rage noo, saving the planet by wearing used clothes – vintage, they're called.'

'How's that saving the planet? And I see this vintage premise clearly doesna cover ties.'

'There's vintage, and there's shite. I wouldna be seen dead walking aboot wae something like that on. I suppose if there's an emergency and the lights go oot like they did in thon *Titanic* film, we'll be fine. We can jeest follow your tie tae safety.'

'Aye, get it a' oot while you can, Annie. You'll no' be

laughing when you see the table o' folk I'll be sat at. German aristocracy, I'm thinking.'

'There's no' so many o' them aboot these days, I fancy.'

'Now that jeest shows your ignorance on the subject o' anything that goes on past the *Welcome to Kinloch* road sign.'

'Oh aye, and just how is that?'

'Oor ain dear monarch is near as German as you get. You can hardly say she's no' the aristocracy.'

'Maybe not, but sometimes it's hard tae tell who someone is or whoot they do jeest by looking at them, right enough. I canna say that for you, mind.'

'How so? Is it my proud naval bearing, the tan you get at sea that nae amount o' holidays in foreign climes can match?'

'Naw, it's the smell o' fish and your kipper tie.'

Hamish sucked angrily at his pipe, desperately searching for a retort that wouldn't come. 'You're jeest a scunner, Annie – and getting worse wae age intae the bargain. I'll be happy if you don't attempt tae muscle in on my company the night. In fact, I canna think why you were invited in the first place.' He sent a cloud of blue tobacco smoke into the air.

'I'll have you know I was invited by that captain himsel'.' She nodded at the old fisherman with a triumphant smile.

'Mair likely the bosun, I'm thinking.'

'No, nor the bosun. I was invited by Captain Magnus Banks. After me putting on such a fine day for the guests when they were ashore.'

'I suppose it was a passable event. Though auld Lamont was fair puggled wae whisky on that accordion. He didna know his Gay Gordons fae his Dashing White Sergeants by three o'clock. Could you no' get wee Roger?'

'No, he's away in Tenerife.'

'Poor soul. Here, talking o' dashing white sergeants, you'll see yours the night.'

'He's an inspector now, Hamish.' Annie stared across the loch at the hills beyond, her face taking on a mournful expression.

'And whoot have you got the glums aboot? Nae doubt the fact that the inspector's wife is wae him, I'll venture.'

'Nothing of the kind, Hamish! I was thinking, here's us enjoying oorselves while poor Mr Pearson's lying in the mortuary.'

'Well, no' all of him.'

Annie looked at Hamish. 'Whoot dae you mean?'

'Sure he was minus his heid, and other parts tae.'

'You're a wicked man, Hamish.'

'It wisna me that did it!'

'No, but you're fair wallowing in the gore o' it all. He was a lovely man – jeest wanted tae be up the hill wae his birds.'

'He wisna too clever at keeping an eye on one bird.'

'Eh?'

'Och, you know fine. If he'd spent mair time wae his binoculars on his wife rather than looking for a hoopoe, he might have kept her oot o' the arms o' Peter Scally.'

'I'm no' speculating on any o' that, and neither should you.'

'If Mr Daley was on the case, that sleekit bugger would be behind bars, and no mistake.'

'You cannae go throwing aboot accusations like that. Someone might take them seriously.'

'Aye, wae good cause, tae.'

Annie looked him straight in the face. 'It was you, wasn't it?'

'Whoot was me?'

'You that telt the polis aboot this *affair*, between him and Maggie Pearson. Oh, Hamish, it's written a' across your face.'

He took one last puff of his pipe and tapped the bowl on the heel of his shoe, sending the ash onto the pier below. 'I'm telling you, Peter Scally's a rogue. He'll get himself arrested again, you mark my words.'

'Och, you stupid auld bugger. The only one likely to get arrested is you if you keep flicking up your kilt like that. Half the toon got a look at something naebody wants tae see, jeest there.'

Hamish looked about, carefully adjusted his tie and made no response.

The captain's launch skimming across the calm waters of the loch towards Kinloch from the *Great Britain* contained not only the eponymous captain, but also the team of technicians who had managed to put the great cruise liner's electrical systems to rights.

'I'd like to thank you all for getting your work done so quickly and efficiently,' said Banks, addressing the six-man team. 'We've managed to stay pretty much on schedule, though we may be a little late leaving for Belfast. I'll make sure you all get a bonus for your efforts.'

'Much obliged to you, Captain,' said the team's foreman. 'Glad to have been of assistance.'

At the rear of the launch, one of them sat quietly, nursing the large canvas bag containing his tools. Had anyone taken much notice, they'd have seen that the bag was almost empty. But as the team had been vetted prior to their trip to Kinloch, and as security was busy, no one was bothered. As he looked out at the oily blue waters of the loch he smiled at the thought of the five sets of red digits now shining unseen in various nooks and crannies of the ship that lay in their wake.

If a job's worth doing, it's worth doing well.

Symington was fretting following Scott's call. She'd been wrong about Patrick O'Rourke. According to Scott, he was planning to buy a piece of land in County Antrim and return to his roots as a rich man, not the scared wee boy from a family ruined by hatred, division and death, who had crossed the Atlantic with his mother so long ago.

In order to keep his cover intact, Scott had taken a beating from the Irish-American, who suspected the undercover police officer of trying to steal from him. But the newly minted inspector was convinced that he wasn't their man, and Symington trusted his instincts.

She looked at herself in the full-length mirror in her hotel room. Her first visit had been an official one, and she had dressed appropriately in her best uniform. Now, she'd discarded her buttons and braid for a little black dress and matching short jacket. She'd also applied some make-up, and wondered when she'd last had the chance to dress up. Her new promotion had sent her far from friends and family; her flat in Glasgow's West End was more akin to a dormitory than a home, as all her efforts, her very being, were focused on work and banishing a past that still haunted her.

Symington took a deep breath and dropped her fully charged mobile into the small clutch bag she would take with her. It contained little else other than some lipstick, face powder and a tiny bottle of Chanel No. 5.

Maybe Brachen was right – but he couldn't be. Someone

had killed Cameron Pearson, and they'd had a reason. The neat explanation that the drone man had fallen to his death may or may not be true. But there was something about the guarded nature of Brachen's comments that niggled at her.

Then there was the man captured on the town's CCTV. What had he done to Peter Scally, and why? She had a forensic team in Scally's house, but whether they would be able to throw any light on what had happened she didn't know. At the very least, she supposed, they would be able to confirm whose blood was caked around the basin and on the threadbare carpet on the lounge.

Symington wished she had Jim Daley at her side. She'd become used to his steady thoughtfulness and reassuring physical presence. Often she wondered why he wasn't higher up in the management structure, though having looked at his file she knew that his temper had held him back from promotion more than once. She'd also read a lot about John Donald, and his cold dead hand was all across Daley's career, poisoning his prospects. She recalled how shocked she had been when she discovered the true nature of the man she'd replaced.

As she sprayed a puff of perfume behind each ear, and wrestled with her earrings, she wondered more about Daley. She wanted to share her worries with him, but knew that he had more than enough to cope with. Liz's predicament had reminded her of her own problems in the past. Despite Scott's recent intervention, she still couldn't be sure that the threat posed by the man who had occupied her thoughts, her worst nightmares, for so long would not raise its head once more and ruin everything she had worked for.

The secret she now shared with Scott was a potentially

ruinous one. It was the biggest regret of her life. Sometimes she just wanted to come clean, to tell all. But not only did she stand to lose her career; her liberty too could well be at stake.

But tonight Carrie Symington had more pressing things on her mind. The motorcyclist she'd hit when driving home from a watch night out, unaware that her drinks had been spiked, and all that followed must take second place to the here and now.

Could she honestly say that the passengers, crew and guests aboard the *Great Britain* were safe? No. She despised Commander Brachen and his patrician superiority. She was the product of a solidly middle-class family from North Yorkshire, who now found herself in this remote yet alluring part of the country with a weight of responsibility she didn't deserve bearing down heavily on her slender shoulders.

She took one last look in the mirror, patted down her short black jacket, and with clutch bag in hand left the hotel and headed for Kinloch's old quay.

52

Captain Banks stood proudly on the pier, passing time with the locals waiting – mostly patiently – for a launch to take them to the party.

'Pleased to meet you,' he said to the old man with the slanting eyes and the olive skin that ended at the top of his forehead to reveal a milk-white bald head. He wasn't sure whether it was the odd contrast of colour between the old man's scalp and his face or the shade of his tie that was most remarkable, but he slipped easily into his default mode of welcoming smile and well-honed bonhomie. This was something his life had consisted of for as long as he could remember. Smiling at crude jokes, or enduring painfully boring guests at the captain's table as he progressed round the world on one ocean or another, simply to entertain those willing to part with enough money for the privilege.

'She's a fine vessel, right enough,' said Hamish, shaking the captain's hand enthusiastically. 'I'm a mariner of some repute myself,' he added, as Annie looked on.

'Aye, an' a drinker o' even mair repute,' she muttered.

'Sorry, madam?' said Banks, taking her hand and bowing deeply.

'I was jeest hoping that yous have plenty whisky on board to entertain those who like a drop or two,' she replied in her best phone voice, usually reserved for those booking a room at the County Hotel.

'We're well stocked, don't worry . . . Annie, isn't it? I remember visiting your establishment this afternoon.'

'Aye, that's right, your honour,' she said with a curtsey. 'Mind you, it's easy tae misjudge a party one isna used tae, if you know whoot I mean.' She smiled.

'Pure poison,' said Hamish in a stage whisper.

'Sorry, sir?'

'Hamish, Captain, jeest call me Hamish. I was referring to the make o' whisky the lady beside me stocks behind her bar.'

'Well, you're looking no' too bad on it, and you've been sampling it for longer than jeest aboot anybody.' Annie's withering look was enough to make even Hamish decide not to respond.

'Only the best malt whisky for our guests,' said Banks.

'None o' that Speyside stuff I'm hoping, Captain.'

'Not a fan, Hamish?'

'No. The only decent malts is fae the West Coast – here, to be precise, though they concoct a fair enough brew o'er on Islay if you can stand the peat.'

'I'm certain we have something for every taste.' Banks looked up as another launch arrived. 'I think this is your transport,' he said. 'I'll see you all aboard.' He smiled again as a steward guided the small gathering left on the quayside down to the pontoons.

'Jeest a fine man,' said Hamish as he moved forward alongside Annie in the line.

'Poor bugger's likely blinded, whoot wae having tae stare at that tie for mair than a minute or two.'

338

'Och, not at all. He was likely jeest thinking tae himself, well, if anything happens tae me my vessel will be in fine hands wae this upstanding matelot.'

'Who?'

'Me, you daft woman.'

'One mair comment like that an' you'll no' need a boat back off the ship.'

'How no'?'

'Because you'll have tae swim hame.'

'Chief Superintendent,' said Banks, 'I'm so glad you could make it. I hardly recognised you out of uniform.'

'Not something I'm very used to seeing myself, these days,' replied Symington. Her smile faded. 'I wonder, is it possible to have a word with you – in private, I mean?'

'Shall we head to the end of the quay?'

'Yes, that would be fine.'

As they walked along the line of short people still shuffling towards the pontoons Symington made small talk while Banks waved and smiled beatifically at those about to be his guests.

Once they were out of earshot, Symington stopped. 'I'm worried, Captain Banks.'

'About what, Carrie?'

'Something feels wrong. I questioned Majid with Brachen. I think the only thing he's guilty of is foolishness, to be honest.'

'I knew they'd found him, but I'm afraid Commander Brachen and his team keep as much from me as they can. I know very little of what has happened.' Banks sounded concerned.

'The drone man – the second man who was seen on the

hill – has been spotted in the town. I think he's still here, but Brachen isn't interested.'

'I was under the impression that he didn't exist. Well, according to Brachen, at any rate.'

'Oh, he does, and we've reason to believe he's taken a local man captive – violently, too.'

Banks thought for a moment. 'I'm so sorry to hear that, but I have to say, with all the security that surrounds us, I can't see what he could possibly do to threaten the *Great Britain*.'

'Did you believe the paparazzi story?'

'One has to take the advice of those in the know, Carrie. We have some of the UK's best security people on this trip. I'm a mere merchant captain, for all my braid and buttons – a glorified steward, really. Though one that can sail a boat, admittedly.'

'Still, there's something wrong, and Brachen is determined to ignore it.'

Banks looked around. 'There's a hotel on the corner. Why don't we have a quick snifter in there while we wait for my launch to return? My chief steward is more than able to take care of hosting until I arrive, and this is quite an informal gathering.'

'More informal than you might think by the look of some of the people I've just seen heading across to your vessel.'

'Yes, please do tell me. Who on earth is the man with the kilt and the big orange tie?'

'Now, it'll take maybe two drinks to describe him alone.' Symington smiled as they crossed the small roundabout and went into the hotel beyond.

*

Daley looked at the screen carefully. One name on the crew list had caught his attention. As a police officer, certain things raised suspicions, and a change of name was one of those things. He reached across the desk for his phone and called Kinloch Police Office.

'Good evening, sir,' said the familiar voice of Sergeant Shaw. 'How are things, Jim?' he continued in a more muted tone.

'You know the score. It's been a tough few days.'

'We're all thinking of you, sir.'

'Much appreciated, too. With a bit of luck, everything will be okay.' As he said this, Daley felt like crossing his fingers, but resisted the temptation. 'Can you get me details on someone, please? I'm working on something for the chief super – is she about, by the way?'

'No, off on a jolly to the *Great Britain*. It's the local reception there tonight.'

'Is Brian still on board?'

'Yes, but he's on radio silence. Chief Superintendent Symington has a secure line to him that security on the ship can't monitor, sir. He called here earlier, but that was a one-off.'

Daley thought for a moment. 'So all communications from the ship are via their own links?'

'Yes. She got permission and the means to have direct contact with DI Scott from above.'

Daley smiled at the mention of Scott's temporary rank. 'I'll give her a call. Is she on board yet?'

'No idea, sir. There's a bit of a crowd, the last time I heard. I think more people from the town are attending than they initially anticipated.'

'I don't doubt it.' He gave Shaw the name of the crew member who had raised his suspicions. 'Get back to me when you can on that. I know you'll be busy.'

'Just a bit, but I'll get to it ASAP, sir.'

'Any news on the Pearson murder?'

'Not that I know of, sir. I'll ask for you, if you like?'

'No, it's okay. None of my business, I suppose.' Daley ended the call and looked down his contact list to find Symington's number. He dialled again.

'Get ready, Mr Scally. Soon it will be your time to make a move.'

'And what do you want me tae dae?'

'You, my friend, will do what you do best. You'll lie. When the time is right, you will go to the hotel across from the pier. There you will cause a diversion – make a scene.'

'By doing what?'

'I don't know, I'll leave that to you. I know you to be a very imaginative man when it comes to creating an illusion.'

'Ach, you talk in riddles, man.'

Cabdi walked across to Scally, who was still seated on the amp. The big Somali was now carrying the old brass telescope like a cudgel. 'You will do what I tell you to do, or you will die. The bargain is simple.'

'Right. I go and make a fuss, eh?'

'Go and pretend you're drunk. I'm sure that's nothing new to the people you know.'

'I like a drink. So what?'

'You're right. You do much worse things than that.'

'So what will you be doing when all this is going on?' Scally folded his arms and looked away from his captor.

'That is none of your business. Just do as I ask, and do it well, or your fate will be the same as that of the birdwatcher, yes?' Cabdi waved the telescope in front of Scally's eyes.

'You're a bastard,' spat Scally.

'I am a man of faith who believes in the right path. You, on the other hand . . .'

'Right, right, I'll do it.'

'Oh, you will, Mr Scally, you will.'

Symington was just taking her first sip of gin and tonic when her phone rang. She removed the mobile from her bag and, without looking, rejected the call.

'Quite right, Carrie. Switch the bloody thing off, if you want my advice. I do it all the time, otherwise I'd spend half my life in some place or other across the globe answering calls from head office in London.'

'I know exactly what you mean.' As she placed the mobile back in her bag, Symington turned the sound off on the device, but left it on vibrate. 'So, how's this trip been? I mean with the passenger list you have, it must be some responsibility?'

'Oh yes, but that's something one gets used to in this job. Though I must admit, our current guests are somewhat out of the ordinary.' Banks took a sip of his malt whisky.

Symington studied his face. Certainly in his fifties, but he'd looked after himself. He was tall, broadly built, but with no sign of middle-age spread. His uniform was well cut and fitted to a frame of which a much younger man would have been proud. His hair was still thick, grey at the sides with threads of silver through a colour that would once have been red or auburn, but had faded with the years; something she'd noticed before in people with that hair colouring.

'Are you married?' asked Banks, putting down his glass.

'No. I used to blame my job, but somehow I don't think I'm the marrying kind.'

'Oh, that's a shame. You can't beat a family. It's security – peace of mind. We all grow old, Carrie. I know that must seem like a long way off to you now, but the years fly in, trust me. There comes a moment when hearth, home and family become the most important things in your life.' His face was serious, showing none of the forced charm she reckoned must be part of his job.

'Where are they? Your family, I mean?'

'In deepest Buckinghamshire.' The smile returned. 'My wife's a pillar of the community. We live in a small village, you see. The kids are away at school – not my choice, but there you are.'

'Public school?'

'Yes. Oh, nothing fancy like Eton or Harrow, but they're growing up to be proper little Englishmen, nevertheless.'

'And you're not happy about that?'

Banks's face was now hard to read. 'Delighted! I mean, where I came from you worked on the fishing boats or you were poor. With the state of the fishing now, everyone's poor.'

'So, life was tough in the northeast of Scotland?'

'It was, but let's not waste our few moments of peace and quiet discussing my ancient history. You're from Yorkshire, if I'm not much mistaken?'

'Yes, North Yorkshire.'

'The best bit.'

'A small village near a market town – though I didn't have the luxury of a private education.'

'I'm not sure it's a luxury, just a way of turning out men

and women who come to think they are superior to the rest of the country in every way. My wife – though I love her dearly – is an inveterate snob. Nothing would do but our children being hived off. To be honest, I'd have liked them to go to the local school so that I could spend more time with them when I'm at home.'

'So you don't see them as much as you'd like?'

'No, not really.' He took another drink. 'Oh, we do the normal things – well, normal for my wife's world. Skiing in February, a little villa in Tuscany for a couple of weeks in the summer . . .'

'But still not enough time?'

He looked at her with what she perceived to be a great sadness in his eyes. 'No, not really. In fact, I feel as though they're strangers to me, sometimes. My work, by its very nature, takes me away so much of the time that the years have slipped away so quickly that I feel I hardly know them.'

'Different when you were young, then?'

'Oh, yes, very much so.' The smile again, but behind it his eyes were still sad.

'Life's never what you expect, Magnus. I've learned that much for sure.'

'That, Carrie, is undoubtedly true.' He looked at his watch. 'We have plenty of time for another swift one before my launch gets back. Same again?'

'Yes, please.' Symington nodded her head as her companion left for the bar. She was by no means as regular a drinker as she had once been, and already the soothing notes of the gin were having the desired effect. The murder of Cameron Pearson was still preying on her mind, though, as was the situation with Scally and the mystery drone man. She was sure that everything must tie up somehow, but she couldn't make the connection. She was thankful that once this night was over the *Great Britain* would be sailing for another port and she could get back to some sort of normality, albeit a normality perhaps without Jim Daley. She tried not to think of that.

The group containing Hamish and Annie was taken through the ship towards the ballroom, located almost at the centre of the vessel. White-coated stewards hurried to and fro, and the distant sound of a string quintet could be heard entertaining those already at the party.

'Noo this is how you dae a function,' said Hamish, making sure his tie was straight. 'No pished auld accordionist here.'

'I told you, he was the only man I could get at short notice,' said Annie.

'You'd have been better served wae me on the mouth organ.'

'Aye, fun for a' the family. You'd have fair got the party going, I'm sure.' She looked doubtfully at the kilted man beside her. 'I hope you've brought it wae you. I mean, anyone can get scunnered o' classical music. I'm sure there'll be a procession o' folk jeest fair demanding you get up and gie us a few tunes tae get the party off wae a bang.'

'Dammit! I left the bloody thing at hame. I could have stuck it doon my sporran, tae.'

'I was joking!'

'Well, you might change your mind when they start up wae one o' they dirges – Beethoven or the like. I've got tae say thon classical music fair sends me tae sleep. Give me the skirl o' the pipes any day.'

'If you fall asleep that can only be a bonus,' said Annie.

They were ushered into the ballroom, where a majestic chandelier hung down from a high ceiling. The space was huge, with tables and chairs set on a raised gallery round the dance floor. A few couples were already waltzing to the quintet playing on a small stage at the far end of the floor.

'Damn me, you widna think you were on a ship at a',' said Hamish, open-mouthed.

'No, it's grand, right enough,' replied Annie. 'I shouldna wonder if the duke and duchess come in at any moment.'

'Aye, they'll likely get the green light tae come doon now you're here,' Hamish said, removing the pipe from his sporran.

'No smoking, I'm afraid, sir,' said a steward, staring beyond Hamish's pipe to his tie.

'I'll no' be smoking, son, jeest having a sook.'

'No vaping either, I'm afraid. Though there is a dedicated place on deck should you require it, sir.' The man shifted his gaze from Hamish's tie and took the tray of drinks he was carrying to a table beyond them.

'This bloody vaping thing again. Naebody will explain whoot the hell it is.' Hamish gave Annie a bewildered look.

'It'd take too long tae explain. Jeest you do whoot you always do an' take a sook at your pipe. Mind, don't get drunk and forget you're in a no-smoking zone.'

'See you, you're a right smart-arsed . . .'

'This way, sir, madam.' Before Hamish could finish what he was going to say they were shown to a table.

53

Acting Detective Inspector Brian Scott was perched on the end of the king-size bed in his cabin as Ella knelt before him with a stick of concealer, applying it to her husband's face.

'I feel like a right tit,' said Scott.

'Don't you move. This is a delicate task. Now the blood's away and I've put some concealer on your mush, you can hardly see the bruises.'

'But I've tae head doon tae this affair wae make-up on! Have you any idea how that feels for a man?'

'Och, away, men wear make-up a' the time noo.'

'No' where I come fae, they don't.'

'We're in the twenty-first century, no' the eighteenth, Brian. Anything goes, these days. And anyhow, no one will notice a thing under the lights in the ballroom. I'm mair worried you come up against that bruiser O'Rourke again.'

'I was playing a part, Ella. How many times? I'm mair than a match for him, given an even playing field. I had tae convince him I was drunk, and jeest got the wrong room. Aye, and find oot what he was at, tae. He'll no' gie us any bother.'

'It didnae look like that when you were lying on the floor near unconscious.'

'I fell awkwardly, that's all. He buggered off then – most probably regretting the whole episode.'

'So, what have we to do tonight?' Her expression turned serious. 'Don't go near thon sheik again, neithers. I'm surprised that Symington didnae whip you off here and boot you back doon tae constable after that carry-on. I mean, "you'll need tae pitch your tent somewhere else". I've never heard the like.'

'Well, what dae I know aboot Arabs, save what I read in the comics when I was a boy?'

'I don't understand why they chose you to go undercover.'

'I've done mair o' that than you think.'

She leaned back, admiring her work. 'There, hardly a mark, and not a soul will know you've got a wee bit o' make-up on.'

'Gie me that hand mirror oot your bag.'

Ella reached into the depths of her handbag and produced the mirror. 'See for yourself, man.'

'Fuck, I look like thon Boy George. I cannae go oot in public like this!'

'Boy George indeed. He's a good-looking man. You're nothing like him.'

'If my faither was alive, he'd gie me a good hiding if he saw me like this.'

'If your faither was still alive he'd be doon the pub as usual, no' giving two monkeys what you looked like.' She licked her finger and removed a smear of concealer from his eyebrow.

'That's disgusting!' said Scott, screwing up his face. 'Keep the contents o' your mooth tae yourself. I'm no' wanting them spread across my face.'

'How times change.' She winked at him.

'We're past a' that stuff, noo.'

'Speak for yourself. Right, get your jacket on and we'll go and *observe*. Though what, I do not know.'

'See, that's how you'd never make a good polis. You've got tae be ready tae handle any situation. I've had my fair share o' surprises in this job, let me tell you.'

'So have your bosses.'

'Huh. I faced it all wae candour and bravery, I'll have you know.'

'Like the time when you just joined up and that poor taxi driver stopped you in Hope Street because the lassie was having a baby in the back o' the cab?'

'I was young then.'

'Lost your dinner, if I remember.'

'Jimmy was sick a' o'er a tramp!'

'That's excusable. I mean, the stench o' some o' they poor folk.'

'Oh aye, there's always an excuse for Jimmy. You've always had a right soft spot for him – going right back tae the start.'

'I've always liked the man – and so have you!'

'You'll be oot licking his face before long. Here, is that how you've always hated Liz, eh?'

'Aye.' Ella hung her head. 'You've the right o' it after a' these years, too. Here's me been hankering after big Jim Daley and you never noticed. Some detective you are.'

Scott looked momentarily stunned.

'You stupid bastard. I've always loved you – though only the good Lord knows why.'

'You think I was bothered? I was just aboot tae get up and jump aboot for joy.'

'Well, make sure you don't smudge your make-up.'

He smiled at her. 'You're a right bitch, Ella Scott.'

'And you're a hopeless bugger.' She returned the smile. 'C'mon, you observe while I get a glass o' something sparkling.'

The van carrying the team of technicians was about thirty miles out of Kinloch when the driver cursed. 'What the bloody hell is this?' he said, slowing the minibus to a halt. 'Can I help you, officer?'

'We'd like a look round your vehicle, sir – just a routine security check,' said the policeman in the hi-vis jacket.

'Listen, son, we're the team that's just fixed the electrics on the *Great Britain*. I suppose this roadblock is extra safety checks for the vessel, right?'

'I'm not permitted to say anything about that, sir. If you pull in at the side of the road there, we'd like to take a quick look. Won't take more than a few minutes, then you'll be back on your way.'

The driver turned to his passengers. 'You all heard that, lads. Can't be helped. We'll soon be back on the road, and I'll get you boys to Glasgow airport in plenty time.'

As the minibus moved slowly towards the verge, the man at the back picked up the canvas bag from under his seat, cradling it on his lap. 'I'll nip out the back doors,' he said to the driver.

'Yeah, okay, mate. It'll save you having to get past this lot. C'mon, lads. The quicker we get this shit done, the quicker we can be on our way.' He waited as the work party exited the minibus and watched in his rear-view mirror as the man who had been seated next to them exited the vehicle.

Two policemen gathered everyone at the front of the minibus, while another with an excited spaniel on a lead entered the vehicle.

'Here, what's this all about? I hope that bloody dog doesn't piss all over my bus!' The driver folded his arms and shot the policeman beside him a dirty look.

'As I said, sir, it's a spot check. You guys just drew the short straw. Right, is that everybody?'

The driver looked along the line. 'Yeah, that's us. Eh, no, wait.' No sooner had the words left his mouth than the dog in the van began to bark.

In the fading light, a figure was making its way down through the thick bracken towards the rocky beach that bordered the sea.

'What the fuck is this all about?' said one of the men, looking bewildered.

The officer with the dog leaned his head out of the van. 'Quick, the dog's picked up a trace on the back seat.' In seconds, two constables were wading through the high bracken in pursuit of the man who had just disappeared from view onto the beach below.

The minibus driver scratched his cheek and looked at his remaining passengers. 'Something tells me we might not make that flight, lads.'

The Kinloch party were together in the gallery overlooking the ballroom on the *Great Britain*. Hamish was screwing his face up at the cocktail he'd just been handed, while Annie was deep in conversation with Charlie Murray. As more of the ship's exalted guests entered the ballroom, Hamish spotted two familiar faces.

'Brian, Ella, we're o'er here!' he called as Scott and his wife entered the room.

'Shit,' said Scott. 'This'll no' do my cover any good. I'd

better get o'er there and shut Hamish up. Come on, Ella, don't dawdle.'

'Steady on, man. I cannae go at a gallop wae these heels on. The last time I'd heels was at oor Betty's wedding.'

Scott raised his eyes and made a beeline for the Kinloch party. 'Hamish, Annie, Charlie, how are you all, eh?'

Charlie Murray was about to speak when Hamish interrupted him.

'Can I ask you a personal question, Brian?'

'Eh?' said Scott.

'I see you've taken tae wearing the make-up.'

Scott glared at his wife, who'd just hobbled up to the table. 'Noo, I want you tae listen. I'm undercover, so jeest pretend yous don't know me and Ella, okay?'

'Man, if that's a disguise, you're no' on the right track at all, Brian. You look like that pop star I mind fae ages ago.'

'Boy George,' said Annie. 'Aye, you're the spit o' him right enough, Brian. Are they shoes murder, Ella?'

'Aye, and I've only come doon fae the cabin. I think I'll need tae slip them off once we're at oor table. We're o'er there, near the captain, wherever he is.'

'Right, yous don't know me, or Ella. Have you got that?' Scott stared at Hamish. 'Where on earth did you get that tie?'

'Full o' the questions, eh? I'll tell you aboot my tie when you tell me why you're sneaking aboot made up like a Christmas tree, Brian Scott.'

'Later. We need tae get a move on. Hurry up, Ella!'

'Jeest take one o' they shoes off an' clonk the bastard o'er the heid wae it, Ella.'

'Don't tempt me, Annie,' Ella called back as she was hurried away by her husband.

'What's that all about?' said Murray, draining his cocktail.

'I don't know how you can drink that bilge,' said Hamish. 'Reminds me o' the beer they serve at the Douglas Arms – pish!'

'Whoot dae you think's up wae Brian, Hamish?' said Annie, leaning in conspiratorially to the old fisherman, better to be heard above the quintet.

'Och, it's strange whoot promotion can dae to a body. I mind when Erchie Lang got made up tae skipper o' the *Girl Nancy*. Got tae be he wouldna speak tae anyone but other skippers. Damn me, he even applied for membership o' the Gentlemen's Club.'

'Did he get in?'

'Nah. You know fine that's a place populated by doctors, teachers, businessmen and the like. And I have tae say, I never met a fisherman that smelt so much like the creatures he was after in my life. Even in a suit he smelt like a full net.'

Annie looked sadly across the dance floor and up to the gallery where Scott and Ella were now in deep conversation with a striking woman whose diamond necklace sparkled under the lights. 'Dae you think Brian's turning intae a snob, Hamish?'

'Och, I widna be surprised at all. There's one thing for sure. He'd make a better snob than he does an undercover polis, that's a fact.'

Three decks below the ballroom, in various places amongst the engines, fuel tanks and electrical panels, five sets of numbers blinked red in the darkness.

54

'Now is the time, Mr Scally. Do as I tell you and nothing will happen. Do not, and things will end very suddenly for you. I hope you understand?' Cabdi glared through the gloom of the old net shed.

Scally remained on the amp, his face a picture of misery.

'I will give you three seconds to muster your courage. Maybe we should have brought some whisky for you, no?'

'What are you going tae be at when I create this *diversion?*'

'That's none of your business. Just do what you have been asked, and count yourself lucky you are not the one lying dead in the sea. That was the fate of your friend, yes? Everyone in the bar where I met you was talking about it.'

'Right, I'm going!' With a defiant look Scally got stiffly to his feet. 'How dae you know I'll not just go o'er there and grass you up, eh?'

'Because you are a coward, the lowest kind of man – barely a man at all.' Cabdi flashed the smile that always looked more threatening than appealing.

The older man sighed and walked to the door. He unlocked it and pulled it open, wood scraping along the grimy concrete floor.

'I will be watching you. You have fifteen minutes, then I follow. Do your job, Mr Scally, and do it well.'

Scally closed the door behind him and stood for a few moments taking in the sounds and smells that had been familiar to him since childhood. Fishing boats bobbed at the old quay across the harbour, while the line of people awaiting transport to the *Great Britain* had dwindled to only a couple of dozen. Still, he could hear their excited chatter as they waited for the launch that would take them to the big party on the cruise ship.

Overhead he watched a gull hover, wings outstretched on the light breeze. The bird was different from the gulls he normally saw in and around Kinloch. It was smaller, shorter-necked, with distinctive markings. 'Bugger me,' said Scally to himself. 'The American gull.'

The irony of it all was not lost on him as he took his first steps up the new quay and onto the promenade. He eyed the hotel in front of him. He'd enjoyed weddings, retirement parties, family dinners – various nights out – in that very place. Now – well, now he wasn't sure if, once he had entered the building, he would ever leave.

He thought of Cameron Pearson. First, the face of the boy he'd tormented at school came to mind, then the youth with whom he'd gone for a few pints while chasing girls to the music of Bill Haley, Elvis Presley and countless others. The small coffee bar that had been their haunt was now long gone, as was the large cinema, built during the war to entertain locals and the thousands of servicemen and women who made Kinloch their temporary home. So much gone now – a different town in so many ways.

Then he recalled the last time he'd seen Cameron Pearson's

face, and everything seemed to fade away. All he could hear was the sound of his own footsteps, the rasp of his breath and the pounding of his heart as he neared the King's Hotel.

Daley picked up his mobile and called Symington again – still no reply. He decided that she either had her phone on silent, or had left it in the County Hotel. He supposed that what he'd discovered wasn't that urgent, but certainly worth looking into. All the same, his instincts told him that he had to do something.

Reckoning that his boss must be on the *Great Britain* by now, he dialled the switchboard number Sergeant Shaw had given him. The call was answered quickly. Daley announced himself as the local chief inspector and who he was looking for. He was left to listen to the patriotic hold music while the operator tried to locate Symington. As the last bars of 'Land Of Hope And Glory' faded, the man on the other end of the line came back.

'DCI Daley, I'm afraid Chief Superintendent Symington hasn't yet arrived on board. She's expected soon, though. Will I have her call you when she gets here?'

'Yes, please,' replied Daley. He considered asking for Brachen, but reasoned that the arrogant Royal Navy Commander would probably scoff at his findings. 'Can I speak with Captain Banks?'

This time the reply was instant. 'Again, sorry, sir. Captain Banks is meeting guests on the quayside before coming back to the ship.'

'Right, I see. Don't worry, but please tell the Chief Superintendent that I'm on my mobile if she'd like to ring me when she gets a chance.'

Daley clicked off the call and thought for a few moments. If Symington wasn't yet on the *Great Britain* she might just be still ashore, not on a launch. He looked down at James junior who was playing with a toy car on the rug by the television. 'Right, James, we're going for a wee run in the car, son.'

'Yay!' said the little boy as Daley fetched his coat from the hall. 'Where are we going, Daddy?'

'I just need a quick word with someone. Then we can go to the shop and maybe get an ice cream.' He smiled at his son, who was shrugging on his jacket. For a second, he reminded Daley of his own father, who'd put on his jackets in exactly the same way. Only when he donned his own coat did he realise that he too shrugged himself into the garment in exactly that fashion. The thought, this insignificant connection, almost made him cry. But he smiled to himself as he hauled James into his arms. He could have raised the alarm, sent a blue light to find Symington, but he knew how sensitive anything to do with the *Great Britain* was, and what he had found couldn't really condemn in any specific way. It just wasn't what he'd expected, and that, for some reason, had raised his hackles. To be honest, Daley wasn't even sure that his mind was working properly. Maybe the drama of the last few days had affected him more than he'd thought.

But, not being a man comfortable with sitting around waiting for things to happen, he made his way down the front steps of his house, his son in his arms. He strapped the child into the back seat of the SUV, got behind the wheel, and was soon heading down the steep hill and into Kinloch in search of Carrie Symington.

*

Scally crossed the road at the roundabout, doing his best to ignore the last guests awaiting transport to the *Great Britain* as they threaded their way towards the pontoons.

He hesitated under the canopy of the King's Hotel before entering. There were two bars in the establishment, a large bar where guests could eat as well as drink, and a smaller, more intimate cocktail lounge. He took a deep breath and opened the door to the bar.

The place was as he expected, bustling with customers, locals anxious to witness and pass comment on the members of their community who'd been lucky enough to bag a golden ticket to the reception aboard the cruise ship. He made his way into the large bar first, searching the long room for the person Cabdi had described.

'Aye, free drink an' food a' night, and a chance tae shake hands wae a duke. Canna be bad,' he heard a woman at the nearest table comment to her friends.

'I don't give a damn aboot any duke,' one of them replied. 'I'd be off tae bag myself a billionaire. I saw a few crackers in the toon earlier. Imagine a life wae money like that.'

Scally couldn't see who he was looking for, and as he left the bar he ignored the scowl of the barman busy polishing glasses. He crossed the lobby and entered the lounge. It boasted spectacular views across the loch to the hills beyond, and for a moment he stared out at them, deep in thought.

'Can I help you?' asked a woman he didn't know behind the bar. She spoke with a foreign accent, and Scally reckoned her to be one of the Polish community who had arrived in the town over the last few years. Quickly, he scanned the room, and sure enough, sitting at a table near the window was the person Cabdi had told him to seek out.

'Aye, a whisky, please – a large one.'

'What kind?'

'The cheapest,' said Scally, searching in his pocket. In the net shed and during his walk along the promenade he'd had the chance to think what he might do to cause a distraction. He looked at his watch – he had more than ten minutes before Cabdi was likely to do whatever it was he'd planned. He paid for the drink and knocked it back in two gulps. 'I'll take another o' the same, please.'

As the barmaid put the glass to the optic, he knew it was time to carry out the tall man's orders. Time for one last dram, he thought.

55

The two police officers looked left and right along the beach, but there was no sign of their quarry. Across the Atlantic, a purple hue was forming over the isle of Islay, the setting sun turning the sea into molten gold.

'We've lost him, sir, over,' said one of the constables into his radio.

'Then bloody well find him!' shouted the inspector, his voice distorted over the Airwave radio. 'And be careful, McCann. He may be armed for all we know. If he's had explosives he could have a weapon.'

Inspector Mauchlin was twenty miles further up the road from Kinloch. His team's job was to check vehicles, to look for anything worrying or suspicious travelling to or from the town at the end of the peninsula – and they'd found it.

He took his phone from his pocket and called his superior. 'Sir, one of the technicians working on the *Great Britain* has left traces of explosives in the van he was travelling back in. He's made off, but we have two men after him.'

'This man was working on the *Great Britain*, you say?' Assistant Chief Constable Brown's face was etched with concern.

'Yes, we believe so, sir. I'm not at the locus, but my men are questioning his workmates now. They've all just left the vessel after correcting an electrical problem, apparently.'

'Right, leave it with me. Good work, Mauchlin. Make sure your men take care, and await my instructions.' ACC Brown clicked off the call and pressed another button. 'Get me Chief Superintendent Symington in Kinloch – and quickly!'

Daley was driving round the loch as his son hummed an unidentifiable tune in the back seat. He saw the small straggle of passengers still waiting on the quay and pulled up alongside them.

'You wait there, James. Daddy's just going to have a quick word with someone.' He left the car, locking it as he went. A few yards away, a steward was ushering guests down to the pontoons as a motor launch on the loch slowed ready to come alongside. Daley flashed his warrant card.

'Yes, sir, what's the problem?'

'I wonder, has Chief Superintendent Symington been taken over to the ship yet?'

'No, I don't think so, sir.' The steward consulted the notes pinned to his clipboard. 'No, definitely not, sir. I haven't checked her off. I think I saw her and Captain Banks going into the hotel across the road a while ago. I suppose they're still there.'

Daley thought for a few moments. 'Can you do me a favour? My son's in the car there, and I'd be grateful if you could keep an eye on him while I nip into the hotel. I just need to have a word with the Chief Superintendent.'

'Certainly, sir. That won't be a problem.'

*

'I canna say I'm overly entertained,' said Hamish as he looked at the old watch on his wrist. 'Thon dirges are fair putting me in the glums. I canna shake them, for some reason.'

'We're in esteemed company, Hamish. You canna expect them tae be playing Jimmy Shand,' Annie told him. 'Anyway, how come you're so glum? You were fine at the pier.'

'Och, I don't know. You know fine I'm prone tae a bit o' melancholy noo and again.'

'But something must have brought it on?'

'Ach, I don't know. Don't worry, I'm jeest a havering auld fisherman. A decent dram would set me up better. As far as I'm concerned you can pour these cocktails o'er the side.'

'They're champagne cocktails, Hamish. Likely expensive champagne, tae.'

'Och, I've never been one for champagne, nor any o' they foreign drinks. It's like knocking back lemonade. Potent, mind you – one minute you're shipshape and Bristol fashion, the next you're on your arse, no' knowing jeest where you are. Happened tae me at a wedding once in Tarbert. They were handing oot champagne as if it was water. By half eight I didna know if it was New Year or New York.'

'So you don't like foreign drinks?'

'No' in the slightest. For a start, you never know jeest whoot's in the bloody stuff. They telt me years ago that they French fellas jump up and doon tae tread the juice oot o' the grapes wae their bare feet. Well, I'm here tae tell you, I'm no' keen on finding a Frenchman's bunion in my glass, that's for certain sure.'

'You seemed tae enjoy it fine the last time we had that wine tasting in the County.'

'Aye, well, that was another matter. The drink was free,

and it's a well-known fact that any drink tastes better if you've no' tae reach intae your sporran tae pay for it. Especially in the County!'

Annie eyed him up and down. He'd already spilled something on his tie, which made it look even worse. But she did note that his expression was one rarely to be seen across the face of the man she'd known all her life. He looked down in the dumps, fretful even. 'Here, I'll catch the eye o' one o' they waiters and get you a whisky.'

'Aye, but you're a fine lassie, Annie. It's a wonder tae me how some handsome young man hasn't swept you off your feet long since.'

'I'm sure he will, one day,' she said, looking sadly across at Brian Scott, who was deep in conversation with a tall blond man, his arm round his wife's shoulders.

'Och, maybes you're jeest looking in the wrong direction,' said Hamish. 'Time tae get the compass oot and set another course, I'm thinking.' No sooner had the words come from his mouth than he shivered, dropping the unlit pipe from his hand, and sending it spinning onto the thick carpet below.

'Whoot happened there? You looked like you were having a fit!'

'No, not at all,' said Hamish as he retrieved his pipe from the floor and stuck it back in his mouth, brow furrowed. 'As my dear auld mother used tae say, it was someone walking o'er my grave.'

'Fuck, I better get you some whisky before one o' us cuts our own throat.' Annie caught the eye of a steward, who obligingly made his way to their table.

'It's no' often I'm unhappy at sea, and that's a fact. But for some reason, the night I feel right uneasy.'

'We're in the loch on one o' the biggest ships I've ever seen, man.'

'Aye, so we are, so we are, Annie.'

'Can I get you something?' The steward was hovering.

'Dae you have such a thing as a decent malt whisky?' asked Hamish.

'Yes, we certainly have, sir. What would you like?'

'A good West Coast malt – nane o' that Speyside rubbish, mind. It was us that taught them to make whisky, and I'm no' sure they've got it right yet.'

'Certainly, sir. What about a Springbank, or a Glen Scotia?'

'Now you're talking, son. Man, they still know how tae make whisky in the wee toon. Thank you, either would be perfect.'

Annie hoped that the imminent arrival of one of his favourite whiskies would cheer the old man up. But as soon as the steward left, the worried expression returned to his face.

'Whoot's that thon quintet are murdering noo? I recognise it fae somewhere,' he said.

'It's Mozart,' said Charlie Murray, a dainty sandwich in his paw of a hand. 'His *Requiem*, if I'm no' much mistaken.'

Hamish took another silent draw of his unlit pipe. 'Aye, maybe mair appropriate than you know.'

'Right, will someone pass me the bread knife,' said Annie.

56

Patrick O'Rourke was drunk. He knew that, though for most people it would have been hard to discern. His gaze was still steady and his speech wasn't slurred. Mind you, he thought, I've had a lot of practice.

For a moment he recalled his father staggering around in their cramped front room, shouting at his mother. Her pride and joy were three china horse figurines that took pride of place on top of the black-and-white TV. They were the only hint of something different in an otherwise dowdy, functional room. He could still see his father swiping them to the floor where they smashed against the old grate. One of the ornaments had been a foal, and for some reason the sight of it lying headless on their living-room floor, the mixture of anger and sadness on his mother's face, and his father's slurred expletives had never left him.

He was furious with himself for assaulting the hapless drunk who'd been in his room. It had been stupid and could easily jeopardise what he'd come to do. There had been too many self-immolations in his family, and he didn't want to add to their number. He stared into his glass of Bushmills as the scenes in the quiet cocktail bar played out unnoticed around him. Only when he heard raised voices was he roused from his reminiscing.

'You have had the drink, now you must pay!' The barmaid was shouting at the small elderly man beside the bar who was busy draining his glass. As the woman opened the hatch, no doubt ready to eject this troublesome customer, without warning the old man threw the glass at her. His aim, though, was poor, the glass missing the barmaid by inches. It crashed against a table and shattered, sending two young women screaming from their table.

O'Rourke could feel his temper rising, but remembering the assault on his fellow passenger earlier in the day he forced himself to remain in his seat, though he wanted nothing more than to get up and throw the man who had disturbed his thoughts bodily out into the street.

Just as the unwanted customer started to shout and swear, a large man appeared through the door of the lounge and grabbed the miscreant by the collar of his faded jacket, almost lifting him clean off the floor.

'Phone the police office and tell them that DCI Daley has made an arrest and to send officers, will you?' Daley called to the barmaid as he brandished his warrant card. His heart was thumping in his chest, and he felt unsteady on his feet, but all the same he managed to keep hold of the struggling man, who was still shouting and swearing. As he held the man as tightly as he could, he heard a voice at his side.

'It's okay, Jim. You shouldn't be doing this.' It was Symington. Expertly, she caught one of the old man's arms and twisting his thumb sent him howling in pain to the floor, where she straddled the prone figure, making sure his movement was restricted, but ensuring he could still breathe. 'Settle down, Mr Scally. Your night out is over.'

Realising that he was beaten, Scally stopped struggling.

'I'm telling yous, this is no' whoot it looks like!' he said.

'And what does it look like, apart from an obnoxious man who's had too much to drink, Mr Scally?' Symington looked up at Daley, who had taken a seat on a stool at the bar. 'You okay, Jim?'

'Fine,' replied Daley, not mentioning that he'd been grateful the bar stool was so close at hand.

'Well done, Chief Superintendent.' The voice belonged to Captain Magnus Banks, who was now standing over the senior police officer and her captive. 'You were certainly paying attention at the self-defence classes – good job. You beat me to it by some distance.' He looked up. 'And good to see you too, DCI Daley. Hope you're feeling better. This is the last thing you needed, I imagine. It's age. Comes to us all, sadly.'

Cabdi had watched Scally's progress along the promenade, and checked his watch to make sure that the old man had the time he'd allotted him to create a diversion. He saw him enter the hotel and waited.

When the agreed time had elapsed, he scraped the net shed door open and left the building, making sure that his cap was pulled low over his eyes. As he took long quick strides towards the hotel, he turned his face to the loch, shoulders hunched in the hope of making his distinctive frame more anonymous.

When he reached the roundabout at the head of the old quay, he hesitated. A procession of cars seemed to come from every direction all of a sudden, making it impossible to cross the road. As casually as he could, he leaned against the black railings of the promenade, head down, staring into the oily waters of the loch and waiting for an opportunity to proceed towards the hotel. Horns sounded and people called out of cars as the last straggle of guests made their way onto the motor launch ready to be taken to the *Great Britain*. He could feel the pistol in the waistband of his trousers as he stared at a graceful swan gliding across the water in his direction, no doubt in the expectation of being fed bread by anyone lingering on the promenade.

Still staring at the wash of the waves against the pier and a set of old stone steps leading down to the water at his side, he flinched as he heard another distinctive sound: a police siren.

Having to make a split-second decision, he realised he had little choice. He made his way quickly down the steps, almost slipping on the slick, seaweed-covered stone. At least he was out of sight, he thought. Silently, though, he cursed Scally and considered the possibility that the sly old man had betrayed him, however unlikely that seemed. He knew the man was a coward, but perhaps he'd underestimated his deviousness.

He had to think. He was so close – but he had to think.

'See your friend keeps staring across at us,' said Ella Scott.

'What friend?'

'Annie, who else? I swear that woman's besotted wae you, Brian.'

'Och, you're havering, as usual. You thought Janet Donegan doon the close fae us when we first got hitched was madly in love with me. I was sick o' hearing aboot it.'

'I'm no' so sure. Mind how when it was sunny and we was doon in the drying green she used tae appear wae her baby doll nightie on tae hang oot the washing?'

'I've seen you hanging oot the washing in your dressing gown, dear – or that onesie thing you wear, the one wae the tail and ears.'

'That's first thing in the morning, Brian. She was parading aboot at three in the afternoon! See if I didnae know you better, I'd have sworn you were at it.'

'Mind you, she had a nice big red setter.'

'Eh?' Ella suddenly looked furious. 'A what?'

'A dug – an Irish setter. Are you going deaf, or what?'

'Och, I thought you said something else.'

'Filthy mind, that's your problem. Was her husband no' a sailor?'

'Aye, he was. Mind you, he spent mair time on than off when he was at hame, that's for sure. You could hear them right up the close stairs.'

Scott shook his head. 'This is just typical of you. Here we are in the lap o' luxury, and all you can talk aboot is something that didnae happen thirty years ago.'

Ella looked around, seemingly unimpressed by her husband's reasoning. 'Still, it's nice tae see her and Hamish here. They must be sick o' the sight o' the County Hotel. And don't look now, but he's coming o'er, Brian.'

'Bugger. I telt him that I was busy.'

'Och, I widnae worry, It's no' as though he'll attract much attention wae that tie. And his sporran's near at his ankles.'

Hamish approached the Scotts' table like a crab, side on, looking in the other direction.

'Can I have a word with you, Brian?'

'What is it, Hamish? I telt you, I'm working undercover,' replied Scott, his smile not matching his tone.

'Jeest thought I'd tell you something, that's all.'

'I know, you've sacked your tailor.'

'I've got a terrible feeling in the pit of my stomach. In fact, I've no' felt like this since my dear auld mother died.'

'Ach, we all get down sometimes, Hamish. Get a dram or two down you, you'll be fine.' Though Scott's words were of encouragement, he could see the old man was troubled.

'Aye, you're likely right, Brian. But I'm damned. This second sight is a curse.'

'You and your second sight. Get o'er there and keep Annie company. She's looking right lonely.'

'I'm right fond o' you, Brian – your wife, tae. And as far as Annie's concerned, well, she's like a daughter tae me . . . Don't be telling her that, mind.'

'That's very kind of you, Hamish. But I've got tae get back to work, okay?'

'Aye. Message received and understood. But mind, it's no' the only message I'm getting right noo. That's all I'll say.' Hamish sidled off the way he came, his tie and the low trim of his sporran attracting much comment.

'What's up wae Hamish?' asked Ella.

'He's got a bad feeling.'

'About what?'

'He doesnae know.'

'If that's the case, why are you looking worried?'

'He's got the sight, Ella.'

'Dae you no' mean that he *is* a sight?'

'I'm serious, woman. That auld man knows stuff. I'm telling you.'

57

In a private dining room, Sir Edward Chapelhouse, Commander Brachen and Annabelle Tansie of the Security Service sat at one end of a long mahogany table, normally used for the captain and his officers. In front of them sat a conference phone, looking more like a small alien spacecraft in the middle of the table.

'I understand your concern, ACC Brown, I do,' said Chapelhouse. 'But my security team here tell me that there is no way that explosives could have made their way onto this vessel. Everything has been checked rigorously – including the maintenance team.' He looked up at Brachen and Tansie. 'I'm right in saying this, yes?'

Both nodded. 'Yes, sir,' they said almost in unison.

'So why then did this man make a run for it?' said Brown, his voice loud through the device on the table.

'Who knows? I mean, how clever are these dogs of yours? He's been working here working amidst all sorts of fuel and electronic equipment. And remember there are armed Marines on board – his bag could well have come into contact with one of them, picked up some residue that your bloody animal has sniffed out. Must say, though, it would have been a damned sight easier if you hadn't let the bugger go.'

'We've stepped up the search, sir.'

'I should think so.' Sir Edward took a breath. 'You must understand, ACC Brown, that on board this ship are some of *the* most influential people in the business world. They may not be household names, but collectively they have the potential to make this country money – a great deal of it. And we all know how much that's required. We've already had this thing with the press and that bloody drone, now a dog smelling a trace of explosives. I think people are getting carried away. I will not have this operation – or my guests – unsettled in this way. By all means continue the search for this man, but I'm sure there will be a sensible explanation as to how this has came about.' Sir Edward cocked his head, awaiting a reply from ACC Brown. 'Are you there, man?'

'The blasted idiot's put the phone down on you, Sir Edward,' said Brachen.

'Bloody cheek! Typical of the police force these days – above their station to a man, if you ask me. Get them to reconnect him, will you, Commander. And tell the bugger I'm not happy with him!' He stood. 'Meanwhile, I need a drink.' He stormed out of the room, leaving Brachen and Tansie at the long table.

'What do you think, Annabelle?'

'I think we need to find out more about this maintenance guy, and quickly.' She took a phone from her pocket and typed quickly with both thumbs. As she stared at the screen, a puzzled look crossed her face.

'Something wrong?' asked Brachen.

'You know how the call with ACC Brown ended abruptly? Well, now I have no wi-fi.'

Brachen sighed. 'It'll be some problem at comms. I'll get a

handle on it. Come with me and we'll sort it out. I'd like to speak to this ACC Brown without Sir Edward peering over my shoulder.'

'Good idea.'

The pair left the dining room and headed for the ship's communication office.

Officers arrived and took charge of Peter Scally. He was pliant now; quiet, not protesting in any way. As he was pulled to his feet by one of the uniformed constables he looked at Symington.

'Can I speak tae you?' He looked about. 'In private, like?'

'Anything you have to say you can tell the officers here. Had I not had my back to you, I'd have arrested you on the spot when you came in. Where's your friend?'

'The big fella, you mean? He's no friend o' mine.'

'You look a bit knocked about, Mr Scally. Was that him?'

'I canna say.'

'Why?

'Because he'll kill me, that's why.' Without warning, the old man broke down. 'He's got something planned – for all of yous, I'm sure. He's got a gun, tae.'

'Come with me, Mr Scally. Excuse me, Captain Banks.'

'Of course,' he replied, a concerned look on his face.

Daley followed her. 'Ma'am, my son is in the car across the road. I'll check on him and come back.'

'No need, Jim. I can handle this. You're off sick, remember?'

'I need to have a word with you.'

'Urgent?'

'No, just niggling at me. Speak to Scally first, then we can talk, okay?'

'Sure. I want to have a word with him and get to the bottom of this second drone man. If you hadn't spotted him we wouldn't have known anything about him.'

They parted, Daley heading back to his car while Symington ducked into the back of the van along with a constable handcuffed to Peter Scally.

'Can't work it out,' said Petty Officer Hodges. 'Everything just cut out about ten minutes ago – phone, wi-fi, the lot.'

'And you have no idea why?' said Brachen impatiently.

'No, sir. My men are on it now, but everything seems to be in order – certainly at this end.'

'So we've no way of communicating off the ship?'

'Radio comms are still working, but that's all.'

'Where's bloody Banks?'

'Still on shore, sir. Meeting local guests at the pier, I believe.'

'Keep working on this, Hodges. I want everything up and running again as quickly as possible.'

'Of course, now our system is jammed anyone can get a signal on their mobiles and so on. They just have to hook up to the local 4G network, sir.'

'But we'd jammed that for security purposes.'

'Yes, sir. But that's gone down with everything else.'

Tansie was looking at her phone. 'Yes, he's right. I've got some signal from the local mobile network. It's not good, but it's there.'

'What should we do?'

'I think we should take a RIB across to the pier and get Banks on board. I'm uneasy. At this point I think I should take charge. It's part of the protocol. Sir Edward will just have to lap it up.'

'Good, do that. I'm still not convinced about all this, but we'd better make sure.'

'Systems do go down, sir. And there's been a lot of electrical work done. Wouldn't surprise me if one of the civilian technicians has caused this.'

'You go get Banks, Annabelle. I'll get some bodies over from the frigate. We'll have a poke around. What do you think?'

'Too many things going on, to be honest. But everyone and everything has been so closely vetted. We'll just keep Sir Edward out of the loop for the time being.'

'Agreed. I'll keep in touch by radio, Annabelle.'

She nodded her head and hurried off.

'Hodges, get me the frigate on the radio.'

Daley wandered back across the road towards his car. There were now no more than twenty guests standing patiently on the pontoons waiting to be taken to the *Great Britain*.

'Your lad's fine,' called the steward with the clipboard. 'I've been checking on him.'

'Much obliged,' said Daley. 'Everything going smoothly?'

'Yeah, just fine. Be perfect if I could find Captain Banks, mind you.'

'He's across in the hotel. There's been a bit of a rumpus, I'm afraid.'

'Yes, I saw the police van arrive. Not Captain Banks, I hope?'

'No, you're okay there,' said Daley, getting into his car. 'I'll go and get him. The last launch is about to arrive.'

Daley smiled at him, then closed the door. 'You okay, son?'

'Why did the police van come, Daddy?'

'Oh, just some silly man. Nothing for you to worry about.'

'You said we'd go for ice cream.'

'Yes, and that's exactly what we're going to do.'

He started the engine and pulled out, heading towards the roundabout. He noticed a group of boys on bikes shouting over the railings on the promenade. As he drove towards them, he could see how animated they were.

James junior chuckled in the back seat. 'Ha, we're going round again!' he shouted, and clapped as Daley swung the car in a full circle round the roundabout.

'Yeah, it's fun, James. Daddy just wants to have a look at something, son. Hold on.'

He parked just beyond where the boys were leaning over the railings and got back out of the car.

58

The ballroom was filling up. Excited locals waved at their fellow townsfolk as they were shown into to the opulent space, heads craning here and there, taking in the room and those in it. Many were gazing up at the glittering chandelier.

Annie observed them with a critical eye as they arrived. 'Well, I didna think Jessie Duncan would be getting an invitation tae something like this.'

'She's got an OBE,' said Hamish.

'Aye, for cleaning up beaches. It's hardly climbing Everest, is it?'

'Does a right fine job, oot in all weather, so she is. That beach at Firdale is immaculate, and so is the òne at Machrie.'

'She doesna dae it by herself, Hamish. There's a whole squad o' folk helping her.'

'Aye, but she was the woman who started it all.'

'And what about that carry-on wae Jimmy Kirkhope?'

'Thon was jeest a misunderstanding.'

'Aye,' said Annie. 'And I'm a polar bear. I saw one o' they photographs and there was no misunderstanding whoot I saw, and that's for sure.'

'They can dae a' sorts wae pictures noo. That great-niece o' mine shows me photos on her phone thing. Her wae rabbit ears and big teeth, the lot. Och, a photo canna be trusted these days, at a'.'

'Trust me, there were nae big teeth nor ears in these pictures, Hamish.'

'Och, you're getting right cynical, Annie. Leave the woman tae enjoy her night.'

'And you're still in the glums, I see.'

'Wae good reason, tae. I canna shake this terrible mood – it's jeest fair overpowering, so it is.'

'You should have stayed home and gied your tie a rest.'

Hamish took another drink of his whisky, desperately hoping that it would make him feel less perturbed.

Unseen by Hamish, Annie, or anyone else aboard the *Great Britain*, the numbers on five devices placed around the ship started to blink, and the message ARMED flashed across their screens.

Magnus Banks had discovered Patrick O'Rourke in a dark corner of the bar. He attempted to make conversation with him, but soon realised that the man was the worse for drink.

'I'd better leave you to your night, Mr O'Rourke. Sometimes it's good to be alone with your thoughts. I know the feeling well. The last launch will be leaving now, but just let us know when you want to come back and I'll get someone to come over and fetch you. Not a problem.'

'I've tried to phone my wife twice – nothing. The line just breaks up.'

Banks considered this.

'Why not send a text? Must be something up with our

communications.' He smiled. 'I'm sure they'll have it fixed quickly. I can give your wife a message, if you like?'

'I'll be back soon enough. Just working through some old memories.'

'Yes,' said Banks. 'We all have a surfeit of those.'

'You ain't kidding, Captain.'

Banks wished him a good evening, gave the barmaid a large tip, and walked out into the fading evening sunlight. He looked across at the *Great Britain* out on the loch. Lights had appeared all over the ship, giving her a festive air. He smiled at her sleek lines and the way the huge craft dominated its surroundings. There was little doubt that she was the smartest vessel he'd ever had the pleasure to command. This made him happy, but the happiness was tinged with great sadness.

Movement on the promenade caught his attention. Suddenly he heard the screams of children and saw the tall figure of Daley standing stock-still, his hands in the air.

As if from nowhere, a figure emerged from the loch onto the promenade. The man was tall and thin, and he was pointing a weapon straight at the big police officer.

'Tell me what happened, Mr Scally. I don't have any more time for this nonsense!'

'I canna. The man is a maniac. He'll find me and he'll kill me!' Scally began to sob convulsively.

'You're drunk, Peter. You need to tell me what he wanted you to do.'

'Jeest like I says. He wanted me tae go tae the hotel and make a fuss, that's all – a diversion, he called it.'

'So, you just did this without question? Why did he want a diversion?'

'We've seen quite a lot of you over the last few days, Mr Scally,' said DS Potts at Symington's side. 'Too much, I think.'

'Listen, I've been through a lot today. That big bastard assaulted me, made me carry on that way at the hotel. It's him you should be after, no' me!' He broke down in tears again. 'I don't know why he wanted tae make a diversion. If you think me and him are in this together, you can think again. Anyway, I've the right to have a solicitor present. I want a doctor, tae.'

Before Symington could reply, the door swung open.

'Ma'am, come with me, please. It's urgent!' said Sergeant Shaw.

Symington hurried out of the room, leaving Potts with Scally. 'What's so urgent, Sergeant?'

'We have a situation on the promenade ma'am. A man with a gun. A tall black man – I think he's the one we've been looking for. Our second drone man.'

Symington swallowed hard. 'Draw weapons, Sergeant Shaw. Get a team organised – now! I'll get onto HQ.'

'Yes, ma'am.' He hesitated. 'There's something else.'

'What?'

'He has DCI Daley, ma'am.'

Daley stared at the tall black man in the red cap. 'I'm Detective Chief Inspector Daley,' he said, mouth dry. 'Whatever you're trying to do, you won't succeed – you'll end up dead. The security surrounding the *Great Britain* is tight, and they won't mess about, trust me.'

'So tight I'm standing here pointing a gun at you,' said Cabdi.

Daley was surprised by the man's perfect English; for some reason, it wasn't what he'd expected. 'You've been lucky so far, but your luck is about to run out.'

'You think?'

'You're stuck in a small town with police, Royal Marines and Security Service personnel everywhere. What do you think you can achieve?'

'You assume that you know why I'm here.' Cabdi edged closer to Daley, the pistol held out in front of him in both hands. 'Who is left in the hotel?'

'I don't know what you mean.'

'It's not a difficult question. You tell me you're a police officer – surely you can answer it?'

Daley shrugged. A few feet away in the car, he could hear James wailing. 'Give this up, sir. I've told you, you don't stand a chance.' Movement over the gunman's shoulder caught Daley's eye, and for a split second he looked in the direction of the pontoons.

Noticing this, Cabdi backed off slightly, arm out and upright palm facing towards Daley as though urging him to stay still. He looked over his shoulder and spotted figures moving across the street from the hotel. 'You haven't told me the truth, Mr Policeman. I think you've known all along who was in there.' He raised the gun to eye level.

59

Brian Scott was surprised to feel the phone vibrate in his pocket. He knew that Symington was the only person who could contact him through the ship's signal screen. He answered the call with a finger in one ear to block out the noise of the quintet and the rabble of voices around him.

'Brian, I need you to find Commander Brachen. Tell him we've a problem onshore and we need his assistance.'

'What kind of problem?'

'One serious enough for you to identify yourself as a police officer. Just tell Brachen we have an armed situation and we need backup. I have to go, Brian.'

Scott was about to ask another question when the line went dead.

'What's up wae you?' asked Ella.

'You stay where you are. I've got tae find this Commander Brachen.'

'Just typical. How many nights oot have I had wae you that have been spoiled by the polis?'

'That's 'cos I am one. Go over and have a word wae Annie and Hamish while I'm away. I shouldnae be long.'

'Great, a date wae Fran and Anna. You know how tae treat a woman, Brian.' She watched her husband hurry off. Hamish caught her eye across the ballroom floor. The old man put his head in his hands and Ella saw Annie move to comfort him. She decided to take her husband's advice and make her way round to their table.

'Whoot's the matter, Hamish?'

'I'm feeing terrible, Annie – jeest terrible.'

'I'm going tae get some medical help. They'll likely have the best doctors in the country on here.'

'Jeest let me be for a whiles, that's a' I'm asking.'

'But you've been awful all night!'

'I know. Och, I'm jeest fair buggered in my heid.'

'Well, we've known that for a while, but I've never seen you like this.'

'Nothing's right, I'm telling you, nothing's right at all.'

Ella arrived at their table. 'What's up with you, Hamish? I saw you across the floor. Is it a headache?'

'He's jeest no' himself, Ella. Been moaning the whole night that something's wrong. I don't know what to dae with him.'

Ella leaned into Annie's ear. 'Dae you no' think it's something tae dae with the drink?' she whispered. 'You've no idea how bad oor Brian got.'

'Aye, I've a fair idea, Ella. But no, he's no' even had that much to drink.'

'Maybe that's the problem.'

'I'm still here, you know,' said Hamish, drying his eyes on his orange kipper tie. 'Tell me, Ella, where's your Brian away off tae at such a rate?'

'He got a phone call fae the office, Hamish. But he does that all the time. Weddings, funerals, parties – you name it, I'm left on my ain while he rushes off tae the latest emergency.'

384

Hamish turned to Annie. 'See, I telt you something wisna right.'

Cabdi stared into Daley's eyes, the gun still levelled at the detective. 'The child in the car, he's yours, yes?'

'No. I don't know who he is.'

'I think not. Come with me.'

'No.'

'You have to trust me, Mr Daley. I will not harm you or your son. And in any case, your choices are limited.'

Daley searched the man's face. 'Yes, he is my child and that's my car.'

'Then we are going on a journey, Mr Daley. But don't worry, it is a very short one. Get into the car.'

With the gun trained on him, Daley got into the driver's seat, while Cabdi climbed into the front alongside him. James was still howling in the back, and Daley turned to him in an effort to calm him. 'It's okay, James. We're just taking this nice man somewhere.' Still the little boy screamed.

'What's your name?' said Cabdi, the pistol held low, out of James junior's sight.

'James,' he sobbed.

Cabdi smiled at him and took off the red baseball cap. 'You have this – go on, it's a gift.' He handed the little boy the cap. 'It's yours. Put it on.'

James stopped crying and grabbed it. Without further prompting, he put the cap on his head, where it flopped down over his eyes, making him giggle.

'You remember me, James.' Cabdi turned to Daley. 'I want you to take me to where they are boarding the launches, but not the direct way – from the other end. I know the layout of your town. I've studied maps.'

'And what if I say no?'

'Then you will have made the biggest mistake of your life.'

Daley took a deep breath, and just as sirens once more sounded on Kinloch's Main Street he pulled away along the promenade, past the second pier, and turned right away from the seafront.

'I'm not at liberty to tell you where Commander Brachen is, sir,' said the young naval rating.

Scott fished into his pocket for his warrant card. 'Detective Sergeant Scott, son.' He thought for a second. 'Well, I'm actually an acting inspector, but that's no' important at the moment.'

The young sailor stared at Scott's ID, looking confused.

'Come on, son. This isnae rocket science. Just tell me where he is!'

'He's in the power facility with a search party, sir,' blurted the young man.

'And what's he doing there?'

'Looking for something – that's all I know.'

Scott thought for a moment. 'Right. Come on, take me doon tae this power facility.'

'I'm not sure I should, sir.'

'In that case you're under arrest,' said Scott.

'But I'm in the Royal Navy, sir!'

'I don't care if you're in the royal family. Just you get me tae this Brachen, aye and quick smart. Haul your yard arm, or whatever it is you navy chaps get up tae.'

Finally the sailor relented. 'Yes, Inspector.'

'Eh? Oh aye – try not tae confuse me, son. Oh, and this power facility. Dae they not call them engine rooms any mair?'

Brachen was with a team searching the electrical heart of the ship. 'This is where he was, according to the other workmen, chief.'

'Yes, sir.' The Royal Navy engineer was on his hands and knees, a small bright torch in his hand. 'I can't see anything, sir. Looks okay.' He got to his feet. 'There's one more fuse board across there, sir. We can check that out, too.'

Along with two armed Marines they made their way across the small space to a panel with buttons, switches and a monitor screen. The engineer turned it on and peered at it in the gloom. 'All appears in order, sir. No malfunctions, or alerts. If he's done anything, I don't think it's in here.'

'What about behind the console, chief?'

'Bit tight, but I'll have a gander, sir.' He knelt down and craned his neck in order to see behind the panel. 'Sir, there is something here.' His voice had tightened suddenly.

'What?'

'I can't see it properly, but there's a red glow. It's some kind of device, Commander. I'm sure of it!'

Brachen heard the change of tone in the engineer's voice. It had gone from one of routine procedure to a note of panic. He put the radio to his mouth. 'Brachen to Tansie, over, come in.'

There was silence for a few seconds before Annabelle Tansie's voice crackled over the radio. 'Go ahead, over.'

'We've found some kind of device on an electrical board. Don't know if it's viable, but I'm taking no chances.'

'I'm nearly at the pier, over.'

Brachen thought for a moment. 'Stand by, Tansie. Out.' He turned to the engineer. 'You keep looking. You have the areas where this man worked. Let me know the minute you find anything else.'

As he was leaving the room he saw one of his ratings coming towards him, followed by a man he vaguely recognised.

'Sir, this man is from Police Scotland – Inspector Scott, sir.'

'You'll have to come with me, Scott. We're in big trouble.'

'What kind of trouble?'

'I've good reason to believe that there are explosives on the ship.'

'Shit,' said Scott. 'There's also a problem on shore – an armed man. We need your help.'

'I'm afraid the police will have to deal with that themselves. We're about to be blown sky bloody high, Inspector.'

'Fucking boats, I hate the bastards!' Scott took the phone from his pocket and pressed the screen to call Symington.

The armed police team arrived on the seafront. Symington looked around, but there was no sign of Daley or the gunman. She saw the distinctive figure of Captain Banks at the head of the pontoons. 'Potts, get over there!' she shouted to her acting DS, pointing to where Banks was standing.

'Yes, ma'am,' he said immediately, looking in the mirror to make sure that the van carrying the armed team was following.

Symington swung in her seat with the sudden motion of the car. She looked at Potts behind the wheel. He was pale, and she could see sweat breaking out on his brow. She was beginning to wish she'd left any problems on the *Great Britain* to those on board and had the experience of the redoubtable Brian Scott at her side. Her phone rang just as they were pulling up alongside the pontoons.

'Listen, it's me.' Scott's voice was urgent, no preamble.

'Yes, Brian.'

'They've found explosives on this tub.'

'How the hell could that happen with their security?'

'I'm buggered if I know, but they have. You won't get any assistance from here.'

Symington bit her lip. 'But half of Kinloch is on that ship, not to mention the VIPs.'

'They have bomb disposal men from the frigate on it now, but I don't think they've a clue what they're dealing with. Aye, and I think they're trying tae hush it up. What's the situation you're attending – this man with the gun, I mean?'

'Don't worry about that, Brian. Just try to keep yourself – keep everyone safe.'

There was a short pause on the line. 'You're not telling me something.'

'It's okay, I'll deal with things here, DI Scott.'

'Tell me, ma'am!' Scott shouted down the line.

'The gunman has Jim, Brian.'

'But he's off sick!'

'It's a long story. Please, do what you can over there and leave this with me.' She listened. 'Brian, are you there?' The line had gone dead.

60

Daley was driving down the Glebe Fields. The situation was surreal. In the passenger seat Cabdi had the gun pointed at him, while joking with his son in the back.

'Where now, Mr Daley?'

'If we turn right here we can drive down to the far end of the Back Road and from there onto the seafront, as you wanted,' said Daley.

'Yes, good. Just keep driving and all will be well.'

'How can all be well? You're going to try to kill people.' Daley tried to keep his voice as conversational as possible, trying not to alarm his son.

'Keep driving, Mr Daley, that's all I ask of you. You have my word: do this, and no harm will come to you and your son.'

'If you try to harm him . . .' Daley left the rest unsaid. 'I'm pleading with you – whatever it is you think you can do, please think again. Nothing, no cause, is worth this.'

'You are always so sure, you people. Everything in your world is black and white, when in reality all the shades are grey.' He turned to James. 'When you are a big man like your father, you will see all the colours, not just your red hat, yes?'

The child smiled back at him, pushing the cap Cabdi had given him up so he could see. 'You're funny. I like you,' he said.

Daley drove on, as the thought that his son was as good a judge of character as his wife crossed his mind.

Brian Scott was tearing up steps and along gangways. He found a lift that he thought would take him back to the ballroom, but when the door opened a group of chefs eyed him curiously.

'This is private place,' said one man bearing a set of trays, in broken English.

'Where's the ballroom?' said Scott in the usual manner he deployed when addressing foreigners: shouting slowly.

'Not my job,' replied the man, moving on. But as he passed Scott the policeman grabbed him and pulled him towards him, sending trays flying and attracting the attention of the entire culinary staff.

'You come with me and show me the ballroom, right fucking noo!' Scott flashed his warrant card. 'Police, get it?'

The man nodded, laid down the rest of the trays, and stepped into the lift after him. When the doors closed he eyed Scott with a worried expression and punched a number on the panel.

'Quick as you can, there's a good man,' said Scott by way of encouragement.

'We have to change at next floor, get other lift.'

'Right. Go for it, man!'

The lift stopped again and the kitchen porter beckoned Scott to follow him. They ran along to the end of another passageway where three lifts doors faced them in a line. Scott's guide pressed the up button, and the pair waited anxiously for a lift to arrive.

The door to their left was the first to open, so both men hurried into it, the porter pressing another number on the panel as the doors swished shut. 'You are in a hurry – arrest someone?'

'No, no' exactly, son,' said Scott, watching the numbers rise.

They had reached four when the lift juddered and the lights flickered off. The lift stopped and an eerie blue emergency light filled the small space. Scott pressed the doors open button, but nothing happened.

'Lift is broke,' said the kitchen porter with a shrug.

'You must have been top of the class in your school, eh?' said Scott, now pressing the alarm button repeatedly. Not only was he on a boat, but it was full of explosives, with his wife and some of his best friends on board while he was stuck in a lift. 'No' my day, son, eh?'

The kitchen porter looked at him in the blue light, an apologetic look on his face.

Sir Edward Chapelhouse looked as though his face was about to explode. It had taken on a crimson hue that any doctor would have baulked at. Commander Brachen stood before him, a Royal Marine with a machine gun slung over his shoulder at his side. 'You incompetent fool! How on earth could this happen?' he snapped.

'Let's not worry about that at the moment, Sir Edward. The safety of the passengers, guests and crew is now my only concern. It's time to abandon ship, sir.' Brachen jutted his chin defiantly.

'I'll damn well decide when it's time to abandon ship, Commander!'

'With respect, no, you won't, sir. This is now an emergency operation, and that leaves me as the ranking naval officer in charge of the operation. All decisions will be mine.'

'We'll see about that! Get me the Foreign Secretary!'

'Our comms are down, sir. We only have radio communication and that's localised. The frigate is making its way into the loch now. I'll be ordering that the *Great Britain* be evacuated as soon as possible.'

'But you have no idea what these devices are?' Sir Edward's face became redder.

'Sir, I'll say again, one of the maintenance engineers had a bag that bore traces of explosive. Now we have found two devices. My men are isolating power from areas of the ship just in case they are being enabled through the vessel's electrical system in some way. So far we have had no success. The two devices we have located are armed. Fortunately the timers are zeroed, but we can't guarantee that will remain the case. In the meantime, though, there is absolutely no other course of action to be taken to ensure the safety of those aboard. My officers will be ready to implement evacuation soon. My decision is final!'

'Think about it, man. You'll make our country a laughing stock. Have we received any threats, demands? How do we know this isn't some sophisticated prank?'

'Whoever is behind this has gone to great lengths to conceal their actions. We can only respond in the way I describe. Please make ready to leave the vessel, Sir Edward.'

'You'd better be right, my boy. Because if you're not, you can take off that uniform and burn the bloody thing!' Sir Edward strode away from the Royal Navy commander. 'If what you say is correct, then how are they to be ignited?'

'We have no idea yet, sir. What we have to do is avoid any panic. I've made arrangements to take the duke and duchess off by launch now. But everyone will have to be ferried to the frigate as quickly as possible. We'll use everything at our disposal, sir, but how quickly it can be done, I don't know.'

'There seems to be no end to the things you don't know.' He paused to pick up a glass of whisky from the desk before him. 'One way or another, Brachen, we're all going to go down with this ship.'

Annabelle Tansie ordered the RIB to stop while she observed from the other side of the loch what was happening on the pier and pontoons. As she stared through her binoculars all she could see was a launch alongside, a few figures still not on board. Despite the gathering gloom she could make out the distinctive uniformed figure of Captain Banks, but just as she spotted him her attention was grabbed by a procession of flashing blue lights making their way along the promenade.

'Bell, get me Kinloch Police Office. I can't see any gunman, and I need an update fast!'

'Yes, ma'am!' the man in the combat gear replied.

As she peered she saw the lights stop at the pontoons and police officers disembark from the vehicles. 'Chief, take us round behind the pier as discreetly as you can.'

On her command the RIB began a wide arc, now out of sight of the old quay, heading slowly for the shore.

Ella Scott was watching two stewards. The one with the fancy braid was talking in an urgent fashion to the other, his hand over his mouth, looking around furtively as he did so. As she continued to observe them, she saw the one she assumed to be the junior man run off, leaving his well-adorned companion looking uncomfortable in his wake.

'I'm nae detective, Annie, but I'm sure something's

going on. First oor Brian takes off, noo all they waiters are looking dead shifty – take a look.'

Annie gazed around the large ballroom, and sure enough, the men and women who had greeted them with warm smiles now appeared to be on edge, grim looks passing between them. 'What could be the matter?'

'I'm no' sure, but I hope it's got nothing tae dae with my husband.'

'Och, no. We're in safe hands wae Brian aboard. There's no' much he can't handle, I'm sure.'

Ella looked at Annie doubtfully. 'I wouldnae count on that,' she said with a raised eyebrow. 'But I'm glad you've got so much faith in him.'

'Oh aye, Brian – and big Jim – are well respected in the toon, let me tell you.'

Talk about starry-eyed, thought Ella, but turned her attention to Hamish. 'How are you feeling now?'

'Och, jeest as though I'm staring intae the abyss; as though I'm on a fishing boat being sucked doon by a whirlpool.'

'Fuck me, you're the life and soul, Hamish,' said Annie. 'If you start tae go under they can always catch a hold of your tie and pull you back up. I mean, it's bound to stand oot in all this gloom that's surrounding you.'

As Hamish and Annie nagged at each other, Ella took in the scene before her. She watched as a man in Royal Navy uniform went from one steward to the next, whispering in each one's ear.

'I wouldnae give him a hard time, Annie. I think your man might have a point. There's something going on, and by the look o' some o' the stewards, it isn't good. Where the hell's Brian when you need him?'

With a jolt the lift carrying Brian Scott and the kitchen porter began to move. The lights came back on, and the floors counted up on a dial at the side of the console.

'Well, at least that's something,' said Scott as the lift came to another stop, pinged, and the doors opened.

'This way, Mr Police, please. We go along here then at ballroom.'

'You're a fine man,' said Scott as the pair took off along the corridor.

His mind was working overtime. For no reason he could hear his mother's voice in his head. *When it comes doon tae it, son, those close tae you are all that matters.* He could see her sitting in the scullery of their rundown tenement flat, wiping flour from her hands on her apron. The memory brought a tear to his eye as he followed the small man in kitchen whites. Aye, you're not wrong, Mother, he mumbled to himself.

61

'Stop the car!' said Cabdi.

Daley looked at the tall African. 'So, what now?'

The gun still pointed at the policeman, Cabdi reached into his pocket. 'Do you understand?' he said, searching Daley's face for an answer as he showed him something in his big hand.

'Yes – yes, I think so. But why?'

'There is no time for why. You must do what you think is right. But you have your son to think of. Surely your first duty is to keep him safe. If you choose to follow me . . .' Cabdi left the rest unsaid.

The RIB carrying the security team from the *Great Britain* drifted into the steps beside the old quay, engines off. The chief petty officer in charge of the craft brought her alongside expertly, nudging the bottom step as another crewman jumped onto its slick surface with a rope in order to secure the vessel.

'Well done, chief,' said Tansie. 'Now, everyone,' she went on, addressing her team. 'We don't know what we're facing, so everyone follows my directions to the letter, right?' They nodded in agreement. 'Right, with me.'

The dark-clad figures made their way up the sea steps beside the quay as silently as they could. The seafront was strangely empty of people. Even the white swan that had observed everything at such close quarters had made her way out into the middle of the loch, as though sensing all was not well. The sky above Kinloch was fading from day to night, the last red glow of the setting sun casting long golden shadows across the loch. The town's lights would soon hold sway, shining under the full moon that was already casting its reflection on the rippling water.

Symington climbed quickly out of the police car, her protective vest emblazoned with POLICE in bold white letters at odds with the smart designer dress she was wearing.

'Captain Banks, what happened to DCI Daley?'

'I'm sorry?' Banks looked mystified. 'I'm afraid I haven't seen DCI Daley. There's some kind of problem on board. I have to get everyone off this launch and send it back to the ship. We've just had a radio message.'

'But I don't understand. We were told that DCI Daley had been taken hostage by a gunman.'

'I heard some children screaming, but I assumed it was just high jinks. Where did this happen?'

'The other side of the old quay.'

'As you'll notice, it's not easy to see from here.'

Symington looked round, and sure enough, unless she stood on her tiptoes, she was unable to see much on the other side of the pier. She did notice that there was no traffic on the road, and assumed that the famous Kinloch bush telegraph had been busy. As she watched, she saw disgruntled partygoers being shown off the launch. She put her radio to her mouth. 'To all stations, DCI Daley is not at the locus, repeat, not at the locus. I want everything on this, over.'

Shaw replied from Kinloch Police Office. 'I'll have everyone search, ma'am. We'll use the town's CCTV system and check his home, over.'

As she thanked Sergeant Shaw, Symington felt the phone in her pocket vibrate. She grabbed it and looked at the screen.

'Not bad news, I hope,' said Banks as he helped an elderly woman with a fur stole and a disgruntled look on her face from the launch.

'No, no – it's okay.' She began to turn away from Banks. 'I'll need to get moving – find DCI Daley.'

'Yes, of course.' Movement from across the pontoons caught Banks's eye. 'What the hell?' Without warning, he made a grab for Symington, pulling her off her feet and holding her round the neck, a knife glinting in the setting sun. 'I'm very sorry about this, Carrie. Wrong place at the wrong time, I'm sad to say.' He dragged Symington back to the edge of the pontoons as policeman drew their weapons and passengers on the launch began to scream.

'Let her go, sir!' shouted DS Potts, his hands shaking slightly as he held the gun before him. He heard footsteps from behind and turned his head to see a collection of figures with machine guns and helmets running towards him. 'What's going on?' he shouted.

'So, Annabelle,' said Banks casually, as though he was a mere observer of events rather than protagonist. 'You've caught up with the game at last!'

Tansie showed Potts her identity card. 'We'll take over from here, officer,' she said.

'Ma'am?' said Potts, giving Symington a questioning look.

'Do as she says!' shouted Symington, then let out a yell as Banks's grip tightened and the knife pressed into her neck.

'What can you do, Magnus? You have a knife. Give this up, man!' Tansie shouted.

'But I also have this.' Banks delved into his pocket and produced an old-fashioned mobile phone. 'As you know, there are explosives all over the *Great Britain* – more than enough to destroy the ship and just about everyone on it. They're handily placed, I assure you. This phone is linked to them. I press one button, and – well, I don't have to elaborate, I'm sure.'

'But you'll die too, Magnus.'

'Some prices are worth paying. Payment for a dead father and brother – the debt of a nation torn apart by the British. Fuck you and fuck Great Britain!' He held the phone high in the air, his thumb moving to the keypad.

'Stop!' shouted Tansie

A single shot rang out. The captain staggered, an exit wound blossoming in the middle of his forehead, and both he and Symington tumbled into the loch.

Cabdi threw the gun to the ground and raised his hands above his head. He watched as policemen and Royal Marines pulled Symington coughing and spluttering from the water, the motionless body of Captain Magnus Banks floating at her side.

Tansie and two Marines ran up the pontoons towards him as red dots danced across his torso from the many weapons trained on his chest.

When she reached him, Tansie looked the tall man straight in the face, her gun held out before her. 'Handcuff him!' she said, and the two Marines descended on Cabdi, bringing him to the ground and complying with her order.

He spat as he was shoved into the police van by his captors, Tansie following them in.

As the van moved off, Tansie stared silently at the Somali on the opposite seat.

'What, are you going to shoot me now?' he asked, a broad grin spreading across his face.

At that, she leaned across to the tall African and enveloped him in a hug. 'You mad bastard, you mad fucking bastard,' she mumbled into his shoulder, as the Marines looked on expressionless.

62

Liz Daley went to the kitchen to get her husband and Chief Superintendent Symington coffee, James junior wobbling unsteadily after her, still wearing the red cap Cabdi had given him.

Symington took in the scene from the big picture window. The loch was empty now, save for a small shellfish boat chugging its way towards the pier and a yacht navigating its way past the causeway. The *Great Britain* had moved on with as little fuss as possible. None of the locals or VIPs aboard – apart from Brian Scott and his party, that was – knew anything of the danger they'd faced. The killing of Captain Banks was covered by the story of a crazed gunman with a grudge against the man, the culprit spirited away from Kinloch under the auspices of the Security Service. It had merited comment in the national newspapers and on television, but the lines had been intentionally blurred and names withheld. No doubt the British Government had ensured that the event made as little a splash as possible, and it was soon lost in the never-ending news cycle.

'I'm sorry, Jim. I should have answered your text messages. You were the first onto this.'

'No, I wasn't,' said Daley slouching in his recliner. 'Cabdi

– or whatever his real name was – had been an MI5 plant for years. As deep cover as you'll get. Not a job I'd fancy.'

'Who would?'

'Brian, maybe?'

'Please. He's nearly scuppered our relationship with half of the oil states in the Middle East. Possibly not my best decision.' She thought for a moment. 'Though I really wanted him beside me in that van when were heading to the pier.'

'Now bravery is something he's good at: diplomacy – not so much. Anyway, he might be the full time sub-divisional commander soon.'

'That's defeatist, Jim.'

'I feel defeated.'

'You're going for more tests tomorrow, yes?'

'Yes, flown up on the wee plane, to hear my fate, no less.'

'I could have driven you.'

'No, Liz offered, but it's better this way. Twenty minutes each way in the air, a damn sight better than that road.'

'Don't. Brian never shuts up about it, and he's living here!'

'You can always rely on Brian.'

'Indeed.'

'Thanks for coming up, I appreciate it. Captain Banks turned out to be quite a complex character – or Magnus Kelly, I suppose I should say.'

'Yes. Lost his father to drink, his mother to suicide, and his brother was killed resisting arrest by the army – only fourteen. The records of it all look pretty murky to me. Most of it is redacted. That kind of thing is bound to affect anyone, especially a child. They found a journal in his cabin. Most of it railing against the imperialist British, but it's clear he had a difficult relationship with his mother. It was strange.' She stared out of the window again.

'But why all of a sudden? That's what I don't understand.'

'Who knows? His real goal was to do the dirty deed in Belfast harbour. A massive strike against the state. It would have been headline news all over the world. He was clever, too. Hoodwinking the Islamic terrorist cell, the disappearing crewman. All designed to get security's eyes off the ball while his accomplice worked on the ship. But so different from the man I met. And it all backfired on him in the end – big time.'

'But to be brought up away from all that by his aunt – a model student, the very highest reputation as a sea captain, all thrown away in an act of madness.' It was Daley's turn to look out of the window. 'I suppose circumstances make people do strange things.'

'Well, his intention was to kill and maim, mainly to rekindle the troubles in Northern Ireland.'

'A breath on dying embers.'

'You think?'

'Who knows?' Daley shrugged. 'These days, anything is possible.'

'Listen, I know you're worried about your health. But honestly, what they think you have can be managed. I've checked: nothing to stop you coming back to work if the diagnosis is right.'

Daley sighed, looking at the floor. 'I can't shake the feeling in my gut. My father told me he was going to die, even when the initial prognosis was good. It was as if he knew somehow. I've wondered about it for years. Now I know what he meant.'

'Here we are,' said Liz, bringing in freshly brewed coffee

and cakes on a tray, doing her best to smile through her yellow and purple bruises.

Symington watched Daley watching Liz as she busied herself with pouring coffee. She could see a mixture of anger and hurt on his face, and something else that was hard to define. Still, they drank the coffee and ate the cakes to the pleasant accompaniment of small talk.

'Right, Mr Scally,' said DI Scott. 'So . . . on the day Cameron Pearson went missing we have a picture of your movements.'

'Oh, aye?' said Scally defensively.

'Your van is here, here and here,' said Scott, pointing to a number of screen grabs taken from the town's CCTV cameras. 'I'm told this road you're turning on to takes you up to the hill?'

'So? I'm a birdwatcher.'

'You were spotted there by . . .' Scott looked at his notes. 'A Mr Hines, who was walking his dog. He said you looked furtive, Mr Scally.'

'My mind was occupied, that's all.'

'And then we have this.' Scott pushed a piece of paper across the desk. 'Phone records. If you look carefully you'll note two calls. One from Mr Pearson's mobile to yours, and then just over an hour later you called his number.'

'I'm a friend of his. I phone my friends, that's whoot folk dae.' He shook his head. 'You polis should be asking thon African that gave me a good kicking.'

'And then there's this, Mr Scally.' This time DS Potts picked a clear plastic evidence bag from the floor. In it was a small hacksaw, its blade still stained with blood. 'Found in your shed, sir. The blood on the blade matches that of Cameron Pearson.'

'Circumstantial – nothing but circumstantial. Yous are jeest putting things together to make it look like it was me.'

'So, having you on the hill at the same time Mr Pearson went missing, two empty petrol cans in your van, and a hacksaw blade with Mr Pearson's blood and bone fragments a' o'er it, and it's just coincidence?' Scott sat back in his chair. 'And you've been having an affair with Mr Pearson's wife for years.'

'Jeest Kinloch gossip!'

'Mrs Pearson has confirmed it herself, Mr Scally. We've also found bone fragments in a fire set on the hill. Marks still visible on them were made by the very same hacksaw that was found in your shed. Also traces of Mr Pearson's blood and DNA were found in the back o' your van.' Scott leaned forward. 'Mr Scally, I think Mr Pearson thought of you as a friend. He had a real fright up that hill. He called a man he thought he could trust tae help him home. But help wisnae what you had in mind. You just saw opportunity, eh? And I'm going tae charge you.'

Scally looked at the solicitor at his side. 'Come on, you. You're meant tae be defending me!'

The solicitor looked at his client and shrugged.

63

The morning was bright and clear. A fresh breeze bearing a hint of autumn swept across Kinloch, deep within it a whisper of the winter to come.

'I wish you'd let me drive you – or come with you, at least, Jim,' said Liz as she pulled into the car park at the small airport just outside the town.

'We've spoken about this. I'm up and down on the plane in minutes – and it's paid for by the NHS. I'll be back before you know it.'

She leaned sideways to kiss Daley on the forehead and looked hurt when he turned his head away. 'Sorry. I'm just wishing you well, nothing else,' said Liz.

'I have to sort my head out, and so do you. The future's pretty uncertain right now. We've got to take things one step at a time, Liz.'

She brushed away a tear. 'I'd better get back. Ella will want to get on with her day, not have to keep James occupied.'

'And who knows what bad words he's learning off Muncle Brian.' Daley smiled. 'Things will work out one way or another,' he said enigmatically, then got out of the car and walked towards the terminal building without looking back.

'I love you, Jim.' The words on Liz's lips were almost silent.

Brian Scott was in the bakery, wondering whether to pig out on two bacon rolls or go for the healthy salad on wholemeal bread option.

'That'll be you then, Brian,' said a voice from behind.

'Eh? Oh, hello, Hamish. Nice tae see you better dressed.'

'But I'm jeest in my bib and braces.'

'Better than thon kilt – and the tie.' He stopped to place his order. 'Two bacon rolls and a large cup of coffee, please. Here, do you want anything, Hamish?'

'Jeest a small mug o' tea, if you don't mind. I'm no' feeling that hungry, tae be honest wae you.'

'Still in the glums?'

'Aye, jeest worse, if anything. I canna shake them.'

Scott collected his bag of rolls and handed Hamish his tea. Once he'd paid, they headed out into the sunshine on Main Street.

'It's a fine day for oor Jimmy tae fly up for his tests.'

'You think so, Brian? Tae me it feels as black as January the fourth.'

'Why that date?'

'Because that's when I usually take a rest fae the drink after the New Year. Och, fair grim it is.'

'I remember.' Scott looked reflective.

'Mr Daley – are you sure he's off tae the hospital the day?'

'Aye, he went on the morning plane about half an hour ago. Why dae you ask?'

'It's jeest this dream I keep having.'

'What dream?'

'I told him myself. Him on a boat – strange tides. Aye, and I keep dreaming aboot teeth.'

'You do?' Hamish had Scott's attention. 'What did he say when you mentioned this?'

'Jeest fair brushed it away, man. But there was something aboot him that made me shiver.'

'Here, drink your tea and away doon the pier and potter aboot. And cheer up, man!' Scott patted Hamish's shoulder and made his way back up the hill to Kinloch Police Office. Try as he might, though, he couldn't get what Hamish had said out of his mind.

The sea below was blue, but looked cold as Daley stared through the plane's window. The trip reminded him of his first case in Kinloch. He'd flown down on that occasion and the sea seemed as uninviting now as it had that day. So much had happened in his life since then; many faces passed across his mind's eye, but only the blue eyes of Mary Dunn stared into his soul.

'We'll be landing at Glasgow Airport in a few minutes. Please make sure your seatbelts are secure,' said the voice over the loudspeaker.

They bumped down on the tarmac and taxied to a halt. A transport ambulance was waiting on the tarmac. Daley watched as two frail patients were helped from the plane and into it.

He walked across the concourse, through the bustle of tourists and business people heading in various directions. Again he was reminded of the past, of his days spent at the airport as a young uniformed constable. He smiled at the memory, and the thought of friends he'd known then and not seen for so long.

He made for a car hire desk, produced the necessary documents, paid the deposit with his credit card and was shown to his vehicle. He'd picked a black Mercedes SUV. He made himself familiar with it, and was soon heading away from the airport.

The roofs and spires of Paisley brought back more memories. This time, Liz's face in the Paris nightclub, long, long ago. He smiled at the thought. *We met in Paris*, she told her friends, always omitting the fact it was a down-at-heel nightspot rather than the French capital.

He parked the car on a piece of disused land on Abercorn Street that had once been a factory. Other cars were dotted about. A boy approached him, no more than eleven or twelve years old, dressed in fashionable clothes intended for an older male.

'Three quid tae watch your motor, mister.' He held out his hand.

'Or you'll pan in the windows, right?'

'Naw, I'll keep an eye on it. You're no' fae here. This toon's a fucking nightmare.'

Daley smiled, reached into his pocket and handed the lad a fiver. 'You're right. I'm not from here, son. That car better be pristine when I get back.'

'Cheers, bud. Since you gave me a five spot, I'll clean your window for you.'

Daley nodded and walked away. Such were the entre-preneurial skills in the old mill town's young; some things never changed. Given the chance, some of these kids could be captains of industry. More likely, though, they'd be brought low by drugs, drink and crime. It always made him depressed.

Scott swallowed the last morsel of bacon roll and instantly wished he'd had the salad. He washed it all down with a gulp of coffee, and swung round on the chair in Daley's glass box, still troubled by what Hamish had said. Why the old man was dreaming about teeth when Scott knew Jim had discovered that Liz had been assaulted by a dentist he couldn't fathom. But he also knew the old man had the knack of seeing things others couldn't.

He picked up the phone and dialled a number he remembered well from his days in Paisley CID.

'Royal Alexandra Hospital,' said a bright woman's voice on the other end.

'Outpatients clinic, please – cardiology,' Scott replied. He waited for a few moments and this time a man answered the phone. 'It's Detective Inspector Scott at Kinloch Police Office,' he said in his best phone voice. 'I believe my boss DCI James Daley is with you for an appointment at the moment. Can I speak tae him, please? It's quite urgent.'

'Hold on, Inspector,' said the man on the other end of the phone. Scott drummed his fingers as he waited to hear Daley, but instead the same voice sounded in his ear. 'I'm sorry, Inspector, we have no record of Mr Daley on our list for today.'

'Are you sure?'

'Yes, quite sure. I've looked at the computer and his appointment isn't until next week, sir.'

'Right,' said Scott. 'My mistake, son. Sorry tae have bothered you.' He put the phone down, feeling suddenly very uneasy.

He thought for while as he finished his coffee and headed out of the glass box. 'I'll be back in a while, DS Potts. The empire is a' yours. But mind and no' sit in my seat. It's like musical chairs in here already.'

Leaving a smiling Potts, he made his way out of Kinloch Police Office and into his car.

64

The bar on Paisley's Old Sneddon Street was more rundown than Daley remembered it. A skinny elderly man stared at him with rheumy eyes as he counted change in his hand, no doubt searching for enough money to buy another drink. Two youths were standing at a fruit machine, cursing as they lost money with another roll.

'Can I help you, mate?' said a bored-looking barman.

'Just a soda water, please,' said Daley. 'Quiet in here, eh?'

'This is as good as it gets till the weekend. Even then there's only a dozen or so. Pubs are buggered in this town; half of them have shut.'

'Sad. I remember this place when you couldn't get in the door.'

'No' in my time. I'm just doing this to pay my way through uni. Bugger this for a job.' He passed Daley's drink across the bar. 'Ice, lemon – an umbrella?' He smiled.

'You're fine.' Daley made his way past the lads at the fruit machine, then to an area of tables where in the dim light a rotund man with a bald head sat, half-finished pint in front of him.

'You've fair put on the beef, Jimmy,' he said.

'Always a cheery word, Mr McLean. You're hardly

Twiggy yourself.' They shook hands warmly and Daley took the seat opposite him. 'How's things, Billy?'

'Just as you see them, I'm sad tae say. I'm still up in Gallowhill, though my daughter wants me tae go intae a *sheltered community*.' He spat out the words with disgust.

'But you've still got your ear to the ground, Billy.'

'Oh aye. But this has cost me a few quid, Jimmy. Inverkip's no' just next door, know what I mean?'

'Here.' Daley handed him a bundle of rolled-up notes, hidden in his large fist.

'That'll do nicely,' said Billy, quickly counting them under the table.'

'How long have you been doing me favours?'

'A good quarter of a century, anyway. No' much business from you lately, mind you, what wae you stuck doon in the sticks. You must miss the action up here, Jimmy?'

'I've more than enough action to cope with, thank you.'

'How's Brian?'

'Brian is still Brian. Though he's off the bevvy.'

'Naw, you're kidding!' Billy looked horrified, almost as though somebody had died. 'That's a shame. What the fuck does he dae with his time?'

'If I told you, you wouldn't believe me.' Daley looked at his watch. 'Anyhow, Billy, I'm short on time. Are things as we expected?'

'They were half an hour ago. Here, I'll just check.' McLean pulled a mobile phone with a cracked screen from his jacket and dialled a number, mumbling when the call was answered, and ending it quickly. 'Yup, all's as I said.'

'Good. Thanks, Billy. It's just like old times.'

'No, it's no', Jimmy. Those days have gone, my friend.'

Daley bid his old informant farewell and left the bar.

'Tell me his name, Lizzie,' said Brian Scott, standing in Daley's lounge.

'No, it's none of your business. I'm not making a complaint. I've told Jim and I've said the same to Carrie. I just want to forget the whole thing.'

Scott rubbed his chin.

'What aren't you telling me, Brian?'

'The big man. I checked a while ago, and he's not got an appointment at the hospital today. It's next week. So what do you think he's up to?'

Liz looked momentarily confused. 'What? You know Jim: he doesn't lie, Brian.'

'No, he leaves that tae you.'

She smiled at him sarcastically. 'Why, thank you so much.'

'I want tae know where this boyfriend of yours lives. You know Jimmy as well as I dae. He might no' be a liar, but his temper's off the scale. And it simmers, tae.'

'He's in no condition to go after anyone.' Suddenly Liz looked worried.

'And when did anything like that matter tae him, eh? I know he's been brooding about what happened tae you. You must have seen it yersel'. Tell me where this bastard lives!'

'Keep your voice down, Brian. James is having a nap.'

'Tell me, Lizzie, or I swear I'll arrest you for withholding evidence.'

'Oh, yes, that would look great in the papers: *Police Inspector Threatens Beaten Woman*. Think about it, Brian.'

'Listen tae me. If you care one jot aboot Jimmy, you'll tell me. He only told me the bare bones.'

'So you wouldn't go after him, you mean.'

'Whatever. Tell me, Lizzie, and tell me now!'

The sky was still blue when Daley drove into Inverkip past the honey-coloured buildings on the seafront. Though the season was almost at an end, there was still a forest of masts in the exclusive marina and some tourists taking in the scene.

Daley drove slowly past rows of pontoons until he had almost reached the end of their line. He pulled up and got out of the hire car. He could smell the telltale aroma of wood and coal being burned on the air, a sure sign that the nights were drawing in.

He walked down the wooden slats of the pontoon until he reached a large cabin cruiser. Its sleek sweeping lines made it look as though it was sailing at top speed out to sea, but in reality it was tied to two bollards. He looked at the name of the boat and smiled: *Wisdom* was written above the black silhouette of a large tooth, roots and all. Water lapped gently at the side of the expensive craft, making it bob gently at its moorings. Above the squawking of the gulls and the putter of a small motor boat heading out of the marina, Daley could hear drilling from within the vessel and a song on the radio – Journey, one he remembered from his youth. A man was humming tunelessly.

Gripping the hand-rail, he stepped on to the deck.

'Mr Manston, are you there?'

Brian Scott spoke quickly into the phone. 'I want someone tae go and see this Manston, right now. I have information that he assaulted a woman who's now in Kinloch. And make it quick, tae; he's a right slippery bastard!'

He put down the receiver and grabbed his mobile from the desk. Again the call to Jim Daley's phone went to voicemail. 'Listen, Jimmy, I know what you're at, man. Don't be fucking stupid. There's too much at stake, you hear me? I've put in a call tae Renfrewshire and they're on their way tae find this bastard. You stay out of it!' He clicked off the call and flung the mobile across the desk.

Daley aimed a last kick at Alexander Manston's stomach as he lay helpless and bleeding on the floor of the cabin. 'You bastard!' said Daley, struggling to catch his breath, eyes wide with fury. 'Never, never come near my wife, or do to anyone what you did to her again, have you got that?'

Daley leaned forward, his hands on his knees, gasping. His chest was tight, and he could feel the room start to spin. Desperate for air, he began to make his way out of the cabin.

'You won't get away with this, you bastard. Your wife's a slut and she deserved all she got.'

Daley turned back and loomed over the recumbent man. He knelt down and lifted his head off the floor. He looked into Manston's bleeding and battered face.

'I don't care what happens to me. Next time I'll kill you.' He pushed Maston back down and got unsteadily to his feet, dozens of tiny white dots playing across his vision.

He staggered off the cabin cruiser and onto the wooden slats of the pontoon. He felt dizzy, and he couldn't breathe.

The last thing he saw was the blue sky tumbling out of sight as everything went black. He fell heavily onto the wet pontoon, and lay motionless as the distant wail of police sirens sounded across Inverkip.

A Note from the Author

Two strange things happened: one during the writing, the other on completion of this book.

I had just finished the passage about the arrival of the *Great Britain* in Kinloch, when a huge vessel of similar function entered Campbeltown Loch in real life. An all too unfamiliar sight, I'm sad to say. For a look at this please seek out the wonderful photography of Raymond Hosie, the man responsible for the cover image of this book.

Then, a week after I'd sent the script to my publisher, I sat back to watch the news – to find Gatwick airport under attack by a drone. Life does indeed sometimes imitate art.

In such uncertain times, I wish the government was doing more to develop our trade prospects. Surely now is the time to show everyone what these islands have to offer regardless of the outcome of this agonising paralysis in our body politic. In generations to come, whatever your view, this period will be looked back upon with mouths agape at such ineptitude and lack of foresight.

As John Lennon said, 'Strange days indeed'!

Acknowledgements

As always to my wife Fiona and those I cherish. To my editor Nancy Webber, I owe you many thanks. Also to Hugh Andrew, Alison Rae, Jan Rutherford, Neville Moir and all at Birlinn/Polygon, thank you for helping Daley et al go from strength to strength.

To fellow author and friend Douglas Skelton who is as wise and kind as he is talented. Indeed, to all those who are the bulwark of my existence. To our lovely friends and neighbours, especially Mary Anderson, who make this wee community so special. To Ronnie Kelly with whom I always raise a glass or three on our annual pilgrimage to Oban, and who spreads the word of the great game cricket wherever he can. It's been a long time, old pal.

I make my best attempt at a deep bow of gratitude to David Monteath who narrates the DCI Daley audiobooks with such aplomb – in between stints on *Game of Thrones*, *Vikings* and more. It is no wonder he is known as 'the king of narration'.

To all the journalists and bloggers who have written such kind things about the books, I can't thank you enough. Every writer needs help from those willing to spread the word, and they all do so magnificently.

To the readers: thank you for coming back time after time and telling your friends, and taking to the dinner table, the water cooler or social media to share your thoughts. Again, this is invaluable to anyone who has to trust his or her wits in order to live by the word.

My gratitude, too, to the army of booksellers who stand in stores or work in other ways to promote my work – you carry on a proud and, I trust, continuing tradition. In addition, a special mention for Vikki Reilly who hasn't forgotten big Jim and Brian, even though she's found pastures new.

As always, thank you to the people of Kintyre. They continue to be my inspiration. I hear now from so many who have travelled there, or intend to (you'll love it!), after reading the books.

Finally, to my departed friend, our hybrid Scottish wildcat Wee Boy, who came through with me every morning and curled up in front of the fire while I battered away on the keyboard. He lives on in Hamish the cat. On my return from hospital at the end of 2017, he sat at the end of the bed every night until I went to sleep. It was such a simple thing, but unconditional devotion – a rare quality indeed. The first time I wrote without him at my side I wept buckets. I'll miss him always.

D.A.M.
Gartocharn
May 2019

419

The DCI Daley thriller series

Book 1: *Whisky from Small Glasses*
DCI Jim Daley is sent from the city to investigate a murder after the body of a woman is washed up on an idyllic beach on the west coast of Scotland. Far away from urban resources, he finds himself a stranger in a close-knit community.

Betrayal, fear and death stalk the small town of Kinloch, as Daley investigates a case that becomes more deadly than he could possibly imagine.

Book 2: *The Last Witness*
James Machie was a man with a genius for violence, his criminal empire spreading beyond Glasgow into the UK and mainland Europe. Fortunately, Machie is dead, assassinated in the back of a prison ambulance following his trial and conviction. But now, five years later, he is apparently back from the grave, set on avenging himself on those who brought him down.

Book 3: *Dark Suits and Sad Songs*
When a senior Edinburgh civil servant spectacularly takes his own life in Kinloch harbour, DCI Jim Daley comes face to face with the murky world of politics. To add to his woes, two local drug dealers lie dead, ritually assassinated. It's clear that dark forces are at work in the town. With his boss under investigation, his marriage hanging by a thread, and his side-kick DS Scott wrestling with his own demons, Daley's world is in meltdown.

Book 4: *The Rat Stone Serenade*
It's December, and the Shannon family are heading to their clifftop mansion near Kinloch for their AGM. Shannon International, one of the world's biggest private companies, has brought untold wealth and privilege to the family. However, a century ago, Archibald Shannon stole the land upon which he built their home – and his descendants have been cursed ever since.

When heavy snow cuts off Kintyre, DCI Jim Daley and DS Brian Scott are assigned to protect their illustrious visitors. But ghosts of the past are coming to haunt the Shannons.

Book 5: *The Well of the Winds*
As World War Two nears its end, a man is stabbed to death on the Kinloch shoreline, in the shadow of the great warships in the harbour.

Many years later, the postman on Gairsay, a tiny island off the coast of Kintyre, discovers that the Bremner family are missing from their farm.

When DCI Daley comes into possession of a journal written by his wartime predecessor in Kinloch, he soon realises that he must solve a murder from the past to uncover the shocking events of the present.

Book 6: *The Relentless Tide*
When Professor Francombe and her team of archaeologists find the remains of three women on a remote Kintyre hillside – a site rumoured to have been the base of Viking warlord Somerled – their delight soon turns to horror when they realise the women tragically met their end only two decades ago.

It soon becomes clear that these are the three missing victims of the 'Midweek Murderer', a serial killer who was at work in Glasgow in the early 1990s. DCI Jim Daley now has the chance to put things right – to confront a nightmare from his past and solve a crime he failed to as a young detective. However, when Police Scotland's Cold Case Unit arrive, they bring yet more ghosts to Kinloch. *The Relentless Tide* is a tale of death, betrayal, Viking treasure and revenge set in the thin places where past, present and future collide.

Can Daley avenge the murder of his colleague and friend?

Book 7: *A Breath on Dying Embers*
When the luxury cruiser Great Britain berths in Kinloch harbour, the pressure mounts on D.C.I. Jim Daley. The high-powered international delegates on board are touring the country, golfing and sightseeing, as part of a UK Government trade mission. But within hours, one of the crew members vanishes and a local birdwatcher goes missing.

The lives of the ship's passengers and the residents of Kinloch, as well as the country's economic future, are soon in jeopardy. And as Daley faces a life-and-death struggle of his own, D.S. Brian Scott – reluctantly back at sea – comes to the fore.

Could this be Daley's last throw of the dice?

One Last Dram Before Midnight: The Complete Collected D.C.I. Daley Short Stories
Published together for the first time in one not-to-be-missed volume are all Denzil Meyrick's short stories and novellas.

Discover how DCI Daley and DS Scott first met on the mean streets of Glasgow in two prequels that shed light on their earlier lives. Join Hamish and his old mentor, skipper Sandy Hoynes, as they become embroiled with some Russian fishermen and an illicit whisky plot. And in present-day Kinloch Daley and Scott investigate ghosts from the past, search for a silent missing man, and follow the trail of an elusive historical necklace that still has power over the people of Kinloch.

All of the DCI Daley thrillers are available as eBook editions, along with an eBook-only novella and the short stories below.

Dalintober Moon: A DCI Daley Story
When a body is found in a whisky barrel buried on Dalintober beach, it appears that a notorious local crime, committed over a century ago, has finally been solved. However, the legacy of murder still resonates within the community, and the tortured screams of a man who died long ago still echo across Kinloch.

Two One Three: A Constable Jim Daley Short Story (Prequel)
Glasgow, 1986. Only a few months into his new job, Constable Jim Daley is walking the beat. When he is seconded to the CID to help catch a possible serial killer, he makes a new friend, DC Brian Scott. Jim Daley tackles his first serious crime on the mean streets of Glasgow, in an investigation that will change his life for ever.

Empty Nets and Promises: A Kinloch Novella
It's July 1968, and fishing-boat skipper Sandy Hoynes has his daughter's wedding to pay for – but where are all the fish? He and the crew of the *Girl Maggie* come to the conclusion that a new-fangled supersonic jet which is being tested in the skies over Kinloch is scaring off the herring.

First mate Hamish comes up with a cunning plan to bring the laws of nature back into balance. But little do they know that they face the forces of law and order in the shape of a vindictive fishery officer, an exciseman who suspects Hoynes of smuggling illicit whisky, and the local police sergeant who is about to become Hoynes' son-in-law – not to mention a ghostly piper and some Russians.

Single End: A DC Daley Short Story
It's 1989, and Jim Daley is now a fully fledged detective constable. When ruthless gangster James Machie's accountant is found stabbed

to death in a multi-storey car park, it's clear all is not well within Machie's organisation.

Meanwhile Daley's friend and colleague DC Brian Scott has been having some problems of his own. To save his job, he must revisit his past in an attempt to uncover the identity of a corrupt police officer.